Sins of Arrogance

LUCY MONROE

LUCY MONROE LLC

For Arianna Fraser, who has become a dear friend but first made me fall in love with her unhinged heroes.
This story is for you because I know Mick is right up your alley.
Wishing you endless story ideas and all the best, all the time!

Divorce, Mob Style (Step 1: Kill the Mistress)

He broke her heart. She's about to break the rules.

KARA

My heels clack a staccato rhythm on the marble floor of the hallway leading to my father's office. There's no hesitation in my steps, nothing to indicate the turmoil inside me.

Am I really going to pull the lever on this?

Do I have a choice?

A normal woman, from a normal family would have this discussion with her husband and then an attorney. But I'm an Irish mob princess and my father's word is law.

I have to convince him that a divorce between me and Mick is the best thing for the syndicate as well as myself. Beyond that, I want him to kill the woman my husband calls friend.

Neither are going to be easy sells. The former because my father doesn't believe in divorce and the latter because Mick is going to oppose killing Dierdre.

Unfortunately, he has a stronger position with my father than I do.

Mick is da's right hand man. I'm just his daughter.

But I'm not giving in on either. My marriage is ending and Dierdre will no longer be a threat to me and my son.

One way, or another.

CHAPTER ONE

Let's build a Ghost

8 Months Earlier

MICK

Brogan, boss of the Shaughnessy Mob and my father-in-law, follows me into the strategy room.

This is not a conversation I want to have at the mansion, regardless of the new security measures I employed after a recent breach.

My top three lieutenants follow close behind. Brice shuts the door when we're all inside and leans against it.

"Okay, I'm here. What's this about, Mick?" Brogan plants himself in the chair at the head of the long conference table, arms crossed.

I put my finger up in a sign for him to wait while Conor scans the room for listening and video recording devices and Rory sets up the portable signal jammer.

Overkill? Maybe.

But that's the way I lean when it comes to security. Especially after discovering not one, but two different infiltrations by other organizations into our mob in less than two years.

Conor gives me a thumbs up and takes out his earbuds. "Clean."

"We're secure." Rory steps away from the device placed in the southwest corner of the room.

Building joists, pipes and vents affect the jammer's performance and he tested for the ideal spot before we had our first meeting in here.

This is the first time I'm looping my father-in-law into my plans.

"What do you know about whisper guns?" I ask Brogan.

"What the hell is a whisper gun?"

And that's my answer. He knows nothing. Which means we start from the beginning.

"Imagine a firearm that doesn't leave a trace." I cross to the table where I lay out the mockup schematics in front of him. "No sound signature. No powder residue. No rifling marks on the bullet." The electromagnetic charge causes the spin for accuracy. "No casing left behind."

Brogan frowns. "Sounds like sci-fi bullshit."

"It's not." I tap the printout of the internal barrel design. "This is real. Magnetic rail propulsion using neodymium magnets instead of explosive force. The projectile moves fast enough to kill, but silent. Close-range only."

For now. But the plan is for that to change once we get the initial tech perfected.

Brice steps away from the door. "Think of it like a cross between a railgun and a ghost. No bark. No footprint. Just a body hitting the floor."

The six-foot tall Black man came with me from Ireland and is my top lieutenant. So did Conor. Five-feet-eight inches of deadly accuracy with a rifle, he's our sharpshooter.

Rory was born here. Worked on the docks, connected to the Shaughnessy Mob, but not a soldier. He wanted something different though. We met over a pint and a dead body.

He kills up close and with a knack for keeping the scene clean.

All three run crews under me. Our ranks are the deadliest in the Shaughnessy Mob. Which is not a coincidence. Like draws like. My men all have a code of honor they know I'll kill them for breaking, but none of us feels guilt about doing the things we need to in order to protect the mob and our interests.

Brogan leans forward, interest sharpening. "And this is your idea?"

"Not originally," I admit easily.

I don't have to be the first to the table, I only care about being the best when I get there.

My father-in-law makes a "continue" motion with his hand.

"I saw a weapons prototype at an arms showcase in Istanbul two months ago. Off-the-books presentation. Russian engineer, desperate for backers, acting the maggot fired too many shots to impress his protentional clients. Sloppy build, it overheated after four."

Brogan will understand my Irish slang. The man was a total fool.

"Totally banjaxed," Conor says with disgust. "And it was his only prototype."

"Practically melted the demonstrator's hand off too." Rory's eyes gleam with gratification from the memory.

The engineer had been so desperate for cash that he'd stuck around to bargain for the schematics of the nonfunctioning gun. It had fired two shots with non-lethal force and enough accuracy to hit the target, if not the center of it.

The third shot had gone completely wild and the fourth had given him third-degree burns and lost any chance for him to get backers on his project.

Once we had the schematics and all the research documentation, we torched his lab and put the engineer out of his misery.

I was going to offer him a job – not running the project, because he'd already shown his inadequacies for that – but his knowledge of the tech would have made him an asset to the research team.

However, while Rory was scrubbing the hard drives, he came across some sick shite and we ended up killing the engineer instead.

"Mick saw the potential." Even after nearly eight years in New York, Brice's deep voice still has a hint of a Dublin accent.

"The concept is game changing," I say. "Zero noise." Unlike gun suppressors that cannot dampen all the noise from a shot. "No forensic trail other than the unique character of the ammo itself."

Instead of gunpowder, the bullets have to have a ferromagnetic core to work with the magnetic acceleration of the firing mechanism and barrel.

We have a supplier, but I'm looking into building our own refinement facility to decrease the chances of the ammo tracing back to us through a third party.

But without barrel striations, the bullets cannot be matched to an individual gun, or person pulling the trigger. And the heat of the firing propulsion burns any residual DNA on the ammo itself.

I let that settle. Let Brogan consider what a gun like that would mean for hits and close-range protection.

It has taken me two months to figure out and source the necessary pieces for research and development without tipping anyone off to my interest in the field. With my most recent hire, I've got everyone I need on board.

Except Brogan.

"Forensic-proof. AI-detection proof." The zeal in Rory's voice makes Brogan sit back a little. "So quiet even the most sensitive monitoring equipment isn't going to read the shots for what they are."

Some men watch porn. Rory watches videos of weapons being fired. He probably gets just as turned on doing it too.

"It's the kind of weapons tech that changes how syndicates can operate." These weapons won't just make us money, they'll make the Shaughnessy Mob and its allies virtually untouchable.

Brogan whistles low. "So, you want me to believe this isn't sci-fi bullshit. That it's something we can actually build?"

I lock eyes with him. "We're not going to build one. We're going to build *hundreds*."

And they won't burn away the flesh from the hands firing the guns.

"But first we have to develop one," Brogan says, showing why the Shaughnessy businesses have thrived under his leadership. "What kind of investment are we talking here?"

"First, we need to rehaul the Bunker for security and usability and then we have to outfit and staff the research lab."

Brogan looks around the room we're in. "This place *is* secure. Built like a Cold War panic room. And we've already got a weapons development lab. What else do you think you need?"

"A facility built for today's warfare, not what we faced in the last century." I press the button on a remote and the large screen taking up most of one wall comes to life. "And a clean lab designed for the kind of projectile technology we'll be testing."

Financial line items and figures I've memorized fill the screen, including subtotals for the different stages of the project and an overall projection of total cost.

Brogan's indrawn breath says there's nothing wrong with his eyesight.

"This kind of ghost tech doesn't exist. Yet." I pause, letting that one word sink in. "But I'm not the only one who saw that demonstration."

"Just the one smart enough to lay hands on the research and failed prototypes before anyone else could," Brice adds.

I meet my father-in-law's gaze. "The first weapons manufacturers to the table will control the market. That advantage doesn't come cheap."

Brogan's eyes narrow, but he nods. "I'm listening."

"Initial facility expansion, clean lab conversion, full electromagnetic shielding, airflow partitioning." I point to a number on the screen. "We're looking at a baseline of $20 million, just to make designated space in the Bunker safe for development. Security retrofits will push that to $35–$40 million."

Rory whistles. "For a bunker that already exists?"

Doling out information on a need-to-know basis, I haven't walked my guys through the numbers. I trust them, but only a foolish man doesn't take precautions to protect an endeavor of this magnitude.

I might be a sociopath, but I'm no muppet.

"Not like this," I say. "I'm talking independent air systems, laser-coded hall locks, neural-gated access points. The same shite they use to protect experimental defense labs in Nevada. Only better. Because no one, and I feckin' mean *no one* can know it's here."

Brogan rubs his chin thoughtfully. "I assume the original engineer is in a holding cell."

"Dead," Rory says with satisfaction.

He really hated what he found on the Russian's hard drive.

"And the other potential backers?" Brogan asks.

I shrug. "Neutralizing all of them would have drawn attention to our interest in the whisper gun technology."

My risk assessment said that was more problematic than the fact other people knew about the failed demonstration. Magnetic propulsion gun technology is not entirely new, only undeveloped for close range, personal weapons.

Brogan grunts approval and I switch to the second slide. "Then there's the talent."

A photo pops up of a LatinX woman in her late 30s in glasses, her dark hair in a tight bun and wearing a lab coat. Her expression is guarded, but there is banked rage in her gaze.

The picture is from the moment when her male colleague was being awarded a medal of excellence from DARPA for the work he stole from her and published as his own.

"Dr. Ximena Morales. She should be the head of experimental ballistics for a NATO defense initiative but her less talented male colleague was given the job over her."

"Let me guess. She's not coming over for the pension plan," Brogan says in a dry tone.

"No." Not even close. "She's coming for $1.5 million upfront and the opportunity to kit out a lab to her specification, no red-tape involved."

But more importantly to Hex, she's coming because I offered respect and recognition of her intelligence and work. I made it clear to Dr. Morales that she wasn't in the running, but the only physicist/weapons systems engineer I wanted on this project.

Brogan raises his eyebrows. "I presume the signing bonus is only part of her hiring package."

"We'll pay her half a mil a year to stay. Add another $2 million annually for her handpicked team of four weapons engineers, two materials chemists, and a robotics tech."

Brogan grunts. "Two-point-five million a year, just for staff?"

"They're not staff," I say coldly. "They're the reason no one will be able to match what we're building. We hire the best and not only do we get the prototype faster, we know they aren't out there somewhere working for somebody else."

"Let's say we fund it," Brogan says. "How long before we see a return?"

I flip to the final screen. The whisper gun mockup appears. A sleek, unassuming matte-black shape surrounded by a glowing field of numbers.

"Base cost per unit: $5,000–$7,000, depending on material fluctuations. That's graphene-lined barrels, neodymium-magnet rail propulsion, and phase-shifting gel lined grips."

Conor whistles this time, not tonelessly though. He whistles *The Foggy Dew*.

Brice rolls his eyes at his fellow lieutenant. "And sale price?"

"Conservative estimate? Fifty grand. That's black market. If we go bespoke, offer to elite buyers, private militaries, states looking for deniable assets, we can easily push into the six-figure range. *Each*." I let that sink in. "We sell a thousand units in a mix of base price and bespoke, and our initial investment is returned."

"With a working prototype, we can sell a thousand guns like that before we're even in production," Brice muses.

Rory nods. "Our problem will be limiting our output and buyers."

"And that's the primary reason we need to do this," I say.

Brogan leans back in his chair. "Explain."

"It's about dominance," I say, voice low. "No striations. No muzzle flash. No GSR. A gun that doesn't make a sound and leaves no trace. That makes *us* untouchable. Everyone else fights for scraps. We set the rules."

Brogan exhales through his nose. "How much, total?"

"$75 million with access to an additional ten percent for necessary budget adjustments."

My boss doesn't flinch. It's not even the biggest investment we'll make this year, but it is the most important.

Brogan drums his fingers on the tabletop while he thinks. "Developing these whisper guns is going to put a huge assed target on our backs."

He's right. This is the kind of technology everyone is going to want a piece of. "If word gets out. It won't."

"You think it's a risk worth taking?"

"I think someone is going to take that risk. Protecting the mob..." And more importantly, my wife and son. "Means we're the ones that have to do it first."

CHAPTER TWO

Tattooed Husbands, Tankinis, & Trouble

The Present

KARA

"Come on, Fitzy. You can do it!" I give my son an encouraging smile and beckon him to me.

He looks from me to his father, standing a few feet to my left in the deeper water off the shore. Fitz peers suspiciously into the water shimmering in the mid-August sun.

Only deep enough to reach my ribcage, he can see all the way to the bottom, but his sturdy little body remains firmly on the dock.

"Here, Fitz. I'll catch you." Mick's soft Irish lilt still makes my heart flutter after seven years of marriage.

But that's nothing compared to the way my nether regions react to his muscular, tattooed body covered in nothing but board shorts, the barbell through his right nipple on display. Even the frigid waters of the bay can't cool my ladybits.

You'd think that after this long, I'd be immune. I'm not.

I've learned to accept that regardless of what my heart may feel, and my mind might think, my body will always respond this way to Mick.

It's the one area of our marriage we are on an entirely level playing field.

My husband craves my body as much as I pine after his nonexistent love.

No matter what time he comes to bed at night, he always initiates sex. Do I make sure I get to sleep early enough to take advantage of that when the time comes without being tired and sluggish?

Yes, yes I do.

On the rare occasions he's around during the day and our son is otherwise occupied, Mick turns on the seduction then too. There's no question he wants me.

However, the heated passion and sensual touches stay tucked safely behind our bedroom door.

What can I expect when I got married as part of a deal between two powerful mob families?

That's what I tell myself anyway. Only, some days, my heart is feeling salty and tells me that I deserve more. Like when we spent our seventh anniversary apart last month. Mob business.

He sent me seven dozen white roses and a diamond tennis bracelet. No card.

Which is not what I need to be dwelling on. Because today, I'm doing my best to give off nothing but positive vibes for Fitz.

Three weeks ago, Fitz and I were playing together in the water with my sister, while our cousin sat on the dock, soaking in the summer sun.

Then without warning, Róise was jerked into the water by a diver and kidnapped right in front of us. None of us could reach her in time.

I didn't even try. I love my cousin like a sister, but my son comes first, last and always. Heart pounding in terror that our enemies would hurt my son, or take him from me, I grabbed Fitz and rushed to get out of the water.

It felt like treacle slowing my limbs, but we made it to the shore as men tore across the yard, trying to reach the water in time.

They didn't reach Róise, but her mafioso fiancé followed and got her back.

Róise's fine now, but my son? Not so much.

Fitz has been clingy and terrified of swimming in the bay ever since that day.

Micks answer?

Exposure therapy. Not what he calls it of course. "He's going to be mobbed up one day. He has to learn to overcome his fears."

So, in an attempt to get our son past his trauma response, we're swimming together as a family. Or at least we're trying to.

Fitz is still dry and on the dock.

He'll let us carry him into the water, but this is the first time he's ventured onto the dock. And he's a lot closer to the shore than the spot where Róise was yanked into the bay.

"Mommy, you should come up here with me." Green eyes so like his dad's entreat me.

"Fitz," Mick says in the tone our son never ignores. "Ye need to come to me."

"But what if the bad men come and take mommy?" Fitz demands, his little fists against his hips.

"I'll kill them," Mick replies without a second's hesitation.

"But what if they get away fast like the bad man with Róise?"

Fitz has started showing more of the Shaughnessy temper over the past six months, but this defiance toward his dad is something new.

"I increased underwater security and the number of guards patrolling our water access." Mick speaks to our son with an adult frankness that Fitz finds less jarring than I do. "Your mam is safe and so are you."

Fitz glares at his father. "But what if we're not?"

Unperturbed by our son's defiance – thank goodness – Mick puts his arms up. "Come to me now, *a mhac*."

The Irish endearment that literally just means *son*, sounds different in Mick's voice than it does in mine. I speak *Gaeilge*, but my accent reveals my American roots.

Mick's is pure Dublin.

With one last wary look at the water, Fitz leaps toward his father.

Mick catches the small body easily and swings him toward me. "Your mam said you learned a new swimming stroke. Are you ready to show me?"

Worry wars with the need to impress his dad in Fitz's gaze.

"I can swim across the pool," Fitz says, clearly angling to shift our location.

He's proud of his new skills, but even that pride won't make him let go of his father.

Mick lifts our son until their faces are parallel. "Look at me, Fitz."

Identical green eyes stare back at each other.

"I will never let any harm come to yiz. Not you, nor your mam. You will always be safe when you are with me." It's more reassurance than I expect from my husband.

I'm not sure why. He's a good dad and has always shown an affection and patience for Fitz that he doesn't show anyone else.

Our son's shoulders lower and his body relaxes in his dad's hold. "What about when you're not here?"

"Then you have to trust me that I've taken the precautions necessary to keep yiz safe."

One thing about the way Mick speaks to Fitz: our son has a truly impressive vocabulary for a newly turned six-year-old.

Fitz nods and then looks at me. "You're not scared, are you, mommy?"

"No, *mo stóirín*. I'm not."

Fitz won't like being called my little treasure for many more years, but he hasn't decided he's too big for the endearment yet. And I'm using it until I can't anymore.

His little brow furrows as Fitz considers my answer.

What Mick hasn't mentioned to our little boy, is that it's not just a matter of increased security. The man who betrayed us by looking away from the sonar monitoring system at the *opportune* time (on purpose) is no longer on our payroll.

He's no longer breathing either, but that's beside the point.

Or maybe that's the only point? Hopefully the method of his demise will discourage other soldiers from selling out the Shaughnessy family.

I don't know the details, but I do know that even though it's been a couple of weeks since it happened, several soldiers who witnessed the execution are jumpy when my husband is around.

Some even avoid him altogether if they can.

Mick begins moving away from the dock, parallel to the shore. "Your mam can stay near the dock and you can swim to her."

Fitz's body bows like he's trying to throw himself from Mick's hold. "No! Mommy, come with us! The dock's not safe!"

That's it. My son is going to start seeing a children's therapist. No matter what my husband or father says.

Mick pulls Fitz close and speaks quietly in his ear. After a few seconds, our son's rigid body relaxes and he nods.

My husband raises his head, so our gazes meet. For once, I can easily read the concern in his usually inscrutable emerald gaze. "Fitz will swim toward you from the dock and I will keep pace with him."

I nod and dive into the water to swim past them. When I'm about thirty feet away, I stop and turn to face the two males I love most in the world.

Even if one of them doesn't love me back.

Fitz is smiling, obviously relaxed now. Clearly, he identifies the danger with the dock and not just the water in the bay. Which is good to know, but no less concerning.

He leaps from his father's hold and starts swimming a butterfly stroke toward me.

Mick calls encouragement, moving more swiftly through the water than I ever can unless I'm swimming, staying in easy to reach distance with our son.

Fitz stops in front of me and treads water, too short for his feet to reach the bottom. "Did you see mommy? I'm fast. Just like a dolphin."

The way the swimming technique resembles that marine mammal is the biggest reason Fitz wanted to learn it. "You looked just like a dolphin, *mo stóirín*."

"Ye did well." Mick's voice is laced with approval for our son's swimming feat. "That's not an easy stroke to learn."

"Mommy taught me." Fitz grins at me.

And my heart warms.

The look of heated approval Mick gives me is less joyous but no less impactful to my foolish heart.

My husband swoops our son up into the air. At six-one he can easily stand in water that is only chest-deep for him, while it's almost up to *my* chin.

Fitz whoops and Mick laughs like he hardly ever does, the sound real and happy. My mobbed up husband smiles a lot because he has the charming Irishman thing down pat, but it almost never reaches his eyes.

And his affability act does not stretch to frequent laughter either.

When we were first married, I thought all those smiles were genuine. Now, I know better. My husband is not the genial Irishman everyone believes him to be. I'm not really sure who he is, only that I wish he would let me in so I can find out.

"Micky!" A woman's voice calls from the shore.

A voice I don't recognize. I turn to look.

Standing next to my father on the lawn is a woman, her willowy frame encased in a well-tailored, designer suit-dress. Black hair cut in a stylish bob frames an almost ethereally beautiful face.

"Who is that?" I ask the back of my already moving husband's head.

"Dierdre Kelly."

Kelly, as in the other family that leads the Northside Dublin Syndicate in Dublin along with Mick's family, the Fitzgeralds? What the heck is she doing here?

"You never mentioned her before." I would remember.

My husband doesn't bother to answer. He doesn't stop to put on his slides when he steps onto the shore either. It takes me a few seconds longer to step out of the surf, but I still take a moment to slip my feet into sandals.

The white sand is too hot from the summer sun to walk barefoot. Reaching down, I scoop up Fitz's shoes as well.

When they reach the grass, Mick lets a squirming Fitz down to run toward his grandfather. Brogan Shaughnessy, Boss of the largest Irish mob in New York, is a more doting grandfather than he ever was as a dad.

I reach the small group just in time to hear Dierdre say, "Micky, I have to admit that of all the places I expected to find you, having a family swim with your sweet wee boy and innocent young wife wasn't one of them. How terribly domestic of you."

There's so much to unpack in that statement. Not least of which is how she makes *innocent* sound synonymous with *stupid*. And her emphasis on the word *young* makes it sound like Mick is twenty years older than me, not a mere eight.

That's not even a decade. Although that eight-year gap was intimidating to an 18-year-old bride, it's seven years on. Our difference in ages hardly registers anymore. I'm a wife and a mother. Hardly innocent.

And seriously, what is up with her calling him Micky?

Suddenly the buzz of conversation around me stops and I realize three sets of eyes are fixed on me expectantly. Fitz is staring in fascination at Dierdre Kelly, but she, my husband and my father are all looking at me.

"Sorry. Did I miss something?" I ask.

My father's lips flatten with irritation. "Kara, this is Dierdre Kelly. Dierdre, this is my daughter, Kara."

Oh, introductions were made while I was lost in my thoughts. There was a time not so long ago that it would have sent my stress skyrocketing to think I messed up.

But I'm working on the perfectionism that plagues me with the help of my secret online therapist. She's not the only online secret I have. I'm also attending university through distance learning courses.

My father would tell me I don't need either a therapist or higher education.

I don't know how Mick would react. I've never asked him, but keeping him in the dark so he doesn't tell my father feels like the safest course of action to me.

"Pleased to meet you, Miss Kelly." I reach my hand out to shake the Irish beauty's.

She barely touches my fingertips before pulling hers back, her carmine painted lips twisted in a moue of disapproval. "Wet."

"That happens when you're swimming." Do I sound as unimpressed by the prima donna as I feel?

"It's Dierdre, please," she says, ignoring my comment. "We're practically family, after all."

"We are?" I ask, nonplused. "How?"

"Micky's family and mine are very close." She gives Mick an appreciative once over. "Though we aren't actually related. We've been friends since I was a wee lass in pigtails."

I can't imagine this sophisticated woman wearing pigtails, even as a little girl.

And the way she looks with a little too much interest at my husband in his board shorts, his tattoo covered muscles glistening with water from the bay, makes it clear she definitely doesn't see him like a brother.

Whoever this woman is to my husband, she and I are not going to be besties.

The coolly assessing look Dierdre turns on me makes me wish I had stopped to put on my swim wrap and not just my sandals.

My wet tankini doesn't hide any of my body's imperfections. Well, except the faded stretch marks on my stomach from my pregnancy. They're the reason I wear a tankini instead of a bikini.

I'm rarely uncomfortable in my own skin though. I like my curves, even if I'm too rounded and jiggly to be mistaken for a gym bunny.

But right now, standing before the perfectly coiffed woman almost as tall as my dad in her heels, it's hard not to feel short and pudgy.

"What are you doing here?" Mick asks Dierdre.

Dierdre's mouth turns down in a pout. "Aren't you glad to see me?"

"Of course," Mick replies with a smile.

I draw comfort from the fact it's his charming persona smile, not a genuine one. I didn't used to be able to tell the difference.

When we were first married, I mistook Mick's charm for some kind of affection for me. After our son was born, I learned the difference between the façade and real affection.

Mick adores our son.

Which makes it impossible to lie to myself about him adoring me. He doesn't.

But sometimes when he smiles at me, it reaches his eyes. So, I know he likes me. Maybe even holds some affection for me.

Like my dad.

Not love.

Casual affection that doesn't impact either of their thoughts when I'm not directly in front of them.

My therapist is helping me work through that too.

"Let's go inside and I'll tell you all about it." Dierdre shoots a significant glance my way. "It's not something for the ears of a stranger."

If my sister were here, she'd be rolling her eyes at the drama queen. I'm tempted, but the six years between me and Fiona means I have to control the urge.

I'm a mature woman with a child.

Sometimes that reminder isn't all it's cracked up to be.

Mick jerks his head in acknowledgment and heads toward the house without another word. Or a look back at me to see if I have Fitz in hand.

Why would he? Our son is my responsibility during Mick's work hours.

And I never shirk my responsibilities.

FML

I grit my teeth in frustration. I can't even say the F-word inside my own head. Just the acronym. Because I'm the good girl. The obedient one.

I willingly sacrificed my life and dreams in marriage for the good of the mob at the age of 18.

But I resurrected those dreams, didn't I?

I might be a *good girl* who can't curse inside her own head, but I'm also the woman who is attending online university in secret and is only nine months from getting my degree in computer science.

Not that I'll ever be allowed to do anything with it, not in the Shaughnessy Mob anyway. My father's firmly stuck in the Dark Ages in his views on the role of women in the family business.

But maybe outside it. My specialty is programming and well...hacking, but I don't want to make a career out of that outside the mob. Too risky considering who I am.

But lots of programmers work remotely and with Fitz starting first grade in the fall, what's to stop me from filling my days with something more challenging than shopping and coffee dates with other mob wives?

Maybe I'll have a secret career to go with the rest of my secret life.

The parts of life I choose, not the pieces thrust on me because I was born a mob princess.

CHAPTER THREE

My Wife, My Rules, My Problem

MICK

"I 'll be right back," I tell Dierdre after leading her into the mansion's main living room.

She lets her gaze roam up and down my body. "Don't get dressed on my account."

Her words and attention leave me cold.

The view of my wife walking across the lawn toward the house with Fitz's hand in hers, in contrast, has blood surging to my dick.

Ignoring her innuendo, I leave Dierdre and jog toward our quarters before my Pavlovian reaction to my wife becomes obvious and the daft woman thinks it has something to do with her.

I'm sliding into my suit jacket, after a quick shower, when Kara steps into our bedroom.

Her eyes widen upon seeing me. "I thought you were meeting *in private* with Dierdre."

My wife doesn't roll her eyes when she says *in private* but her tone leaves no doubt how unimpressed she is with Dierdre's refusal to talk in front of her.

"I needed a shower, and I don't take meetings half dressed."

"I'm sure Dierdre wouldn't have minded." Turning toward the en suite, Kara shrugs out of her swim wrap.

Her swimsuit bottoms cling to her generous ass and my dick predictably takes immediate notice.

"Where's Fitz?" I ask, not having heard his boisterous tones before she came into the bedroom.

The walls on our room are sound dampening, but when the door is open, noise travels easily from the front room despite the distance.

We have the entire second floor in the west wing of the mansion for our private use. Set up like a luxury apartment, besides four bedrooms, three bathrooms and a kitchen, it has its own communal living area and saferoom too.

"He wanted to swim in the pool with Enoch."

Two weeks ago, Brogan accompanied Miceli De Luca to destroy the compound of an enemy. When my father-in-law came back, he had Hope Dobbs and her two children with him.

Esther is sixteen and Enoch is eight. Despite their two-year age difference, the two boys became immediate friends.

My wife is slower to trust their mother. So, it surprises me she left our son in Hope's care.

"Fi and Zoey were already swimming and promised to bring Fitz back when they're done," Kara says, like she knows exactly what I'm thinking.

She reads me better than anyone else, but she still doesn't *know* me. And if I can help it, she never will.

I straighten my cuffs. "I'm surprised you didn't stay with them."

Kara prefers the bay, but she loves to swim. Brogan has discouraged the family from using the bay for swimming since Róise's kidnapping though. However, I don't want my son hampered by unresolved fears.

So, Kara and I are working on getting him used to being in the bay again. "He's afraid of the dock."

Kara stops in the doorway to the en suite and turns to look at me over her shoulder. "I don't think it's that cut and dried. He was fine standing on it by himself."

"But he didn't want you near it alone."

She nods, chewing on her bottom lip and then meets my eyes, her hazel gaze dark with worry. "I want to get him therapy."

"Aye. Better that than to let his fears fester."

Face slack with shock, Kara turns around completely so she's facing me. "You'd be okay with it?"

What does she think? I would deny my son the medical care he needs? Is that why she hides her ongoing visits with the therapist she started seeing in the "luxury treatment center" when Fitz was still an infant?

She thinks I won't approve?

Her father wouldn't, which is why I don't mention that my wife has weekly video calls with a mental health professional. But hell, anything that will prevent her from going back to the dark depression she fell into after Fitz's birth is a good thing.

She tried to end her own life and damn near succeeded. Thirty minutes later and I wouldn't have gotten to her in time. Her heart would have stopped for the pills she took.

Never again.

If talking to her therapist once a week helps, then I'll make sure my wife always has that option. No matter what Brogan has to say about it.

Even if I personally don't understand the need to talk about her innermost thoughts and feelings with someone. Despite my disguise of normalcy, I don't have feelings like other people. And if I shared my deepest thoughts, I'd be locked up in a not so luxury mental health facility.

"It will have to be someone connected to the syndicate though," I warn Kara. "Someone who knows better than to share our business with outsiders."

She shakes her head at me. "Doctor-patient confidentiality would prevent that from happening regardless."

"I trust family bonds over HIPAA compliance." With the right incentive, even a doctor can turn informant.

It's happened before and will happen again.

Kara sighs, but nods. "I'll see if my therapist knows a child psychologist she can recommend."

That's one of the many things about my wife that I admire. She doesn't lie unless she has no other choice. So, she doesn't refer to the woman as her *former* therapist, or imply they aren't still in touch.

Nor does she offer the fact she continues to see the doctor weekly. Kara hides a clatter of shit from me and her father, but she doesn't outright lie about it.

"You'd better get back down to your friend. She's probably wearing a pattern in the carpet waiting to have her *secret discussion* with you." Kara uses air quotes when she says *secret discussion*.

It's the second time she's mentioned the fact that Dierdre won't tell me why she's here in front of my wife. And that's cause for concern.

When she first started showing signs of jealousy during her pregnancy, it didn't bother me. I'm possessive and would kill a man who made a move on my wife. Her expressing the desire for other women not to flirt with me was reasonable.

Unfortunately, Kara often thought women were flirting when they weren't. If one of the household staff smiled at me, it could lead to an emotional rant from Kara.

I minimized my time with women who worked with us in either our mob businesses or legit ones. But then Fitz was born and I thought Kara's emotions had evened out.

When I started working on a deal that required a lot of legal support, I spent many hours sequestered in my office with our lawyer. She happened to be an attractive woman in her early thirties, but all I saw was her brain and ability to give legal advice.

Kara threw a fit and demanded her father fire the lawyer. Brogan refused.

I found my wife unconscious on the floor of our bathroom three days later. She'd taken nearly a full bottle of sleeping pills.

Now, I pay attention when Kara shows anything more than mild annoyance. Not because she's exhibited jealousy since then, but because since that time, her feelings have been almost as locked down as mine.

"You know there's business I don't share with you." I watch closely to gauge her reaction to my words.

Her kissable lips twist in a frown, but there's no fervor of banked fury in her hazel eyes. "Are you saying her reason for being here has to do with business?"

"I don't know."

"And if it's not, will you tell me then?"

"Is it important to you that I do?" I ask, my senses on high alert.

Kara sighs again and her shoulders sag. "No, I suppose not. What's one more secret between us? It's not like we love each other."

I'm not capable of loving her. Obsession may be part and parcel to my nature, but not love.

However, Kara used to believe she loved me. She never said it, but it was there. Both her father and grandmother commented on it during Kara's jealousy episodes.

However, somewhere along the line, she stopped.

I don't know why exactly, but it doesn't surprise me. A heart as pure as hers can't stay fixated on a monster. Even one she doesn't know exists.

At some point her atavistic instincts must have sounded the alarm to her heart.

~ ~ ~

"I'm sorry I didn't come for the wedding." Dierdre looks up at me through her lashes. "It would have been too hard to watch you marry another woman."

I incline my head, not convinced. Sure, there'd been plenty of craic about me and Dierdre getting married one day.

We dated. We had sex. But I wasn't her first and she wasn't mine.

There was no romance. No great love.

The only person I have ever loved is my son. I'm not sure Dierdre has ever loved anyone.

When my da got the chance to tighten the ties between the Northies and the powerful Shaughnessy Mob in New York, he took it.

Marriage to Kara offered me something marriage to Dierdre never could: the chance to become second in command.

And I didn't even know it would go down that way when I agreed to the marriage.

The promotion from assassin for my former mob to captain, running my own crew under Derry Shaughnessy – Fergal's oldest son and underboss, was enough incentive to leave Ireland.

The death of both Fergal and Derry in the same year offered me something more. The chance to be underboss and eventually, the Boss of the Shaughnessy Mob.

As his "disturbed" youngest son, my father would not have made me a captain. And there was no chance I would ever be second-in-command in the Northies, much less the boss without my older brothers dying.

I don't have a lot of scruples, but killing family *is* one of them.

Don't think my da knows that though. He was as happy about getting me out of Dublin as he was about the marriage alliance with the Shaughnessy Mob.

I make him nervous.

Da is one of the few people who knows the real me. He recognized my lack of the moral restraints other people are born with before I started school. He's the one who taught me to project a relatable persona to cover the sociopath within.

Other kids learned manners. I learned to mask the monster who felt no remorse about breaking the arm of a boy who knocked my sister off the monkey bars and made her cry.

Brigid was five. I was eight. The boy who knocked her off so he could play on them was ten.

While he writhed on the ground crying and screaming for the teacher, I told him I would kill him if he ever touched her again.

Da took me out of school and got me private tutors after that.

My brothers were all made between the ages of nineteen and twenty-one. I had my first kill at the age of eleven.

It wasn't for the mob. It was for my dog. Animals made more sense to me than people. They still do. Toby was my friend and confidant. He loved me unconditionally and without judgment.

He was the only living being that could.

I sliced the throat of the man who hit him while driving three sheets to the wind. Da never allowed me to get another pet.

Now, Fitz has a cat. A bundle of chaos my son lets sleep in his bed. If someone hurts Gobby, I'll kill them myself.

"It took a long time for me to get past losing you," Dierdre adds.

"I'm sorry to hear that." I'm not.

I don't feel anything at all in response to her words, but those are the words to say in this situation.

I've perfected the art of knowing the correct response whether, or not, I think it's a valid one.

Except when it comes to my wife. At first, Kara was as easy to predict and appease as anyone else. Easier even. But not anymore.

She used to follow me around like Toby and I didn't mind that she was always there. I liked it.

It felt right.

But things changed after Fitz was born and taking care of him took precedence. She still dropped in to see me when I was working from my office on the estate, but not as often.

And after she got back from The Marlowe Center, she stopped coming to my office at all. That's when I started stalking my own wife on the CCTV in the mansion.

Unbeknownst to my wife, I installed cameras in the main living area and bedroom in our apartment.

Being able to check on her throughout the day settled something inside me that had been feral since her brush with death and trip to The Marlowe Center.

Then Kara's seventeen-year-old cousin stood up to Brogan and insisted on going to college like her deceased father had promised her that she could. Kara stood up for Róise, but something changed in her when her cousin got accepted to the fine arts university.

She pulled away from both me and Brogan emotionally.

Emotions aren't my thing, so at first, I didn't think it mattered.

When I realized how much I didn't like the distance she'd created between us, I assumed it would change back after she started secret online courses for university. That her resentment about having to marry at eighteen, when most women had their whole lives ahead of them, would dissipate.

She'll get her degree next spring, just like Róise, but nothing has changed between us.

Kara never visits my office anymore unless Fitz is asking to see me. Often as not, she'll send our son to me with one of his guards. Always with instructions to send Fitz back to her when I need to.

Always.

Like she needs me to know she's not shirking her duties.

Feck if I know how to change that either.

Dierdre moves a few inches closer. "How are things between you and your child bride?"

"Kara will be twenty-five next month. She's not a child."

"She was only eighteen when you got married."

"Still not a child." If I'd had my way, the marriage would have taken place a couple of years later.

I was no keener to get married at twenty-six than Kara was at eighteen.

But that wasn't an option. Fergal Shaughnessy would have offered the deal to another mobster if I'd refused to marry his granddaughter two weeks after she graduated high school.

Too bad he didn't die until a year later. A lot of things would have gone differently in the beginning if Brogan had been the boss already.

Dierdre's mouth twists with distaste. "Not technically, but I'm surprised you were okay with marrying a teenager."

"My marriage gave me the path forward I wanted." And once I set my eyes on Kara, she was never going to marry anyone else.

Eighteen years old, or twenty-eight. As long as she was an adult, she was going to be mine.

"Without me."

What is the point of this conversation? "Yes."

Dierdre flinches, like my words hurt her. Again, I'm not convinced. She's always been a little dramatic.

"Ye didn't tell me you were coming to New York." Dierdre and I stay in touch with texts and the occasional phone call.

She's a good source of information on what's happening in Dublin. Dierdre tells me things my da and brothers wouldn't.

"There was no time." She grabs my forearm. "I'm in danger and da wanted me to get a move on."

"Why are you in danger?" And why is she in New York and not a safe house?

And why the feck is she touching me? I pull my arm from her grip and step back, putting some distance between us.

She frowns, but stays where she is. "The Odessa Mafia tried to have me kidnapped. They want leverage on a deal that has stalled between them and da."

Her da is the leader of the Kelly crew. My da leads the Fitzgerald crew. Between them they make up the Northside Dublin Syndicate. The Northies.

"The Northies are doing business with the Odessa Mafia now?"

She shrugs. "War makes opportunities for organizations that can keep their supply chains stable."

"Why didn't you tell me about the attempted kidnapping?" Why didn't my father?

There's too much business happening in Dublin I don't know about. I'm going to have to fix that.

Dierdre is no longer an adequate source.

"It only happened yesterday. Da thinks I'll be safer here, with the Shaughnessy Mob."

"Does Brogan know about the danger you brought with ya?" I demand.

"I didn't bring it with me. No one knows I came to the States. Da laid a false trail to a safe house. One of my second cousins who looks like me is staying there to keep the fiction going."

There's not an ounce of remorse in Dierdre's tone to indicate it bothers her that the other woman could be taken in her place.

That's one of the reasons she and I have always gotten along. Selfish and ruthless, she's entirely predictable.

Kara is the only person I have trouble reading and predicting behavior for.

"That does not answer my question."

She shrugs. "Ask my da. He's the one that made the arrangements."

"Did you bring security?"

"Of course."

"How many?" And why wasn't I told that soldiers from another syndicate would be remaining on premises?

"Only two. Our fathers are certain your men are up to the task of keeping me safe."

"Your safety is not my men's priority." The safety of my wife and child come before everyone else.

Which I'm sure the men understand after the last demonstration I gave them.

Brogan thinks he comes first, but the men understand now. If Brogan dies, so will they. If Kara or Fitz are harmed in any way, they'll still die.

But slowly and in so much pain, they'll be begging me to kill them.

Just like that fecker, Troy, who thought taking money from an Aryan militia group to betray the family was a good idea.

He put my wife and son in danger.

Now all the soldiers know what a feckin' stupid thing that was to do.

CHAPTER FOUR

Trust Issues, Spyware, & Other Love Languages

MICK

"Why didn't you tell me you were bringing another security risk into the household?" I don't bother with pleasantries.

My father-in-law and I are the only ones in his office and I'm not feeling pleasant.

"How many times do I have to tell you, boyo? Hope Dobbs and her children are not a security risk. Her husband died like all of the other AOG bastards when we razed the compound."

"And if she decides to cozy up to another Aryan cult?"

A feral glint flashes in Brogan's blue eyes. "That's not going to happen. She's staying right here."

"You're pretty feckin' possessive over a houseguest." I don't bother to point out that the woman is twelve years younger than him.

I'm not a hypocrite. A psychopath? Yes. A hypocrite? No.

"She risked her own safety to protect my niece. Hope deserves my protection in return."

I don't bother to argue. If Brogan wants to watch out for Hope, that's his lookout.

As long as she doesn't put the only people that matter to me at risk. Kara and Fitz.

Brogan waves his hand at one of the chairs in front of his desk. "Sit down. You know I don't like it when you loom over me."

My boss doesn't like feeling at a physical disadvantage. It's smart. I don't either.

I sit down, but don't relax. "When were you going to tell me about two soldiers from another mob staying in the barracks?"

"Do I need to remind you that that other mob is not only our ally, but your own family?" Brogan drawls sarcastically.

"Kara and Fitz are the only family that matters to me." I'll burn down my old mob to keep them safe without a second's hesitation.

I won't kill family for ambition, but I will kill *anyone* for the sake of my wife and son's safety.

Brogan's mouth shifts into a sardonic smirk. "I notice you didn't include me in that list."

I shrug. I won't grieve if he dies. I'm not wired for that kind of emotion, but I'm loyal. And that's all Brogan has to worry about.

"Did you know the Odessa Mafia tried to kidnap Dierdre when you agreed to let her come here?" I don't do a damn thing to hide my disapproval.

"I know that's what her father told me."

That makes me pause. "Ye don't believe him?"

"Did you believe her?" Brogan asks me, instead of answering.

"She doesn't have any tells when she lies."

"Which is not the same as saying you believe her."

"No. It's not."

"The timing is suspect. We're developing new technology for silent guns and suddenly one of our Dublin friends needs to stay in my house?"

"Ye think we have another mole?" I ask.

Brogan scowls and shakes his head. "No fucking way. I looked every one of our men in the eye when they renewed their pledge of loyalty."

I had too. If one of them is spying for my family's mob, they're a better liar than Dierdre. Because the very absence of any tells makes me distrust *everything* she says.

Which is only one of the reasons I think she has ulterior motives for being here.

Brogan's scowl darkens. "We didn't use a shell company when we sourced the Neo magnets through your contact in Myanmar."

Ko Naing has a strict face-to-face, one-on-one policy. Insisting on dealing with me personally, he won't even take a call from Brogan. I respect that level of caution.

Besides we need access to Neodymium without going through government channels. Most sources in China and the United States – the biggest producers – are connected to government entities.

Unfortunately, my father also does business with Ko Naing.

The Burmese man is discreet, but my da could have a spy in his operation. I do.

Trusting a business partner to be completely transparent is a fool's game and I'm nobody's fool.

Expecting other people to take the same precautions, I'm hyper vigilant about watching for indicators of spies in our ranks. Which is why Troy and his fellow spy for the AOG pissed me off so much.

Unfortunately, both men were inducted into the mob before I came to America. Both had the personal approval of Brogan's father and both were too damn good at covering their tracks.

Just like the mole working for the Columbian cartel we identified last year.

Both situations still fill me with rage.

I've personally vetted every single one of our soldiers now, but I should have done it when Brogan made me second-in-command.

Which is why all soldier's phones are now equipped with listening devices and spyware.

Even if they use a burner to make a call, or text, if it's done within the vicinity of their primary phone, the content of the call or text is fed into the AI program developed by our new Cosa Nostra allies. The AI monitors communications for suspicious speech patterns and behavior.

Like using a burner cell to make texts and calls.

No one but Brogan and I know it's on the soldier's phones.

We weren't surprised when our blackgloves discovered a back door in the program that would have allowed the Italians to spy on us too. I would have tried the same thing.

When the hacker closed the backdoor at my request, he put an alarm on its lock. When the Italian's tried to use it to access our coms information, it triggered a warning to us and a virus to the server hosting their AI that did just enough damage to warn the Cosa Nostra not to fuck with us.

It was my idea for every monitor in their network to flash: Nice try, *gléas*.

I personally texted the message to Miceli. He texted back a frowning devil, horse and hole emojis. His own version of fuck off, asshole. We're all good.

"Most likely scenario is that Dierdre is here on a fishing expedition." The Northies aren't going to know we're working on whisper guns from the magnets alone.

Much less how close we are to a working prototype.

But we're not the only ones working on the technology. Civilians, governments and other syndicates all want a piece of that pie.

It wouldn't be a far reach for my father to guess where our business is headed. It's conceivable he sent Dierdre here to gain information.

It makes sense, even if I don't like it.

"You'll need to keep an eye on Dierdre. She'll reveal herself to you in ways she won't to the rest of us. It's clear as day that woman wants you back in her bed."

Brogan is right. On all counts.

But that doesn't make it a good idea. "Kara won't like it."

Brogan grimaces. "She's better now. You don't have to worry about my sensible daughter throwing a jealous fit."

No, she'll just pull further away.

Or not.

What if jealousy triggers Kara's desire to stake her claim on me? Maybe she'll start visiting my office again if she thinks she needs to check up on me.

A tiny voice in the back of my head questions the wisdom and ethics of using Dierdre to spark my wife's battened down emotions. I think it's what exists of my conscience.

I ignore it like I've been doing for most of my life.

CHAPTER FIVE

Family Dinner & Other Bloodsports

KARA

E arly enough for Fitz not to be cranky with tiredness, Sunday dinner is usually one of my favorite times of the week. It's the one time our powerful mob family feels almost normal.

Not only do both Mick and my father stop working early to be at the table by two o'clock sharp, but there is no business talk at the table on Sundays. Per *mamo's* decree.

My grandmother is a stickler for timeliness and tradition.

It's an Irish tradition *mamo* brought from the Old Country. One even my grandfather didn't mess with.

Like he messed with everything else.

My hand presses against my lower belly in a self-soothing reaction to the memories that try to surface. Concentrating on my surroundings, I push them back.

No clinic. No callous disposal of embryos with female DNA. No fertility controlled sex life.

I was four months pregnant with my son before I had penetrative sex for the first time with my husband.

No. Darn it. I am not going there.

In a desperate attempt to stem the tide of memories that don't want to be suppressed for some reason today, my eyes latch onto the view across the lawn.

The afternoon sun shimmers on the bay, turning the boats into hazy blips of bobbing color. A soft breeze lifts strands of my hair and carries the scent of sea salt and grilled meat from the terrace.

My father's contribution to family tradition. Brogan Shaughnessy, wealthy boss of the Irish mob, turns steaks on the barbecue. He only does it during the summer months, but I remember how much my mom loved it.

At least I think I remember that. Is it a real memory, or part of the movie that plays in my head when *mamo* tells family stories?

Does it matter?

Dad does his thing at the grill and it makes me feel closer to the mom I lost at the age of six. Another good thing about Sundays.

It's also the one day a week that Mick almost never returns to work after eating, despite it being served several hours before our usual dinnertime.

My family is gathered around the long outdoor dining table shaded by an enormous cream-colored sail attached to sturdy trellises on three sides. The scent of the climbing roses mixes with the other smells of summer and I breathe in deeply.

Finally, the painful memories disappear into the haze on the water.

I smile at the sight of Fitz climbing up beside my grandmother with a bowl of fresh watermelon chunks. They're both fiends for it and grab for a chunk at the same time.

The good boy that he is, Fitz offers it to *mamo*, who insists he eats it. Of course.

She's the opposite of her deceased husband, my grandfather, in almost every way, but especially how she dotes on the children in the family.

My gaze shifts to Fi leaning into Zoe, whispering something that makes them both snort into their wine. I love seeing my sister come out of her shell. Before Zoe, Fi was a silent guest at the dinner table, even among family, only opening up around *mamo*, me and our cousin, Róise.

Róise doesn't live here anymore, but we have new people living in the mansion to fill the empty space at the table.

Hope and her two children. Esther, the teenager, is coaxing Enoch, Fitz's new best friend, to try a shrimp from the cocktail platter. Their mother is hovering at my father's side, her expression filled with a worrying amount of hero worship and adoration.

I suppose that to a woman raised in a white supremacist cult and married off to an abusive man nearly old enough to be her grandfather at the tender age of sixteen, my father must seem like a hero among men.

But his feet of clay will crush her heart if she doesn't watch out. I should know.

And then there's her.

Dierdre's high-heeled sandals click against the stones of the terrace as she walks toward us, Mick at her side.

Where he has been presumably since leaving our apartment to speak to her three hours ago.

She's got her arm through his, clinging possessively and I have to school my features into passivity.

Nothing to see here.

Mick pulls out her chair and Dierdre slides into the seat one over from me like she belongs there, all long legs and artful disinterest. She's wearing a breezy designer sundress and sunglasses too big for her face.

Her lips curve like a woman with a secret. Or several.

Mick doesn't greet me, but his hand rests on the back of my chair when he takes the empty seat between Dierdre and me.

"So," Dierdre says, tilting her head toward me with an air of insouciance I don't trust for a second. "This is family dinner."

The words are innocent enough, but this woman is trouble.

"New York summers are something else. It's not like this in Dublin, is it, Micky? So hot." She fans her face with her hand, her eyes now fixed intently on my husband's face.

He makes a sound that could be agreement or a grunt.

Dierdre doesn't seem bothered by his taciturnity. But then she knows what he's like. They're practically family after all. The sarcasm inside my head is strong, but I keep it there.

Twirling her wine glass by the stem, her eyes flick toward *mamo*, then back to me. Cataloguing. Assessing.

Mamo came over from Dublin herself to marry my grandfather over five decades ago at the age of eighteen. Just like Mick came here to marry me.

Only I was the teenager in that wedding ceremony.

"Micky and I used to sit out like this in the summer. The view from the rooftop of his building was breathtaking," Dierdre says with a warm gaze directed toward *my* husband. "You remember those nights, don't you, Micky? Back then, what we got up to wouldn't have been appropriate for a family dinner."

A sick feeling invades my stomach and the breath catches in my chest. But I keep my smile fixed. Polished. Impervious.

They'd been lovers. This Irish beauty and my husband.

He had a whole life before I met him, I remind myself. I know he wasn't celibate, but having one of his ex-girlfriends sitting at my family dinner table is sending my appetite to the bottom of the bay faster than a concrete boat.

Mick's fingers twitch against my chair. But he doesn't confirm, or deny Dierdre's claims. That's confirmation in itself, isn't it?

Mamo stiffens beside Fitz. "Your conversation leaves something to be desired at the dinner table, Miss Kelly."

Zoey raises an eyebrow. *Mamo* might scold her family, but not a guest. She spent years as a mob boss's wife and hiding her irritation is second-nature to my grandmother.

Unless someone comes for one of her own. Then *mamo's* Irish temper sparks.

"Dierdre, please, Maeve. We're practically family." She completely ignores my grandmother's admonishment.

Oh, to have that kind of confidence for real, and not a put-on façade for the sake of appearances.

Mamo's eyes narrow to slits.

Fi notices because she's hyper attuned to the emotions of the people around her. She goes still, pulling away from Zoey slightly, like she's going into self-protect mode. The smile drops from her face.

I want that smile back. My sister is finally happy and the harpy intent on stirring up trouble isn't going to steal it.

Shaking my head infinitesimally at my grandmother, I focus on the love I have for Fi so my smile is real before I turn it on my sister. I wink at Fi, letting her know I'm fine.

That the Irish beauty claiming past intimacies with my husband isn't getting to me. For a second, even I believe it.

Then Dierdre opens her mouth again. "Of course, that was years ago," She waves her hand dismissively. "We've stayed in touch, though, through texts. And calls here and there. It's nice to have...history."

I glance at Mick. His eyes are on me, not Dierdre. Is he worried I'm going to snap again? I won't.

I might *feel* like dumping the platter of cold prawns over Dierdre's head, cocktail sauce and all. But I won't.

The past is the past. And we are living in the present, as my therapist would say.

I may not be as confident as Dierdre on the inside, but I'm definitely not the same insecure woman at twenty-four that I was at nineteen.

"I'm sure you understand." Despite Mick's lack of a response to her words so far, Dierdre blithely goes on, the smile she directs at me saccharine sweet and just as bad for you. "Old friends."

"Sure," I say lightly. "I'm a big believer in keeping tabs on dangerous people."

Her smile falters for half a second, then rebounds as she places her hand on Mick's forearm. "Well. That's one way to put it. But Mick knows I'm not dangerous to him."

The look she gives me says I'm in a whole different category.

Mick doesn't pull away from her touch.

Five years ago, I would have drawn into myself and spent the rest of the meal telling myself I wasn't enough.

That's not where this is going today. I lower my hand below the table and slide it over Mick's upper thigh, stopping when the back of it brushes against his sex.

Luckily, Mick dresses to the right, so I don't have to reach across his lap and make my movements obvious. To the others it looks like I'm resting my hand in my lap.

No one else at the table knows where it actually is. Except Mick.

My husband sucks in a breath and I feel the bulge against the back of my hand grow. That quickly.

Dierdre's eyes narrow. I'm pretty sure she can guess where my hand is right now too.

I smile back, all teeth.

Having made my point, I go to pull my hand away, but Mick twines his fingers through mine and keeps it against him.

Showing she is and will always be on my side, *moma* pushes the basket of yeasty rolls toward Dierdre. "Here, take one and pass it to Mick."

"I don't eat carbs at dinner, even when the meal happens at lunchtime," Dierdre replies, but she takes the basket, having to remove her hand from my husband's arm to do it.

Showing no such compunction, Mick snags two, putting one on my plate, before passing the basket over to Enoch.

"I love the smell of freshly baked bread and the taste even more," I say, taking a bite.

"Enough of that, we've yet to say grace," my father protests as he sits down.

Unconcerned, I finish chewing the yeasty goodness as I bow my head and let my father's recitation of the familiar *Gaeilge* words wash over me as Mick's penis grows steel hard against the back of my hand.

I smile to myself. This is *my* family. *Our* traditions.

No matter what they shared in the past, Mick is *my* husband.

Unsurprisingly, our new houseguest dominates the conversation over dinner. Though every time she looks in my direction, it's like she sucked on a lemon.

Mick hasn't let go of my hand and he's still hard.

I wonder if Fi and Zoey are up for some nephew time after we're done eating?

As we're finishing up, Hope asks Dierdre, "What brings you to New York, Miss Kelly?"

"The Odessa Mafia tried to snatch me right off the street. Who knows what they would have done to me if my bodyguards hadn't stopped them?" Dierdre replies dramatically.

Hope's innocent gaze turns horrified. "That must have been awful."

"It was terrifying. My father sent me here because he knew Mick would keep me safe." Dierdre puts her hand right over Mick's heart and gives him a look that I'm sure is meant to convey frightened vulnerability.

It doesn't sit naturally on her face. The woman's a viper, not a mouse.

Unfortunately, the mask I can see through so easily is opaquer to my son. He leaps from the oversized chair he shares with my grandmother and rushes toward me.

Throwing himself against me, he bursts into tears. "They can't have you mommy!"

Climbing right into my lap like he hardly ever does anymore, he clings to my neck with both arms.

Finally shaking off yet another unsolicited touch from Dierdre, Mick shoves his chair back and drops to one knee beside our distraught son. "No one is taking your mam from you. I promised you, didn't I?"

"Is it wise to make promises to a child like that?" Dierdre asks sotto voce. "I don't know a lot about children, but making empty promises to calm them down isn't a kindness."

"If Mick makes a promise, he keeps it," my father says firmly, concern softening his harsh features as he watches my son sob in my arms.

At least he's not telling Fitz to pull himself together like he did me after my mom died.

"I'm only pointing out that our world is dangerous and our children need to realize that. As the missing family members from this table can attest."

Alluding to the violent deaths of my beloved aunt and uncle at a table full of people who still miss them is a low blow I won't forget. But I'll never *forgive* the way she's so clearly trying to increase my son's hysteria.

And it's working. Fitz's sobs turn to incoherent wails amidst a few recognizable words demanding his da keep me safe.

Mick tries to pull him away from me to reassure him, but Fitz's little arms are like barnacles. He's not going anywhere.

"I will always protect you and your mam," Mick vows again as he stands.

Then he leans down and slides his powerful forcarms under my thighs and along my back, lifting both me and our son like our combined weight is nothing.

When I know for a fact, it's more than average something.

Without a word to anyone else at the table, including his awful ex-girl-friend, Mick takes long, confident strides toward the house.

The movement stops Fitz mid-wail and he looks up. "You're carrying me *and* mommy?"

His voice is still tear soaked, but at least he's talking and not wailing.

"Aye. I'm strong enough to carry yiz both and I'm strong enough to keep yiz both safe *mo leanbh*."

"Strong enough to carry us up the stairs?" Fitz tests.

Mick nods. "Strong enough to carry you as long as I need to."

By the time we reach our apartment, Mick is breathing a little heavier, but he's not panting. I don't know about Fitz, but I'm impressed.

So are my ovaries, which are sparking like an ungrounded wire.

It's almost enough to make me forget how tolerant my husband was of Dierdre's familiarity.

Almost.

CHAPTER SIX

Daddy's Armed. Mommy's Dangerous.

MICK

My strategy is working faster than I expected it to.

My usually reticent wife has never once touched me in an even remotely intimate way with other people around.

But in staking her claim, she did the unthinkable. And I was more than happy to capitalize on her unexpected behavior, keeping the back of her hand pressed against my hard cock throughout dinner.

She didn't once try to pull away after the first time. Not until Fitz launched himself at her.

My son's distress deflated my erection faster than an ice bath. If Fitz wasn't so upset, I'd ask Fiona to watch him so Kara and I could have some time alone.

But Dierdre has Fitz riled up good and proper.

I set Fitz and Kara down on the sofa. "Look at me *mo leanbh*."

Fitz obeys me instantly and I take that as a win.

I shrug out of my summer weight suit jacket and indicate the gun holster under my left arm. Then I put my left foot on the coffee table and lift my pant leg so he can see the small pistol holstered there.

I switch feet and show the double knife holster on either side of my ankle on my right leg.

After that, I reveal the hidden knife in my belt buckle and the razor wire that slides out of my leather belt. "I am always prepared to keep you and your mam safe."

"What if you aren't with her? What if you're working and the bad guys come for her?"

"There is not another man alive badder, or scarier than me," I promise our son. "And when I'm not with yiz, I always make sure at least six men are watching over you."

"And mommy too?" Fitz stresses.

Where is this coming from? Why does my son believe I value his mother's safety less than his? "Aye."

"Even when she goes somewhere without me?" Fitz asks doubtfully.

"Next to you, boyo, your mam is the most important person to me in the world." As the words leave my mouth, I realize where some of my son's fears stem from.

I've said something similar to him many times believing it would give him comfort. Now, I realize it has caused him to create a narrative in his mind where I don't value Kara's safety as much as his.

The way that Kara looks down at our son and doesn't meet my eyes tells me she buys into the same narrative.

Feckin' hell.

I'm not a man made to comfort others. Present situation a glaring example of that truth. But I cannot leave either of them believing that I won't burn down the world to protect Kara.

"I will never let anyone take your mommy away from us," I promise Fitz before lifting my wife's chin so our eyes meet. "Ye are *mine* Kara, now and forever. I will always protect you."

Her eyes soften like they do sometimes. "I know."

But she doesn't know. Does she? Neither does Fitz. Words are not enough and they're not my strong suit anyway.

I pull out my phone and send two texts. One to the head of security and one to the group message stream for the entire team dedicated to watching over my wife and son.

I get seven immediate responses. All of them affirmative. Not that I expect anything less. These men know their lives are forfeit if anything happens to their charges. They knew it long before I had to teach that lesson to the rest of our soldiers.

"From now on, when I'm not here, there will be security both inside and outside the apartment. Two of your guards will be visible at all times."

Kara's mouth drops open, but whatever she wants to say gets swallowed as our son nods enthusiastically. "Even when mommy is alone."

"Even then," I promise him.

My wife is not nearly as happy about the change as our son. I'm not sure why. There's no material change in her routine. The guards were always there, she just didn't see them.

"Did you think yiz didn't have guards with yiz at all times?" I ask her.

"Why would we have guards inside the house?" she asks back.

But clearly she didn't.

She still thinks I don't know about the little outing she arranged with Róise for her cousin's twenty-first. Kara has no clue that the minute she left the estate, I got an alert from her tracker.

She only got that far without me knowing because my wife is scary good at disabling alarms and hacking security footage. I had eyes on her the minute they reached the dock of the mansion further down the coastline.

After following them into the city, I watched over them the entire time they were there and made sure my wife made it safely back to the estate.

Then I told our blackgloves to take the mansion security firewalls to the level of a nuclear weapons facility. Should have done it sooner, but Kara's the only one who ever managed to hack through the ones we had.

And she had inside access. Regardless, even she won't find a way in now. Unless she gets physical access to the server room, and we beefed up security to that too.

"Because what happened to Róise will *never* happen to yiz." My wife is never leaving the estate without me knowing again.

Fitz draws in a sharp breath. "You promise, da?"

"Aye."

"Double pinky swear." Fitz shoves his arms out, crosses them and extends both of his pinkies.

What the feck is this? I look to Kara for an explanation. And of course she has one. There's nothing about our son she doesn't know.

"Enoch taught him. You cross your arms, and twine your pinkies and swear to keep your promise."

I do as she says, curling my pinkies around my son's smaller ones. "I double pinky swear to always protect you and your mam."

Fitz throws himself against me and hugs tight. "Thank you da!" He pulls back, grinning. "Can I go play with Enoch now?"

"Aye, if you want." I text the man stationed outside our door and Fitz's personal bodyguard who is on standby when my son is with me.

Less than a minute later, Kara and I are alone.

She's looking at the door as if she can still see our son through it. "I'd feel better if I knew Fi was watching him too."

"Then text her."

Kara nods, but doesn't move to grab her phone. "I still want him to see a child psychologist."

"Aye." A pinky swear isn't going cure my son of the trauma of seeing Róise disappear from the dock right in front of him.

"You're a lot more accepting of the idea than I expected you to be." Her gaze shifts from the door to me, her pretty hazel eyes filled with questions.

"I'm not an unreasonable man, *mo chuisle*."

"That's not what the soldiers who hide behind bushes when they see you coming think," she teases me.

She's the only person who ever does. The only person I would allow to.

"If my soldiers are jumping behind bushes to avoid me, they need another lesson in doing their jobs."

"Yeah, sure. That's exactly what they need. Another reason to fear you."

Something goes cold in my chest. "What do you know about my lessons to the men?"

"Only that since you dealt with Troy, the men avoid you to a near comical level." She sounds amused.

Not distressed by the truth she's married to a monster. She has no idea what went on at the warehouse. And she never will. I promised to cut the tongue out of any man's mouth who so much as breathes a word about it around her.

"Not all the men." My crew doesn't avoid me.

They know better.

I don't tolerate weakness.

"If you say so," my wife sasses. "I better text Fi."

"I'll do it." If she texts her sister, Kara is as apt to end up joining them as to stay here with me.

And that would feck with my plans to drown myself in her tight pussy. Before Kara can argue, I send the text to Fiona.

She texts back immediately that they're all going to play a game of croquet.

Good. That should be enough time.

I drop my phone and pick up my wife.

She gasps but immediately wraps her arms around my neck. "I could get used to this."

Yeah. I don't think so. My wife is too independent to let me carry her around and keep her attached at my side like I want to. I crave her full attention, only ever really okay with sharing it with Fitz.

Everyone else only exists in our world because it would hurt her if they didn't.

I carry her straight into our bedroom and kick the door shut behind me. My hands don't shake, but they should. They would if I was a normal man.

I married Kara for what that marriage would give me. But now I crave her for her own sake. All the damn feckin' time.

When she put her hand on my thigh, pressed against my cock like she owns it? The howling wind inside me quieted.

Even the monster recognizes the truth. She does own us.

Somehow, after seven years of marriage Kara still doesn't realize that though. Not really. Or this afternoon wouldn't have been the first time she made a move like that.

It almost makes me want to thank Dierdre for coming to New York.

Kara's fingers trail up my nape, soft and trusting. She doesn't speak. Doesn't need to. She's watching me with hunger and fear twisted together like silk and barbed wire.

Doubt she even realizes the fear is there. It's atavistic, not conscious. But the hunger has her arousal perfuming the air around us.

I drop her onto the bed. She bounces once, her tits jiggling in a way that tells me she's not wearing a bra under her sundress. Her hair falls across her face like a veil and I want to wrap it around my fist and yank it back.

The flush of arousal pinkens the swell of her breasts above the neckline of that sweet little dress. Her nipples already hard, creating shoals in the fabric and begging for my mouth.

I love her tits. So damn lush and sensitive. Nipples as big and dark as raspberries. I could spend hours sucking them, watching her tremble while she tries to hide how much she needs me.

But not tonight. My patience burned to cinders the second our son left the apartment.

"Ye started something at dinner," I growl, pulling my shirt over my head.

Her eyes go wide when they land on my chest.

She's seen me naked more times than I can count, but it's the same look of voracious hunger every time. Like just looking at me sends her pussy spasming.

Our gazes locked, I undo my belt. "And I'm going to finish it."

Hers drops to follow the motion. She swallows.

Kara's breath stutters, but she doesn't look away. "You seemed fine with letting her touch you."

My hands still. "Ye want to talk about Dierdre now?"

Something not good flashes in her expression before it's gone, replaced with unmistakable hunger. "I don't want to talk at all."

CHAPTER SEVEN

My Wife's Pussy, My Religion

MICK

Kara shifts up onto her knees and reaches behind her neck to unhook the halter top. Then her hands lower and there's the soft swish of a zipper going down.

She lets the dress fall away from her body, revealing her bountiful tits, the sweet swell of her tummy, the thin silver lines attesting to her pregnancy with Fitz. Then she pulls it off completely, tossing it to the floor as she settles back on her arms, her legs stretched out toward me.

No shame. No hesitation. Just all that soft, pale skin and those full tits rising with every breath.

Fuck me.

I cross the room in two steps, grip her ankles, and yank her to the edge of the bed. She gasps, but her thighs fall open like they're begging for me. Moisture turns the gusset of her panties dark, and I haven't even touched her yet.

"You're soaked," I rasp.

"Whose fault is that?"

It had better be mine. Always and forever. No one else touches this woman but me.

I sink to my knees and press my mouth to the heat of her through the thin cotton. She arches, whining low in her throat. The scent of her hits me like a punch to the gut – sweet, musky, mine.

I want to tear these panties off with my teeth. I want to push her down and hold her there while I fuck her so hard she forgets her own name. But I can't.

I won't.

Because if she ever sees what's inside me, the part that wants to pin her, to mark her, I don't know if she'll ever look at me the same way again.

Unable to hold back everything, I press a hot kiss just above the wet cotton, sucking at her pussy lips through it. I don't drink to excess. I don't do drugs, but I get drunk on her taste.

She moans, writhing on the bed, pressing her feminine flesh toward my mouth.

I indulge us both until the frustration of even the slight barrier her panties make is too much. I want her bare for me. Dripping. Open. But I can't let myself forget she's not just a body, not just a wet, greedy cunt I want to live inside.

She's Kara. My wife.

I force myself to draw my knife instead of ripping her panties from her body. That would hurt her. Yanked hard enough to tear, even cotton will leave angry marks like a rug burn.

I did it once before. Right after she got pregnant, when we finally got to have penetrative sex for the first time. The marks lasted for three days and she winced when they brushed against something...or someone. Me.

I'll never do it again.

Pressing the tip of the lethally sharp blade of my knife between the fabric and her hip, I slice upward not even brushing the silky-smooth skin underneath.

Another quick slice on the other side and I can pull the panties from her body. I draw them upward, rubbing over the swollen little clit that is now peeking out of its hood and begging for attention.

She bucks her hips, hungry for more, but I bring her panties to my nose, mainlining her pheromones for several deep breaths.

"Michael!" She draws my name out in demand.

Hell, I love when she calls me by my given name. She's the only person who does and she only does it in the bedroom.

I tuck her panties into my pocket and Kara surges up from the bed, cupping my face between her hands, and kissing me like it's the only way she can breathe.

Her tongue tangles with mine, needy and messy and real. She moans into my mouth and shifts so she can rub her soaked pussy against my chest, dragging her slick over my skin.

I'm going to lose my mind.

If my cock was out, it would already be inside her slippery, tight folds.

She breaks the kiss, panting. "I need you inside me, Michael. I want it hard. I want to feel you after."

Teetering on the edge of control, I close my eyes for a beat, swallowing the feral snarl that threatens to rip from my throat. "Ye don't know what you're asking."

"Yes, I do," she gasps with certainty. "I trust you."

God help me. A woman like her shouldn't trust a man like me. And her trust shouldn't make my cock throb like it's about to tear through my pants.

But it does.

"You'll have to wait. I want to taste your sweet honey straight from the source first." I spread her thighs wide and bury my face in her pussy.

Her cry is instant, sharp and breathless. "Michael!"

Both tangy and sweet, she tastes like fucking salvation.

I flatten my tongue and drag it from her slick entrance all the way to her clit. Her thighs quiver against my shoulders, and her hands fly to my hair. She grips tight like she needs something to anchor her.

She always responds like this. Always melts the second I touch her. It's a damn drug, the way her body yields, the way she writhes when I suck her clit into my mouth and lap at it like it's the only thing keeping me alive.

She bucks, and I hold her down with an arm across her pelvis. Not as hard as I want to. Just enough to keep her still while I tongue her until she's panting my name.

"Please, Michael. I can't..."

"Ye can," I growl, the words muffled against her heat. "You're going to come all over my mouth, Kara. Give it to me."

She shatters.

One minute she's begging, the next she's gone, head thrown back, thighs locked around my head, screaming as her pussy pulses against my tongue. Her orgasm rolls through her in waves, and I keep licking until she jerks and tries to pull away.

Too much. Too sensitive. But she tastes too good to stop.

Only when she's sobbing my name do I finally let her go.

I rise, shoving my pants and briefs down in one motion. My cock springs free, flushed and hard and aching to be inside her. Kara's eyes drop to it, and she licks her lips like she's starving. I almost come from that look alone.

"Get on your knees," I rasp. "Hands and knees, baby. Let me see you."

She doesn't hesitate.

She turns, presenting herself with the confidence established intimacy. Ass high, thighs parted. I can see everything – her swollen pussy, her juices, the way her inner lips glisten in the low light of the bedroom.

My control slips.

I grip her hips tight enough to make her gasp and line myself up. I should go slow. Should let her adjust.

I don't.

I shove in, hard and deep, burying every inch in one savage thrust. Only then can I stop. But it nearly fucking kills me.

Kara cries out, arching under me. Not in pain. In need.

"Yes," she gasps. "Just like that. More."

Her voice is wrecked, her breath catching with every stroke. I thrust harder, faster, chasing the edge like a madman. Her ass ripples from the impact. Her pussy squeezes me so tight I see stars.

"You're mine," I grit out. "No one else gets this. No one else gets you like this."

"Yes. Michael. Yes, yours..." She slams back against me, matching my rhythm.

She wants this. Needs the same filthy, ruthless pleasure I do.

I reach around and palm her tits, one hand cupping the heavy globe, fingers tweaking her nipple while I keep pounding into her.

"Ye drive me insane," I growl into her ear, leaning over her. "Ye know that? I think about fucking ya every time I see you walk across the room."

"I love it," she moans. "I love when you lose control."

She doesn't know what she's saying.

I never lose control. Not fully. Not with her.

Because if I did, she'd be pinned to this bed, unable to move while I fucked her until she couldn't breathe.

I slide my hand between her legs and rub her clit as I thrust harder, faster, deeper. She starts to come again, shaking and gasping, walls milking me like her body doesn't want to let me go.

And I don't go. Not yet.

I slow just enough to drag it out, her pussy still fluttering around me, still so damn hot and wet it takes everything in me not to give her every dark, unholy thing I fantasize about.

When her moans fade to whimpers, I pull out, flip her onto her back, and thrust in again.

I need to see her.

Her eyes are glassy, lips parted, flushed and swollen and perfect.

"More," she whispers. "Please."

God help me.

I fuck her slow and deep now, grinding in circles with every stroke. I watch her unravel. Watch her melt under me. Her breasts bounce with every thrust, and I can't stop touching them, squeezing them, sucking on them until her back bows and she claws at my shoulders.

I hold her like she's fragile even as I drive into her like she's the only thing keeping me grounded. Because she is.

She comes again, this time silent. Just her mouth open in a soundless cry and tears leaking from the corners of her eyes. She clings to me like she'll drown without something to hold on to.

I let go.

My climax tears through me, white-hot and brutal. I bury my face in her neck and groan as I pulse inside her, my cock jerking with every spurt.

We stay tangled like that for a long time. Her breath is ragged. Mine is worse.

And the monster inside me?

Still there.

Still hungry. Always feckin' hungry.

For her.

CHAPTER EIGHT

Mo Chuisle, Mo Dhiabhal

KARA

He collapses on top of me, his weight pressing me into the mattress like he's trying to fuse us together. For a few seconds, I can't breathe. Not because it's too much, but because it's not enough.

I don't want him to move. Not yet. I want this. All of it.

The stretch, the soreness, the wet heat between my thighs. The scent of sex and sweat on my skin. The way his heart pounds hard against my chest, like maybe – just maybe – it beats faster for me.

He calls me *mo chuisle*. His pulse.

That means something, right?

His breath is hot against my neck as he whispers words I can't quite make out. Not English. Not Gaeilge either.

Just Mick. Raw. Bare. Unmasked.

He doesn't say anything else. Instead, he presses a kiss to the side of my throat, then another to my collarbone, and another, softer still, right over my heart.

My eyes burn.

Because this? This version of Mick – the one who touches me like I'm breakable and sacred all at once – only comes out after he's been inside me. After I've been wrung out and made to take every inch of him. Like now.

I stroke his back with trembling fingers, feeling the tension slowly drain from his body. He's always so tightly wound. So armored. But after sex, when he's empty and satisfied, the mask slips. And for a few precious minutes, I get to see the man I want to believe is hiding underneath.

"Stay," I whisper, my voice barely audible.

He stiffens just a little, barely noticeable. But I feel it. I'm tuned to him like I'm a Mick-receiver.

"I'm not going anywhere," he murmurs.

But he doesn't mean what I want him to. He'll stay physically, but this softened version of him will disappear soon enough.

He rolls onto his side and pulls me with him, keeping me wrapped in his arms, one hand curving around my hip possessively. His other hand cradles the back of my head like he's afraid I'll disappear if he lets go.

His cock is still inside me, softening but not fully gone. Like he's anchoring himself inside my body.

Maybe he is.

I tuck my face against his throat and breathe him in. Salt and soap and sin.

"I like this," I say before I can stop myself. "When you hold me after."

Mick doesn't respond. His fingers just tighten on my waist. That's answer enough.

I shouldn't push. I never push. Not anymore.

But something about what we just did, how primal it was...it makes me reckless. Makes me want.

"You're different when we're like this."

"Different how?"

I press my lips to his chest, right over his heart. "You touch me like you feel something."

He doesn't speak. Doesn't move.

I don't need him to say he loves me. I gave up hoping for that a long time ago. But right now, in this moment, I want something. Anything.

He brushes a kiss to my temple. "I feel everything with you."

And somehow, that hurts more than if he'd said nothing at all.

Because it's a nothing answer. We both know he doesn't feel *everything* with me. And his words imply, maybe he doesn't actually feel anything.

Except sexual need.

But is sex a strong enough glue to hold two people together without love?

What happens if he finds someone else he wants like this? An image of Dierdre flashes in my mind's eye but I force it away.

He *had* Dierdre, according to her. And he still chose to marry me.

For ambition's sake, but he still chose me over her when he agreed to the marriage contract. And again when he left Ireland to follow through on it.

I let my eyes slide closed and my body relax on that thought.

MICK

The tension leaves Kara's body and seconds later, she's asleep in my arms.

Her breathing evens out, and that soft, sated expression replaces the fire that burned so fiercely in her hazel gaze while I was inside her.

My wife looks peaceful.

So feckin' trusting.

She shouldn't.

If she knew what I was thinking right now, she'd throw herself from this bed and run.

I stroke my hand down her bare back, slow and steady, and try to pretend to myself it's soothing. But my cock's already getting hard again. Still semi erect from earlier, it thickens with every second I stay inside her.

I could push deeper right now. She's wet and warm and open for me, her pussy still so tender from the last round that I know it would take almost nothing to make her come again.

I could wake her with it. Or not.

I could fuck her slow and deep until she came in her sleep, muscles clenching around me without ever knowing why. I could take her while she dreams, over and over again, until her body gives out and she can't walk straight for days.

The idea sends blood surging into my dick.

But I don't move.

Because I'd rather die than see horror in her eyes when she wakes up. She and Fitz are the only two people I never want to look at me with fear.

I love him.

And Kara? She's the addiction I have no intention of trying to kick. She is *mine*.

The need to own every inch of *mo chuisle*, every sound she makes, every look she gives, rides me like a speeding roller coaster barely clinging to the rails.

She's not mine because we're married. She's mine because I've given her a place inside me no one else touches and I've carved out a place inside her that belongs to me alone.

But sometimes, like now, there's a tightness in my chest I can't explain. Not just lust. Not just protectiveness. Something else. But it's not love.

A man like me can't love.

But one thing is undeniable, Kara makes me want to burn down everything just to keep her close.

My hand slides over the curve of her ass. Soft, full, perfect. My cock is hard again now, steel and need pressing against the slippery heat of her cunt.

I want to take her.

Again.

Forcing my body to stillness and my hand up to her back again, I press my mouth to her shoulder and breathe her in.

"I'll keep you safe, *mo chuisle*," I whisper. "Even from me."

She shifts in her sleep, her leg sliding higher on my thigh, opening herself to me in irresistible temptation. She's warm, soft, and still slick with everything I gave her earlier. Her pussy pulses faintly around my dick.

I could fuck her.

Right now. Slow. Deep. Let her wake up with me already moving just enough to draw those soft gasps from her lips, to claim her even in her sleep.

I've thought about it thousands of times. I've never done it

But feckin' hell, I want to.

Instead, I let my hand drift further down on each pass on her back until I'm caressing her ass again. She doesn't stir.

Not until I slide my middle finger between her ass cheeks and press gently against her tight little rosebud, just enough to tease. I've never taken her this way.

I never will.

But touching her like this is almost enough to make me blow my load inside her without a single stroke of my cock.

She whimpers. Half-asleep. Dreaming.

Her thighs part further, her body canting back, seeking more of my touch. Controlling the temptation to push my fingertip past her sphincter muscles makes sweat bead at my temples.

"Michael," she murmurs.

My control shatters. That single utterance tells me she's not fully asleep.

At least that's what I tell myself.

I push my cock deeper into her heat, letting her feel the thickness of it, the promise of what's coming.

"Mmm...yes..." Her voice is slurred, honey-thick with sleep and sex.

But there's no fear in it. No hesitation. Only need.

I roll my hips.

Her breath catches. Her body shifts, spine bowing as I fill her. Lips parting in a soft moan, her eyelids flutter but they don't open.

"Yes," she whispers again.

Definitely awake now. Just enough. And she's still saying yes.

"You always want me," I murmur into her hair, thrusting once, deep and slow. "Even when you're sleeping."

Kara tilts her head up, eyes barely open. Dazed. Glowing. "Only you," she breathes.

Fuck.

I start to move, and she pushes forward to meet me, sleep-heavy but eager. There's no rhythm, just instinct. Just our bodies finding the beat we always fall into.

She clutches my shoulders. I grab her hip with one hand, slide the other between our bodies to cup her tit. She whines when I pinch her nipple, louder when I lean down and bite the side of her neck.

"Mine," I growl.

"Yours," she gasps, shuddering.

She comes fast, hard, her body clamping around my cock like she's trying to drag me with her.

I let her.

I thrust deep and stay there, groaning as I spill inside her again, my vision going white for a second with the force of it.

When I come back to myself, she's still gasping, still shaking. I wrap myself around her, still inside, and pull her close like I can keep the world away if I just hold her tight enough.

She drifts off again before I can say a word.

And I lie there in the dark, my arms around my wife, my cock still pulsing inside her – and that tight feeling in my chest that won't go away.

I don't know what it is.

But I know I'd kill to keep it.

CHAPTER NINE

High Heels & Low Blows

KARA

I'm enjoying a rare moment of me-time when I hear what has so quickly become the unmistakable harbinger of Dierdre's arrival.

Click. Click. Click.

It has been four days since Dierdre's arrival and I am not ashamed to say I have avoided our houseguest as much as possible. Because every time we are alone together, she always gets a dig in.

Heck, she's pretty good at drawing blood in the company of others too.

A memory that starts off innocuous and quickly devolves into, "But you don't want to hear about that do you? If I were you, *I* wouldn't want to hear about how close my husband was with the lover he had to give up to marry me."

A comment that should be a compliment, but is anything but. "You're so good with children. I guess that's the benefit of Micky marrying someone so much younger than him."

One of my favorites? "Women in alliance marriages are so lucky they don't have to keep up their figure. It's not as if you have to worry about your husband moving onto someone else...permanently."

It's my favorite because it's the one zinger that never hits its target. My husband is way too addicted to my curves for me to think he wants me to change them.

Here she comes again, her high heels tapping a determined rhythm across the marble floor of the foyer. Will she turn off to visit Mick in his office? Again.

She sees more of my husband than I do. When I brought that up last night after he came to bed, he did the whole, *you don't have anything to be jealous of, you're my wife* thing before making me insensate with pleasure.

Which is his answer to pretty much any conflict between us. Sex so good, my body hums from it the next day.

But it's the words that stick with me long after he goes to sleep. They're code for, "You're being unreasonable, just like before."

The *just like before* might be something my brain tacks on. Despite weekly therapy, I've never managed to forgive myself for trying to abandon my son. If I had died that day, my sweet little guy would have grown up without his mom just like I did.

So, I'm hypersensitive to any emotion that resembles the chaotic, pain-filled thoughts that plagued me the first six months of Fitz's life.

Well, damn. Dierdre is definitely heading in this direction. And too quickly for me to vacate the sunroom before she reaches it.

There goes my peaceful respite.

If I hadn't taken off my shoes and started reading a book, maybe.

But it took too long for the click-clack of her heels to infiltrate my conscious mind.

After a more exhausting session than usual with my therapist, I needed to get out of my own head. And I do that best while reading a book where I can immerse myself in someone else's thoughts and experiences.

I really needed that after I signed off with a bruised heart and mind filled with confusion.

"What is it you want from your marriage, Kara?"

I know what I want, but isn't the more achievable and therefore important question, what can I have?

My therapist doesn't think so. She asked if my marriage is the type of future I want for Fitz? After that gut punch, she gave me the name of a child psychologist to reach out to for Fitz and told me my homework was to write down the three most important things I want from my marriage.

Not three things I believe I can have. Three things I want. My emotions started spiraling, and not in a good way, after one.

I want Mick to love me like I love him and that is never going to happen.

Dierdre appears in the doorway to the sunroom looking too sexy for eleven in the morning. Her dark red, backless sundress leaves most of the flawless skin of her upper body on display. The tightly fitted bodice pushes her modest breasts into prominence and the swirling skirt emphasizes her tiny waist.

"Good morning, Miss Kelly. Did you need something?"

Her mouth twists in a moue of displeasure. "I told you to call me Dierdre."

I incline my head, like I do every time she makes the demand. Neither agreeing with nor denying her request, but my actions speak for me.

I don't use her first name and I don't plan on *ever* using it. Petty? No. It's a boundary I set, something I've given myself permission to do.

I will not pretend friendship with someone who so clearly sees me as a rival. It's a big departure for me and not one my family is used to.

Fi loves it though. Every time I call Dierdre *Miss Kelly*, my little sister gives me a discreet thumbs up. Since *moma* also continues to use the more formal address, I'm not worried I'm disappointing her.

Hope also calls Dierdre Miss Kelly, when she speaks to her at all. Which is not often. All three of the kids avoid Dierdre too. Even my usually gregarious little boy gives monosyllabic answers when she tries to talk to him.

The only people in this house who enjoy Dierdre's company are my husband and father. Which seems to suit the Irish beauty just fine.

I have no doubt she's used to getting her way. Too bad for her, this isn't Dublin and she's not the reigning mob princess. Worse for her, I'm no longer a mob princess. I'm a mob queen.

Because my husband and son are the next in line to run this mob, that makes me the senior ranking woman in the Shaughnessy Mob, something *mamo* regularly reminds me of.

Dierdre sinks artfully into an armchair without being invited.

"I hope I didn't make things...awkward last night." Her tone laced with innocence so false, it might as well be sugar free sweetener.

Unsure which particular memory she dredged up with my husband that she's referring to, I say, "Not at all."

She crosses one leg over the other, posing even now, with no one but me in the room to appreciate her practiced movements. "It's just we have so much history."

"That's usually the case with *older* friends." Forced by my own adherence to good manners, I put the e-reader down on the occasional table beside me.

Her eyes narrow. "I'm sure you meant old friends."

The way she says old friends sound like *past lovers*, or is that just me?

"Did I? Would you like a glass?" I indicate the pitcher of iced tea on the serving tray. "Green tea is filled with antioxidants that can help keep older skin looking youthful."

"What are you implying? I don't need anything to help me look younger."

"Of course. With your fixation on me being younger than you, I thought you might appreciate the—"

"It's not your age relative to me that I find so..." Dierdre cuts me off before I can finish, but then flounders in her umbrage, unwilling to say the word on the tip of her tongue.

"Objectionable," I offer. She's certainly implied as much.

"Concerning," she counters.

She's been very careful thus far not to say anything that can be pointed to as a direct insult.

"I'm not sure why me being nearly a decade younger than you would be so concerning?" I pause and then give her a commiserating look. "You shouldn't let the fact that you're over thirty and unmarried get to you. I know mob culture can be backwards, but we don't live in the last century. A woman doesn't need a husband and family to have a satisfying life."

Which is something I believe strongly, but not a sentiment I think Dierdre will appreciate.

Her murderous expression tells me I'm right. "My *concern* is how much younger than Micky you are, not me."

"But you're the same age, aren't you?" I ask, doing my own imitation of false innocence.

"Yes," she grinds out. "But that's not the point."

"What exactly is the point?" I pour myself a glass of tea and take a sip, giving her plenty of time to answer.

"It must be..." She waves her hand like she's looking for words, when I have no doubt she'd come in here with every word already planned.

Hopefully my question got us back on script. As fun as it has been to give her a little of her own back, I would still rather be reading.

"Exhausting," she goes on, her eyes filled with pity. "Always watching. Always wondering."

Refusing to let her get to me again, I arch one brow. "Wondering about what exactly?"

My post-partum depression fueled jealousy notwithstanding, the only thing I've ever had cause to wonder about is whether or not my husband will ever love me.

"A virile, powerful man like Micky...you've got to be curious what he does so many hours of the day away from you."

So, she noticed how little time Mick spends with me. It's hard to miss. But it's also not uncommon with mob men at his level. The mob comes first, family second, no matter what kind of lies my father likes to tell himself.

"Not particularly." Which is true.

I'm neither interested in the details of Mick's legitimate business dealings nor the gritty ones related to his role as the Shaughnessy mob underboss.

Even back when we were first married, and I used to hang out in Mick's office – I still struggle with memories of how besotted I was – the details of his work didn't interest me.

I just wanted to be in the same room as him, which is my own pathetic truth to live with.

Dierdre's scoffing laugh is the first real thing in her demeanor since she came into the room. "Is that the line you've been taught to toe? It must be different in Ireland. I wouldn't stand for my husband having *friends* on the side."

"Mick can have whatever friends he likes," I answer with deliberate obtuseness. "Though outside of his crew, I don't think he has many."

He and Róise's fiancé, Miceli De Luca, underboss to the Genovese Family? But even with the family ties soon to be cemented, that relationship is still primarily business.

"Maybe you're not as smart as I thought. I wasn't talking about boyos to drink at the pub with."

"I didn't think you were, but why should I dignify your nasty innuendo with an answer? If you think *my husband* lacks the integrity to keep his marriage vows, that's a you problem."

"You think he's faithful?" she scoffs.

"You don't?" I counter.

Dierdre shifts in her chair. Something about this conversation isn't going the way she expects.

It's probably the part where I'm not intimidated by her. Insinuations of Mick's supposed roving eye don't hold any weight after the way he wrecked me last night...and the night before that...and the night before that.

"I just think it's sad, that's all. For both of you. A man like Micky? He should be with a mature woman who doesn't get all teary eyed when he gets cold or quiet."

"Mick doesn't do cold and quiet with me, and even if he did, it wouldn't send me crying into my pillow."

"You're very loyal, but you don't have to pretend with me. I know him." She pauses. "*Intimately.*"

"Correction you *knew* him." I leave off the intimately.

"You know we stayed *in touch* after he left Ireland. And not just through texts. He's been back to Dublin many times since he came to work in New York."

She wants me to believe Mick has been having sex with her when he visits Dublin?

Not likely.

Allowing myself to believe otherwise would be way too detrimental to my mental health. But I'm not burying my head in the sand.

Mick's a starving man with an insatiable sexual appetite the first few days after he gets back from any trip, including the ones to Dublin.

No way is he getting his rocks off while he's away.

Ignoring her blatant innuendo, I choose to focus on something else Deirdre said. "He didn't just come to work for the Shaughnessy mob. He married into it. New York is Mick's home now."

She doesn't like hearing that, but the anger glinting in her gaze quickly turns to calculation.

"It worries me," she says, clearly intent on ignoring the words she doesn't want to hear, just like I did. "He's a powerful man who deserves someone who doesn't flinch when he gets a little brutal in the bedroom."

One thing I never do, is flinch away from Mick and his sexual appetites. However, I'm not about to discuss my sex life with this woman, or any other one, for that matter.

Neither my sister, nor my cousin, knows about the early months of my marriage when I wasn't allowed to have my husband inside me until the male embryo had implanted in my womb through IVF.

I lost my virginity to Mick's thick, long fingers. It was both amazing and overwhelming at the time.

But that doesn't mean I ever want to discuss the lack of penetrative sex in my marriage until I was pregnant with the great-grandson Fergal Shaughnessy was so adamant on getting.

One to carry the Shaughnessy name into the next generation.

Not that *seanathair* planned that particular outcome to begin with. I think, at the time, he still hoped my uncle would remarry and give him more grandchildren.

But then Uncle Derry was murdered while I was still pregnant and my father ascended to the position of heir apparent. My father renegotiated the deal with Mick, offering more than a chance to run his own crew.

He offered Mick the chance at being underboss and eventually boss if he allowed our son to take the Shaughnessy surname.

Mick insisted on Fitzgerald for a first name so our son would carry Mick's surname too, even if it wasn't as a last name.

"Nothing to say?" Dierdre taunts with some impatience when I've been lost in memories too long.

"About?" I feign ignorance.

"Micky's bedroom proclivities." She makes her eyes comically wide. "Are you trying to say he doesn't let that side of him out with you? Oh...I then...I shouldn't have said anything."

That ship sailed thirty seconds after she arrived and she called my husband Micky.

"I'm not saying anything at all. I was raised to respect the privacy of others. Weren't you?"

"I wasn't trying to pry. I'm just looking out for my *friends*. That's all." She does the whole wounded routine.

Accusing eyes. Hunched shoulders. Caught breath.

And none of it lands because of how blatantly false her claim is. If she was looking out for Mick, we'd be having a very different conversation.

If she considered me a friend...I can't even create a scenario with that one.

We aren't friends and never will be.

No friend would try to make me doubt the strength of my marriage. What she doesn't know, is I don't need any help in that department. I go there all on my own.

Way too often.

But trying to make me believe Mick is having sex with other people? That's a nonstarter.

And I'm definitely not picturing her red painted nails digging proprietarily into Mick's forearm.

Huh. Looks like Dierdre's not the only one playing fast and loose with the truth today.

I'm done playing. "But we aren't friends, are we *Miss Kelly*?"

Her eyes fill with tears and she sniffs. "I want to be, but it's obvious you don't. I'm so alone here. Even with Micky watching over me, I'm scared."

This piranha scared? In another lifetime maybe. In this one, not so much.

When she sees her amateur dramatics aren't having their intended effect, she stands. "If you think I should leave, I will."

I don't bother to respond. Whatever I say, she's going to twist to fit the narrative she's already created of this discussion. I'm just a bit player; this drama wasn't for me at all.

It was for someone not even in the room: Mick.

Who I'm sure Dierdre will seek out, her crocodile tears shimmering in her eyes and wearing her wounded dignity like a snug fitting hoodie.

CHAPTER TEN

Damsel Piranha in Distress

MICK

A soft knock sounds on my office door and anticipation thrums through me.

My crew texts they're on their way before they get here. The other men knock like the soldiers they are. Three, quick, firm raps.

Kara?

Before I call to enter, the door opens.

Not Kara. My wife would never walk into either my or her da's office uninvited.

The sleek black hair framing a familiar face peeking around the door comes as no surprise.

Spoiled by her parents and raised to see herself as mob royalty, Dierdre has a flexible relationship with other people's boundaries.

This is not her first visit to my office in the last four days. It's not even the first time she's entered without being given leave to.

She pauses in the doorway, framed in the afternoon light like she thinks she's walking onto a stage. Shoulders drawn in just enough to suggest fragility. Lips glossed pink instead of her usual red.

Eyes glistening with moisture, but not red. Because no matter what she wants me to believe, she hasn't cried.

"Micky..." Her voice trembles.

I lean back in my chair and say nothing.

"I'm sorry," she breathes. "I shouldn't have gone looking for Kara, but I'm lonely here and I didn't want to interrupt your work."

"That's never stopped you before," I say dryly.

"Don't tease." She sniffles. "I just. I didn't think she'd be so..." She trails off, like it hurts her too much to say the word.

I don't jump in to fill the silence. Dierdre has something she wants to say and she'll say it. If I show any sympathy at this point, it'll only encourage the dramatics.

She likes performing a damn sight too much.

Dierdre bites her lip and blinks at me. "Your wife. She's just so *jealous*."

She says the word like it should trigger something in me and my first thought is, who in the hell leaked information to my former mob about my wife's hormone driven jealousy after she gave birth to our son?

Or did they do a deep dive and discover her stay at The Marlowe Center? Like I told Kara, HIPAA be damned. If somebody paid someone enough, or had hackers on level with ours, they could learn she'd been a patient and gain access to her file.

The question is, why would the Northies go to all that trouble? Or have they been spying at that level since I left Ireland? And if they have, how in the bleedin' hell did I miss it?

When I don't react, Dierdre comes around my desk to stand beside me and settles her hip on the edge. Curious where this is going, I don't move.

"I suppose I can't blame her." Dierdre trails her hand down my arm. "You are something special. Someone like her, naturally she'd be insecure about a man with your appetites."

As if Dierdre knows anything real about my sexual proclivities. Did I fuck her with less care than I give Kara? Aye. Dierdre likes rough sex.

But I was never tempted to fuck her until she couldn't walk. Or lock her away so I didn't have to share her.

The only woman who triggers that kind of possessiveness in me is my wife. And the only woman I would temper what I crave with what is good for her is Kara as well.

Dierdre folds her arms around her waist and bites her lip.

I stand, dislodging Dierdre's hand from my arm and take a step away from her. "My wife has no reason to be insecure."

"Of course not. But that won't stop her worrying, will it? She doesn't know you like I do. "

"Did Kara say something to you?" As soon as I utter the words I want to knock myself upside the head.

Of course my wife wouldn't say anything to Dierdre. And asking that question implies I'm worried. I'm not.

I'm just...curious.

"She doesn't want me here. The way she looks at me? She's jealous. Trust me, one woman recognizes that emotion in another."

I don't think so. Kara and Dierdre are so different from each other, they might as well be different species.

Dierdre slides closer to me her perfume a cloying cloud between us. "And you know I'm used to getting more than my fair share directed at me."

"Kara is fine." Where is this going?

"I didn't come here to cause trouble." Dierdre turns her head, rubbing her finger delicately under her dry eye as if disposing of a tear. "But if Kara doesn't want me here, I can go. I understand. I can't stay somewhere I'm not welcome."

She waits.

There it is.

She wants me to ask her to stay. To what end? She's already our guest. She and I both know that's not going to change anytime soon.

We may suspect her of spying for the Northies, but that's all it is: suspicion. They're our allies. Refusing her sanctuary would put that at risk.

She knows it.

I know it.

So, what's her endgame here?

Dierdre shifts so her skirt rides up her thigh, then drops her gaze. "It's just...it's hard. Being here. Not knowing who to trust. Feeling like a burden."

"You're not a burden," I say, voice even.

She's an informational resource.

Her head snaps up. The relief in her expression there and gone so quick, I would have missed it if I wasn't observing her so closely.

"Micky..." She sighs and blinks away moisture that never had a risk of spilling over. "I'm so glad you feel that way. But you're the only one. And I can't..."

Again she lets her voice trail off.

"Can't what?" I need this interview over so I can get back to work.

"You must realize how isolated I feel. How uncomfortable I would be dining with the Shaughnessy family with Kara looking at me like I'm filth."

"Kara is too well mannered to look at you like anything other than a guest at her father's table."

"You think so? I know she's young and so *sweet*, but she can get her point across. Believe me. She did this afternoon."

Good for Kara.

"Maybe I should return to Ireland. I don't think I can spend any more days, much less weeks being treated like a pariah."

She's gone from being looked at like she's filth to being treated like a pariah in two sentences. What's next, claiming someone in the family wants to kill her?

I bite back a sigh. I have better things to be doing, but for now, Brogan and I want Dierdre here. That means bridging the divide between her and my wife.

"I'll speak to Kara." She's the perfect mob daughter and wife.

She does what she has to do for the good of the family. I'll ask her to reassure Dierdre that she's welcome here.

"Only if you think it's best. I don't want to make her uncomfortable. And it's obvious that my being here does that. I respect your marriage."

I raise a brow. "Do you?"

A flash of hurt. "You used to trust me."

I don't answer.

Because I trust her to be exactly what she's always been: ambitious, slippery, and useful.

And if she thinks I'm defending her out of sentimentality?

That's fine.

If she thinks Kara's jealousy gives her leverage?

Let her think it.

Because eventually, Dierdre will reveal what the hell brought her to New York. When she does, I'll know if my family are still allies.

Or if they've become my enemy.

CHAPTER ELEVEN

Dinner, Dierdre, & the Death of Illusions

KARA

Dierdre's machinations come to roost just before dinner.

Mick arrives while I'm still working with Fitz on the word list he needs to recognize by sight going into first grade. He learned to read last year, but there are still words on the sight list he's unfamiliar with.

That was an interesting conversation with his Kindergarten teacher.

She was annoyed I'd taught Fitzy to read, saying it made things more difficult for her. As she had to keep him occupied while teaching the skill to the rest of the class.

I suggested the teacher allow my son to read books at his reading level on his own while she worked with the rest of the class.

Mick shocked me by saying maybe we should send Fitz to a military academy with advanced academics near Boston. I countered that if Fitz went to Boston to go to school, he wouldn't be living in the dorm, because I was going with him.

For a couple of weeks, I thought that was what was going to happen. Then my father negotiated a marriage alliance between my cousin, Róise, and Don De Luca's brother, Miceli.

Suddenly, there was no more talk of sending me and Fitz out of state and Mick gifted a library of age-appropriate books to our son's Kindergarten classroom.

I found out later that Mick wanted to get us out of New York in case war broke out between our mob and the Cosa Nostra.

Not that he told me that at the time.

No, he just let me think my company was disposable.

I never told Fi or Róise that's what went down. There's a lot I don't share about my marriage with my innocent sister and cousin.

Mick ruffles Fitz's hair. "Get washed up for dinner, *mo leanbh*. I want to talk with your mam for a minute."

"But look, da!" Fitz points to the stack of flashcards on his side of the table. "I won all of them."

Fitz loves to learn, but add an element of competition by making it a game where he "wins" the cards he gets correct? And my sweet son gets laser focused.

Mick's smile for our son reaches his eyes, the pride there easy to read. "That's grand, *mo leanbh*. You'll be the smartest boy in first grade."

From someone else, that might be hyperbole. But not Mick. He doesn't give empty praise to our son. Or anyone else. He genuinely believes Fitzy will be the smartest kid in his class.

Chances are, Mick's right.

There are a lot of things I still don't know about my husband after seven years of marriage and having a child together. But how scary smart he is, isn't one of them. If only his emotional intelligence was equally impressive.

"Mommy taught me," Fitzy is quick to point out.

"Aye. Your mam is smart as they come, isn't she?"

Teaching our six-year-old to recognize words by sight makes me smart? Who knew? I would have said it indicated patience.

A few minutes later, Fitz is playing in his room while his da and I get ready for dinner.

And talk, apparently.

I'm not feeling either smart *or* patient now. But angry? I'm fizzing with it.

I can't believe what I'm hearing. "Are you seriously asking me to apologize to your ex-girlfriend for her misunderstanding and causing an issue?"

"You don't need to be jealous of her, Kara. You're my wife." Mick adjusts the cufflinks on the new shirt he changed into for dinner.

Why? Was the other one sweaty?

What from?

His *chat* with Dierdre?

"I know who and what I am," I grit out. "And I'm not jealous of her."

Okay, that's a total lie. But it was true before this conversation started. Mostly.

"When you repeatedly refer to her as my ex-girlfriend, that tells me you're jealous. And you know there's no reason to be."

Do I though? Do I really know that?

"Believe what you want." I turn away to brush my hair into a sleek ponytail.

Why do I straighten my natural curls?

There's no answer to that question in the eyes of the woman staring back at me from the vanity mirror. But the man pulling on a suit jacket in the background might be one.

I started straightening my hair right after we got married. I thought it made me look older. Now, it's habit.

But somehow the sophisticated woman staring back at me, eyes pools of uncertainty, is a stranger.

I smooth my dress and face my husband so our gazes meet.

So, there can be no question I mean the words I'm about to say. "I am not going to apologize when I did nothing wrong."

"Perhaps she misinterpreted something you said."

"You said that already."

Mick's lips flatten. "We both know you have a tendency toward jealousy. It's not unreasonable in the face of an ex, but it is unnecessary."

My eyes narrow to slits. "I had pregnancy and then postpartum hormones raging through my body when my jealousy was an issue. I'm nearly twenty-five now. And I'm not walking around looking like I have a ball shaped condo attached to my front."

"You were beautiful pregnant."

Mick so rarely turns the Irish blarney on me. But really?

"False flattery isn't going to convince me to apologize to Dierdre. She was in the wrong. I don't expect her to say she's sorry, but I will not say those words to her."

"You admit there was an argument then?"

"I admit that your *ex-lover*," I say the word with deliberate emphasis, daring him with my eyes to comment on it. "Tried to convince me you're screwing around on me."

"Are you sure that's what she said, and not the way you interpreted it?"

"Gah!" I throw my hands in the air. "Even if I did misinterpret *her* words, nothing *I* said to her could be construed as me telling her to get out of my father's house."

"It's not about what you said, but how she took it. I'm not asking for you to abase yourself. Just say you're sorry and that you want her to stay." Mick's expression says he clearly expects me to give in.

I don't. "No."

His head jerks like I landed a strike right under his jaw.

Why? Because I'm standing up for myself? Allowing the real me that's been hiding behind the Stepford wife and daughter he and my father expect me to be to show herself.

He takes a calming breath, which I know is for effect because the only time Mick *isn't* calm, is when we're naked in bed together. "You know this is hard for Dierdre, being away from her family and everything she knows."

"But she's not is she?" I pick up my perfume to spritz myself. "She has you."

"Don't do that." Mick indicates the bottle of *Portrait of a Lady* in my hand.

Róise got it for me as a gag gift after I started doing things like breaking into our security feeds so we could leave the mansion undetected.

You've played the lady too long, cousin mine. It's time you spread your wings a little. Róise's words, infused with love and acceptance, ring in my head.

I wear the perfume as a reminder that being a lady isn't all I am. I'm also a secret student. A mom. And a darn good friend to my sister and cousin.

Besides I like the woodsy scent with floral hints and just a suggestion of raspberry and cinnamon.

I almost ask Mick why not, but then a burst of saltiness has me defiantly spraying the perfume on the back of my neck and pulse points.

He grimaces.

"You like this perfume. Or did you lie about that too?"

"Too? I don't feckin' lie to you and I do like it. It's just..." He shakes his head. "Never mind."

Shrugging, I put the perfume bottle back on the vanity and slip on my heels. I don't wear heels during the day around family, but I always wear them to dinner.

It's expected.

And darn if my feet aren't itching to kick them off at that mental reminder.

Mick lays his hand on my shoulder stopping me from leaving our bedroom. "She'll be uncomfortable at dinner if you don't make things right with her."

I shrug off his hand. "If her comfort is so important to you, then you apologize to her."

"I already told her I wanted her to stay."

Did he really?

He doesn't see the wince his words cause. "She should be fine then."

This sigh isn't faked for my benefit. It's filled with pure, Grad-A masculine irritation. Wow.

This is really important to him. And that? Makes me dig my heels in like they're set in concrete.

Schooling my features to hide the emotions jumbling my insides like rocks in a tumbler, I turn and look back at him over my shoulder. "I have nothing to make right."

Mick's gaze turns calculating. Seven years ago, I wouldn't have known what his nearly blank expression meant. I do now.

So, I'm prepared.

Or I think I am until he opens his mouth. "If Dierdre's uncomfortable around you then maybe she and I will have to have dinner privately until things settle down."

Expectation fills his green gaze. He thinks he just laid down a Royal Flush to my Full House.

My stomach cramps and my throat goes tight. No matter what I claim to myself, or to him, we both know I've never completely rid myself of the jealousy that turned so self-destructive after Fitz was born.

I do my best to pretend, even to myself, that it does not exist. And Mick is intentional about doing nothing to trigger it. Usually.

I used to think that meant something.

That he cared, at least a little, about my feelings.

Right now, this minute, I know it never meant anything at all. Betrayal stings my insides, a swarm of wasps bent on destruction.

My husband is willing to use insecurities that stem from circumstances neither of us can change to manipulate me into doing what he wants.

Mick didn't choose me. I didn't choose him. Love wasn't part of the equation when we got married and love on only one side only makes that equation impossible to solve.

We never had a romance. Despite the white dress, hundreds of guests who wished us well, and all the trappings of a woman's dream day, our vows sealed a business transaction.

Not our hearts.

No matter how much I wish we'd started out differently, I will always be the clause in the contract he couldn't strike out.

But his threat to have dinner with Dierdre isn't a single shot fired. It's the whole darn magazine.

Because he knows how important eating dinner together is to me. Mick's not just a mobster, he's second in command for all the Shaughnessy holdings as well.

He works long hours. Unlike our son, I can't go to Mick's office and demand his attention. I used to...well, not demand his attention, but just hang out with him. Reading. Playing on my phone.

Just being there. So freaking pathetic, but it took an unsuccessful attempt to end my life and someone asking me in group therapy at The Marlowe Center what I *did* when I spent all those hours in Mick's office before I realized it.

Because I didn't *do* anything. Not anything that *required* being in the same room as my husband.

I had no other reason to be there than my pathetic belief that if we spent enough time together, the feelings getting so big inside me would jump to him by osmosis or something.

Looking back, it shocks me he never asked me to get lost. Another action I misinterpreted.

But now that I've stopped haunting his office like a teenaged bride specter, dinner is pretty much the only time I see Mick until he wakes me in the night for sex.

Not making love. I can't lie to myself about that.

It was never making love.

Just sex. Sex that causes seismic shifts in my heart, mind and body, but still...just sex.

And even sex that good isn't enough to make up for the little bits of my soul I lose every day in this marriage.

"Do what you want, Mick, but don't expect me to make excuses to Fitz. If he asks, I'll tell him you'd rather have dinner with your friend than your family."

CHAPTER TWELVE

The Doormat Has Left the Building

MICK

What the fuck just happened?

I thought I had the perfect leverage to gain Kara's cooperation. I didn't think I'd have to use it.

As the highest-ranking woman in the Shaughnessy Mob, insincere apologies are nothing new to Kara. She knows how to play the game to keep peace when another syndicate leader's wife or daughter takes umbrage over an imaginary slight.

How is this any different?

Dierdre's a source of information and must be tolerated until I can get that information out of her.

Realization blinds me like the muzzle flash of a Ruger 57 shooting 5.7mm ammunition.

I didn't explain that to my wife.

Kara doesn't usually require an explanation to cooperate when it's for the good of the mob, the family, or both. But I didn't couch it in those terms, did I?

I made it about Dierdre's feelings which I give feck all about. And somehow I expected my wife to know that.

But she's not an emotionless monster like me. Kara feels things and that matters to me. Believing I'm a better man than I am, she assumes that Dierdre's feelings matter too. And didn't I feckin' feed that fear?

Bleedin' hell. I'm not a stupid man, but I should have led with the explanation and then none of the other shit would have been necessary.

I swiftly catch up with my wife before she opens the apartment door, Fitz's hand in hers.

Pressing my hand against the door, I look down into her beautiful, closed off face. "Your da and I need Dierdre to stay for the next little bit."

Instead of lighting with understanding and acceptance like I expect, Kara's pretty hazel eyes darken with displeasure.

"Will you be eating dinner with us, Mick?" she asks, right there in front of our son.

"That's up to you," I lobby back.

Her expression stony, she shakes her head. "No, it is not."

"Do you have to work, da?" Fitz asks, my little guy's voice tinged with the disappointment he's trying to keep off his face.

Bleedin' feckin' hell with demons dancing on a man's grave.

"Of course I'll be eatin' dinner with ya." My wife well and truly won this round.

And as frustrating as that is, part of me, the pole between my legs to be exact, is impressed.

Removing my hand from the door, I step back and let Kara open it. Two of her security team are waiting in the hall and they accompany us to dinner.

My family doesn't need security when I'm with them, but their presence reminds our son that I keep my promises.

Maybe I need to figure out a way to remind my wife of the same thing. I promised fidelity. I will never break that promise. Not only because I am apparently now Kara-sexual, my cock reacting to no one but her.

But also because although I may not experience normal emotional reactions, I do have my own code of honor. And I don't break my promises.

Placing my hand on the small of Kara's back, I answer Fitz's question about the nutritional merits of broccoli. My son is looking for a reason to strike it off his "foods I eat" list.

Kara steps a little faster, trying to dislodge my hand, but I keep pace with her.

I don't usually touch her like this in public, not because I don't want to. But she and Fitz are safer if both of my hands are free to pull a weapon to protect them. Or defend them with my bare hands and in that case, two is always better than one.

But we have two guards with us and I've seen the way Kara looks at Róise and Miceli. Like she yearns for the same small touches of affection that come so naturally to the Italian underboss with Kara's cousin.

I'm not a touchy-feely guy outside the bedroom, but I don't like my wife looking at another man like he's all that.

If she wants me to hold her hand, I'll hold her feckin' hand.

And when she tries to step away from my touch again, that's what I do, keeping her pinned to my side with her hand in mine.

"Da!" Fitz exclaims mid sentence on reason twenty-four that broccoli is not a superfood. "You're holding mommy's hand."

"Aye. So are you."

"Yeah, but I always hold mommy's hand. You never do."

KARA

I always hold mommy's hand. You never do.

Fitz's words echo in my mind, pinging against every lonely memory from my marriage.

No, my husband never holds my hand and I have no idea why he's doing so now.

I want to rip it away, but our son is watching us both, his dear little face lit with joy. At least someone's happy about my husband's small dose of public affection.

When we reach the dining room, Mick pulls my chair out for me like he always does. I sit down, forcing a smile and a greeting for everyone already seated.

Mamo taps the bevel of her Tiffany watch and my smile turns to a grimace.

Then I mouth, "Sorry."

We're five minutes late sitting down, which means everyone else is already here. Except Fi. She and Zoey are having a picnic on the beach for two.

My sister practically gets hives at the idea of going to a restaurant, or anywhere else with a lot of people. So, her girlfriend arranges romantic at home date nights.

It's incredibly sweet. And Fi is so happy, she glows. That's all down to our cousin Róise, who negotiated Fi's freedom from an arranged marriage by agreeing to one of her own.

When and if my beautiful little sister marries, she will be the first woman in four generations to do it for love.

"Am I to take it that everything is sorted with our houseguest?" My father gives me a pointed look. "I assume that's why you're late."

"That issue is indeed why we're a few minutes tardy for dinner," I agree. "But if by sorted you mean, I talked to her. That did not happen."

My father's eyes widen in shock before they narrow in anger. "I expect—"

His voice abruptly breaks off at the click of heels drawing near on the terrace stones.

Why am I not surprised that Dierdre got over her pique and decided to join us for dinner after all?

In a magenta dress that covers very little of her decolletage and none of her shoulders, she stops theatrically for everyone to take in the magnificence of her beauty.

Seriously, did this woman go to the drama school of overacting, or what?

Her expression is reticent, like she's been dragged here against her will – despite the perfect makeup and the fact she clearly timed her dramatic entrance.

"I wasn't going to join," she says with faux-shyness, "but your *mamo* insisted."

Mamo's snort is not well concealed, but she doesn't gainsay Dierdre.

Hope leans toward me from the right and whispers, "Maeve told Dierdre that she wasn't holding with a prima donna eating on a tray in her bedroom and if she wanted to eat, it would be at the table with everyone else."

I duck my head to hide my smile. *Mamo* is my hero.

Brogan stands to pull out a chair for Dierdre. "You're always welcome at our table, my dear."

Hope stiffens beside me and my heart squeezes for her. Falling for my dad is not a good proposition. Even if he returns her feelings, he's not going to be considerate of them.

The mob always comes first.

No exceptions. I should know.

Dierdre looks around the table, her lips twisting in disappointment when she realizes she can't sit beside Mick.

He's to my left and Fitz is once again in the oversized chair with *mamo* at the end of the table near him. Hope's son is across the table, in the chair closest to Fitzy.

Their oblivious chatter brings a smile to my face despite the tightness in my shoulders.

Hope's daughter Esther is seated across from me. Since no additional chair was added, because with my sister and Zoe's absence it wasn't needed, that leaves the only two empty chairs across the table and opposite the end where Mick's sitting.

Dierdre smiles coquettishly at my dad as she sits down. "Thank you, Brogan. You're so sweet."

I sip my water and breathe through my nose.

One second.

Two.

And then I smile.

Because I have never in my life wanted to stab anyone with a salad fork more than I do in this moment – and this family believes in table manners.

Her eyes pointedly moving right past me, Dierdre smiles at Fitz, the way some adults do.

With condescension. "Aren't you lucky to be the spitting image of your da."

Fitz eyebrows draw together in a scowl. "I look like my mommy too. Everybody with eyes says so."

"Fitzgerald Shaughnessy," my dad barks. "Apologize right now."

Fitz presses his lips together and lifts his chin mulishly. No apologies coming from that quarter either.

"He's only speaking the truth, son," *mamo* chides. "Fitz has his father's red hair and green eyes, but the shape of them, his mouth and cheekbones are all Shaughnessy."

For once, my father doesn't have a ready comeback. The fact Fitz resembles my side of the family is a great source of pride to him. To deny it now would be to deny that pride. He's not going to do that, not even for our forked-tongued houseguest.

"Oh, I can definitely see you in your grandson," Dierdre gushes, bypassing my donation to the gene pool completely.

"I think Fitz is a very lucky boy to look like both of his parents," Hope says, putting herself firmly on my side and surprising everyone at the table.

I mean. I know she's got inner strength because she's the one that risked her own life to warn my cousin about the AOG's plans to "bring her back to the fold".

But since she arrived, she's been quiet. Unlikely to join most conversations much less cast a verbal vote that might be taken as siding against my father.

The look on his face is even more surprising than Hope's words.

Instead of angry, my dad looks stunned and then pleased. Proud even.

Because Hope spoke up?

If that's the case, I'm going to bring him a delirium of joy going forward. Because I'm done conforming.

I did everything right, submitted to emotionally devasting conditions regarding having a male heir, stood beside my father and husband in all ways. And what did it get me?

A marriage that is an emotional wasteland and a father who shows no pride in me, only expectation. He has no idea that he should even consider putting me, or Fiona, first sometimes.

That as his children, we deserve his protection before anyone else. Even the mob.

Róise's kidnapping crystalized that truth for me, when I didn't hesitate to put Fitz ahead of either her, or Fi. His safety was the only thing I cared about in that moment.

If it had been my father in the water that day, he would have protected his most important current asset of the moment: Róise.

"Mick, I need you in London next week to oversee a negotiation with one of our European clients." My dad's frown says he's not happy about the timing of this trip.

Which implies it is both urgent and necessary.

The buzz around the dining table continues as if my dad didn't just drop a conversational bomb between the grilled swordfish and rosemary potatoes.

Fitz chatters away, telling *mamo* how he and Enoch played super spies today, but all I hear is the echo of my dad's voice.

London.

For how long? Does it matter?

What will be materially different with Mick gone? Well, nightly sex for one thing, but is that such a bad thing?

You starve a fever right? And love is nothing but a fever of the heart.

That's what I'm telling myself when I realize both my dad and Mick are looking at me with expectation.

"I'm sorry, I missed that," I say automatically, knowing I missed *something*.

"I was saying you should go with Mick. Some time away from the family is always good for a marriage." My dad's smile is all white teeth and false generosity.

As if he's gifting me Paris Fashion Week, not another week of loneliness in a five-star prison.

Been there, done that. Burned the t-shirt. The week I spent in Paris on what was supposed to be my belated honeymoon, turned out to be a cover for a meeting between Mick and our other European clients, the ones not on the books of our legitimate businesses.

"Mick is free to go, of course." Like that would ever be in any doubt, or that I would have any say in the matter. "But I won't be tagging along to act as window dressing for another business trip disguised as a romantic getaway."

My belated honeymoon in a nutshell.

And every trip we've taken since then.

But now things are different. I have a life, maybe one that my dad and husband know nothing about, but I have one all the same. School. Self-defense lessons with my cousin and sister.

I'm getting really good. Who knew?

And of course, there's Fitz. I don't want to leave him behind this time. Not with Dierdre here.

There's something off about her. Besides the fact that she so obviously has the hots for my husband and would be happy to see me get hit by a bus.

My father's brows beetle, his displeasure cast in the slant of his lips. "It wasn't a request, Kara."

I set down my fork. "Neither was my answer."

Mick tenses, and Fitz goes still, glancing between the adults like he's sensing a storm front rolling in.

"You don't want to go to London with your husband?" Brogan asks, the even tone of his voice belying the storm seething in his blue gaze.

"Not really, no." I swirl my water glass. "I've stayed in the suite. Ordered room service. Waited around while Mick took meetings."

"You think I ask him to travel for fun?" my father snaps, his voice lowering just enough to make my skin prickle.

"No. I think you ask him to travel for you," I reply evenly. "And I think you send me along so I can smile and look pretty when the situation calls for it."

My father's jaw flexes, his hold on his fork now white-knuckled. But he doesn't reply.

So, I go for broke. "And I know that you don't care whether it's a good experience for me, or how much your business disrupts my life. But that matters *to me*."

Mamo makes a small sound, barely audible over the clink of silverware.

"This is not the place to discuss personal family matters," my father says freezingly.

"Considering the fact that this is the only time I see you unless I make an appointment, I would say that family dinner is the perfect time to have a personal conversation."

Brogan Shaughnessy looks like I smacked him in the face with the swordfish before our chef got a chance to cook it. "We have guests."

I open my mouth to reply, but Mick lays his hand on my thigh and squeezes. "We can talk about the trip later."

"There's nothing *to* talk about," I reply, with zero remorse. "I am not going to London."

Fitz watches me with awe, not worry in his bright green gaze. I wink at him and he smiles.

A strangled sound comes from my father's end of the table. I ignore it.

The doormat version of Kara Fitzgerald has left the building.

"Why can't you go to Lunnon, *athair mór?*" Fitz asks. "I don't want my da to go."

I have to swallow back totally inappropriate laughter. If anyone doubts that my son has both his father and me in him, that should seal it.

Only Mick is audacious enough to challenge my father. And it's the Shaughnessy blood that makes me stubborn enough to do it.

I might not have shown that side of me for a while, but she's always been there. Biding her time.

"That's a wonderful idea, Fitz." I smile sweetly at my father. "You have fewer family commitments than Mick. Your daughters are all grown."

Brogan's mouth drops open and he stares at me like my head just spun around three times while I laughed maniacally.

"You allow your grandson to question your decisions, *ceannaire?*" Dierdre asks, scandalized, using the Irish term for chief.

Boss, but a shade more emphatic.

"No, I do not. Fitzgerald Shaughnessy, you do not question me." For the first time in memory, my father levels a harsh glare at my son and speaks in a tone better suited to dressing down one of his soldiers. "Ever. It is disrespectful."

Fury explodes like a grenade in my chest and I jump to my feet, shoving my chair back and knocking Mick's hand away. "If you do not like the manners I have instilled in my son, you take it up with me."

My father doesn't stand, but the look of chilling disapproval he sends toward me is meant to cow me. "Then *you* tell your son to apologize. To both Dierdre for his comment earlier and to me. I will not tolerate that kind of rudeness at *my* table."

He doesn't say it, but he definitely expects me to say I'm sorry too.

Going hot all over, my entire body flushes with anger. Fitzy's future unrolls in my mind's eye like a terrifying movie.

Us teaching him to be like me, tolerant of anything his grandfather, the boss, wants him to do. Us teaching him to be like Mick, willing to do whatever heinous act is necessary to further the mob's interests.

And never, ever having a say about his own life.

"I will not."

My father regards me coldly. "You will, or you will both leave the table."

Disbelief that my father would say such a thing to me wars with pain at the knowledge that if I don't change something, it will always be this way for Fitzy too.

Swallowing back tears, I say, "It doesn't have to be this way."

"There's a hierarchy in the mob and it must be respected."

Feelings I've kept locked away for so long leak out of the cage I've kept them in, adding to the cauldron bubbling in my gut.

"Kara, *a ghrá*. It's alright," *mamo* says soothingly. "Fitz has excellent manners and it will not hurt him to remember them with his *athair mór*."

I blink away tears and shake my head. "No. Brogan isn't acting like Fitz's *athair mór*, he's behaving with all the cruelty of a *ceannaire*. But my son is not one of his soldiers and I won't have him raised to believe his feelings don't matter. That he's not allowed to have an opinion in a family discussion."

"This is not a family discussion, Kara," Brogan points out, almost patiently. "We are discussing business."

"Then you should have saved it for your office," I fire back, not even a little appeased.

Every bit of softening in Brogan's demeanor disappears. "You dare to tell me how to behave in my own home?"

"I thought it was my home too, but it never has been, has it?"

"Is she always this dramatic?" Dierdre asks in a whisper meant to carry.

The woman whose picture is next to Drama Queen in the Urban Dictionary thinks *I'm* dramatic?

Brogan's face tightens, but he doesn't reply. He's staring me down. A tactic he's used to great effect in the past.

But I am beyond being subdued by his disapproval. When you're never enough, eventually you stop trying to be anything.

"Fitz..." My husband's voice sends a dagger straight through my heart.

Betrayal nearly takes me out at the knees. So, it takes a second to parse what Mick is actually saying.

"...have nothing to say you are sorry for. You used a respectful tone when you asked your *athair mór* a question. If I go to London, you *and* your mam will be coming to. I made ya a promise and I don't break my word."

Now our son is looking at Mick like he's one of Fitz's favorite Marvel heroes. And *mamo* mouth is round with shock.

I'm clenching my teeth so hard my jaw hurts, but I will not cry in front of Dierdre Kelly. I didn't expect Mick to take my side.

He didn't take your side, a voice inside my head taunts, *he took up for your son*.

He's still talking like he plans to take me (and Fitz now) to London. I'm not sure how I feel about that. Is it better, or worse than the trips that came before?

"You'll not be taking my heir out of this country," Brogan says with arrogant implacability.

The quality of Mick's stillness beside me changes and the temperature around the table drops into the Arctic zone, sucking all the summer heat out of the air. "If I go *my* son goes with me."

The shock on Brogan's face when I stood up to him was almost comical, the look on his face now? Is not funny at all. He looks surprised, but there's a tendril of fear in his gaze too.

Something I never thought I'd witness in my father's face. Ever.

Whatever he sees in my husband's expression has him spooked.

"Yes, well...we'll discuss this later."

Mick slides his hand into mine and tugs. Not sure how to process the last five minutes, I sit. I stood up to my dad. Mick stood up for Fitz.

And my dad backed down.

Mick's arm slides along the back of my chair, his fingertips settling on my bare shoulder. The barely there touch sends electric zaps straight to my ladybits.

He just doesn't touch me out of the bedroom. So this? Tonight? My body doesn't know how to process it any better than my brain with my roiling emotions.

A show of solidarity with me? Or possession?

Brogan challenged Mick's right to make decisions for our family. He challenged mine too, but I wouldn't and didn't expect anything less.

Telling Mick he couldn't take Fitz out of the country was overreaching and my father knows it.

Dierdre sighs and shakes her head. "Micky, I know you're a doting father, but there's something to be said for discipline."

The look she gives me tells everyone at the table who she blames for my son's supposed lack of discipline.

Ignoring her, Mick reaches for his wine and asks our son if Gobby, Fitz's spastic cat, has brought him any more *gifts*.

When Gobby gets out of our private apartment, the cat steals things and brings them as tribute to my son. Once it was *mamo's* favorite crochet hook. Another time, the little monster found one of Brogan's cufflinks.

Fitz launches into a story about Gobby stealing Enoch's LEGO and bringing it to him.

And me?

I pick up my fork and resume eating like nothing happened.

Like I'm not mentally adding *don't stab the guest* to my personal growth mantras.

CHAPTER THIRTEEN

The Devil's Bride

KARA

Dierdre monopolizes the conversation over dinner and I make no attempt to change that. Normally, I would make sure everyone at the table felt included. Not this evening though.

I'm too lost in memories.

The moments that led us to here.

The day I turned sixteen and my birthday gift from my grandfather was a contract marriage. My father didn't put it that way, of course.

Even Brogan Shaughnessy has enough sense not to imply an arranged marriage is any kind of gift for his teenage daughter. No, he made it clear that it was my *duty* to both my family and the mob.

My obligation to give the rest of my life to serve as a guarantor of a contract between two powerful mob families.

I didn't learn about what exactly that would entail until two years later.

Home from school for the Thanksgiving holiday weekend, I'd been inundated with plans for the wedding. Did I like this color? Would I prefer this cake?

As if any of my preferences mattered. I tested it once, just to see. Knowing my grandfather was not fond of chocolate cake, I said I wanted devil's food cake with chocolate mousse filling for my very American wedding cake.

The caterer was instructed to bake a vanilla cake with a raspberry coulis and custard filling.

I didn't care about cake flavors after *moma* took me aside and explained what was required *after* I said *I do*.

Neither my father, nor my grandfather wanted to discuss an eighteen-year-old's future sex life with her husband.

Honestly? Even if I'd been thirty, I doubt they would have been up for the task.

Seven Years Ago

"It will be alright, *a ghrá*." *Moma* pats my hand soothingly. "Once you become pregnant, you and your husband will be able to enjoy normal marital relations."

"What are normal marital relations?" I ask, shock moving the words from my head to my mouth.

Moma stares at me. "Ach. Don't the girls at your fancy school talk?"

I nod. They do talk, but what they say doesn't give me comfort. "They say it hurts. That boys don't always listen when you say no, especially if they're your boyfriend."

Won't a husband be worse?

"If you ever say no to Michael Fitzgerald and he ignores you, you tell me." The militant glint in *moma's* eyes tell me she's not kidding. "I'll sort it, even if it means making you a widow."

I believe her. "But won't that make *seanathair* angry?"

I've never called my grandfather by anything less formal. He's definitely not a grandda. It's either *seanathair* or sir.

"You listen to me now, girl. The women in our world may marry for the sake of the mob, but we're Irish. We don't stand for our men abusing our good nature."

Don't we though? Isn't arranging a marriage for me less than a month after I graduate high school an abuse of my good nature?

Not for the first time, I wish my father was more like Uncle Derry. My uncle made an iron clad promise to my cousin, Róise, that she'd never have an arranged marriage.

Maybe if my mom were still alive, but probably not. She moved here from Chicago to marry my father and strengthen ties with the Doyle-Byrne Mob. Their current boss is my second cousin, or something, but I've never met him.

His father took exception to my mother dying in childbirth after being told not to get pregnant again. But *seanathair* insisted my generation had to have a male heir.

My mom and aunt had only given birth to me and Róise at this point. The plan failed on every level when my sister was born. Not only did my mom die, she'd done it giving birth do another daughter.

As far as I know, relations with Chicago have been tense ever since.

"...and we know how to handle it if it happens." *Moma* is still talking.

She digs into the embroidery basket she keeps beside her favorite chair and pulls out a box with the tree of life carved on the lid. "Your *seanathair* believes this is where I keep medications and necessessities for that time of month."

"Isn't it?"

Moma taps the side of her nose. "It's much more practical. She opens the box and pushes aside a box of tampons and a package of pads.

Lying on the brown velvet lining is a dagger. Beside it is a small prescription style bottle with no label and a glass vial with a stopper lid.

"If your man lays a hand on you, you tell him you'll cut his balls off in his sleep if he does it again. You show him how sharp you keep that dagger and he'll believe you."

I can't imagine threatening Michael Fitzgerald with a dagger. I'm not like my moma. I don't make waves.

She pats my hand again, like she knows what I'm thinking. "Like I told you, *a ghrá*, if your husband gives you that kind of trouble, you tell me and I'll sort it."

She points at one of the pill bottles, "That's blood pressure medication with the unfortunate side effect of causing a man's bod to stay limp."

I swallow. "But why..."

"If your man is randy too often and you're not feeling it, you can give him one of these in his morning coffee for a few days. He'll not be beggin' favors when he can't get it up, you mark my words."

Unwilling to even think about my grandmother using the medication on my *seanathair*, I point at the vial. "What's that?"

"Ethylene Glycol."

"What's it for?"

"The final solution."

"What...I don't..."

"My *máthair* gave this box to me when I wed your *seanathair*. Women in our family have not always been lucky when it came to the men we were induced to marry."

I stare, my mouth opening and closing, but no words coming out.

"A few drops of the Ethylene Glycol in something sweet and it'll not be detected. When your husband has a stroke, there'll be no reason to suspect your hand in it."

"But what about a post mortem?" I like true crime podcasts, but I've never heard of Ethylene Glycol poisoning.

"We're the mob, dear. We don't do post mortems."

I'm sure *moma* means our little chat to be comforting, but all it does is increase my anxiety before the wedding. What she's really saying is that if my future husband mistreats me, I can't rely on the men in my family to protect me.

Never as detached as her son to my wellbeing, I don't doubt that *moma* will kill to protect me. But the fact that she thinks it might be necessary?

That scares the crap out of me.

With no real idea what to expect and her dire warnings ringing in my head, I spend the last semester of high school hiding my fear from my friends and family when I see them.

I've gotten so good at it, my smile doesn't slip once on my wedding day.

And Michael's is completely absent.

He doesn't smile during the ceremony. He doesn't smile when we're pronounced husband and wife. His face is void of emotion when we cut the cake and that doesn't change when we share our first dance under the ballroom chandeliers.

It's disconcerting. And confusing.

I don't know my groom well, but from what I've seen, Michael's blessed with more than his fair share of Irish charm. And his smile gives me butterflies when it's turned on someone else and makes my heart race the few times it's turned on me.

Until now, I have no inkling why the men whisper about him and call him *an diabhal*. Devil.

But this Michael is intimidating. Downright scary.

Where is his easy smile? Today of all days, I need to see it. But it doesn't break through once.

I can't stop thinking about it the entire helicopter ride to Martha's Vineyard.

Why is he so somber? Did he not want the marriage?

I mean, I know it's an alliance, not two people in love, but I never thought he didn't *want* to marry me.

Is there someone he had to leave behind in Ireland and today was the reminder that he would never see her again? Never have the future they wanted?

My stomach twists in knots, a feeling I've never experienced before, making it hard to breathe.

Jealousy.

We're both silent on the short drive from the helipad to the Martha's Vineyard house.

Bittersweet warmth surges through me when the large white, two story beach cottage comes into view. The Shaughnessy family has been using this place for vacations for three generations.

Or what we call vacations: mob business with our allies masquerading as family bonding time.

Like our home on Long Island, there's a smaller building meant to barracks whatever soldiers are on security, but there are no quarters for live-in staff.

A groundskeeper, cook and housekeeper come daily, when we're here. I don't know what their schedule is when we aren't. I suppose that's something I'm going to have to know.

Moma will teach me.

Despite the business that went on behind closed doors, some of my best memories are playing in the lush grass with my cousin and sister while Aunt Charity and *moma* sipped iced tea on the terrace.

Sometimes Uncle Derry would join in, chasing us down the path to the beach, making us scream with laughter. After Aunt Charity's death, he stopped doing it.

Everything changed after Aunt Charity got shot four years ago. Including me.

Conor, one of the men Michael brought with him from Dublin, opens my door and I step out of the SUV.

Michael is already headed toward the front door, his stride brisk. Gathering the folds of my wedding dress up so I won't trip, I rush to catch up.

Gravel crunches under my heels, some of it skittering around my feet and I have to hop-skip not to fall. Family tradition says I must stay in my wedding gown until Michael takes it off of me.

But right now, I really wish I was wearing tennies and jeans.

I'd settle for ballet flats, but *moma* would not hear of me ruining the line of my dress.

Another piece of gravel rolls under my shoe and I stifle my surprised cry, but a squeak escapes, sending heat rushing into my cheeks.

Maybe Michael didn't notice.

He stops and turns back toward me. So much for not noticing.

"You alright?" he asks.

Am I? No, not really. I'm about to have sex for the first time, or something close to it, with a practical stranger.

But that's not what he's talking about, is it?

So, I answer the way I've been taught to. "I'm fine."

I reach him and keep going, grateful for the smooth steps leading to the porch when I reach them.

Michael grabs my elbow and keeps me steady as I go up, but when we reach the top, he pulls his hand away.

I give him a tentative smile. "Thank you."

He jerks his head in acknowledgment.

"We'll be in the guest house if you need us, boss," Rory says from behind me.

When we come with the family, a full compliment of my grandfather's soldiers joins us and there are perimeter guards at night.

But it's just me and Michael, not the mob boss. We don't need that level of security.

And I'm glad.

Honeymooning with a stranger is going to be hard enough without a bunch of men watching our every move.

We stop at the front door and Michael reaches out to unlock it.

"Do you have a girlfriend?" Ugh. I can't believe I just asked that.

Seanathair would say it's none of my business. Even *moma* would be mortified I asked the question with as much subtlety as a brick to the face.

Michael pushes the door open and then meets my gaze, his green eyes giving nothing away. "Nah."

Relief floods through me, but the shoulders that relax at his answer tense up when he steps around me, making no move to carry me across the threshold.

What's one more dream that will never be fulfilled? I'm the granddaughter of one of the most powerful mob bosses in America. This is my life.

Married for an alliance to a man who could care less about romantic wedding traditions.

Of course, I don't bring it up.

I'm not that girl anymore, am I? Brash. Willing to break the rules and try anything.

Bad things happen when you break the rules. People die. That's what *seanathair* says. No one in the family was breaking the rules when Aunt Charity and Fiona got shot that night.

But the men who shot them were.

Now, my aunt is dead and my sister has panic attacks when Brogan drags her out of the house. Not that he calls them that.

He and *seanathair* say she's throwing a tantrum. But Fi doesn't scream and stomp her feet. She cries silent tears and has trouble breathing.

Not a tantrum.

Taking a deep breath I step forward and stop as soon as my gown clears the doorway, unable to take another step.

Memories of laughter and the family we used to be hit me like a storm blowing in off the ocean. That cozy chair by the fireplace is where Aunt Charity sat and read.

A massive bouquet of roses dominates the small square table by the window where we used to work on jigsaw puzzles when it was raining.

The scent memory of heather and honeysuckle, from when Aunt Charity had vases filled with them all over the downstairs, almost overpowers the fragrance from the roses.

For a moment, I'm more in the past than the present, but the scent of roses is too cloying and sweet to give way to memories.

It's not just the bouquet by the window either. There's another one on the hearth and an arrangement on the counter in the open plan kitchen.

There are even white rose petals scattered on the floor in a path leading to the stairs.

And the bedrooms on the second floor.

Champagne I'm too young to drink chills in a freestanding silver *glacette*. I wonder whose idea that was?

Michael doesn't push me; he simply pulls the door shut behind us and then steps around me.

Throat dry, my heart pounding practically out of my chest, I suck in a deep breath and let it out. It doesn't help.

"Michael...I'm...I mean..."

CHAPTER FOURTEEN

Buttons & Blushes

KARA

"Mick."

"What?" I stare, my brain blank.

"I am called Mick."

"Oh. I'm Kara." I nearly smack my own forehead.

Of course, he knows my name and that I don't use a nickname. We just got married. The priest asked him if he took Kara Doyle Shaughnessy as his wedded wife. To have and to hold from this day forward.

It's that having and holding thing that's making my brain mush and my insides shake with nerves.

"My father calls you Mick, but I didn't want to presume." Why am I even trying to talk? Everything coming out of my mouth makes me sound ridiculous.

Worse, I sound like a prim schoolteacher from the last century, not an eighteen-year-old who spent more time on her smartphone than studying the last month of high school.

Maybe that's good. I doubt Mick wants a reminder he's married to a woman eight years younger than him with no life experience.

"You are my wife." He says the words like they're an explanation.

"Um, yes?"

"Are you in some doubt?" His emerald-green eyes reflect humor for the first time today.

"N-uh...no." Convincing. Not.

"After tonight, there won't be any question," he promises darkly.

"But we can't...you know."

"I cannot penetrate your beautiful body with my bod, nah. But I will make you mine tonight, Kara."

I suck in a breath. Choke on it and then start coughing.

Amusement flares briefly in his gaze again, but then disappears quickly. "There are many things we can do that will give you pleasure that do not require intercourse."

"Oh, uh...sure." My face is so hot, I feel sunburnt.

Suddenly the champagne looks more like a lifeline than romance. Finally able to move again, now that I have a destination in sight that is not the bedroom, I head toward the *glacette*.

Mick catches my arm and stops me. "Nah."

I blink up at him. "No what?"

"No champagne."

"If I'm old enough to get married, I'm old enough to drink a glass of champagne to toast that marriage." Or a bottle.

Not that anyone else seems to agree with me. My glass at the reception had been filled with sparkling white grape juice. Tasty, but not exactly a fortifier for the night to come.

Mick tugs me toward the stairs. "You are not getting legless on our wedding night."

"I don't want to get drunk." Lie. "But a small glass to toast our..."

Union. Mary, James and Joseph, I can't say that word. Or any other word right now.

Because Mick's finger is pressed against my lips, shushing me. "I didn't drink at the reception either."

Is that supposed to make me feel better? Maybe if he was a little tipsy, he'd fall asleep without doing his marital duty.

Seriously, Brogan called it that just the day before yesterday. He wanted to make sure I remembered that though I *could* be intimate with my husband, we *could not* fully consummate our marriage until after I got pregnant.

That's one conversation I never want to repeat. We were both as red as tomatoes by the time it was over.

Digging my heels in, I try to stop again. "Maybe we should talk for a while. I bet there's still a Scrabble game around here somewhere."

What the heck am I saying? This isn't a family vacation, not that we've been on one of those since Aunt Charity died. This is my wedding night.

A dark chuckle is the only answer I get to my suggestion.

So, no Scrabble.

"You don't have to be afraid of me, Kara."

I'm not afraid of him. I should be. He's Mick Fitzgerald. *An diabhal.* The son of a powerful mob leader in Dublin with a reputation as a killer. There are rumors he got made when he was still a child.

But I don't believe that. Not even in the mob, do they expect children to kill.

His control is legend. According to *mamo*, he never loses his temper or his composure.

He will smile while slitting your throat. At least that's the rumor. And that one? I believe, along with every other story about his ruthlessness.

I should definitely be afraid.

But I'm not. Nervous? Yes. I have no idea what happens next, but I'm shaking because I want him to touch me.

Whatever that means, however that plays out.

"I know the rules," I say, my voice barely above a whisper. "We're not supposed to... not until after the IVF."

Something flickers in his eyes. Irritation? Regret? Hunger?

"Aye. But it doesn't mean tonight has to be cold. That I can't make you scream my name with ecstasy."

Mick shifts and suddenly I'm being lifted high against his chest and he carries me up the stairs and into the primary bedroom.

Something settles inside me. Because he remembered. Tradition. Honor. Me.

When he sets me down beside the bed, the scent of roses has grown stronger and I realize the entire bedspread is covered in fresh petals too.

Mick turns me to face away from him and I see myself staring back from a mirror as big as a life-sized portrait.

My cheeks are flushed and my eyes are wide. My husband stands behind me, but he's not looking at the mirror. He's looking at me, his expression inscrutable.

I see his arm shifting and feel his fingertips on my back. They trail across my shoulder blades.

"So soft. Like silk." It's as if he's talking to himself, not me.

Then he starts undoing the buttons on my wedding gown. Thirty-six tiny pearl buttons that took Fi nearly five minutes to do up this morning.

Mick's deft hands finish in less than two. He doesn't fumble. He doesn't pause. Each button slips free like it was made to obey him.

And suddenly I can feel the air on the skin of my bare back.

"No bra?" he asks, his voice husky.

"No." I could explain that the modiste insisted the off-the-shoulder design would look better with support sewn into the bodice.

She assured me that my larger than average boobs would not shake like jelly when I walked. She'd been right.

But she'd said nothing of how I would feel when my new husband tried to peel the satin down my body with nothing to cover my naked breasts.

Without even thinking about it, both my hands came up to press the dress against my chest so it will not slide down and off.

Mick doesn't frown. Or look impatient.

In fact, one corner of his mouth tilts in something like a smile and he slides his big hands around my body and places them over mine. "Feeling shy?"

"I am shy." At least I am now, and he knows it.

He never met the other Kara. The daredevil. The girl who leaped for the next adventure without looking where she might land.

Mick's been here the past year getting to know the business. Brogan told me he was here to get to know me too, but that's a lie.

I never saw Mick alone. We didn't date or take walks on the shore to talk. He wasn't here for me, no matter what my father claimed.

He's not even in this room for me.

This is all about cementing an alliance.

He leans down so he can speak close to my ear in his panty melting Irish brogue. "There's no need to be shy with me."

"I can't help it." But that's not true.

Being quiet and holding back from people is a choice I deliberately make. There's less chance of losing someone else I love when I don't add any to the number.

Now that I'm married, I have no option but to get to know my husband. We'll be living together, sleeping in the same bed.

He kisses me right below my ear. "You'll get used to me."

Doubtful. I shiver, everything inside me ultra focused on the feel of his lips and how close they remain to my skin.

His hands curl right over mine to cup and squeeze my breasts.

And I forget how to breathe.

Wow! That's...I don't know what it is. Weird? Wonderful?

My nipples suddenly ache. Like whoa. I press my palms harder against them. Oh, that's good.

"That's right, *a stór*." He calls me treasure and my insides melt into a puddle of goo. "Like that."

Mick's hands guide mine into circular motions, abrading my tight peaks through my bodice.

It's not enough.

An embarrassing whimper escapes out of me.

"Fuck." Mick nips the side of my neck.

The use of that single word sends a burst of pleasure right to my core.

Mick usually uses the more Irish and softer word, feck. Is he losing a tiny bit of his control?

He starts tugging downward. "Let's get this off."

My arms stubbornly stay up. He kisses down my neck, taking my earlobe between his teeth and tugging.

Gasping at the burst of alien sensation fizzing through me like the champagne I didn't get to drink, I lose my grip on the dress.

Mick tugs the satin down, leaving nothing between my own palms and my sensitive nipples.

I groan as the gown drops into a pile of billowing satin and crinolines around my feet.

My gaze locks on the two of us together in the mirror again. He's still fully dressed in his wedding tuxedo. I'm only wearing a tiny pair of white lace panties, a garter belt and sheer silk stockings.

My breath catches and I bite my bottom lip, excitement warring with vulnerability.

"*Tá tú chomh álainn.*" You are so beautiful.

Does he really think that?

I've never felt beautiful. "I guess every bride is on her wedding night."

He growls. Like really growls at me. "You are the most beautiful woman I have ever had the privilege of seeing naked."

How can that be true? But the expression on his face in the mirror is fierce.

I swallow. "Thank you."

His fingers skim my arms, my waist and down my belly, slipping into my panties and brushing over my trimmed pubes.

Oh, gosh. I never knew the hair there could be *sensitive*. Every follicle is hotwired to my clitoris and it pulses with pleasure.

I thought that was just a thing romance writers made up. The pulsing clitoris thing. I read a bunch in preparation for my wedding night, but honestly didn't believe it would or could feel like this.

I've touched myself, but Mick's fingers on me feel different.

He breathes out like he's trying to keep a leash on something vicious inside him. "You're so bleedin' tempting."

My breath catches. It doesn't sound like a compliment, more like a warning.

Mick grabs me up into his arms and tosses me on my back on the bed. My breasts bounce and stinging pleasure knots my tender nipples.

He rips my Manolo Blahnik white satin heels right off my feet and tosses them aside but then he steps back.

CHAPTER FIFTEEN

Devoured

KARA

Mick's eyes close for long seconds as he breathes in and out. I scoot into a sitting position but that does nothing to make me feel less vulnerable.

When his eyes open the heat in them burns me, but his movements are controlled. He removes his cufflinks and shirt studs, one-by-one and lays them on the dresser. His gaze never leaving mine, he shrugs out of his shirt.

My mouth goes dry.

His white undershirt stretches taut over the sculpted muscles of his chest, but then it's gone too. And I can't get enough air no matter how much breath I take.

His right nipple is pierced. I've never seen a man with a piercing and if I'd thought about it, I wouldn't have thought I would like it. I would have been wrong.

Really, really wrong.

His biceps bulge, making the tattoo on the left side of his chest ripple. It's a skull with a scythe dripping blood below it. Fascinated, I try to read the Gaelig under it.

Noticing where my eyes are focused, Mick smiles, but there's nothing nice about it. "*Ní bionn sé, stop chun an scaidín a ghéilleadh.*"

It's not a delay to stop and sharpen the scythe.

The Irish proverb is about taking time to learn before rushing in headlong. *Moma* has used it many times with us girls.

Why do I think he doesn't mean the words that way? And why does that turn me on even more?

He's the scythe, honed to killing sharpness.

Celtic markings interconnected with a dagger, a gun and brass knuckles – that look like they're part of the symbols – cover the right side of Mick's chest and shoulder before flowing down to meet and surround the tattoo on his bicep.

They're stunning and perfectly shaded, but without a speck of color on any of them.

It's all black ink contrasting with the lighter tones of his skin, giving him the air of an ancient warrior.

Dark. Dangerous. Mesmerizing.

He walks toward me, wearing nothing but snug black briefs that do nothing to hide the raw power of his body or the size of his hardon.

Relief that we can't have intercourse wars with curiosity and unfamiliar desire. What would something like that feel like inside of me?

Even my own finger feels too big sometimes.

I scoot further back on the bed, a deer cornered by the hunter. Only, I want him to catch me. No matter how afraid I am of the unknown, something deep inside me craves Mick even more.

He comes down beside me on top of the rose petal strewn duvet. "I'm going to devour you."

There's no chance to answer because he starts with the devouring, his mouth eating at mine in the most carnal kiss I've ever experienced.

I've never had sex, but I've been kissed and it was nothing like this dominant possession. The brutal passion frees my own and I kiss him back, sliding my tongue against his and moaning.

His hands are everywhere. My breasts, my stomach. Between my legs.

I rip my mouth from his. "Too much," I pant.

His hands still; his jaw goes taut. "I can do slow for my sweet virgin bride." It sounds like he's talking to himself. Not me.

His hands run down my hips, over the white lace panties I picked out with shaking fingers weeks ago.

"Lie back," he commands.

Part of me wants to do exactly what he says when he uses that tone of voice. But most of me is frozen with indecision.

He doesn't repeat himself or wait for me to comply, but grasps my hips and tugs me down until I'm lying flat beside him.

"I'll take care of you," he promises.

I swallow and nod.

Then he starts touching me again, but this time he goes slow. His fingertips skim every inch of my skin, leaving goosebumps of pleasure in their wake.

My sides, my stomach, my shoulders and down my arms. He even traces between my fingers before rubbing a circle on my palm. Back up my arms to trail lightly over the column of my neck and over the contours of my face.

Is this part of making love?

I never thought of my husband touching my face on our wedding night. *That* wasn't in any of my romance novels.

Maybe I read the wrong ones.

His fingers tunnel into my updo, kneading my scalp and sending shudders through my body as my muscles turn to goo.

When he cups my breast and brushes his thumb over my engorged nipple, I moan. "*Michael.*"

His hand stills and he leans down to whisper in my ear, his voice low but implacable. "You will always call me Michael when you share your body with me."

Something cracks inside me. A fissure in the protective wall around my heart.

My husband wants something special between us, something as intimate as his touch on my body.

Mick belongs to the mob, but Michael belongs to me.

"Michael," I breathe.

His hand trails down, down, down until he runs his fingers over the gusset of my soaked panties. "It's time for these to come off."

"Mmm...hmm..." I agree, floating in a haze of bliss. And then I force myself to say, "The garter has to come off first."

But he's already sliding his hands under me to work on the tiny clasps that hold it together in the back. They give way before his deft fingers just like the tiny buttons on my wedding gown.

He turns his attention to the slide buttons attaching my stockings to my garters. Then he pulls the garter belt from my body before brushing his fingers over the skin revealed by its absence.

Fingers sure, he rolls my stockings down my legs, caressing the front and sides of my thighs, knees and calves as he does so.

Without removing my panties, he flips me onto my stomach and starts the gentle touching all over again. I'm moaning and trying to hump the bed by the time he turns me back over.

"Now, you feel me everywhere." It's not a question. It's a statement.

"Yes, Michael. Everywhere."

"Almost," he says darkly before ripping the seam down the center of my panties.

Two more pulls and a sharp sting at my hips and then the soaked lace is gone.

He leans down and presses his nose right into my mons, inhaling deep. "You smell so fucking good."

Mick's tongue swipes over my clitoris.

Bucking up for more of the delicious sensation, I cry out.

But my devil refuses, sliding back up my body to cup and knead my breasts before latching on to one of my nipples and sucking hard.

The sharp sensation contrasts with all the tender touches and a starburst of pleasure explodes in my core. Was that a climax? It sure felt like the pleasure I give myself alone in my bed late at night.

But Mick is far from done. He plays with my generous mounds and tender peaks for what feels like hours, driving me toward another detonation before backing off and then doing it all over again.

I'm unraveling.

Tears are tracking down my temples and I'm begging him to, "Do something!" when he shifts back down my body and puts that talented mouth on my most intimate flesh.

A single nibble on the bundle of nerves at my apex and I shatter.

With an animalistic sound, Mick devours my nether lips like he did my mouth earlier. And I finally understand what the term "eating her out" means.

With greedy tongue and teeth, he forces another body melting orgasm from me before he kisses me softly, right on my swollen clitoris.

Again, the tone of his movements shifts as one of Mick's fingers slides into me to the first knuckle. I'm so boneless, I don't react. He gently sucks on my labia on one side before moving to the other to do the same thing, his finger moving in tiny increments inside me.

The pleasure slowly builds again, but it's different now. All of my body's defenses are down. I welcome every touch, every hot breath against my intimate flesh as the low buzz of ecstasy vibrates along my nerve endings.

Mick lifts his head. "Tell me if I hurt you."

"Yes," I sigh. "Will."

But I cannot imagine pain coming from his touch when my body is surfing on the tsunami wave of the endorphins he caused to crash through me.

Sliding up my body, his expression changes slightly, fire banked in his green gaze. He looks at me like I'm a task he's about to complete with brutal efficiency.

And even that doesn't spark anxiety in me. How can it after the surfeit of pleasure he's already wreaked on my body?

Then he kisses me, owning my mouth, no trace of gentleness on his lips or tongue. I taste myself on him, tangy and different.

His finger slides further into me up to the second knuckle. It stings a little, but even that morphs into something I enjoy.

The heel of his hand presses down on my pleasure spot as he slides his finger deeper. The pressure builds, then sharpens. Another sting, this one quick and biting.

Still kissing me, he swallows my gasp of surprise. I try to press my butt deeper into the mattress to get away from the sting and then I'm tilting my pelvis upward, craving more.

When I climax this time, I nearly pass out from ecstasy fueled exhaustion.

Only then does his hand still and his mouth lift away from mine. "It's done."

I feel hollowed out and at peace like I haven't done since my aunt's death.

Present Day

I come out of my memories with a snap.

Because all the wonder and vulnerability of my wedding night ended with Mick leaving to take care of business.

And that's the way it's always been. The mob first, me somewhere down the list of his priorities.

Maybe Fitz has that first spot now, but I know I'm not second. Or third. I'm not even sure I'm in Mick's top ten.

CHAPTER SIXTEEN

A Scythe Well-Honed

MICK

The last bite of her dessert is barely off her fork before Kara wipes her mouth with a linen napkin, rises from the table, and walks out.

She doesn't look back.

Not at Dierdre, who has been shooting her alternating looks of disapproval and wounded reproach throughout dinner. My ex is clearly still playing the victim role and it's working.

At least on Brogan, who spends most of dinner paying attention to Dierdre as Hope grows quieter and quieter.

Kara doesn't spare a glance for her father, who's nursing a whiskey and acting like he didn't just put a feckin' match to a powder keg.

Not at me.

The only person she acknowledges is our son, who jumps up to follow her after kissing Maeve's cheek.

"See you tomorrow, Enoch!" Fitz waves, but sidesteps Brogan like his beloved *athair mór* is not there.

However, he smiles at Hope. "See you tomorrow, Auntie Hope."

Auntie? When did Hope Dobbs get promoted to family?

From the warm approval on my wife's beautiful face when she looks back over her shoulder to nod at our son, I think the promotion happened just now.

Fitz is no more forgiving than me.

And it won't be his grandfather's chastisement of himself he's taken issue with. It will be the way Brogan upset Kara.

Fitz is fiercely protective of his mam.

As he should be.

And tonight, it's his mother's example he's following.

Leaving the rest of us without a backward glance. I'm not aware of what I did to earn my little man's ire, but sure as certain, it's something to do with his mam.

Then he turns his head and the look he gives me asks, "Are you coming?"

"Excuse me," I say to the table at large and stand to go.

"We have business to discuss," Brogan blusters.

"It will keep." My father-in-law stepped over a line tonight and I'm letting him know it.

Fitz's suggestion that Brogan go to London instead of me grows on me as I follow my wife and son. Brogan may be the boss, but within my family? He doesn't override me, or Kara.

He needs a lesson in the cost of forgetting that fact.

I catch up with Fitz and Kara on the stairs. Fitz hops up one stair at a time while Kara patiently slows her pace to stay with him.

She is everything a mam should be.

Everything a man like me could ask for in a wife too.

In the beginning, Kara was nothing more than a clause in the contract that allowed me to advance to captain.

Now, she's my obsession.

And it all started on our wedding night, when I had to leave her or break the terms stipulated in the contract.

Seven Years Ago

My bride breathes shallowly beside me, boneless and sated, while my body buzzes with energy and *need*.

I don't feel need. I get aroused. I have sex, or I beat off. I don't *need*.

Living without sex since signing the contract has not been a hardship. No matter how many times Dierdre tried to renew sexual relations, I was never tempted.

I don't break my promises and one of the clauses in my contract with the Shaughnessy Mob is fidelity.

Dispersing my thoughts like mist in the sun, Kara's silky, tight heat flutters around my middle finger. My dick's so hard it's pressing against my stomach.

Need. Desire. Crave.

To be inside that soaked, grasping tunnel. *Bleedin' feckin' hell.*

I should leave now.

Because that is the one thing I cannot do. I agreed to no penetrative sex until after she is pregnant with my son.

I thought it would be easy. Lust has never driven me. Sex is a bodily function, not a daily, or even weekly necessity.

Kara is a sweet woman. Shy. Not someone to get like this over.

I need to pull my finger out of her and roll away. Get up, dress and walk out like the composed bastard I've always been.

But I don't.

I feckin' can't.

Keeping my own breathing even with more effort than it should take, I stay exactly where I am.

Taking in my fill of the bride who was just supposed to be part of the bargain. A contract guarantor.

A pretty pink blush covers her usually milky-white skin from her mouth-watering tits right down to the pussy I want to taste again. Her lashes flutter as she tries to recover and her hips make an aborted movement.

But my hand holds her in place.

Those innocent hazel eyes fly open, widening as she seems to realize, all at once, that I'm still buried two-knuckles deep in her hot cunt. She tries to press her thighs together in knee-jerk reaction that's no more successful than when she tried to shift her hips.

But it jostles my finger inside her, and her channel tightens as she moans.

Fuck it.

In one swift move, I pull my hand away from the glistening apex of her thighs and move to straddle her. I have to force myself to settle my ass over the gentle curve of her lower abdomen when all I want is to bury myself between her sweet, juicy thighs.

But her big, soft baps will have to do. Those tits were made to be fucked.

And my cum can't go anywhere near her newly claimed pussy.

My hand is drenched with her, and I suck her juices off my finger while she watches, her lips parted, her eyes hot.

As much as she clearly likes seeing me taste her, the blush across her chest turns rosy red.

Fuck me, I want more.

I want inside her.

Now. Not in a month or two after she's gotten pregnant. *Now.*

My control – which until this very moment I would have said was absolute – is fraying by the second.

And it's her fault.

She's not supposed to be like this. Sensual, sweetly responsive and utterly wrecked by a single finger. She's supposed to be a means to an end. A condition. A clause.

Instead, she's temptation wrapped in skin softer than silk. She's heat and innocence, and I'm a man who knows how to take what he wants.

But not this.

Not yet.

With herculean effort, I stay where I am and grab her hand.

"Now, it's your turn," I say roughly, dragging her hand to my cock.

She blinks at me, that blush surging into her cheeks now. "I don't know what to do." She swallows, her fingers flexing. "I read books, but..." Her voice trails off.

The smile I give her has nothing to do with humor. "Don't worry, *a stór,* I'll show you."

I wrap her small hand around my girth. Her fingers don't touch, but I cover her hand with my own and press to get the pressure I like.

Precum drools from my cockhead, sliding down to wet her fingers. I guide her hand up and over my head, then back down, lubricating my dick with my own precum.

An idea forms and as fast as it does, I act on it, reaching behind me to soak my hand with her essence.

Kara cries out, her hips canting.

But I shake my head. "Not yet, greedy girl. You've already come."

Multiple times.

"Now it's your turn," she repeats my words back to me.

I spread her juices over my dick, sliding under her fingers and around them. "Bleedin' right it is."

Then I swipe my forefinger across my leaking tip and press it to her bottom lip.

She gasps, the sound small and startled.

Taking advantage of her parted lips, I slip my finger inside. "Taste me."

She doesn't hesitate, sliding her tongue around my finger and humming.

Feckin' hell. She likes it.

Then she blushes and tries to turn her head away. I'm not having it. I keep her in place with my finger once again buried in her wet heat. Only this time, it's her hungry mouth instead of her hungry pussy.

"Don't be shy." I wrap my other mitt around hers again. "You're my wife now, aren't you? This is yours."

Something flares in her eyes at that.

Possession.

"You like that, don't you?"

She nods, her teeth sliding against my finger. Fuck. I want to feel those teeth on my cock, but that's for another night.

Right now, I'm so hard, a dagger's blade is soft by comparison. And less deadly.

I show her how to jack me without making me come, because that's not happening until I'm cradled between her pillowy mounds.

The lesson goes off the rails fast when she grips me too tight, jerking hard and awkward but with unmistakable enthusiasm.

Her movements are unskilled, but honest. Unfiltered. No practiced technique like past sex partners and it's a fucking turn-on.

I'm no muppet, but I'm feeling like one as my control threatens to shatter.

Fuck. I can't hold back. Giving up on giving my wife her first pearl necklace, I stop trying to control her movements.

Two strokes later, an orgasm rips through me before I can stop it. Like I'm some fucking teenager without any control. Cum erupts from my balls, tearing up my pole and shooting out like a feckin' geyser.

A growl tears from my throat. Then I shout. Her name.

"Kara!" My control disintegrates in the space of a breath.

White heat.

Blinding.

I slam my eyes shut, jaw clenched, riding the wave until it ebbs. My body is still twitching when I finally force her hand away.

"Enough," I snap, harsher than I mean to.

But fuck. I just came like a rocket and all it did was make me want to be inside her more.

She flinches slightly, pulling her hand back to her chest, smearing my cum over her bap, but not the way I wanted to christen those beauties.

Shit.

I climb off her before I do something stupid. Like break the clause in the contract.

I don't renege on my promises.

Not even for a sexy as fuck virgin who just took me apart with the least practiced hand job I've ever had.

Going into the bathroom, I clean up quickly, methodically, like I didn't just lose my mind over a girl who was never meant to matter.

After wetting a thick washcloth with warm water, I carry it back into the bedroom.

Kara's exactly where I left her, lips swollen, eyes questioning, skin still flushed with pleasure. She's looking at me all soft, like I'm someone I'm not. Like this thing between us is something it can never be.

I should be glad. I spend every waking minute pretending to be the charming Irishman with emotions like everyone else.

But I'm not.

I think better of my plan to clean her up with the cloth and toss it at her. "Clean yourself up. I got a text. I need to check it."

The soft glow in her eyes dims, but she doesn't argue. Just starts washing my sticky ejaculate from her hand.

Fuck. "Don't use that on your pussy now it's got my cum on it," I growl before turning away to *check* my phone.

No text came, but I need an excuse to get out of here.

Staring down at the blank phone screen, I hear her get off the bed and pad across the room to the en suite.

I'm dressed in black cargo pants and t-shirt when she comes out of the bathroom.

"Your grandfather needs me," I say, rising and adjusting my jacket like the mind-blowing almost-sex was just a stop along the way to more important business.

It's a lie. There's no call. No emergency.

The only thing pressing is the realization that I came harder with this untouched virgin than I ever have with any of my lovers.

And I didn't even fuck her.

This is the real problem.

Because I want to. If I stay in her vicinity for five more minutes, I will. But I'm not willing to pay the price my lust would cost me.

Her grandfather's trust.

My position.

My sense of honor, as tarnished as it might be.

I don't speak again. I just walk out, shutting the bedroom door behind me with the click of a lock.

I tell myself it's a victory.

But all I feel is weak.

When her grandfather texts at three in the morning to tell me I'm needed on a product transfer in Boston, I leave for the helicopter without a backward glance.

But I don't take Brice and Conor. They're my mates, the only two men on my crew in Dublin I brought with me. I trust them to keep Kara safe.

CHAPTER SEVENTEEN

Lines in the Sand

MICK

Present Day

Rory stops me outside the apartment. "Hex needs to talk to you."

Along with Bryce, Rory and Conor, Dr. Ximena Morales is one of the best recruits I ever made to our syndicate.

If she needs to talk to me, it's about the whisper gun project. And if she called on a Sunday, it's urgent.

With a flash of regret that's been happening more and more when I have to walk away from my family, I nod.

"I'll be back in time to tuck you in for bed," I promise Fitz.

Kara's eyes widen. We both know I don't usually get home until after our son and she have gone to sleep.

I love waking my wife with my mouth between her legs. Not something I need to think about before talking to the gun tech guru.

With a tiny shrug, Kara turns away to take our son inside the apartment.

I don't know what's driving me, but I grab her shoulder and turn her back toward me.

Her mouth is open on a gasp when my lips cover hers. I kiss her until she's pressing into me, her body soft the way I like it.

"Mommy and da kissing in a tree, k-i-s-s-i-n-g," Fitz sings loudly.

Kara's body stiffens and she pulls back.

With another dose of regret, I let her. "Let me guess, another thing he learned from Enoch?"

"More likely he learned it in Kindergarten," Kara says. "Didn't you sing it to taunt your friends when you were little?"

"Nah." I didn't have friends in primary school.

Other than my dog and he wasn't going to sing songs with me, was he?

I reluctantly leave my wife and son to call Hex. The brilliant scientist thinks she's made a breakthrough cooling the barrel, but she needs more materials to run the tests she wants to.

Not an emergency. But not unimportant either.

I hope she's right about cooling the barrel. Doesn't matter how quiet the gun is if it melts in your hand and burns a good chunk of skin along with it.

Brogan tracks me down right after I end my call with Hex. Entering my office, he shuts the door behind him and glowers. "What the fuck was that at dinner?"

I go still and stare him down until he tugs at the collar of his custom-tailored shirt. "Good question. What the feckin' hell did you think you were doing reprimanding my wife and son?"

"She's my daughter. He's my grandson," Brogan blusters.

"You ever talk to Kara like that again and I'll cut out your tongue and have the chef turn it into soup," I promise my father-in-law.

Brogan laughs uneasily. "You've got a warped sense of humor, boyo."

"Do you see me laughing?"

Brogan clears his throat. "Okay, you're right. I shouldn't have been so hard on either of them. I'm just not used to my daughter being so obstinate. Not since she was a little girl anyway."

He's made comments before, about how Kara used to be stubborn and brash. She's still stubborn, even if he refuses to see her quiet rebellions.

Like telling me point blank if I sent Fitz to school in Boston, she was going with him. She meant it.

I didn't want either of them to leave, but for a while there, we were on the verge of war with the Genovese Family.

If it came to war, I would have sent them to Dublin though, so I gave up on Boston as a stopgap security measure.

"When did she change?" I ask.

Brogan rubs his hand over his face. "When my sister-in-law was murdered. Charity was like a mother to my girls. They both took her death hard."

My wife didn't just see her aunt shot, but her little sister as well, but Brogan ignores that fact.

"No child should have to witness the murder of someone they love." Or any murder.

When I kill, I never do it in front of the innocent.

"It's a dangerous life." Brogan shrugs, then frowns. "I only wish Fiona would snap out of it. She's let it affect her for more than a decade."

Fiona survived being shot, but she'd been in a coma for nine days. Her anxiety is understandable, even if it's not something I can experience.

And if Kara used to be impetuous, she's been affected as well, because she's anything but. Her more amenable nature isn't something her father is going to mind though, is it?

"Fi is who she is. She's happy." Even I know that people don't just snap out of childhood trauma.

His youngest needs therapy, but that's not going to happen unless she does what Kara has and sees someone online in secret. Maybe I should suggest it to my wife.

If there's a chance for Fiona to be able to live a less anxiety-filled life, she deserves it.

Brogan frowns heavily. "She could be happier."

"You mean you could be happier using her to secure another alliance."

"That's not happening," Brogan grumbles.

"No, it's not." I respect the hell out of my wife's cousin for negotiating Fiona's freedom from an arranged marriage.

Róise made it a condition for her being willing to enter a marriage alliance with the De Lucas. We needed that alliance to end decades of strife between the Shaughnessy Mob and the Cosa Nostra.

And she took advantage of our need to force Brogan into a promise I would never let him break.

"About London, I need you there the day after tomorrow," Brogan changes the subject.

"You heard Kara. She's not going. I'm not leaving her and Fitz here with a potential spy living under our roof." And even if Dierdre isn't a spy, she's a dramatic pain-in-the-ass I don't want causing trouble with, or for, my wife.

"You'll just have to change her mind," Brogan says complacently.

I lean back in my chair and meet his gaze, making no effort at a pretense of normality. "No."

"What the fuck? You know I need you there, Mick. There's no one else we can trust with this negotiation."

"Are you saying you don't trust yourself to handle it?" I gibe.

"You know that's not what I'm saying. It's your job, damn it!"

"No, my job is to protect my family. Everything else is secondary."

"You don't think I can keep my own daughter and grandson safe?" he demands, offence in every line of his tall frame.

I don't sugar coat it. "Nah."

"Fuck me." Brogan leaps to his feet. "Who do you think you're talking to?"

"Do you have feelings for Hope?" I ask.

Brogan rears back. "What in the hell does that have to do with this?"

"If you do, you lost major ground with her at dinner tonight," I point out.

"I don't know what you think you know—"

I don't let him finish his false denials. "You hurt her by playing up to Dierdre."

"Well, you sure as hell weren't doing it."

"It wasn't necessary." And I already pissed my gentle wife off to the point she barely acknowledged me over dinner.

"I don't agree."

"Clearly."

"You think it upset Hope?" he asks, shocking me.

I didn't think Brogan would acknowledge his interest in the widow with two children.

"I know it did. The question is: how come you don't?"

"She's always quiet."

Which means he noticed she was quieter than usual at dinner and is trying to tell himself it didn't mean anything. I don't give a fuck.

I shrug. "If you want to regain lost ground, take her with you to London. Kara will watch Enoch and Esther."

That's one thing I'm sure my wife won't balk at, regardless of her out of character behavior lately.

Up until dinner tonight, her usual reserve was in place with Hope, but Kara welcomed the two children with warm generosity when they came to live at the mansion.

"Tonight's dinner notwithstanding..." Brogan pauses to glare at me. "You have a better chance of discovering Dierdre's real reason for being here than I do."

"Agreed." I also have a better chance of gathering intel on what is happening with the Northies.

And I'll take out the lot of them if they're a potential threat to Kara and Fitz's safety.

It's time to find out what Dierdre knows and how she knows it.

Which means no matter how much I would rather go back to our apartment, I need to find Dierdre for a soft interrogation.

CHAPTER EIGHTEEN

Earwigging and Interrogation Plans

MICK

Dierdre's not in her room and her security is nowhere to be seen when I come out of my office.

Frustrated that it's closing in on Fitz's bedtime, I search the ground floor of the mansion.

Moonlight filtering through the windows gives the only illumination to the sunroom. So, it's the last room I check. Assuming Dierdre would not be sitting in the dark I almost miss her because I only give it a cursory once over.

I'm wrong. Slight movement catches my eye. Dierdre's curled in the chair that Kara favors, knees tucked beneath her, glass of wine in hand.

The French doors to the balcony are open as are the interior doors to the entrance hall. Is she hoping to overhear conversations?

That would make sense of the lack of light in the room.

With no desire to have this conversation, or any other, with this woman in the dark, I flip on the lights. The standing lamp beside Kara's chair has a full spectrum bulb so my wife can read without straining her eyes.

I had it installed after I found her reading in here with nothing but a small table lamp to illuminate the book's pages.

Bright light reveals Dierdre's startled face and the way her entire body tenses.

But when she sees it's me, her expression shifts into calculated welcome.

I've only got twenty minutes before Fitz's bedtime. So much for a prolonged soft interrogation, but there's enough time to lay some groundwork.

Leaving the door open, I cross the room toward Dierdre. "What are you doing in here?"

"Am I not allowed? Only Kara didn't say anything like that earlier."

"You mean when she was supposedly making you feel so unwelcome, you thought you had to leave the mansion?" I shut the door to the patio and the still warm, muggy air from outside, but don't take my eyes off Dierdre.

So, I see the way her mouth tightens in consternation at being caught in her lie.

But almost immediately, her lips turn down at the corners and she tries to reflect sad vulnerability with her eyes. "I may have taken her words more to heart than I should have."

Too bad for Dierdre, even if her dejected demeanor is real, I don't care. But that doesn't mean I'll let her know that.

I allow a mask of understanding to settle over my features before taking a seat close to her, my posture relaxed and open. I've practiced this posture-expression combo just like so many others and have never had anyone doubt my sincerity.

It is easy to project because most people want to believe you are sincere. Even other syndicate members.

"Why were you sitting here in the dark?" I ask Dierdre.

She shrugs. "Just wanted a quiet place to think."

And she just happened to want to do that thinking in the dark, while sitting in Kara's chair? Dierdre is fully self-involved, but she does not lack most emotions like I do.

Is *she* jealous? She said this morning that me marrying Kara was hard on her. That she couldn't stand to attend the wedding.

I assumed she was playing for sympathy. However, she *didn't* attend the wedding, even though the rest of our families flew to New York to be there.

If she has more feelings for me than I gave her credit for, it should be easier to get the information out of her that I want.

"Thinking about what?" Broad open ended questions are the mainstay of soft interrogation, often revealing more than pointed questioning would.

People go on their guard when answering questions they think could trip them up, but since most people like talking about themselves, broad questions lubricate their vocal cords.

"Memories," Dierdre replies and then sighs artfully. "Your wife has excellent taste in furniture. This is the most comfortable chair in the house."

"Aye." That's on purpose.

Kara told me it's her cozy reading chair. I didn't pay much attention at the time to the width of the chair and the generous matching ottoman.

But now, details about the piece of furniture take on significance my gut says not to ignore.

The fact that Dierdre's feet are curled under her, rather than resting on the ottoman where they would more likely be seen from the doorway. The way the large ottoman blocks the sight of her shoes on the floor from the same vantage point.

She's got her glass of wine to sell her presence in case she's caught, but unless she overpoured to begin with, she hasn't taken a sip from it.

She was definitely sitting in the dark hoping to earwig.

Too bad for her, all our men know better than to discuss anything sensitive in any of the public areas of the mansion, whether they think they're alone, or not.

I've proven to them enough times that they weren't in fact alone and that the punishment for sloppy chatter isn't worth indulging in. Now, our men rarely talk at all when they are in the main areas of the house.

Dierdre makes a sound between a sigh and a hum. "She's a lucky woman."

She's not talking about the chair, but I don't take the bait and pretend like I think she is. "I'm sure Kara would tell you where to buy one just like it to be shipped back to Dublin, if you asked."

Dierdre draws her finger slowly around the rim of the wine glass, making the crystal sing. "I wasn't talking about the chair, Micky."

"What were you talking about then?" I prepare myself for more melodramatic claims about missing me, with the hope it will lead to more substantial topics.

Soft interrogation is all about patience and taking the circuitous route to information.

"I just needed some quiet after dinner. I told you it would be hard for me, and it was. If Brogan hadn't talked to me, I wouldn't have anyone to talk to at all."

"That's a bit of an exaggeration." She'd done her best to monopolize the conversation at the dinner table and no one had made any effort to stop her.

Certainly not my wife, who sat in near total silence throughout the meal after her confrontation with Brogan.

"You think so?" Dierdre wipes at her eyes, like she's hiding tears.

The lack of moisture on her fingertips is apparent in the bright lamplight. I wonder if she realizes that?

The way she wipes them against the skirt of her dress says she's still trying to sell it.

I don't call her on it. "I was glad you joined us for dinner."

Which is true, if not for the reasons she'll assume.

The sound of a soft footfall near the door alerts me to the presence of someone else in the entrance hall. A couple of seconds later, the soldier responsible for locking up at night looks into the room.

I flick my hand at him, telling him to get lost. Like the well-trained soldier he is, he quickly walks away.

"I'm glad, Micky. I feel like we've barely had any time together since I arrived."

"You've only been here a few days," I remind her.

She sighs again and looks at me through her lashes. "Maybe we could have lunch tomorrow, just the two of us? I know family dinner is sacrosanct."

"It's important to Maeve." And I respect that.

Kara's grandmother is a plainspoken Irishwoman who does not suffer fools.

I have no doubt that if I had ever harmed her granddaughter, she would not have hesitated to try to kill me. She might even have succeeded.

"Kara's grandmother doesn't like me. No one here likes me, except you, Micky."

"No one knows you well enough to like or dislike you." Which is a blatant lie.

Sure as certain, Dierdre has managed to get the back up of every woman living in this house, not to mention my son.

But her ego will allow her to believe my words.

"I guess." She shrugs. "I'd still like to have lunch though. Can you make time tomorrow?"

Not usually, no. But this is business. Lunch with her is exactly what I need to lull Dierdre into complacency and letting things slip.

"Aye. Be ready at two o'clock." Getting her away from the house will both feed her ego and provide an environment more conducive to her talking.

One of our businesses is an Irish pub in Queens. I'll send Rory over in the morning to doctor a wineglass and water glass for her use at lunch.

A single drop of a benzo compound developed by one of our Triad connections lowers inhibitions better than a shot of sodium pentothal.

Administered orally, it takes about ten minutes to kick in. Mixing it with alcohol enhances the speed and effectiveness though. Rory can make sure the pub has a bottle of Dierdre's favorite wine on hand.

And we'll have plenty of time for it to reach full efficacy over lunch.

I stand. "I'll see you tomorrow."

She stands with me, stepping into my personal space and lays her hand on my chest and reaches up to kiss my cheek. "I'll look forward to it."

I step back before her lips connect to skin.

Her laugh tinkles, but her eyes don't show amusement. "That's right, you don't go in for the traditional kiss on the cheek."

I don't *go in for* being touched by anyone but my wife and son.

I lock the door to the patio in case our soldier forgets to check this room now that he's done his usual rounds. "Goodnight, Dierdre. Don't go outside now the house is locked up."

"Am I in danger here?" she asks like she's not a shark in a tank full of goldfish.

I answer with truth. "Only if you lie to me."

Dierdre laughs like I'm joking. I don't laugh with her. I don't even give her one of my fake smiles.

She should know better than to believe I'll show any mercy if she's here to harm my family. In any way.

CHAPTER NINETEEN

Business & Fragile Bonds

MICK

When I make it back to the apartment, Fitz and Kara are already in his bedroom. I'm not surprised to find my wife snuggled next to our son on his bed, reading him a Little Golden Book story about Spidey and His Amazing Friends.

Purring, Gobby is curled up on the other side of Fitz.

Kara doesn't acknowledge me standing in the doorway to our son's bedroom. Doesn't even pause when I walk in, like my presence doesn't matter.

I don't like it. I miss when her attention used to fixate on me when I was in a room.

Now, I fixate on her. Whether we're sharing breathing space, or not.

Fitz notices me though and grins. "Hi, da. Mommy said you could read me another story if you got here in time."

But she'd been prepared to put him to bed without me saying good-night. I don't know why that knowledge stings.

I'm rarely home before Fitz's bedtime any night but Sunday. But I told them I would be here to tuck him in tonight, didn't I?

If something urgent had come up, I would have texted to say I couldn't keep my promise to Fitz. And there's not much I can think of that would make me break a promise to my son.

Clearly, my wife doesn't see it the same way.

"Have you got your second book already picked out then?" I move to stand beside Kara, making it impossible for her to stand without brushing her body along mine.

"Yep. I knew you'd come," Fitz says confidently as he pulls a book from under his pillow: Teenage Mutant Ninja Turtles.

My son loves superheroes, but only the cheeky ones.

When it's my turn to read, Kara gives me a look, expecting me to step back. I don't. Giving me a look of exasperation that Fitz can't see, she stands up, trying to keep her breasts and belly from touching me.

It doesn't work. My wife's curves are too luscious for avoidance at close quarters. I don't sit beside Fitz like she had been doing, but lift my son to sit in my lap and then pull my wife down to sit beside us.

She's stiff as a board beside me, trying to keep her distance, but again...not possible on the small twin bed.

Unhappy with the lack of space for him to lounge on the mattress, Gobby jumps into Fitz's lap and he hugs the cat.

Putting my arms around my son, I open the book in front of us so he can see the pictures as I read.

Then I slide one arm around my wife and offer the other side of the book for her to hold. "Will you turn the pages, Kara?"

The glare she gives me could peel paint, but she does it.

Fitz yawns, snuggling into me. "I wish bedtime could always be like this."

"Me too, *a mhac*." Before the birth of my son, I didn't cuddle.

Not even Kara.

However, since she came home from The Marlowe Center, I can't sleep if she's not wrapped in my arms where I know she's safe. Fitz and I bonded in a special way while she was there and he wouldn't sleep unless I rocked him.

I'm not sure when I slipped back into the habit of working such long days and being gone at night sometimes too.

But it was before Fitz went to preschool.

Was that when Kara started distancing herself from me? If I spent more time with her and Fitz would she go back to the way she was?

With no certain answer to that question, I read Fitz his story. He's asleep before I finish and I tuck him and Gobby in before standing.

Kara leans down and kisses his forehead, murmuring a Gaeilge blessing for peaceful sleep before she straightens.

"Good night, mommy. G'night da," Fitz whispers with his eyes closed.

Kara doesn't head toward our bedroom like I expect, but returns to the main living area and puts the kettle on.

"That better be herbal tea you're drinking," I warn her. She needs her rest.

And I need her in our bed.

KARA

Mick's words are like tinder to the hot ball of anger inside me. And it goes whoosh, burning the last of my reticence about speaking my mind.

"What tea I drink is none of your business. I'm an adult and if I want to drink a pot of coffee, I will." Not that I want to.

Because our son wakes with the birds no matter what time I go to sleep.

But I could if I did.

I spin around to face my husband. "Shouldn't you be getting back to Dierdre? I'm surprised you were able to pull yourself away from your ex-girlfriend to tell your son goodnight."

His eyes flicker with surprise.

"I came down to get you, to remind you of your promise." Our son has been so fragile since Róise's kidnapping.

I wasn't going to allow Mick to let him down about tucking him in. So, I left Fitz playing a boardgame with one of our security detail, who has watched him for short times in the past, and went looking for my absent husband.

I'd expected to find him in his office, unaware of the time, not having a cozy chat with Dierdre in the sunroom, while she sat curled up like a kitten in *my* chair.

How much else of my place does she want to take?

All of it, a small voice in my head whispers.

Mick frowns. "I heard a noise, but then the night security showed his face."

It was Frank who clued me into where Mick was and with who. "Yeah, he was with me when I overheard you making a lunch assignation with her."

I'd gone hot with shame and hightailed it back to our apartment, not caring if Mick showed up to tuck our son in, or not. Part of me hoped he wouldn't.

Which isn't fair to Fitz, but just looking at Mick standing there so unconcerned over it all makes my stomach cramp in pain.

"It's lunch." He tunnels his fingers through his hair and sighs. "Not an assignation."

"Funny how you never have time to have lunch with me, but you'll drop everything to take her out for a meal." When was the last time Mick took me anywhere, *just the two of us.*

Bile rises in my throat, a memory of Dierdre saying those exact words less than thirty minutes before echoing in my head.

Just the two of us. Her and Mick.

Not me and Mick. And that's the story of my marriage, isn't it? We're not a couple. We're a contract.

Marrying me was his path to eventual control of the Shaughnessy Mob. Well, marrying me and getting me pregnant with our son.

Fitz's birth guarantees that Mick will become Boss of the Shaughnessy Mob when my father retires at the age of sixty-seven. Or earlier if Brogan dies. Which, in his line of work, is as likely a scenario as retirement.

Sometimes, I can't help wondering if I'm now surplus to requirements.

That's a phrase my English roommate from boarding school used to say. It's kind of perfect for how I feel though. Both in regard to my father and my husband.

Surplus to requirements.

"You have nothing to be jealous over. This is business." Those words are familiar too, only from a long time ago.

They didn't work then, and they don't work now. It all feels too familiar.

And yet, I can't stop my sarcastic retort from coming out. "Oh, yeah. It sounded like business."

Now, it's another voice echoing in my head. Younger and less sure of myself, but still my own. From that bad time after Fitz was born, when I was so jealous of the lawyer who worked for my dad and too closely with Mick (in my opinion back then anyway).

My mouth snaps shut and I shake my head, trying to dislodge the memories, trying to push away the parallels.

"You had nothing to fear then, and you have nothing to fear between Dierdre and me now, *mo chuisle*." Mick's assertion shows he remembers those words too.

Again, his assurances are no more comforting today than they were when I was a young mom. But *I'm* not the same.

I'm not.

And I won't let myself go there again. Not for anything. Turning away from my husband, I pull my feelings back inside, and bury them deep.

I. Am. Not. Going. There. Again.

MICK

Kara doesn't reply, but turns away from me, her posture stiff her shoulders rounded.

Bleedin' hell. I thought I wanted to trigger Kara's jealousy, but underneath it, I assumed she'd know that I don't want any other woman.

I'm jealous of her too. No other man is allowed to touch her and live. It's that simple. But I have no doubts about Kara's faithfulness.

Why is she doubting mine?

I step up close behind her and cup her shoulders, leaning forward to speak softly near her ear. "You know you're the only woman I want."

"Don't you mean the only woman you can have?" She shrugs, trying to dislodge my hands.

I slide them down her arms, and grasping them just above the elbow, I pull her back into me. Let her feel how hard I am. How hard *she* makes me.

Her breath hitches, but she doesn't let herself relax against me.

I lean down and kiss where her shoulder meets her neck, letting my tongue flick out to taste her.

Her skin always smells like flowers, but lately, there's a berries and cinnamon chaser.

The taste though? A bit of salt from sweat and the rest is pure Kara sweetness. I love the flavor of her pussy best of all, but every centimeter of her sates my tastebuds like nothing else can.

I lick a line up her neck, savoring her. Then I tug her earlobe with my teeth. "Only woman I crave."

Kara shudders, but still, she doesn't lean back.

My wife doesn't play hard to get. Something's going on with her and I don't know what it is.

It's not the first time. Kara is emotional, driven by her feelings. I barely have feelings.

"Dierdre is business, Kara."

"Are you trying to pretend I'm something else?" she asks, her breath hitching as I suck on her earlobe.

Spinning her around to face me, I growl, "You are my wife. The only woman who gets to touch me, the only woman I want to touch."

"She touched you. She was your lover." Kara's gaze darts away, like she's ashamed of her insecurity.

I will never feed her jealousy on purpose again. Tomorrow's lunch had better yield the information I need. But I'm not taking any chances. I'll put our blackgloves on her phone and digital footprint tomorrow.

"That was before we ever met and she never made me so hard, I came in my shorts." It's a hard thing to admit for a man who values control like I do, but damn, those first months of our marriage, when I couldn't bury my cock in her tight pussy?

If I didn't keep a physical barrier between me and her near irresistible cunt, I would have fucked her and damned the consequences.

I started using restraints the first month we were married.

Stopping myself from breaking the terms of the contract and fucking her got harder every night we shared a bed. But when her soft fingertips skimmed over my heated skin, it got ten times worse.

Kara loved being bound, my entire focus on her. She still does.

And the satisfaction I found in controlling every aspect of our lovemaking gave me a mindgasm before cum ever erupted from my aching dick.

I reach past my wife and flip the switch, turning off the kettle. "I have a better way to relax you, *a stór*."

She shakes her head, but we're not going there. Sex is the one thing we always get right between us, an invisible tether, tying us together no matter what else is happening.

"Come with me. Be with me." I grab both of her hands and start walking backwards.

She swallows, but she doesn't try to tug her hands away. "Sometimes, I hate how much I want you."

"Does it help to know that I will always want you more?" I ask.

She bites her lip, disbelief shimmering in her vulnerable gaze.

How can she question my desire for her? "I'm the one that wakes you every night because I crave your body. You lay there, sleeping so peacefully and you'd stay asleep until morning, if I let you."

"Fitz wakes up early."

"Kara, I *need* you."

"You want my body."

"Bleedin' hell woman. I'm no liar." I might lack empathy for most people in the world, but I don't lie unless it's necessary.

And it should never be necessary between us. If I can't tell her something, I don't, but I'm not going to lie to her and she knows it.

"I think we define need differently, Mick. If I were gone, you'd find another way to sate your sexual appetite."

The sound that comes out of me borders on demonic. "Do not say that. You will not leave me."

Something in her eyes challenges that statement but she keeps her lips sealed

My control snaps and I yank her to me, lifting her up and carrying her the rest of the way to the bedroom.

CHAPTER TWENTY

Unspoken Pain, Unmatched Passion

MICK

I hip check the door shut and lean down to lock it.

"Fitz's monitor on. Alerts only," I order the smart speaker system.

The monitoring system is programmed to pick up on anomalous noises from Fitz's room. If he has a bad dream and vocalizes his distress, we'll be alerted. If he leaves his room, we'll be alerted.

If the cat jumps off the bed and uses the cat door to leave our son's room and roam the apartment, we won't.

We no longer hear his breathing like when he was a baby, but I'm not ready to give up monitoring him at night altogether. Kara isn't either.

If she were, she would have told me to turn off the system.

I carry her to the bed, but I don't lay her down on it. Instead, I release her legs, letting her feet drop to the floor. She doesn't lean into me, but she doesn't try to move away either.

Her hazel eyes are filled with a pained vulnerability I cannot stand to see.

Cupping her cheek, I slide my thumb over her lips. "So soft. So perfect. *So mine.*"

Her lips part and I push my thumb into her mouth, rubbing over her tongue. Moving her head back, she scrapes her teeth against my skin and then leans forward again before sucking my digit as deep into her mouth as she can get it.

Pleasure so acute it borders on pain rushes straight to my dick.

This woman.

Her breath stutters when I bring her hand to my chest, pressing it flat under mine and guiding her palm over my pecs.

Her fingers twitch. I feel it. Her struggle not to grip, not to cling like she usually does.

She doesn't want to need me. But she *does.*

Just like I need her and only her, regardless of what she believes.

The pike in my pants surges with blood as she allows me to direct her small fingers to brush over the nipple with a barbell through it. She bends her middle finger just enough so her nail scrapes over it.

Fuck.

This is the one thing we always get right and have from our very first night together.

This is where the feelings I don't know how to process find expression. The craving. The need. And something else I don't have a name for.

It's not love, not what I feel for Fitz. Though there's an element of the same need to protect. The same need to care for and see Kara happy.

But it also feels like weakness. So, like every other time it tries to surface, I shove it down deep and focus on what I do understand.

The undeniable, always combustible physical desire between us.

When I can't stand teasing myself with her touch any longer, I walk her backward until her hips hit the side of the bed. She doesn't sit, still fighting the desire raging between us.

She's breathing fast now, lips parted, gaze darting to my mouth, down to the tent in my trousers and back up to my face.

I pull my thumb from her hot mouth. "This is your chance to say *no.*"

She jolts, knowing what that means. If she says no, I don't get out the cuffs

She takes a deep breath and holds it, her eyes closing, before she releases it slowly. She's trying to regain control of her body, but that's not what either of us really wants.

Tonight, I need her surrender. Her trust. And she needs to give it to me, to remember she's safe with me.

Always.

Her and Fitz are the only living beings that I can say that about with absolute certainty.

The war going on inside her is all over her beautiful face.

Even when she's pissed at me for what she calls my high-handedness, she doesn't fight her desire for me like this.

Why is she doing it this time?

More importantly, is her caution going to win?

Will she deny me? Deny us?

The beast of desire rages and claws inside me, snarling its need and pushing against my own control. But this has to be Kara's decision.

Because she cannot meet the monster that rejects the concept of right and wrong, the cold rationality that would justify turning her own body's responses against her.

After interminably long seconds, her eyes open and they meet mine as she nods her head.

And I can breathe again. But it's not enough. "You need to say it."

"Ye..." She clears her throat. "Yes."

Pulling Kara with me because letting her go right now is not happening, I maneuver us two steps closer to the nightstand on my side of the bed. Then I lean down and open the drawer.

And her fingers *finally* dig into my shirt, holding on tightly.

Something I have no name for shudders through me and I retrieve the supple leather cuffs. Padded and lined with black silk, they're the same ones I used that first time with her.

I've used other things since: ties, rope, her underwear on a few notable occasions. But these are the only cuffs. They're *hers* and using them signifies something to both of us.

Tonight, I will take her apart with pleasure and then put her back together again.

The moment Kara sees her cuffs, her pupils blow wide and she follows the movement of my hand as I bring them between us.

I rub the soft leather over her pebbled nipples and she groans.

Tugging at the neckline of her summer dress, I order, "Off."

Kara doesn't hesitate, reaching behind herself to unzip the dress. Then she shrugs it off, revealing raspberry tipped naked breasts and boy shorts that cling to her curves like a second skin.

"Everything," I demand.

Biting her lips, she pushes the boy shorts down, revealing the pretty curls between her legs. The scent of her arousal wafts up from her pussy and I lick my lips.

With a needy little moan, she steps out of her shoes.

"Hands."

She lifts her hands together and I secure the cuffs, buckling each one slowly, and deliberately. I slip my finger between each cuff and her wrist, checking the placement.

They're snug but not too tight.

Tension releases from her body until she sways on her feet.

Fuck. The way she responds to this.

Wrapping one arm around her to keep her upright, I reach for the covers and rip them from the bed. Then I lift her again, bridal style and because I can't not, I kiss her until she's squirming in my arms and my blood is rushing through my veins like liquid fire.

Only then do I lay her down. "Arms up."

She lifts her bound wrists and I attach the cuffs to the hook that pops out from the headboard when I press the hidden lever.

Kara tugs once, but the cuffs don't give and her entire body goes lax.

I lean down and kiss the inside of each elbow before running my hands down her arms. Goosebumps erupt on her skin and she moans.

"Are you wet for me?" I know the answer. I can smell her sweet nectar, but I want to hear her say it.

"Yes."

"How wet?" I push her legs apart, taking in the sight of her juices glistening around the tantalizing pink opening to her body.

"You tell me," she breathes.

Running my forefinger through her folds, I gather her arousal.

She moans softly, her gaze fixed on me.

"So perfect." Lifting my finger near my mouth, I inhale her unique scent.

My mouth waters and I suck her juices off my finger, her tangy essence bursting across my tongue.

Then, because I can't not, I do it again, this time dipping into her satiny heat to coat my finger in her arousal. Her vaginal walls clamp around it and her gorgeous tits rise and fall with her rapid breaths.

Pulling my finger out, I trace up her folds and circle the sweet little clit peeking out of its hood.

"*Michael.*" My name is a plea on her tongue, but she's not ready for more. Not yet.

Withdrawing my hand from between her legs, my gaze roves over the beautiful curves that drive me wild. "Not wet enough yet, *mo stór*. You'll soak the sheet under you by the time I'm done."

Her pupils dilate and her body moves restlessly on the bed. She wants that too.

A river of carnal sensuality runs under the surface of my buttoned-down wife and I am the only one who will ever get to see it surge over the banks of her control

Standing, I begin to strip as Kara watches with avid interest. I take my time, knowing this drives her wild. She is as enthralled by my body as I am by hers.

"Stop teasing me," she husks. "You know I want to see."

I shrug off my shirt and she sighs, her eyes glowing with appreciation. Before our marriage, I had women look at me with lust before, but none ever watched me like doing so fed their soul.

If there's anything left of my own soul, it belongs to this woman. My addiction.

As I shove my slacks and boxers down my legs, my cock bobs and slaps against my stomach. It's so hard, a painful rhythm of blood surges through it with every beat of my pulse.

Kara's gaze locks onto it, and she licks her lips, the heated desire in her eyes turning into an inferno.

She's pissed at me because of Dierdre, but she still wants me.

Almost as much as I want her.

Feeling like the predator that I am, I crawl onto the bed and kneel between her legs, spreading her thighs wide.

Kara's light brown curls are dark with moisture. Her nether lips glisten, inviting my kiss and her swollen and needy clit begs for my tongue.

I trace my finger over her folds again, circling that tight little bud just enough to make her hips buck, but giving it no direct stimulation.

Pushing her foot toward her curvy ass cheek, I make her bend her knee before I press down on her thigh. Then I do the same to her other leg, leaving her in a lewd lotus position completely exposing her pussy to my hungry gaze.

I take my time looking, letting my eyes soak in the sensual beauty that is my wife bound and arranged for my pleasure. Her labia flushes darker, and her arousal perfumes the air around us.

Inhaling deeply, my hunger grows. "Look at that sweet cunt, so ready for my mouth."

"Yes." She shifts a little, but her legs don't move from the position I placed them in.

Good girl.

Shifting my body so I can put my mouth against that delicious flesh I crave, I have to be careful not to rub my straining dick against the bed.

I'm that close to coming and I'm nowhere near ready to fuck my wife. We're just getting started.

Leaning down, I lick her slow and easy, circling her clit with the tip of my tongue without quite touching it. She whines, canting her hips upward and straining against the cuffs.

Feasting on her delicious pussy, my tongue goes everywhere, except where she wants it most.

"Please, Michael!" she cries.

My name on her tongue sends a spear of pleasure straight through my chest. "Begging already, my sweet wife? But I've only just gotten started."

I slide two fingers inside her, curling them until I find the spot that makes her jerk. Then I *stop*.

"Mic—"

"No talking. No begging." There will be plenty of time for that. "Just feel."

I press in deeper and rapidly flick her clit with the end of my tongue. Over and over as I fuck her with my fingers.

She arches, her body tensing, and just as she's about to tip over, I pull back.

"No!" she cries out.

But I shake my head. "Not yet."

Then I bring her to the edge again.

And again.

By the fourth time, she's sobbing. Her thighs are shaking and her body is covered in a fine sheen of sweat.

"Please. Please, Michael. I need it. I need to come."

"Not until I say."

I put my mouth back on her, sliding my tongue inside her tight channel along with my fingers and she screams.

But she doesn't come. Not yet.

Pulling my mouth away from her tangy sweetness, I lift my head. Kara's eyes are closed and tears track down her temples.

"Look at me, *mo chuisle*. Let me see your beautiful eyes and I will let you come."

They snap open, but her gaze is hazy.

I wait until her eyes focus on mine. "Watch."

She jerks her head in what is probably meant to be a nod.

"Good girl. Perfect wife." I return to her swollen, sensitive flesh, but keep my own eyes locked with hers.

Then I close my teeth gently over her engorged clit and suck. I give her three more hard strokes with my fingers and her vaginal walls tighten like a vise.

Kara screams, the orgasm taking over her body, but she keeps her gaze on mine. Such a good girl.

Her entire body bows, thighs locking around my head because she can't stop herself from moving. And that's exactly where I want her.

Finally, she can't keep her eyes open any longer as her body shudders through the ecstasy I give her.

As her muscles start jerking uncontrollably with every flick of my tongue against her clit, I slow my thrusting fingers. But I don't stop.

I want to wring another climax out of her. I *need* to feel her muscles spasm around my fingers, her juices soaking my chin.

I fuck her with my fingers and tongue until she comes again, this time crying my name.

Michael.

Her husband. Her lover. Her man.

I gentle her enough that her thighs fall away from my head and then I stand.

CHAPTER TWENTY-ONE

Bound, Bared, & Bailed On

KARA

My most intimate flesh is still pulsing when Mick shifts his body so his muscular thighs are stretching my legs wide open again.

Muscles like jelly, I give him no resistance.

His shaft bobs thick and angry, his pre ejaculate making the bulbous head glisten. He's so turned on his foreskin is fully retracted and my mouth waters wanting to taste him.

But that's not what's coming next and we both know it.

I tug against my restraints, but I don't want to be free. I don't want to go back to having to think, to having to be Kara, mob princess.

Right now, like this, I'm pure sensation. There is no mask I have to keep up, no fake smile I have to force my lips to make, no perfect words to say.

It's just me and Mick. And he wants me raw and open, like I am nowhere else.

My body is replete with pleasure, but I still want more. I need him inside me.

He presses the tip of his erection against the swollen and sensitized opening of my body. "You're mine, Kara."

"Yes," I whisper, not recognizing my own voice.

His big hands cup my breasts, squeezing and playing, teasing my nipples, forcing more pleasure to spark along nerve ending that connect directly to the pulsing flesh between my legs.

"You will always be mine." His voice is guttural, his eyes filled with primal possession.

For some reason, the agreement I know he expects is stuck in my throat.

It's that word *always.*

Mick's right. I need him. But I need so much more than sex, no matter how mind blowing. I need to know I come first. I need to believe that if *I* asked him to take time off to have lunch with me, he'd make it happen.

And I really, really don't. Because he wouldn't. Because outside the bedroom, I'm just not that important to him.

Not wanting the demoralizing thoughts to impinge on this time, I tilt my hips up and let my body answer so my mouth doesn't have to. My slick and swollen folds suck his head in and we both groan.

"Always," he says, like he knows that's the word stuck inside me and then Mick thrusts deep in one harsh surge.

I cry out, the sensation too much at first, but he doesn't let up and I don't ask him to. There's no slow buildup this time. He claims me like a man who's been starving.

His strokes are hard, deep, relentless. Every thrust sends aftershocks through me. I wrap my legs around his waist, pulling him deeper.

He kisses me then, raw and possessive. Our tongues tangle, the taste of me on his. He kneads my breasts, pinching my nipples until I moan into his mouth.

"You feel that?"

I nod.

"These baps are mine."

I nod again.

He growls, "Say it."

"They're yours. I'm yours."

His thrusts grow even harder and more driving. "Whose pussy am I fucking?"

"Yours." *For now*, flits through my head.

And it's such a shocking, disturbing thought, my body stills.

He doesn't like that, and he grabs my legs, pushing them back so he can go deeper.

His brutal pace is punishing, but I love it, reveling in this moment that not only am I his, but he is entirely mine.

When he swivels his hips to stimulate my oversensitive clitoris, my body lights up like Times Square at midnight.

"Don't hold back," he growls.

And I don't. I can't. I come again, writhing under him, crying out his name.

He throws his head back with a primal yell as he finally lets go, pulsing inside me.

It takes minutes before either of us can move.

He nuzzles into my neck, licking the salty sweat from my skin. "You're mine, Kara. Every inch of you. In every way that matters."

I don't reply, but I don't pull away either. I just breathe.

Eventually, he lifts off me and shifts to kneel beside me. Unbuckling the cuffs, he rubs my wrists and kisses each pulse point before carefully lowering my hands to rest beside me.

After that, he massages my shoulders and arms until I'm barely awake and boneless. I'm so tempted to fall asleep, but I know what comes next.

So, I'm unsurprised when he leaves the bed. The sound of water cascading into our two-person whirlpool tub seconds later tells me he's preparing a bath for me with essential oils and Epsom salts.

Memories of the first time he did this play like a hazy movie reel in my head.

I'd winced from a twinge in my nether regions the morning after a night of passion like tonight.

Mick's eyes narrowed like I'd done something wrong. "Are you sore?"

Not wanting to lie, but unable to say, "No," I shrugged.

"Where?"

I shook my head, unwilling to go there.

"Is it your pussy? Your thighs? Your buttocks, what?"

My face flaming, I glared. "Leave it. I'm fine."

"Tell me."

But I shook my head again.

What followed was a different game from the one we played that had made my muscles sore to begin with. Mick tested my shoulders, my arms, my inner thighs and my buttocks.

By the time he got to checking my most intimate flesh, I'd given away the sore spots with my reactions. I'd tried to control them, but the way he stilled each time let me know he noticed every micro expression, every tiny hitch in my breath.

I was also really turned on.

He gave me an all over body massage, bringing me to a shattering climax once my body was completely relaxed. After, he made me take a soak in a hot bath with Epsom salts and drink a bottle of water while doing it.

I'd enjoyed the sensual massage and the aftermath, but not as much as I enjoy when he binds my hands before torturing me with pleasure. I crave it now. The way I can lose myself completely in his touch, in the ecstasy he wrings out of me.

I don't have to be "good and obedient" Kara. I can scream and beg and even cry and not for a single second does he take his intense focus off of me.

Now. It wasn't always that way.

When I was too embarrassed to pick a safe word, he introduced me to the traffic light system. Red for stop everything. Yellow means I'm nervous, or something is borderline painful or uncomfortable. Green means go.

I yell "green" a lot with even more "pleases."

I've only said red three times. The first time, I wanted to know what he would do.

He untied me (he'd used one of his silk ties that night) and grilled me on what I was feeling, but his hardon never abated.

I finally shamefacedly admitted I'd been testing to see if he would really stop. He didn't get mad. Not even a little.

He never gets angry at me.

And I don't know how I feel about that.

I mean I try so hard to be perfect, but no one is, right?

Anyway, he didn't get mad.

He didn't second-guess me either, when I said I wanted him to tie me up again.

But the second time I said red, I meant it.

"Fuck, Kara. Yes." Ropes of Mick's hot cum splatter against my neck.

He's got my breasts pressed together and slippery with lubricant for him to fuck. It's almost like having him inside me and I love when he comes like this.

My body is on an overload of bliss. I've already come twice and if my husband follows his usual pattern, I'll have at least one more orgasm before he unbuckles my cuffs.

He sits back, resting lightly on my stomach and starts rubbing his semen into my chest. The first time he did this I got a little freaked out.

Just like the first time he tied my hands.

But now, I love it. I feel like we're connected on a really primitive level and that makes me happy.

He likes it too. "That's right a stór. *You're going to smell like me all night long."*

I love going to sleep with the scent of him on me, but I don't tell him that.

He's playing with my nipples, slowly ratcheting up my desire again when his phone rings.

"Bleedin' hell." He jumps off of my body and grabs his phone. "Yeah?"

I don't know who he's talking to or what they're saying, but Mick starts touching me again. But it's like he's doing it subconsciously; his attention is on his phone call.

And I don't like the way that feels.

Suddenly the sensation of his cum saturating my skin makes me feel dirty.

Worse, I feel naked. Exposed.

Which I am, but since our wedding night, I've never felt ashamed to have Mick look at my nude body.

Now he's doing it while talking to someone else, probably making plans to leave me like he did our first night together.

He hasn't done that since, but I realize now it's because he hasn't been needed. No one has called him.

He turns away and crosses the room to flip open his laptop on the desk against the far wall. Mick doesn't sleep nearly as much as I do and he'll work on his computer sometimes after we do what it is we do.

Is it called making love when we don't have intercourse? I don't know. It feels as intimate as anything else could be.

But before Mick, no one had even touched my boobs, so that feels pretty intimate to me too.

Usually, I like that he works in here rather than going into the living room, but I don't like it right now.

Shame prickles across my skin as Mick boots up the computer while talking to the other person on the phone.

"Red." It's barely a whisper and he doesn't hear me. So, I clear my throat and say it again, louder this time. "Red."

Mick spins to face me, his eyes traveling over me like he's trying to see what's wrong. Like maybe I'm hurt. But he doesn't come back to the bed and undo the cuffs.

This time, I yell it. "Red!"

"Hold on a sec," he says into the phone before pressing something on the screen.

Probably the mute button.

Mick jogs back to me and unbuckles the cuffs with quick movements, his brows drawn together. "Do you need to pee, Kara?"

Without replying, I roll away from him and scoot off the opposite side of the bed. Probably making him think his guess was right, I rush into the bathroom, locking the door behind me.

My body still pulses with arousal, but it's laced with embarrassment now. I turn on the shower, flipping it to a lukewarm setting. That's supposed to make the desire go away, right?

I lather my loofah and wash every inch of my breasts before doing the rest of my body. I feel like I can still smell him on me, so I soap up my chest again and rub vigorously.

I think it's working but nothing is helping to wash away the hollow feeling inside me.

I turn the water colder and that doesn't help either. But it's shocking enough to stop the tears trying to fall.

So, that's good.

Finally, I turn off the water and step out of the shower.

My body shaking with shivers, I'm drying off when the handle on the door rattles. "Kara? Let me in."

"I'll be out in a second." I finish drying off and put on my robe, hiding my nudity.

I still feel raw and exposed.

But unless I want to sleep in here tonight, I have to face Mick and pretend like I don't.

I open the door.

He's looming right on the other side. Still naked. Still aroused.

Swallowing, I turn my head, so I'm not staring at his chest. Or anything else. "It's free now if you want it."

"I don't want the bathroom," he says, frowning. "Look, Kara. You didn't need to safe word. All you had to do was tell me you needed the toilet. You need to keep red for when you need it all to stop."

"I did want it all to stop." I try to move past him.

Only, he shifts his body to block my way. "You should know that if you ever tell me you need the toilet, or you've got a cramp, I'll release you from the restraints. You don't need to safe word."

"I never doubted it." And I hadn't.

Mick doesn't want to hurt me. He wants to control me. Sexually.

And I'm pathetic enough that I want that too.

Only not anymore. Maybe. I'm not sure, but what I liked best was knowing I was the center of Mick's focus.

That phone call proved that I wasn't. That I never had been, no matter how he played my body.

"Your hair's wet." He frowns. "Did you take a shower?"

"Didn't you hear it?" It's not really a fair question.

The door was shut and all the walls and doors in the apartment are sound dampening so that after the son I'm not pregnant with yet is born, his cries won't wake Mick in the night.

Mobsters need to get sleep when they can so they're always ready to do their job.

At least that's what my dad says.

Mick says we'll be able to make all the noise we want at night without waking the baby.

"Why did you take a shower?" he asks.

I shrug.

His hand cups my shoulder, big and heavy. "What's going on, Kara?"

"I want to go to sleep."

"We were in the middle of something," he says, like maybe I don't know that.

"And you answered the phone."

"You know I'm on call 24-7."

I duck from under his hand and manage to squeeze by him. "So, go do whatever it is you have to do."

I shouldn't expect anything else. Not after our wedding night when he made it clear that mob business took precedence, even on such a special occasion.

"I'm not going anywhere." He pauses and sighs. "Not yet."

Those two words wound me, and I know they shouldn't. I know I'm supposed to be okay with this. It's the way of life in the mob.

But I'm not okay.

I know Mick doesn't love me, but I'm afraid I'm falling for him. The feelings are so big, they terrify me. Especially knowing they're not returned.

"Don't let me stop you." I dig an oversized sleep shirt out of my dresser.

Because that doesn't feel like enough, instead of the sleep shorts I usually wear, I pull out a pair of soft leggings I sleep in during the winter.

His big hand wraps around my wrist. "Stop. Tell me what's wrong."

I look up at him, my eyes burning again with the need to cry, but I'm not going to. I have lots of experience suppressing my tears.

Even more since going on the hormone treatment necessary before harvesting my eggs for IVF. My emotions are all over the place.

Is that what this is? Am I overreacting because of hormones?

I sigh. "I'm fine."

He curses in Gaeilge. "You knew we weren't done. Why take a shower?"

"Because I wanted to wash you off my body." I jerk my wrist out of his grasp.

"What the fuck? Why?"

Is he really this dense? "Why not?"

"We both like when you go to sleep smelling like me."

"I don't like you answering the phone while we're having sex. But then it's not really sex, is it?" Is that why he didn't ignore his phone?

What we do together in bed isn't as important as real sex? Or will it be the same once he can penetrate me?

"Did you come?" he asks, his voice silky with menace.

He's never used that tone with me before. Is he angry? I let myself look at him, but he doesn't look mad. There's no emotion in his face at all.

"Answer me, wife."

"You know I did." He makes sure of it.

I always come at least once while I'm cuffed, but usually multiple times before he jacks off onto some part of my body.

My chest. The middle of my back. My bottom. Even my face once. Just nowhere near my vaginal opening.

"Did I come all over your beautiful baps?" he demands.

"Yes."

"I may not be fucking your pussy, but it's sex. I claimed your virginity," he says arrogantly.

And he claims me all over again with his fingers every time. I want him inside me though.

"I didn't know waiting until after I got pregnant would be so hard." That's easier to admit than how hurt I am about him answering the phone while I was naked and bound to our bed.

There's no point anyway. My feelings don't matter. Not to Mick. Not to my dad. Definitely not to my grandfather.

"It's only until you get pregnant. The implantation procedure is next week."

"What if I don't get pregnant the first try?" Seanathair insists on a single embryonic attempt.

He doesn't want to risk me having twins because he's seen that dynamic destroy syndicates when the heir to leadership is only minutes older than the brother who will get shunted aside.

"Then we try again."

"By we you mean me, right? You're not the one who has to go through the procedures." All he has to do is ejaculate in a cup.

I have to get my eggs harvested and then implanted with an embryo and hope it takes, so I don't have to do it again. All the research I've done says the discomfort is minimal, but that's what they always say about women's pain.

It's minimal.

I had a friend at boarding school who got an IUD and was in so much pain for a week after she could barely walk. Another friend told me her older sister warned her to take pain relievers before getting her first pap smear.

I'm scared of how much the procedures are going to hurt, but what's the point of telling anyone that?

Even mamo *would just tell me to buck up. She says us Irish women are tough and we have to stay that way.*

I don't feel tough. Maybe because I'm American-Irish? Maybe I'm just weak.

I still have nightmares about the night Aunt Charity died and I hate going anywhere in public with my grandfather because we could be targeted again.

When I told my dad, he said not to be a crybaby. That I had to set an example for my younger sister and cousin. When I told mamo, *she told me I'm too strong to let fear rule me.*

Mick's phone chimes and I pull away. "You better get that."

He's answering as I step back into the bathroom to put my pajamas on.

He frowns when I come out. "I have to go."

I nod and head for my side of the bed. The cuffs are gone from the headboard and I'm glad. I don't want to see them.

CHAPTER TWENTY-TWO

Bound by Trust, Not Just Leather

KARA

M ick didn't use the cuffs the next time we touched intimately. Or the time after that. He kept his sleep pants on though, even though he stripped me bare.

I showered afterward both times, washing his scent off me even though it wasn't as strong as when he rubbed his cum into my skin.

But the next time he wanted sex, he had the cuffs.

Seven Years Ago

Something wakes me. A sound? Movement near the bed brings me out of my dreams. He doesn't turn on the light, but I know he's there.

"Mick?" I ask sleepily.

"You're awake." His voice is flat, emotionless as his weight makes the mattress dip.

I scoot into a sitting position and turn on the nightlight feature on the wall sconce on my side of the bed. Its dim illumination reveals my naked husband kneeling on the bed, the black cuffs dangling from one hand.

The sight of them triggers sensory memories, both good and bad.

Shaking my head, I scoot away from him.

He reaches for me, grabbing my shoulder. "Stop, Kara. You're going to fall off."

Mick stares at me like I'm acting strange.

I stare at the cuffs. "Red."

"Why are you safe wording?" His fingers grip my shoulders more tightly, like he thinks I'm going to run away.

"I don't want to do that anymore." It's not true.

I want to be bound by him and touched by him. I want him to come on me with that wild, nearly out-of-control look he gets, but I don't want to be ignored by him.

The best part of wearing the cuffs is being the center of Mick's focus. The way he looks at me like he's not thinking about anything or anyone else.

No one looks at me like that.

I'm not the key player in anyone's drama in my life, not even my own. But always before, for the time he kept me bound, I felt like I wasn't just the central player, but the only one he could see.

My husband's body vibrates with tension. "The cuffs?"

I nod.

"I don't believe you."

"You're conceited."

"This isn't about conceit. You melt under my touch. Your body craves the pleasure I give you."

"Not that way. Not anymore," I add when he looks unconvinced.

"Because I answered the phone?"

I shrug.

"You're going to have to explain."

Like it's so easy. "I'm sure you can figure it out."

"Nah." His green eyes narrow. "Your brain isn't like mine. Sure as certain, I'd guess the wrong thing."

Are we really that different? "You wouldn't like it if I left you like that to answer the phone."

Something flickers in his gaze. Arousal?

His slacks are already tented, but they have been since I turned on the light.

"I can't let you cuff me. I can't protect you if I'm immobilized."

"No one's going to attack us here," I scoff.

"The men I've killed in their homes would disagree if they could."

The reminder of what he is should scare me. Or at the very least turn me off. It doesn't do either.

Maybe it's being raised as a mob princess, but the men in our world aren't squeaky clean. And he's right about one thing, I wouldn't feel safe with one who was.

"But if I could tie you to the bed..."

That feral light flares again and my voice trails off while images of having him at my mercy flash through my brain. I could taste him then. We haven't done it that way.

I don't know why.

He puts his mouth on me almost every night.

"You wouldn't answer the phone because you aren't on call," he finishes for me.

That reminder does not make me feel better. I wouldn't have answered the phone even if it had been my sister's ringtone. And I never ignore Fi.

She's too fragile.

Knowing I would ignore even my little sister's call for him makes me angry enough to be honest. "I felt dirty. You kept looking at me like I was nothing but inspiration for the spank bank while you talked on the phone to whoever called you."

"Spank bank?" he asks, amused.

And that only frustrates me more. This isn't funny to me. "You know what I mean."

"Nah, I don't. I was looking at you because I couldn't stop even though I was on the phone to your uncle."

"You stopped to look at the computer." And that's when I really started to feel dirty.

"This bugged you?"

Is he for real? "I'm pretty sure it would've bothered any woman to be left naked and tied to the bed while her lover went about his business, like it didn't matter."

"I am your husband, not your lover."

Not the point, but if he's going to harp on it... "Agreed. I can hardly call you my lover when we can't even have sex until after I become pregnant with your son."

"We already went over this."

"Don't try to tell me that any other woman you've called your lover in the past hasn't known what it feels like to have you inside them."

"My past is not relevant to our present."

But he has a past. I don't. He's my first, last and only. It's not fair, but it's the way it is in our world of double standards.

"You are my wife," he adds, his tone implying that's some great honor.

It didn't feel like an honor when he left me on our wedding night.

"I'm just the guarantor for the contract until I give you a son and then that's his role." And only as I say those words do I realize how much knowing that my child will be a pawn in my grandfather's power games just like I am bothers me.

"Arranged marriages are the norm in the mob, that doesn't make you any less my wife." He sounds offended. "Even if I don't stick my cock in your tight, hot cunt until after you become pregnant with our son, that does not change who you are to me."

No it doesn't. Penetrative sex isn't going to make me any more important to Mick than I am right now.

"I don't want to do that anymore." I try to pull away from him.

Only he won't let me go.

Instead, he uses his hand on my shoulder to pull me toward him until I'm sitting across his legs. "We both signed the contract promising we would not have physical intercourse until after you became pregnant."

"So?" I squirm, trying to get off his lap.

He locks his arm around me with more effect than a safety harness on a rollercoaster. "When you touch me it compromises my self-control."

"I don't believe you." It never feels like he's out of control to me.

"I don't lie to you, Kara."

"You would though. If my grandfather wanted you to." And how did we go from talking about sex to this?

"Nah. I wouldn't. I won't always tell you everything and I won't answer if you ask a question I can't give an honest reply to, but I'll never lie to you."

His words hit my heart in a way I absolutely cannot afford them to. "But you're the one who drives me past the point of sanity."

"Touching you does that to me too."

I shake my head, denying his words, but he just said he wouldn't lie to me. "Touching me turns you on?"

"My hard dick doesn't tell you that?" he ripostes.

I shrug helplessly. "You're always hard."

"Around you."

"Oh."

"You washed my scent off of your body," he says, the affront heavy in his tone.

"I told you. I felt dirty."

He tips my head up so our gazes meet. "So now when I touch you, you feel dirty?"

"No. Yes. I don't know." I definitely felt icky when he took the call and left me lying there.

As for the nights since, sex (no matter how limited) makes me vulnerable and somehow washing away his scent makes me feel less owned by him.

He brushes his hand along my thigh. "You have been wearing leggings to bed."

"You're the one that insists we wear pajamas." From the second night of our marriage.

"Fabric is a better barrier than no barrier at all when I wake in the middle of the night and all I want to do is bury myself deep inside your pussy."

He does?

"So why does it matter if I wear leggings instead of shorts?" I ask.

"You tell me. You wore sleep shorts until that night."

I shrug. "I feel less exposed."

"Being exposed to your husband should not bother you," he says with conviction.

My husband may only be 26, but he has the confidence to rival my grandfather.

"It didn't bother me," I admit. I felt sexy and desired when I was naked in front of him. "Before."

"But now it does?"

"Yes." I can't explain it any better than I have.

If he doesn't understand why leaving me that way to answer the phone and go on his computer hurt, I don't have words to make him.

Mick studies me for long seconds before nodding. "Okay."

Then he does something I don't expect. He slides me back onto the mattress and gets off the bed. When he picks up his phone, he taps on the screen for a few seconds. The swish of a text being sent is loud in the now silent room.

After that, he taps and swipes on his screen again, before dropping his phone on the nightstand. "It's off."

"You turned off your phone?" What happened to being available to my grandfather 24-7?

"Aye. Where's your phone?"

I jerk my head backward to indicate behind me. "On the charger."

He walks around the bed and finds my phone tapping on the screen, proving he knows my access code. Then he places it in my drawer. "It's off now too."

"I don't understand." Something warm unfurls in my chest and it's scarier than that idea of the IVF procedures.

"You need my full attention to trust me to bind you." So, he gets it after all.

I nod.

"When I use the cuffs or bind you in any way from now on, I will turn off our phones."

Shock courses through me. "Because I want you too?"

"Because you need it," he corrects.

And he's right. It's not about a preference but a necessity.

Still, I can't help pointing out. "That won't stop my grandfather or uncle from sending someone to pound on our door."

"That's what Conor is for."

"Conor is outside our door?"

"Yes. His instructions are not to interrupt unless there is an emergency."

"Seanathair won't like that." Neither will my uncle or dad, I don't think.

Mick shrugs.

"That doesn't worry you?" I ask.

"No."

"Oh." My thighs clench, but it's the squeeze in my heart that worries me the most. "Does, uh...does Conor know we're going to..." My voice trails off.

"Have sex?" Again, my husband shrugs. "Probably. Does that bother you?"

Not as much as knowing what he's doing that I find so devastating isn't as important to him. Only, maybe it is. If not for the same reasons.

Mick is a highly sexed guy. Getting off might be as necessary for him as being treated like I matter is for me.

He strips out of his clothes, his member jutting from his body like a flagpole.

Everything inside me clenches.

Then he picks up the cuffs and dangles them from his forefinger. "Aye or nay?"

"Y..." I clear my throat. "Yes."

Green eyes flare with desire. "You're sure?"

Unable to say even one more word, I nod.

He turned off his phone for me. He put a man outside our door to prevent interruption. I might be a guarantor to the contract, but I'm not unimportant to the man I'm married to.

Present Day

Since that night, Mick always turns his ringer off, if not his phone when we make love. And the times when he's got me bound? He puts his phone in the drawer until we're done and I've climaxed so many times my womb aches from it.

If that means being sore the next day? It's totally worth it.

But it usually doesn't because Mick's aftercare has grown by leaps and bounds in the seven years of our marriage. It used to embarrass me when he massaged my inner thighs and buttocks along with the rest of my body, but then I began to equate his "aftercare" with actual care.

And I looked forward to it.

I'm not sure anymore that it means anything other than keeping my body prepared for nightly sex, but I still enjoy it.

And tonight is no exception.

He returns to the bedroom and lifts me from the bed, carrying me into the bathroom where he makes sure I pee.

He's militant about that after I got my first UTI. When I'm done, he guides me into the fragrant, swirling water of the bath.

The heat envelops my body and I groan with pleasure as overused muscles find comfort in the hot water. There are two bottles of water.

One for him. One for me.

He brings mine to my lips so I can drink. Alternating between frozen grapes and sips of water, Mick pampers me like I'm really something precious.

When his fingers slide between my labia in the oil softened water, I respond with soul deep passion. And he tenderly makes love to me again in the bath, the water sloshing around us as he takes me on a gentle climb to an orgasm that leaves me insensate.

I don't remember him drying me off or carrying me to bed, but when I wake up in the morning, he's gone like always.

Only this morning, there's a red rose on my pillow. He's done this a few times, leaving the sweet fragrance of the long stemmed rose to tease me from sleep.

I wish that rose meant abiding passion *and* love, but lust based passion is the only emotion I've ever gotten from my husband, or ever will get.

CHAPTER TWENTY-THREE

Intruders

MICK

L asers crisscross the reinforced tunnel, disappearing and reactivating in a precisely timed progression as I pass through.

They're reacting to the DNA specific biometric chip implanted in my bicep.

If anyone attempts to travel the tunnel – without me or one of my three lieutenants assigned to this project – walls will drop at each end, sealing them in with a nonlethal disabling gas, piped in through a duct system completely separate from the rest of the bunker's fresh air supply.

Even Hex doesn't enter or leave the lab unescorted.

After pressing my eye to the retinal scanner, I place my encrypted phone against the digital panel and it reads the passcode only good for the next ten seconds.

Only then does the bank vault worthy, steel door swing inward on silent hinges. It allows me one-point-eight seconds to pass through before automatically closing again.

The NSA would have a lot fewer leaks if they had security this tight, but they don't have my guys working for them.

The whisper gun prototype rests on the long steel table in front of me.

Matte black and sleek, it looks unassuming. From looks alone, it could be mistaken for just another semi-automatic pistol.

But the firing mechanism inside the gun is powered by electromagnetic propulsion, requiring no gunpowder.

Which means it has no barrel flare, no sound and no forensics. The idea is to bring military grade rail guns into personal weaponry. If anyone can make that happen, it's Hex.

There have been some misstarts, but unlike the man who first showed me the weapons tech concept, she's been smart enough not to run tests holding the weapon in her own hand. That's what robotic arms with superheat resilience are for.

Hex claims this weapon is safe for use in the field.

According to the test videos and heat metric measured by the robotic arm, she's right.

Hex comes to stand beside me, giving the gun a look most people reserve for their lovers. "You ready to watch the first test with a human subject?"

"I'm ready to fire it myself."

The brilliant Columbian-American's eyes go wide behind her safety glasses. "I thought we'd start with a lab tech."

She's smart not to risk her own hands, but the fact she was willing to use someone else's says more about her than she'd admit. There's a ruthlessness under the sarcasm. I admire that.

But I don't waver. "Either it's ready, or it's not."

Hex rolls her eyes. "It's ready. I tested it with the robotic arm enough times to make a statistician blush." She flicks a finger toward the casing. "The graphene composite lining in the barrel needed an extra two micrometers."

The scarcity and cost of the product materials dictates minimizing the hardest to source components. Keeping the weight of the gun down is important too.

But the ultimate issue here is effectiveness. Too much cooling of the barrel and there's not enough force behind the bullet.

It has to do with the energy exchange. I don't care about the why though, only the result.

"We also had to tweak the phase-change gel layer in the grip, but we've got it dialed in now," Hex says. "You can fire up to seven rounds without compromising the structural integrity of the gun."

"How long before you can reload the clip and shoot again?" I ask.

She doesn't flinch. "Three-point-seven hours."

So, basically four. Not bad, but not a weapon for long firefights. This is for stealth targets and precision hits. Not the battlefield.

"Is there an indicator on the weapon to let the user know when it is ready for reloading and use?" I ask.

Hex points to a black strip along the back of the barrel. "Color shift display. Each shot will nudge the pigment. After seven, or if you overheat it early, it'll turn deep purple."

"Like a mood ring?"

She winces at my simplified analogy, but nods. "A similar concept, yes. The gun should not be fired again until the section of the casing has turned entirely black once again."

"What happens if the shooter ignores those instructions and tries to reload anyway?" As soldiers in the midst of a firefight are going to do.

"The materials swell microscopically from heat," she says. "Enough to lock the magazine release. Won't budge until the internal temp drops below the threshold. We designed it to protect the user, even if they're not smart enough to protect themselves."

I nod. "Good."

She lifts one shoulder. "Even if it overheats, the grip's layered with that phase-shifting gel. Worst case scenario? The firing mechanism fuses long before enough heat transfers to burn your hand."

I pick the gun up. Light. Cool. Deadly.

"Nice to know it won't explode until after I've used it properly."

Hex grins. "You break it, you buy it. Oh, wait, you already did."

I almost laugh. Almost.

I knew we got the right woman for the job.

Whisper guns will change the playing field – not just for us, but for the entire global arms trade specializing in stealth weapons.

We'll dominate until the other arms dealers catch up. And their chances aren't good for doing that anytime soon. They don't have Hex working for them.

Back-engineering will only take another weapons designer so far. Even figuring out the adjustments have to happen at a micrometer level will be a hurdle because it's so far out of current weaponry science for personal weapons.

"Okay, let's do this." I pull back the slide and lock a bullet in the chamber.

A soft click followed by three low beeps comes through my earpiece before I can fire.

Adrenaline spiking, I clear the chamber before handing the gun to Hex to finish unloading. "Report."

"Sensor trip. Sector 3G. External approach tunnel. No authorized traffic."

The FEDs have not found the Bunker in over a hundred years. The last breach by another syndicate was over thirty years ago. According to Brogan, everyone involved was eliminated.

Does someone know about the whisper guns?

"How many?" I'm already moving toward the lab door.

"Sensors log three bodies."

Not an invasion level force then. A stealth mission by players that don't know about the security upgrades to the Bunker?

Or someone sent to blow it up?

My thoughts lock and load, firing in rapid succession. The external approach tunnels are our weakest link. Brogan insists we keep them though.

Shaughnessy soldiers are trained to seek refuge in them when necessary. But we no longer rely on them being hidden as the primary deterrent to incursion.

The access tunnels got a security upgrade with the rest of the facility before we moved the whisper gun project in.

It's conceivable a rival discovered the access point to 3G watching one of our soldiers.

It's a best case scenario. 3G used to house the dormitories and stash rooms.

Sleeping quarters have been moved to a more secure section in the MNOPs and the old ones now look like they're a forgotten bomb shelter.

The stash rooms are used to store innocuous things covered in layers of dust and grime that would lead infiltrators to believe they've stumbled on a basement that hasn't been used in years.

We're at too critical a stage of development for the whisper guns to rely on misdirection though. "Lock down 3G through 3L. Feed nonlethal into the vents. I want them coughing up their own insides before they get a look at anything useful."

I don't wait for acknowledgment. I'm already moving.

Footsteps silent against the resin-reinforced concrete, I make my way down a parallel access corridor. The walls here are reinforced with smart steel paneling, and biometric sensors scan me, resetting alerts as I pass.

This part of the facility was built two generations ago when Brogan's grandfather needed somewhere to stash bodies and secrets. Before the upgrades it was a bleedin' warren of forgotten rooms, timber reinforced tunnels, and old bones.

The feckin' smell of decomposing bodies had soaked into the dirt walls.

Fresh, clean concrete is a huge improvement. The graveyard is filled in and has been sealed off, the remaining bones dissolved in a chemical bath.

Approaching the access point to a connecting tunnel between me and our intruders, I pull up the security feed on my smartwatch.

Three masked intruders. Tactical gear. American boots. Military posture. Whoever they are, they bypassed the security code on the entrance and didn't trigger a warning until their body weights were detected on the new pressure sensitive flooring in the tunnel.

With a tap on my smartwatch, I trigger the overhead flash-disorientation lights and ear-piercing alarm.

Hands going up reflexively to cover their ears, they stagger.

I smile and cut all the lights and then the sound.

Unworried they'll recover quickly enough to access their own portable illumination, I slide on night vision glasses. Their pupils will be in reactive mode for at least another forty-five seconds.

Wherever they thought they were, they walked into hell. And I am *an diabhal*, it's king.

And if I'm the king of this hell, the interrogation facility is my throne room.

We didn't get rid of the old interrogation rooms. We just replaced the rusted hooks and blood-soaked drains with surgical-grade steel and reinforced soundproofing.

Clinical. Efficient. Easy to clean.

Each one is rigged with remote monitoring and biometric locks – accessible only to me or the people I trust to break someone without killing them too soon.

The last man I worked over pissed himself when I whispered my name in his ear. Reputation is everything.

Especially when it's true.

The one before that bit through his tongue to avoid answering a second question. It didn't save him, but it did save his fingers for a while.

So, he could write the answers I wanted.

I reach the branch corridor just as the first intruder, still coughing stumbles into the laser net and gets lit up like a bug in a zapper – nonlethal, but he won't be walking straight for a week. If he lives that long.

Chances are not good.

The other two fall back and try to turn but between the gas they inhaled and the disorientation lights, they have the grace of drunken seals.

Another tap on my smartwatch and the laser net disappears.

Then I wait.

I catch the first man as he rounds the corner, arm raised, pistol swinging toward the motion-activated light. Too slow.

I grab his arm and twist. The crack of bone is unmistakable. Clean. Satisfying.

He screams – but I've already got him on his knees. A knee to his face and a blow to the back of the head and he's out for the count.

The second man approaches the same corner with more caution, his weapon raised. I put a bullet in his foot as it slides into view. There's a scream and a thud.

Rounding the corner, I kick the gun out of his hand and away from his body. I leave him for my men who should arrive in four...three...two...

"Got him boss."

I'm already sprinting after the third man but raise my fist in acknowledgement.

He's stumble-running back toward the way they came in a fruitless quest to get away.

He has no chance.

The access point is now behind a four-inch-thick steel wall.

I kick him in the back of the knee. His knee gives, but tougher than his cohorts, he doesn't go down. He pivots toward me, gun raised. It's wavering though, his grip unsteady.

He gets a shot off. I don't even flinch. It misses by a mile. He shoots again as I leap forward. Damn, that one was close enough for me to feel the air displacement as it passed by my head.

Grabbing him by the front of his vest, I allow our combined momentum to slam him into the wall hard enough to bounce his head off the concrete. Blood splatters. Not enough.

But it'll do for now.

"Who sent yiz?" I snarl, pressing my forearm against his throat.

He tries to speak. I ease the pressure. Just enough.

"Fuck you," he chokes out.

Well, now. Things just got interesting.

I smile. It's not kind. "You're not my type. Unless you're talking about me fucking you up."

"Do your worst," he snarls.

"You don't know what you're asking for, boyo." Conor comes up on my left. "The boss is deadly savage."

"I didn't expect to find a knitting circle down here." There's sarcasm, but no fear in my captive's voice.

"What did yiz expect to find?" I demand. "And who told you about this place?"

The man just glares at me.

We'll find out if this is bravado, or if he's got a drop of Irish blood running somewhere in his ancestry, when I get him to my throne room.

I slam his head against the wall again, stunning him enough to make getting the zip-ties around his wrists easier. Despite the gas, the flash bang and one already hard knock to his noggin' he's still fighting.

I'd be impressed if he wasn't on the wrong feckin' side.

The itch to force this man and his boyos to tell me what they know settles at the base of my neck.

They're going to learn what it means to dance with the devil.

"Get the other two stabilized for interrogation. They're no good to me bleeding out."

"You got it boss," Conor says. "And this one?"

"We'll be in Interrogation Room 1. Bring the others in to watch once they're stable."

My captive tries to run twice and overpower me once on the way to interrogation. Not sure why I don't just kill him. I've got two more men to question, both of whom showed themselves to be less well trained.

But feck if I'm not reluctantly impressed. It won't stop me from killing him when the time comes, but damned if I don't want to test his mettle some first.

CHAPTER TWENTY-FOUR

Blood's Thicker Than Vintage Clingwrap

KARA

Róise hits the mat again with a solid *thud*. For the second time in five minutes.

"Too much thinking," Fabiana snaps, yanking her to her feet like she weighs nothing.

"I'm *built* for thinking," Róise groans, shifting back into a ready stance. "Not Judo-flipping a mafiosa."

Fabiana smirks. "Your fiancé disagrees. Now again. Less brain. More instinct."

Across the room, Fiona's stiff form mirrors mine as we square off, Zoey stalking around like a smug jungle cat.

"This isn't a fencing lesson," Fabiana barks at Róise. "You're not posing for Renaissance paintings. Drop your weight. Lower. Again."

Róise adjusts her stance and suddenly I'm flipping through the air and landing on the mat with an all too familiar thud.

"Pay attention to what you're doing, not your cousin." Zoey puts her hand out to help me up.

Frustrated and feeling more than a little salty, I grab Zoey's hand in a tight grip. Yanking hard, I kick out and sweep her feet from under her.

Then I roll right on top of her like Fabiana taught us and press my forearm against Zoey's throat. "How's that for paying attention?"

Fiona and Róise are both laughing and clapping.

Zoey grins. "That's what I'm talking about."

"Good job." Fabiana approaches, Róise following behind. "Zoey, show them the sequence for disabling an attacker coming from the back."

With a nod, Zoey leaps to her feet. Her movements efficient and vicious, she demonstrates a series of actions that culminate in a sharp elbow to the solar plexus of one of the padded dummies.

"You know," she says cheerfully, "when I was fourteen, my cousin taught me that. We used each other as live targets. He cried. I didn't."

Fiona's eyes widen. "That's... comforting?"

"Zoey's love language is low-key violence," Róise says, voice dry as she wipes sweat off her face with a gym towel.

"Don't act surprised." Zoey gives Fiona a playful nudge. "You fell for a mafiosa."

Fiona blushes, tugs at her copper red ponytail and tries to hide the smile Zoey's acknowledgement of their relationship brings to her face.

None of us are smiling and my sister, cousin and I are all sweaty and breathing hard by the time we finish practicing the routine on the dummy. I'm hoping Fabiana isn't going to try to make us practice the sequence on each other.

I won't hurt Fiona or Róise. I can't. And I'm pretty sure, they'd feel the same. We already get in trouble for not taking our sparring "seriously enough".

As if my thoughts conjured it, Fabiana announces that we're sparring next.

Fiona ends up with Fabiana because apparently Zoey holds back too much with her too. Fabiana's disgust is real and she threatens to bring in new sparring partners for us at our next lesson.

Apparently learning self-defense is not uncommon among the women of the Genovese Family. Which means we can spar with other women like us. Not *mafiosas*. Which is something anyway.

The Cosa Nostra is so different from the Irish Mob. At least the Genovese Family is. I don't know how the other Five Families in New York treat their women in regard to learning fighting skills and how to use a gun.

I've heard that my cousin's mob in Chicago allows women to act as soldiers too. I wish some of that attitude would rub off on my dad.

I wonder if Mick will take things in a different direction after he takes over as boss? I used to think my husband and father were cut from identical cloths, but now I'm not so sure.

Zoey gets called away to report to Allessio, leaving me and Róise to spar with each other. My cousin and I circle one other, slow and careful. Do her muscles burn as badly as mine?

"You okay?" Róise asks, low enough that Fabiana and Fiona won't hear.

"I'm fine."

She gives me a look. The kind that says *liar*. She fakes a grab and I deflect without thinking, but my timing's off.

"So..." She tries the grab again, breath coming a little faster. "Mick took the news well? About Fitz?"

This time she makes no effort to keep her voice down.

I nod, and keep my hands up. "Better than I expected. He even said he'd handle it if Brogan tries to block the therapy."

"Of course he did." Róise deflects a kick to her thigh. "He'd burn the city for that little guy."

"Good. Fitz needs help processing this stuff." Fiona chimes in sounding way too in control of her breathing for all this exercise. "He needs to learn to *feel* things safely. I don't want him to end up like me."

Everything stops for a beat. Even Fabiana pauses.

I glance toward Fiona. She's staring straight ahead, locked in place; her hands are shaking.

Swiftly crossing the mats toward my sister, Róise right behind me, my heart hurts. Violence and trauma shaped my sister's life, just like it did for me and Róise.

Is it because we were raised in the mob? Maybe. But the only reason my son hasn't had to learn to duck, run and hide is because he attends a school with security dictated by the mob.

Other children his age go to school every day aware that the next mass shooting could be at their school. And they're taught how to respond if it does.

None of that has a single thing to do with being raised as part of a syndicate. And so Brogan reminded us after Aunt Charity's death in his attempt to help Fiona "get over" her anxiety.

Three million children witness a shooting every year, whether at school or in their home. Gun violence is the number one cause of death for children and teens in the United States and only a tiny percentage of those are linked in any way to organized crime.

Knowing this helped me not to hate being born into the mob. It *didn't* help my sister's anxiety levels. In fact, the reality that gun violence is so prevalent made my sister even more stressed about leaving the mansion.

Surprisingly, or maybe not so much, these self-defense lessons are helping Fiona's confidence more than any of our father's lectures.

I pull my sister right into a hug. "Fitz is going to be okay, Fi."

Suddenly Zoey is there, pulling Fiona from my arms into hers. She caresses my sister's cheek. "Your nephew is strong like his aunt. Like his mamma."

"Like Kara maybe, but I'm not strong," my sister whispers.

"You're one of the strongest people I know," I disagree. "You face your fears and anxiety every day and you don't let it stop you from everything."

Fiona gives a watery laugh. "Only some things."

"Which shows just how strong you really are," Róise says forcefully. "Listen, Fi, it's easy to go to a shelter and adopt a cat when you aren't terrified the whole time. But you did it with that terror and you never let Rambo know how afraid you were."

"That cat trusts nobody but you and sometimes my son." I smile encouragingly at my sister.

She returns my smile with a small tilt of her lips.

"Animals have good instincts," Fabiana says. "If the cat trusts you, he knows you'll protect him."

Something flickers in Fiona's eyes. And she stands a little straighter.

My baby sister needs to hear from people who aren't family how wonderful she is. Fabiana is good people, which makes it even more impactful for Fiona to receive affirmation from the mafiosa.

Fabiana claps her hands. "Okay, enough with the chit-chat. Back to work, people. We only have ten more minutes. Let's make them count."

I face off with Róise again, lunging almost immediately and catching her off guard.

We tangle, her hips twist one way, mine the other and we end up grappling. With an unexpected maneuver, she breaks the hold.

But I dive right back in and when Fabiana calls time, we're both panting.

The locker room off the new residents only gym in the Oscuro Building is like that of any other high-end gym, only this one has armed security on the door while we're inside.

Both the entry to the gym and the locker room have biometric scanner based security as well.

Miceli is taking no chances with Róise's safety.

After my shower, I get dressed it the communal area with the rest of the women. I don't know about Zoey and Fabiana, but I'm used to it from my years at boarding school.

There's never been a lot of false modesty between me and my sister and our cousin either.

"It felt like you had some aggression to work out today, cuz." Róise dries her shoulders and arms with a fluffy white towel. "Is everything okay with Mick?"

In no mood to blow-dry and straighten my hair, I pull my curls into a wet bun on top of my head. "We have a new houseguest."

"Who?" Róise asks.

"Dierdre Kelly is over from Ireland."

"As in the Kelly family that runs the Northside Dublin Syndicate with the Fitzgeralds?" Róise asks, sounding shocked.

Her words are so like my thoughts when I first heard Dierdre's name, I smile.

"Yes." I adjust my full breasts inside my bra after clasping the front closure.

"What's she like?" Róise's voice is slightly muffled by the shirt she's pulling on over her head. "How old is she?"

"Mick's age, I guess." I pull on my white textured linen palazzo pants. "They used to be a thing."

"According to her, they're still *good friends*," Fiona pipes up.

No one can do mockery like a teenager and at 18, my sister is in her sarcasm prime.

Róise tucks part of her hem into the front of her shorts so her top blouses over the waistband. "So, she's in New York trying to renew old friendships?"

"She claims it's for her safety. That another syndicate tried to kidnap her."

"You don't believe her?" Róise asks.

Zoey snorts. "That woman has a very distant relationship to the truth."

I finish adjusting my bust under my crisscross halter top. "She tried to convince Mick that I told her I didn't want her staying at the mansion."

Taking a look in the full mirrored wall at one end of the changing room, I nod. The girls look banging and there's a slice of skin exposed between the hem of my halter top and the waistband of my high-waisted palazzo pants.

Frumpy mom vibe is nothing I've ever aspired to. Maybe because I was so young when I had Fitz. Or maybe it's that I crave my husband's attention even if I cannot have his love.

And emphasizing my boobs is sure to get it. Not that I'm going to see him in this outfit with him leaving the mansion to take Dierdre to lunch.

"It was a whole thing." Fiona slides her feet into Crocks.

She practically lives in them, no matter what season it is.

"You weren't even there," I remind my sister.

Zoey adjusts her gun holster. "Hope told us. She was impressed with how you stood up for yourself and Fitz."

"She thought it was amazing that you refused to apologize for something you didn't do. Even though da got angry." Fiona still calls our father da sometimes.

I stopped using the term and started calling him Brogan and the more formal father exclusively when I was at the Marlowe Center. A da would not have pushed me into marriage, undergoing IVF treatments and parenthood as a teenager.

A father might, but not a da.

A da loves his children above others. Like Mick loves Fitz.

Although, it was my grandfather and not my father who ordered the disposal of the girl embryos, Brogan was complicit because he was just as adamant that I provide a male heir to the Shaughnessy line. Despite the risks to my health and mental stability at such a young age, my father insisted I use IVF to ensure giving birth to a boy.

Nearly seven years and my chest still feels like it's being shredded by razorblades when I let myself remember that time and what came after.

"I'm pretty impressed too," Zoey adds. "I know plenty of made men and women who wouldn't have."

Warmth unfurls inside me at the other woman's approval.

Fabiana slides into a blazer that covers her shoulder holster. "It sounds like Dierdre is a real manipulator."

My gut twists. I can't believe I've been talking about something so private in front of her.

Like she knows what I'm worried about, Fabiana winks. "Don't worry. What happens in self-defense training stays in self-defense training."

I nod. "Thank you."

Though I have zero doubts that if something came up that would compromise the Cosa Nostra, she'd take it to her capo without compunction.

I'm pretty sure Róise would too at this point. Her loyalty has shifted from the mob to the mafia and it's no wonder. Miceli protects her with the kind of zeal Brogan reserves for the mob.

"You should bring Hope to the next training session," Róise says.

"I invited her to this one, but she said no," Zoey answers.

Róise frowns. "I'll call her." Hope is Róise's mom's sister. Maybe she'll have more sway. "Tell me more about the vintage clingwrap."

"Vintage clingwrap?" Fabiana asks, her voice laced with humor.

"You know, she's the old model, thin, transparent and sticks where she's not wanted." Róise's tone is pure snark.

I burst out laughing and so does everyone else. Okay, so twenty-one-year-olds aren't slouches in the sarcasm department either.

"She tried to make me believe Mick has other lovers because he has feral needs."

Róise gives the faint red marks on my wrists a pointed look. "I think you've got that one covered."

The first time my cousin noticed the marks, she was livid and threatened Mick's life. I had to admit I like what we do in bed...to a fourteen-year-old. I never gave specifics, but I promised it was something I wanted.

I wonder if Róise has discovered her own kinks now that she's having sex with Miceli. As close as we are, it's not something I'm going to ask.

"Yeah. The one area of my marriage I don't worry about is keeping Mick happy in the bedroom." I pause. "They're having lunch later."

"*Lunch?*" Róise echoes, outraged. "Your husband agreed to *lunch* with his ex while she's living under your roof?"

I shrug, not feeling as sanguine as I'm trying to pretend. "It's business."

She doesn't answer right away, but her eyes narrow. She watches me too closely. I look away.

"Kara," she says gently. "I'd burn Miceli's suits if one of his old flames showed up to stay in our home."

"That's not me." I'm the good girl, and we all know it.

"Before you stood up to da and refused to apologize, I would have agreed, but now, I think Mick might want to start watching out for his wardrobe," Fiona jokes.

I get a picture of making a bonfire with Mick's suits on the beach and the image is way too satisfying. "Maybe."

My sister grins but it slips into a scowl pretty fast. "I hate her."

A year ago, I would have admonished my sister that hating people is wrong. But that was the old Kara. The perfect little doormat.

I don't want to be her anymore. "I hate her too."

"We could accidentally tie her to a training dummy." Zoey cracks her knuckles.

Fabiana gets a positively gleeful gleam in her eye. "Maybe I give her an object lesson in the difference between taking a fall the right way and one that ends up with a broken limb."

The laugh that slips out of me is real. The ache behind it is, too.

Róise steps closer and squeezes my hand. "Anything you need. We're here."

"Yeah, we are uniquely qualified to get rid of the body." Zoey winks.

I nod, blinking fast.

"Next lesson, you pretend your opponent is the vintage cling wrap," Fabiana says sardonically. "I have a feeling you'll attack harder."

Fiona grins. "Oh, I *like* that game. Next time, you're a skinny brunette with a lack of tact. You just see how hard I hit."

We all laugh. But inside? I'm wishing I could throw Dierdre on the mats, just one time. And maybe step on her hand before helping her up.

"I've seen women lose focus because of other women," Fabiana says, going full on serious. "But the real threat is never the ex who flaunts. It's the man who lets her."

I go completely still, the words sinking into my gut like a knife.

She's right.

That's exactly what hurts so much. Not Dierdre's glossy hair or her perfect model's body. Not the casual digs or the way she tries to manipulate me into a corner. No. It's Mick.

It's his tolerance. His *politeness.* His rationalizations.

It's him asking me to apologize to a woman he used to have sex with. It's the way he justifies it all by saying it's *business.*

"Here." Zoey hands me my water bottle. "Don't get lost in your head. Mick looks at you like he's a starving jungle cat and you're the meal he's about to run down and devour."

Róise chokes. "Seriously?"

"You think so?" Fiona asks her girlfriend.

"You're all too close to see it. Whatever Mick and Dierdre's past, that man watches his wife like she's the only woman on the planet, much less in the room."

Wanting to believe that so badly, I ache with it, I drink from my water bottle so I won't pathetically ask Zoey to repeat herself.

Róise frowns and nods. "I can see it. I've noticed over the past year especially that he seems like he wants more from you. But whatever his feelings are, Mick needs to earn the right to stand beside you."

My throat tightens.

"He needs to treat you like you're the only woman in the room," Fiona agrees.

I look at my cousin, who's grown into a woman without losing her fire. She never fit herself into the good girl mold. She stood up for herself and Fiona in a way, I've never been able to.

Only it's not pity in her eyes right now. It's belief. In me.

Fiona's expression mirrors that belief, warming my heart even as a tiny part of me stays drenched in doubt. It's so easy for them.

Fiona knows Zoey loves *her*, not what she can get out of being with my sister.

And Miceli looks at Róise like she's the sun and he's been locked in the dark for his whole life. He protects her like it's his religion.

No one's ever wrapped me in anything but rules, expectations and obligations.

I push a smile out anyway. "I'll try to remember that."

Róise moves closer, her tone gentle. "Maybe we're not the only ones too close to the situation to see the forest for the trees. Maybe Mick doesn't realize he loves you either."

I snort laugh. "Yeah, like he wouldn't know if he felt something that deep."

"You'd be surprised," Róise says.

Is she talking about Miceli? I don't ask. But maybe I should.

But I just shake my head, and plead, "Don't."

I can't afford to start building castles in the sky again. The last time I convinced myself Mick loved me and realized that he didn't, it nearly cost me my life and my son his mom.

I'm never going back there.

"Okay," she says. "But if he forgets who you are, *we* won't."

The burn behind my eyes threatens to spill over, but I blink fast. I don't lose my composure. Not ever.

When I'm sure it won't make moisture trickle from my eyes, I force myself to nod once in acknowledgement of her words.

No matter what my husband thinks of me, my sister and sister-of-my-heart will always love and stand by me.

That's more than a lot of women have.

CHAPTER TWENTY-FIVE

The Knife's Edge of Loyalty

MICK

I tase my prisoner after the second attempt to run and he finally settles down.

Shoving him into the brightly lit steel lined room of Interrogation 1, I say, "I'm beginning to think another mob sent you."

There's a flicker of confusion in his eyes that he quickly douses.

Interesting.

Tasing him a second time, I strip him down to his skivvies and secure him while his neurons are still too scrambled to make him a problem.

I strap his wrists first. Tight. Leather-lined, steel-core restraints that bite down like teeth. Then his ankles. Then the chest harness. I leave the head brace off – for now.

Pain makes most men stupid. I prefer mine just smart enough to be useful.

The stubborn set of my captive's jaw now that he's coming back to himself says it's going to take more than pain to get anything out of him.

Sweat beads at his temples but there's no fear. No anger. Nothing to clue me into how to break him.

Nonverbal interrogation first it is then. Let him sit in silence, the cuffs biting into his wrists, muscles twitching as the last of the taser sting fades from his system.

I crouch beside the pile of his gear and start going through it, slow and methodical. Feels like I'm cataloguing items in a tradeshow display titled *How Not to Die When You Pick the Wrong Bunker*.

His shirt is black tactical weave. Military issue, but not standard U.S. Army. No tags. No logos. Even the seams have been torched – deliberately frayed to remove identifying marks. Someone taught him well.

I pull a ceramic dagger from the boot sheath, holding it to the light. "You always pack this pretty, Boy Scout?"

Barely used. Edge clean enough to split air molecules. The handle's been rewrapped in paracord. Tight and sweat-stained, like he actually trains with it, not just wears it for the look.

"Custom job. Not off the shelf," I mutter to myself, then glance over at him. "You make this yourself, or did Daddy's Black Ops credit card cover it?"

And what the hell is a black ops trained soldier doing on my patch?

No answer. No twitch.

His pants yield a microburner zippered behind a hidden panel in the waistband. The pocket is lined with fine mesh wire. A Faraday cage. Smart.

"Don't want anyone tracking your porn history?" I taunt.

Still nothing. I'd be disappointed at this point if he reacted.

I'm starting to like this guy.

I reach for his wristwatch next, unclip the strap and flip it over. Garmin Tactix Delta. The kind with GPS scrub. Nice, but the next gen is better.

My crew's tactical smart watches were designed by our blackgloves for superior performance on every level.

Under the tongue of his boot, I'm not surprised to find a folded SERE patch with Kevlar cord, lockpick set, handcuff shim, and a razor edge barely the size of a fingernail.

He didn't expect to be caught, but if he was, he came prepared to disappear. Or endure.

"A real prepper, aren't you, Ranger Rick?"

That gets a tiny twitch at the corner of *Ranger Rick's* eyes. Considering his total lack of reaction so far, it's practically a screaming admission that I hit a nerve.

"Not a fan of that one?" I mock. "Tough. You look like the recruiting poster for the Army. Be all you can be."

Nothing.

I almost smile. "Keep that jaw clenched and righteous long enough, it's gonna crack."

Standing, I cross to him, and hold up the laminated card I pulled from his wallet. It's a prayer to St. Michael, the Archangel, the plastic edges worn. This isn't tactical gear and it's the only personal thing on Ranger Rick.

"You got a prayer to the saint of soldiers, but not a dog tag to your name. I've seen cleaner ghosts, but not many. Tell me..." I bend in close, voice dropping low. "How much did they pay you to forget who you are?"

His pulse ticks in his neck, steady but tight. Eyes open just enough to track me. Waiting. Calculating.

I'm impressed in spite of myself.

"I'm bettin' your pals'll be a bleedin' fount of information." Both men were too easy to take down to be trained like Ranger Rick here.

My watch vibrates against my wrist and I check it. Conor and Brice are on their way with the other intruders.

Time to set the stage.

I grab my slap jack and give Ranger Rick's abs a good going over so they glow bright red. He doesn't so much as grunt.

I nod to myself. Then I grab his ceramic knife. Nothing like marking a man with his own weapon.

Digging the tip under his pinky finger, I get it loose and pull. That gets a gusted out breath at least. And a good amount of blood spatter.

Not enough though. I slice a shallow line down Ranger Rick's left thigh. If he lives, it won't take more than a couple of days to heal, but it's bleeding like I want it to.

I do the same to his right bicep and then step back, admiring my handiwork.

He looks tortured good and proper. Ninety percent of interrogation is psychology. And a sociopath who has spent his entire life studying people to mirror, is feckin' aces at psychology.

If I excel at the violence that makes up the other ten percent too, that just makes me well rounded.

Leaving my handiwork to congeal on the floor around Ranger Rick, I go to the cabinet where we keep our compounds.

There's a mix to lower inhibitions. One to increase nerve sensitivity and therefore the impact of pain. I hear the Greeks on the West Coast have something even better. Note to self, contact the Greek mafia and see if we can't do business.

We have drugs to knock our *guests* out. Some with amnesiac properties like Special K, others that let our victims remember every moment they spent in my company.

I grab a bottle labeled in Chinese Hanzi, a benzo compound developed by one of our arms clients. Preparing it for use, I insert two drops into the aerosol dispensing system attached to a breathing mask.

One drop lowers inhibitions, but two will knock Ranger Rick out. Administered as an aerosol it will have immediate effect.

When he wakes up, he'll still be under the influence of the drug. Telling him what I learn from his cohorts should be the final trigger to relax his own tongue.

No use hiding what is no longer a secret.

Humming, I turn back to Ranger Rick.

When I move to slip the breathing mask over his face, he jerks his head away. It takes me a few seconds longer than I want to get it on him and release the aerosol.

But he's slumped forward in the chair, his breathing so shallow, his chest barely moves when the lock disengages on the door.

His pals will have to get a real good look to figure out if he's dead, or not. I'm not giving them the chance.

Conor shoves the man whose arm I broke into the room. He cries out in pain.

"Fuck off y—" His voice cuts off abruptly when he sees Ranger Rick. "Is he dead?"

The color leaches from the dickhead's face as he takes in the scene I set for him.

"Wraith is indestructible," the other intruder says as Brice shoves him into the room too.

Then he sees Ranger Rick and curses. In Albanian.

"Yiz are from Besnik's crew." Just saying the smarmy bastard's name leaves a foul taste on my tongue.

They could be from one of the other Albanian crews, but these two have a tinge of the Gheg dialect to their words, even when they're speaking English.

Besnik's gang is the only local one from Norther Albania.

The man limping on a foot tightly wound with a bandage to stop him bleeding out, looks away from Ranger Rick, then back again and swallows. "Our boss will pay to get us back."

"Not before I get the answers I want." Giving them hope that I might ransom them back to Besnik, gives them incentive to talk in order to live.

But I make no pretense at giving them hope I will show mercy when I string up the guy with the broken arm from the ceiling. By his wrists.

"Take his friend to holding." The cell he's going to is another psychological move.

Smelling like piss, shite and blood, it's soaked in despair. A good setting for him to think about how cooperative, or uncooperative he wants to be with me when it's his turn to talk.

I focus on my now sniveling captive. "Let's start with something easy. Your name?"

If he's foolish, he'll believe me asking is a good thing. It humanizes him and makes me less likely to kill him.

He's wrong.

What I'm really doing is taking away control bit by bit, starting with his identity.

When he doesn't answer right away, I punch him in the kidney.

"Aagh! It's Gjon."

"Who sent you here, Gjon?" I ask, almost friendly.

It only takes two more punches to get him to say Besnik's name.

"How is Besnik's crew getting so much business with weaklings like him working for him?" Brice asks in *Gaeilge*.

"No clue. But Ranger Rick took worse in total silence," I reply in the same language.

"Ranger Rick?"

"If he wasn't an Army Ranger, Wraith was some kind of elite soldier. But he's been trained in black ops too."

"He must be freelance."

"I hope so."

"Why?"

"Because if he's part of Besnik's crew I have to kill him and that would be a waste of a good soldier."

"You think you can recruit him?"

"You think I can't?" My morning just got more interesting. "Care to wager a bottle of Midleton's 40th Anniversary Ruby Edition?"

"You know I'm saving that whiskey for a special occasion."

"I've got just the one. You losing this wager."

"You're a bleedin' pain in my arse." Brice gives me a gimlet stare. "But to win, you can't just convince him to be inducted into the mob, he has to do it."

Brice knows I'll only induct Wraith if I believe he'll be loyal. And that's always an iffy proposition when turning someone.

But my instincts haven't been wrong yet.

"Done." I spit on my hand and offer it to Brice.

He wrinkles his nose, the princess, but spits on his own before shaking.

He's at the sink washing away our combined spit three seconds later, returning to hand me a paper towel to wipe my palm. I consider refusing the paper towel just to mess with him.

But I want to be at the end of my interrogation with the maggot hanging from my ceiling before Ranger Rick comes to.

I wipe my hand on the paper towel, crumple it up and toss it into the biohazard trash bin on the other side of the room. A necessity for a room like this. We dispose of them directly of course, incinerating them in the furnace of the Shaughnessy Mob controlled waste management plant.

Violence is an integral part of mob life, but that doesn't make us barbarians. The people who make it into these rooms are often high risk for carrying infection. I have no more desire than the next man to be infected by blood borne pathogens.

Which is why I don a pair of puncture resistant nitrile gloves before moving onto more persuasive forms of interrogation.

Gjon moans.

I smile. "Strip him."

Brice doesn't hesitate, cutting Gjon's shirt and tactical vest until he's down to his pants. We keep the temperature in here a cool sixty-degrees and goosebumps immediately form on his skin.

My lieutenant goes through Gjon's things while I grab the custom forged obsidian surgical blade out of my private drawer of implements.

Cuts are so clean with this thing, they don't bleed right away and the pain takes just as long to register. Designed for slicing without killing (at first), it's perfect for prolonged, controlled pain.

In other words, interrogation.

Slicing a long stroke from the bottom of one of his nipples to the top of his hip, I watch the perfect, thin line form.

Seconds later, blood wells and he gasps out as the unexpected pain hits.

I nod. "You've heard of death by a thousand cuts?"

"Hasn't everybody? It's a myth." Gjon tries to look tough, but he can't hide the terror lurking beneath the surface. "Nobody can last that many cuts."

"This scalpel makes it possible. It is also very good for cutting away skin." Which is too damn messy for my taste, but this maggot doesn't need to know that.

I make another cut identical to the first on the other side of his torso.

This time, he shouts when the pain hits. "Motherfucker!"

"No desire to fuck my ma, but I am going to fuck you up." I pause and then smile again.

He flinches.

"You ready?" I run the flat of the blade across his chest.

"What do you want? I told you Besnik would pay."

No, he told me his boss would pay for his release. But now he uses the man's name. I already know he works for.

"I'm sure Besnik will be glad to know he gave his name up so easily to save another shallow cut to your precious skin." I would kill my soldier myself if he was this weak.

"You have to know who he is to ask for ransom." He sounds like he thinks he's being clever.

I wonder.

"Who is Besnik to you?" Why is such a useless piece of shite on a job with a man like Wraith?

No way did Ranger Rick pick this pissant for the mission.

A crafty look comes of Gjon's face. He's trying to decide if it's better to tell me or keep it a secret.

I help him out by cutting another line down his unbandaged arm.

"He's my uncle!" Gjon writhes making the chains he's dangling from sway. "I'm his nephew. He'll pay you a lot to get me back."

If that is true, I don't doubt Besnik would pay a high ransom for this man.

"Too bad for you, I don't need money. I want information and if you can't give it to me, I'll cut your still beating heart from your chest and send it to your uncle."

Gjon retches and I jump back, avoiding the vomit that explodes from his mouth a second later.

Weak. So damn weak.

"He's got the right tactical gear," Brice says in *Gaeilge*. "But it's flashy, not useful."

I flick my gaze over to my friend. He's holding up a knife with a neon green blade with hazard logos on it.

The so-called zombie slayer knife is overbuilt with crap materials and breaks under stress. The serrated edge looks cool but it's as effective as a babe's teething ring at hurting the enemy.

No question, despite this man *leading*, the real weapon with him is Wraith.

"You expecting the undead, or are you just terminally stupid?" My voice resonates with the disgust I feel at this incompetence.

I'd be doing his uncle a favor to kill him.

"It's a good knife," he blusters.

I don't bother to reply to that stupidity, but ask, "Who sent you?"

"I told you. My uncle, Besnik."

"Besnik's crew takes outside jobs. Tell me who paid for this one."

"I don't know. You think my uncle tells his men who we're working for? He's too smart for that."

"But you're not just one of his men." I don't call Gjon a soldier, because he's not. "Are you? You're family."

"Do you tell your family that kind of stuff?" Gjon sneers.

I cut him right across the throat. Just for fun. The wound is too shallow to hit anything important but he still squeals like a pig and yanks against his broken arm.

Well, feckin' hell. "He passed out."

Brice hands me the smelling salts without having to be asked. I wave them under Gjon's nose. His head jerks and his eyes open, only to fill instantly with tears. "Please, I don't know who hired the mission."

Mission. Like he's got a passing understanding of what that word means.

"You know something." Puffed up with his own importance, he's the kind of guy that earwigs at doors.

"All I know is that my uncle was speaking in Russian to someone before we got our orders."

More military speak that this maggot has no right to be using.

Russian?

"Did you hear a name when you were spying on your uncle?" I ask.

"Ivan."

I don't bother to say anything to him giving me one of the most common Slavic names for a man. I simply slice one of his nipples off.

"Ilya," he screams. "It was Ilya Darakov."

So, the little piece of shite knew all along who his uncle was talking to.

Ilya Darakov. Shite. A weapons dealer, Darakov does business with my father. But he does business with a lot of people in our world.

"I'm done playing. Tell me everything you know about the mission, or the next thing I'm cutting off is your dick."

Gjon is crying so hard, he struggles to the get the words out, but he manages.

"Something about a prototype gun. High-value. Ilya wants it and anything stored with it."

Darakov knows about the whisper gun? Considering the engineer who showed it to us the first time was Russian, that's better news than it could be. It's entirely possible Darakov was at the demonstration too and tracked the original tech down to us.

But it would have been better news if they'd been after something else entirely.

"Where did you get intel on our tunnels?" I ask.

"Ilya knows about them. Said they've been around for over a century. He told us about a building in Queens to watch."

Brogan isn't going to like hearing that, but believing the Bunker is so secret no other syndicates know about it is foolish. I always figured someone knew, even if I didn't before Brogan inducted me into the Shaughnessy Mob. Which is one of the reasons I upgraded security.

"We didn't think they'd have security like the Pentagon. We thought it was a tunnel that led to a basement the mob used to use as a hideout, not a whole underground facility."

Those words just might be Gjon's death sentence. Right now, the intel is limited to old memories and hearsay. I aim to keep it that way.

Whether I do that by killing him, or not, is undecided.

Too bad the little pissant is Besnik's nephew.

"That doesn't explain how you found the entrance."

"Wraith made us stake out the building until he found a soldier to plant a tracking device on." He snivels some more. "It was boring as hell and he wouldn't even let us go out at night."

Everything Gjon is saying is reinforcing my view of Wraith.

"Who did you put the tracker on?" It has to be someone who comes to the Bunker regularly.

"I don't know his name."

"What did he look like?"

"He's slick. Wears suits. He has brown hair. Oh, and he carries a briefcase."

A pencil pusher? But which one?

Not many come to the Bunker, much less often enough to be tagged.

Wraith will know the name of our man, of that I have no doubt. What I don't know is if he will share that name.

"You think he's talking about that prick, Patrick Mahoney?" Brice asks.

Gjon's eye twitches when Patrick's name is mentioned. The little fecker has been lying to me.

"You know who it is."

"No." Now his eyes are so wide with alarm, the whites look anime sized. "I just remembered! I swear. He said his name into his phone when he answered it."

"Your tracker had sound?" I ask. What else do they know?

"No, but he I was on corner duty when he came a few days ago and I could hear him. The tracker stops working once he's inside the building anyway," Gjon offers desperately. "It took Wraith five days to find the entrance."

"Did it?" Sounds like Wraith would have found it without tracking one of our guys.

Which makes me wonder why he bothered.

"Don't know what the point of the stakeout and tracker was anyway," Gjon says petulantly, mirroring my thoughts.

Once I've learned everything Gjon knows about Ilya Darakov, I ask him about Wraith.

"Who is he?"

"Wraith?" Gjon sneers. "He's just a merc my uncle hires sometimes."

"Let me guess, the times you go out on a *mission*."

"My uncle doesn't think I need a babysitter!" But Gjon's eyes tell a different story.

I switch the scalpel for a six inch long needle-tip Damascus stiletto. "Who does Wraith work for?"

Gjon eyes the knife warily. "He doesn't. He's a merc."

"Mercenaries have handlers."

"If he has one, I don't know who it is. He and my uncle know each other."

"They're friends?" I ask. You can't trust a man you get to turn on his friends.

Ever.

"No. Uncle calls him a fatherless mutt. But he's useful."

I bet he doesn't call him that in front of Ranger Rick.

The infinitesimal change in Wraith's breathing tells me that he knows now what the Albanian gang leader thinks of him.

"From the look of things, Wraith is the only useful man your uncle has working for him."

"I'm useful! I told you everything," the maggot claims.

"That doesn't make you useful. It makes you weak and a coward." I hit him hard enough to knock him out.

Regardless of the complications that would come with killing Besnik's nephew, I'm still deciding if I want to let him live. We have drugs that will make it possible not only to make him forget the past twenty-four hours, but to plant false memories.

He could be useful in recruiting Ranger Rick too.

When I glance over at my future mob soldier, his eyes flutter open, unfocused at first. Woozy. Then they lock on mine. Panic flares and banks just as quickly.

Under the influence of the drug.

Impressive.

But his blown pupils can't lie. The drug is still very much in effect.

"How long were you casing our building?" I ask.

How patient is he? And when did the Russian contact Besnik?

Wraith shakes his head like he's trying to clear it. "Little shit told you everything, didn't he?"

"Everything he knew."

"You think I'm going to tell you more?"

Doubtful. "Will you?"

He starts reciting *Jabberwocky*, one slow word slurred at a time.

Yeah, he's had black ops training alright. Even with the right drugs in his system, overcoming the conditioning he just triggered would take too long.

I don't have the patience when there's another easier man to crack in the holding cell waiting on me. "No. But the other member of your team? It's a safe bet he will."

I have Conor bring him in, dropping his unconscious comrade on the floor before stringing him up from the same chains.

Despite his time in the cell, the second man takes longer to crack than Gjon and I end up giving him a dose of the specialty drug to speed things along.

They deserve whatever I dish out because they broke into our facility, but that doesn't mean I have the patience to dole out the punishment now.

I learn very little more. His name is Luan. He's a high-ranking soldier which comes as a surprise and confirms that Wraith and he are basically bodyguards for Gjon so he can prove himself on missions for his uncle.

Luan also confirms the name of the client: Ilya Darakov.

The whole time I'm interrogating him, *Jabberwocky* is slowly repeated over and over in low tones from behind us.

"Is Wraith a member of your gang?" I ask when I'm sure I've exhausted his current store of knowledge.

Brice will interrogate both him and Gjon again at least twice more to make sure nothing has been missed.

Information is power and we collect as much as we can from every unwilling guest who visits my domain.

"No. Besnik hires him to watch over Gjon, but he'll never be a member of The Albanian Boys."

"Has he refused to be inducted?" If he has, he showed smarts.

Besnik is a piece of shite.

Luan laughs with overblown amusement. Another consequence of the drug. "He's a mutt. His slut mother fucked around while her husband was in prison."

The recitation of *Jabberwocky* stops, jerking my gaze from the now voluble Albanian soldier to Ranger Rick.

The look he's giving the man hanging from my ceiling says if Wraith's hands weren't strapped to the chair, they would be wrapped around his former colleague's throat.

Well now, the first step in turning Wraith into a mobster may have just presented itself.

"Is part of your mission to protect this maggot?" I ask him.

Ranger Rick's expression shifts from stoic to disgust. "No."

I nod. "Good. He's going to die. Do you want to be the one to kill him?"

"What about Gjon?" Wraith asks, no more telltale emotion reflected in his features.

"We're going to drug him and rewire his brain to remember the last twenty-four hours differently. Then I'm going to offer him to Besnik in trade for releasing all claim he has on you."

"Besnik has no claim on me," Ranger Rick snarls. "I'm freelance."

He's got enough conditioning to start reciting *Jabberwocky* rather than answer questions under the influence of our specialty compound, but it's still powerful enough to lower his inhibitions about displaying his emotions.

Otherwise, none of his anger would have shown and I doubt a single word would have passed the man's lips.

"You still work for him. My men don't take outside contracts or have loyalty to any syndicate but ours."

"Your men?" Wraith shakes his head again.

"Aye. Ranger Rick, you've got the right makings for a good Irish mobster."

"Not Irish."

"You know more about who your father is than this piece of shite?"

Wraith's face closes like a vault's door and I have my answer.

"If there's no strong Irishman in your ancestry, I'll be surprised. But Irish blood or not, you've got more in common with a strong Irishman than you do the maggots you've been keeping company with."

Luan squawks out a protest.

But Wraith? Spits in his direction. "You've got that right."

CHAPTER TWENTY-SIX

Bonding through Torture

A Very Mick Style Recruiting Technique

WRAITH

"You want to kill him then?" the crazy Irishman asks me in the same tone he'd use to ask what I want for dinner.

I don't know what all this talk about me having an Irish ancestor is about. But as woozy as my head is, I understand he just offered to let me kill Luan.

The bastard.

I might be one by birth, but Luan is one by choice.

"I want to cut out his tongue and watch him choke to death on his blood." Like my mom choked to death on hers after one of her johns beat the hell out of her.

"No. You can't let him do that. I'm a valuable asset to Besnik. He'll go to war if you kill me."

It's my turn to laugh.

I haven't done that in a long damn time. It's these fucking drugs Mick Fitzgerald, Underboss to the Shaughnessy Mob, gassed me with.

"He *might* go to war over Gjon, but you're as expendable as any other man on his payroll." I refuse to call the gang members soldiers.

They lack the discipline and training necessary for the title. I know what it means to be a soldier and it's not those assholes.

The underboss flicks his head toward me and the big black man that wasn't here when I went under comes over and undoes the straps on my wrists.

Doesn't he realize how dangerous I am? I don't need my weapons to take on these men, but I got caught didn't I.

We breached on bad intel, but I should have been prepared for the gas in the corridor and the flashbang.

Mick hands me my knife, hilt first. "Be my guest."

After Luan dies choking on his own blood pouring down his throat from where his tongue used to be, Mick gives me a nod of approval.

"Why aren't you inducted into one of the syndicates?" he asks me, like that's a normal question too.

I've got my reasons, but all I say is, "I'm not joining the fucking Cosa Nostra."

"Interesting response," the other mobster says, his Irish brogue giving a lilt to his voice.

Mick agrees. "Very. There are more syndicates than the Five Families," he points out.

"Like you all?" I ask.

"Exactly like us. Why work for that asshole Besnik, when you could be part of something bigger? A syndicate that understands loyalty and trains its soldiers so there are no weak links."

"You sound like my Army recruiter." And damned if I don't have that same feeling of destiny as I did the day I met the Staff Seargent.

CHAPTER TWENTY-SEVEN

Sated, Then Shattered

KARA

I can't help it that I keep smiling after finding out that Mick stood Dierdre up for lunch.

And I turn that smile on my husband when he comes into the bedroom where I'm getting ready for dinner.

There are stress lines around his usually stoic eyes.

Rather than put my earrings on, I drop them on the vanity and cross the room to my husband.

Laying my hand against the hard planes of his chest, I look up at him. "Everything alright?"

Rather than answer, he pulls me into a breath stealing kiss.

I'm seriously considering asking Hope to keep Fitz and skipping dinner when Mick pulls away.

"Better now." He gives me one of his genuine smiles.

My heart stutters in my chest. "I'm sorry you had a hard day."

"Not too hard. I might have found a new recruit." His grin turns feral.

Why does his mobster side turn me on every bit as much as his passionate one?

I don't bother asking for details I know I won't get. Instead, I find myself asking, "Want to skip dinner?"

Mick jerks in surprise. "You know we can't do that."

"No, I don't know that." I'm startled too, by my willingness to break the rules, but I *want* to break them this once.

A lot.

"Don't tease me, wife," he growls, still not taking me seriously.

Remembering what Róise said about Mick earning the right to stand beside me, I give him the chance to. "I'm not teasing. We're not children. We don't have to go to family dinner if we have more important things to do."

Like make love.

Mick's eyes narrow. "Speaking of children, what about Fitz?"

"He's with Enoch and Hope."

"You trust her to watch him now?" Mick pulls his tactical shirt off over his head.

My mouth goes dry like it always does at the sight of his tattoo covered muscles. Right now, I just want to lick every single black line inked into his skin.

"Yes." Mostly. "He has his bodyguards watching him."

"He always has."

I nod. "But now I know it."

"Will that make it easier for you to let him out of your sight?"

I give a self-deprecating laugh. "I've been kind of a helicopter parent since Róise's kidnapping, haven't I?"

"You're a caring mam, Kara. Our son is lucky to have you."

"You're a pretty great dad, yourself."

Mick nods in easy agreement, no shortage of mobster arrogance in my husband.

My thoughts about his arrogance and everything else scatter as he undoes his black cargo pants and shoves them along with his silk knit boxers down his hips.

Some days, my husband goes to work in a tailored suit and tie. Others he wears an outfit like this one. I asked once why the different clothes, but he told me it wasn't something for me to worry about.

Since he's come home with blood on his shirts as often as when he was wearing a suit as not, I don't take the tactical gear as an indicator it was any more of a dangerous day than normal.

He's a mob underboss. His whole life is dangerous.

The danger of his job is the least thing on my mind when his heavy erection bobs in front of me.

My mouth waters. I know what I want, but I've never done it.

He's never asked for it. Not even when we couldn't engage in intercourse.

I want to suck him.

But I'm afraid of doing it wrong, so I reach out to grasp him with my hand. Hot velvet covered steel fills my palm and my knees go weak.

Mick grabs me and backs me toward the bed. It's like he knows what my body is going to do before I do.

My knees hit the edge of the bed and Mick is already pressing me down onto it, his body a wall of heat and muscle above me.

I'm still dressed. Not for long though.

"Off," he grits.

I have to let go of his hardon so I can lift my arms. He rips the halter top over my head and flings it across the room, his pupils dilating at the sight of my breasts.

"Such gorgeous baps." He cups them and squeezes, thumbs flicking my nipples until they ache with engorged blood.

I cling to his straining biceps, my breaths coming in short pants and cant my hips upward.

But my palazzo pants are in the way and I whine with frustration. He rips them from my body along with my panties, every movement filled with impatient power.

I'm so wet I can feel my arousal slipping down toward my bottom. More like soaked and he hasn't even touched me there yet.

"Feckin' hell, Kara." His voice is a rasp at my ear as the head of his erection presses against the opening to my body. "You feel that?"

"Yes!" It's all I feel.

And when he pushes inside me in one sharp, glorious thrust, I cry out, my fingers fisting the comforter.

He's thick and deep and he doesn't give me time to catch my breath or get my bearings.

He just pistons into me.

Fast. Deep. Hard.

My body responds.

Instantly. Ravenously. Wonderfully.

Every muscle tightens, a string pulled taut, the tension building so fast my vision goes white at the edges.

This shouldn't be happening so fast. It shouldn't feel this good this quickly. But it always does with him.

I try to say his name, but it comes out a sob.

"Come for me," he growls against my lips. "Now."

The command undoes me.

I break and arch into him as the orgasm crashes through me sharp, sudden, and overwhelming.

Trembling around him, my body convulses with a force that shatters me into pieces only he can put back together.

Like he has so many times before.

Mick groans and drives in deep, once, twice...

And then he follows, hips jerking as he spills inside me, his big body going rigid with his climax.

For a long moment, we stay like that.

His breath is ragged in my ear. Mine is caught somewhere in my chest.

My body is still clenching around him, the aftershocks dragging out like echoes in a canyon.

When he finally pulls out and collapses beside me, I just stare at him wide-eyed, chest heaving.

"Well," I breathe. "That was..."

"Yeah," Mick mutters, draping an arm over his eyes. "Fast."

"It's not the first time." So, why does it surprise me nearly every time the flames burn so hot and fast between us?

You'd think after seven years, I'd be used it.

I'm so not.

"No." He turns his head, looking at me. There's a lazy, satisfied smile on his face.

"Still think we should've gone to dinner?" I murmur.

His body tenses and then he leaps to his feet. "Feckin' hell! Dinner."

"Come on, Mick. It's okay if we miss one family dinner." I'm usually the one who worries about meeting family expectations, but right now?

I just want to lay here and bask.

"It's not that. I had to cancel lunch with Dierdre today, so I'm taking her to dinner."

Every atom of pleasurable contentment disappears from my body faster than it came, the heat still warming my insides turning to ice.

I sit up. "You're taking Dierdre to dinner?" I demand. "After that?"

"One has nothing to do with the other. I told you. I've got business with Dierdre."

"Business more important than making love to your wife?" The words hurt coming out of my mouth, but I want an answer.

"We already had sex, *mo chuisle*."

"You're saying once was enough for you?" It never is.

Why this time?

"I'm saying I have to go. Listen, you stay here and rest. I'll make sure Hope keeps Fitz until bedtime."

"Don't do me any favors." Feeling raw and too vulnerable in my nudity, I stand up and put on my robe.

But when I turn around to face him, Mick's not listening. He's not even there.

He's already in the bathroom, the sound of the shower running through the open door making it clear he has no intention of being late for his dinner with Dierdre.

CHAPTER TWENTY-EIGHT

Dinner, Drugs, and Delusions

MICK

Dierdre prattles on over the appetizers and I let her, waiting for the drug in the wine she's drinking to take effect.

It took more self-control than it should have to leave my wife naked on the bed. It helped that she decided to go to dinner after all and wasn't there when I came out of the bathroom after my shower.

If she still had been, being here would not be a given.

"I'm surprised Kara didn't mind you taking me to dinner." Dierdre plays with the stem of her wineglass and looks at me with what is probably supposed to be understanding. "She's very jealous of you."

"Why do you say that?" I hadn't noticed Kara acting particularly jealous.

At least not after my stupid attempt to trigger her into returning to her more affectionate behavior of our early marriage.

If you had asked me five years ago if I would miss it, I would have said no. A man like me doesn't need affection.

In fact, I pretty much ignored the change in her behavior and when I thought of it, wrote it off as symptomatic of her postpartum depression.

It took another year before I realized the vulnerable young woman I had married was either gone or hiding pretty effectively behind the façade of the perfect mob wife.

"Oh, you know." Dierdre waves her hand and takes a sip of her wine.

"No, I don't know. Explain it."

She gives me an almost pitying look. "I suppose it's something you've learned to live with."

"That is not an explanation."

Dierdre blinks, her focus going hazy.

Good. The drug is taking effect.

"You don't have to pretend with me, Micky. I know how over-the-top jealous she got after the birth of your son." Dierdre waves her hand airily again, misjudges the distance and nearly knocks over her glass of wine.

I grab it and set it to rights on the table.

"Thank you. I'm not usually clumsy, but then you know that."

"What do you know about Kara's behavior after the birth of our son?" I'm supposed to be grilling Dierdre on why she's here and if her da or mine is working with Ilya Darakov.

But knowing how intrusively my old mob has been spying on me is not unimportant. Knowing what Dierdre has learned about Kara is crucial.

"I heard about her hissy fits. The way she demanded you fire one of the women that worked in your office."

"How?" I demand.

"People talk," Dierdre dismisses.

I flick my hand waving away the approaching waiter. "What people?"

"I suppose her insecurity is understandable. Kara's not exactly in your league now. And back then? Recently pregnant and unable to even try to service the needs of her very virile husband..." Her voice trails off in innuendo. "Well, you know better than I do how that must have played out."

"Who did you hear this from?" I demand again.

Dierdre shifts, pressing her waterglass to her cheek like it might cool her. "It's not a state secret, Micky."

"If my people have been talking out of turn, I want to know it," I grind out.

I didn't appreciate how annoying I would find this form of interrogation with her. Things don't usually get to me.

More like never.

But as I've found with so many things regarding my wife, I react in inexplicable ways to the knowledge someone has been talking about her in disparaging terms.

"Don't worry. Your soldiers are every bit as circumspect as you expect them to be," she assures me with a measure of irritation.

Who has she been trying to pump for information?

I pour her more wine, pushing the glass toward her in a silent order to drink.

She obeys and takes a long sip before fanning her hand in front of her face. "It's hot in here. Is their aircon broken?"

"It's fine. If it wasn't one of our soldiers that gossiped about my wife, then who?" I want a name and what I want, I get.

Dierdre rolls her eyes. "Calm down, Micky. Brogan mentioned it when he was visiting last fall."

"I find that hard to believe." Would my father-in-law really be that indiscreet?

"Brian was complaining about Brigid again," Dierdre says, mentioning my sister. "She refused yet another marriage alliance, this one in London."

The fact my sister, at the age of twenty-seven, remains unmarried and unpromised is a source of consternation for my father. He'd have better luck waiting for his oldest granddaughter to come of age than try to push my sister into a mob alliance.

She wants nothing to do with that part of our lives.

"I didn't realize he was trying to arrange an alliance with a mob there." I focus on the truly pertinent piece of information in Dierdre's comment.

"Oh, it wasn't a mob. It was Greek mafia and your sister was having none of it. He couldn't threaten her with cutting off funds because she is self-supporting." Dierdre sounds bitter about that, but nothing is stopping her from using the degree she got from TCD.

And Oisín Kelly has never been stingy with Dierdre's allowance, even allowing her to have her own apartment.

"You never mentioned this to me."

"There's a lot I don't tell you," she says knowingly. "I can't be sure of your loyalties with you living here in America."

I was right thinking I need to cultivate other information sources within my old mob. Maybe my sister would be a good one. There's room there, to play on her discontent with our father.

"Anyway, Brian blamed Brigid's refusal on some teenage infatuation. She has a boyfriend."

And he's still alive? That doesn't sound like my father wanted the Greek connection all that badly.

"She refused to do her duty to the mob. Not like you." She shoots me a look under her lashes. "No matter how hard it was for you to leave me behind."

I don't confirm or deny her assumption. Letting her believe it without confirmation could be useful. "And what did Brogan say about Kara?"

No one could say my wife had not been willing to do her duty by the mob. She'd agreed to more than an alliance marriage to fulfill what her grandfather expected of her.

Dierdre blinks, her head wobbling slightly. "Oh, he sympathized. Said young people these days are ruled by their feelings. Mentioned Kara had gotten a bit overwrought after Fitz was born."

"Overwrought," I repeat softly.

She shrugs one bare shoulder. "He said it like it was funny. *Pathologically jealous* was the phrase. Said she thought you'd been cheating while she was in the hospital, but that she settled down and he was sure Brigid would too."

I was wrong. My father-in-law is *pathologically* indiscreet. How upset would Kara be if I cut out her da's tongue?

I wouldn't make him choke to death on this own blood like the stupid bastard I allowed Wraith to kill earlier. I can be merciful.

Dierdre's smile sharpens. "Was she right? I wouldn't blame you if you had taken a lover." She pauses. "Or still wanted one."

No question who she's suggesting to fill that role.

"I don't break my promises, Dierdre. You know that."

Her red tinted lips twist in a moue. "But forced marriage vows hardly count."

"They do to me." Regardless, no other woman appeals to my libido and hasn't since the first time I touched my wife intimately.

"Pity." Dierdre looks around with a frown. "Where's our food?"

I signal the waiter. He arrives to clear away the appetizers and place our main courses on the table, then melts into the background like he's been trained to do.

He's not one of the regular waiters for the pub. Despite being owned by the mob, I brought in one of the soldiers on my crew to do the serving tonight.

I don't want anyone overhearing what I learn from Dierdre and my men know how to keep their distance. And their mouths shut...unlike Brogan.

Fecker.

Like she's still thinking about it too, Dierdre says, "Brogan said you don't look at other woman, but your little child bride was convinced you did. That it made things difficult."

Kara's jealousy wasn't nearly as difficult as the depression that came with it after Fitz's birth.

And what she tried to do because of it.

What the hell was I thinking trying to make her jealous again?

Feckin' idjit is what I am.

"You never looked at another woman," she repeats. "Is that true, Mick? Not even once?"

"I already told you—"

"That you don't break your promises. I know, but that doesn't mean you don't *want* to."

"I don't want to." I let that settle between us while I chew a bite of perfectly prepared Kobe beef steak.

Yes, it's an Irish pub, but a good steak is a good steak.

"I bet I could change your mind." She pushes her shoulders forward, pushing her breasts together. "Remember how much you loved fucking these."

Shite.

I keep the distaste that washes through me off my face.

The drug lowers inhibitions, making people a lot more susceptible to suggestion and willing to speak freely. It can also result in a woman from my past trying to seduce me at the table.

I'm not even a little turned on right now. Nor am I embarrassed. I don't get embarrassed. But it's a good thing Dierdre's memory of tonight will be hazy.

Because if she remembers this, *she* will be embarrassed. And probably pissed. Rejection doesn't sit well with a woman like her.

Spoiled. Used to getting what she wants.

And that could make her dangerous, even if she's not here to spy on us for the Northies.

Ignoring her blatant attempt at seduction, I ask, "Why are you here Dierdre?"

"I'm having dinner with my very good friend." Her voice is low and flirty.

I manage not to roll my eyes. "In New York. What are you doing in New York?"

Her eyes widen. "I told you. I'm here to stay safe from the Odessa Mafia until my father finishes negotiations with them."

I measure the amount of wine left in her glass. Barely a swallow or two, which means she's already drunk two substantial pours.

We've been here for nearly thirty minutes and the drug is already affecting her, but it will be another fifteen before I'm confident her inhibitions are lowered enough to trust her answers.

Unlike Wraith, Dierdre has no training in withstanding drug induced interrogation, soft or otherwise.

We eat in silence as I wait for the drug to take full effect.

Dierdre tries to stab a prawn on her plate and misses twice. She ordered Dublin Lawyer, but prefers prawns over lobster and insisted the chef prepare it with them.

She hasn't touched the crusty bread it was served with, but she's made inroads in the shrimp tossed in a rich whiskey-cream sauce.

She tries to stab another one again, but when she misses, she drops her fork as if she forgot what she was doing with it.

Perfect.

"I'm curious," I say, voice mild, "why the Odessa boys would want you bad enough to risk taking you on the Northie's turf."

She reaches for her glass, misses and waves her hand. "I wasn't in Dublin. I was shopping in London."

That makes more sense, but doesn't explain why they felt the need to kidnap her at all.

"Why take you?"

"It's mob business. Something to do with shipments or accounts, I don't know. You know how it is. Your da and mine think women are mushrooms and do their best to keep us in the dark."

"But you don't stay in the dark, do you?" It's the reason I continued to cultivate her as an information asset after my marriage.

She always knows the details.

She used to whisper them in my ear at night, between moans and murmurs. Dierdre Kelly collects information the way other women collect handbags. And she always, always knows more than she should.

She winks. "You know me well."

"So?"

"Our das are refusing to budge on the price of a shipment of weapons and have threatened to go elsewhere." Her hazy eyes widen, like the words coming out of her mouth surprise her.

Speaking unvarnished truth probably does. It's not her norm.

"And Odessa thought they would kidnap you for leverage?" Doesn't sound like the way to keep a business relationship strong.

They might get the price they want for the current weapons, but my da will never buy from them again.

"They want a marriage alliance." This time the shock is so strong at speaking the truth, she slaps her hand over her mouth.

"It's not our das who are balking then?" I ask, taking a stab in the dark.

And the bratva doesn't want more money. They want Dierdre.

Even woozy and uninhibited, fury suffused her features. "I'm not a bargaining chip."

"We all are." Even me.

True, if I hadn't wanted what Fergal Shaughnessy was offering, I would have found a way out of marrying Kara seven years ago. I'm glad I didn't, and not because one day, sooner than later, I will be the boss and my son after me.

There is no woman on the planet more perfect for me than my own personal obsession.

"Well, I'm not going to marry a bratva boss nearly twice my age just to provide him with the male heir he didn't manage with his first wife." Dierdre manages to grab her wine glass and drink.

Or tries to. It's empty.

She puts it down with a frown, like she's wondering where the wine went.

I don't want her too inebriated to answer my questions and give another sign to my soldier indicating I want the nonalcoholic version of the wine brought to the table.

Lifting the bottle, I shake my head. "Empty. Here's the waiter with another."

Dierdre gives my soldier a brilliant smile. "Just in time."

He pours her a glass of the nonalcoholic wine and then leaves the bottle on the table before stepping away with the nearly half full bottle in my hand.

Dierdre is so out of it, she didn't even notice my lie.

She takes a long sip of her newly poured beverage. "Ilya Darakov isn't even a pakhan. He's a weapons dealer."

The name hits like an icepick to my brain. "Our das want you to marry Ilya Darakov?"

"It was his idea and he's offering incentives that both our das are finding hard to resist."

"And when you refused to agree to the marriage, he tried to kidnap you?" I ask.

"Not him personally. He sent his flunkies for me." Which seems to offend her as much as the fact her da wants her to marry the Russian.

"Whose idea was it for you to come to New York?" I ask.

"Mine." She gives me a seductive wink. "All mine. But da went along with it. He did not approve of Ilya trying to take matters into his own hands."

"They still want you to marry Darakov though?"

Dierdre scowls. "Aye. The das think they can use the failed kidnapping as leverage for even more concessions."

"Smart."

"You think so? I don't like being bartered like a treasure full of diamonds."

Trust Dierdre to liken herself to precious stones rather than something more prosaic. She still sees herself as the queen on the chessboard.

"What about you? What are you trying to get out of coming to New York?"

"What else?" she asks with a husky chuckle. "I want you, Micky."

"I'm already married."

"There's such a thing as divorce."

More prevalent in the American mob than it is in Ireland. Not that it's common here though. There are plenty of American mob bosses that consider death the only possible end to a marriage.

"I'm not going to divorce my wife."

"You say that now, but think about it, Mick. You've already got Fitz. He's the guarantor of the contract now, not Kara. You don't need her."

"What do you know about the contract?" I demand.

"Please, Mick. It's like you don't know me. I read it of course."

Shite.

Kara will be livid if she finds out Dierdre knows the particulars of our marriage alliance contract. She carries inexplicable shame around the IVF treatments and has never even told her sister or cousin that's how she conceived Fitz.

Between us, she acts like it never happened and I don't remind her. The IVF was hard on my young wife.

I wonder sometimes if that's the reason she never brings up getting pregnant again. She associates her pregnancy with everything she had to go through to get that way and we lost in the process.

It could as easily be that she doesn't want to risk having postpartum depression again.

Regardless of her reasoning, Brogan is not happy his daughter refuses to give him more grandchildren right now.

However, I made it clear to him that if he pushes her on it, I will get a vasectomy.

When he threatened me with one of those uncommon divorces on behalf of his daughter, I told him Kara would stop being my wife over my dead body.

Brogan Shaughnessy is a ruthless man, but he's not like me. He still has sensitivities borne of emotion and those make him reluctant to kill his son-in-law.

If he ever starts to show signs that's changing, it won't be me who ends up dead.

Kara is having our next child when she's ready. If she's *ever* ready.

"Tell me about Ilya Darakov."

Dierdre's eyes soften. "I knew you cared. He's fifty-two, Mick. Old enough to be my father."

But not twice her age of thirty. "When did he approach your father about the marriage alliance."

"Last year some time."

"When?" I press again.

"I don't know, six...maybe seven months ago." She pushes her plate away like the prawns disgust her now.

If she's starting to feel nauseated, my window for effective interrogation is closing.

Ten months ago, we took the whisper gun technology from the weapons engineer and killed him after finding out what a sick bastard he was.

It could have taken a couple of months for Darakov to find out we were the ones who torched the lab and took the prototype.

He's definitely interested in the whisper gun technology, but how much does Dierdre know? How much do my da and hers know?

My gut is telling me, nothing at all.

Darakov wants the alliance with the Northies as a way to get to me. As a competitor in the arms market, he has to know any attempt to do business with us would be suspect.

"Why does he want the alliance with the Northside Dublin Syndicate?" I ask.

"I told you. He wants me to have babies for him." Dierdre shudders. "I don't want to get pregnant."

"Did you tell your da that?"

"No! He'd disown me."

Life in the mob isn't easy for women, but it's not easy for men either.

Certain aspects of our lives are dictated by our births. But this isn't the dark ages.

"Your da wouldn't disown you."

Dierdre shrugs. "As long as I'm an asset for him, he gives me the allowance I need to keep up appearances to attract a suitable husband."

In other words, she pretends to be open to an alliance marriage to keep her substantial allowance coming in.

"It's surprising you aren't already married."

"You know da expected you to marry me. Both our das felt guilty when they saw how heartbroken I was after you left. They understood that I couldn't consider marrying anyone else." The way she says it makes it clear there was no heartache involved.

Just a woman who wanted to keep her lavish lifestyle without being hampered by a mob marriage on the horizon.

"They believe you've had enough time to *grieve*."

She scowls again. "Aye. And now they want me to marry a geriatric."

"Fifty-two is not a geriatric."

"I don't want an old man in my bed. I want you Mick."

I don't have to answer that claim because Dierdre's body succumbs to the drug. Passing out, she falls forward, her face landing in the Dublin Lawyer she pushed away.

Now that I know why she's really here and who wants to marry her, keeping her on Long Island might be strategic.

I just hope she's not too big a pain in the ass to Kara. My wife is strong though. She's not going to be intimidated by someone as fake as Dierdre.

Dierdre wants me, but I don't want her.

Problem solved.

CHAPTER TWENTY-NINE

Shadows Between Us

MICK

The apartment is quiet when I come in, but there's a light from the doorway in our bedroom.

Kara's still up.

I hoped, but it's after ten and she's usually asleep by now.

Checking in on Fitz, I find him out cold, sprawled sideways across his bed with his covers kicked off. I shift him so his head is back on the pillow before pulling up the covers.

Gobby jumps onto the bed and settles herself beside him like the cat has been waiting for someone to sort out her human.

After pressing a kiss to his temple, I head to mine and Kara's bedroom.

The soft click of a keyboard reaches me before I get there. Casting a pale gold halo over her light brown hair, the only light in the room is the lamp on the desk she's working on.

Her shoulders tense, but she doesn't look up when I walk in.

In sleep leggings and an oversized shirt that covers enough to satisfy most nuns, her fingers move fast over the keys. The outfit seems familiar and then I remember.

The third and last time she ever safe worded with me. She'd worn the same kind of clothes to sleep in.

Armor.

Shite.

"Hello, *a stór*." Loosening my tie, I toe off my shoes. "What are you working on?"

"Hey," she says without turning. "How was your dinner?"

Not cold, but not warm either. A shade of polite she uses with people outside her inner circle.

And I don't like it turned on me.

I shrug out of my suit jacket and pull off my tie, tossing it on the bed with an idea for using it later. "Productive."

Kara makes a noncommittal sound in response.

I walk over to her and leaning down with one hand on the back of her chair, I lower my voice in invitation. "You didn't tell me what you're working on."

"Does it matter?"

Her unwillingness to answer pulls me up short. It's not like her.

Is she working on something for school? Maybe Kara doesn't want to tell me since I supposedly don't know about her secretly attending a university with an online program.

"Is this something you have to finish right now?" I ask.

Her hands still on the keyboard. "It's something I'm going to finish right now."

Which is not the same thing. She's choosing to prioritize whatever she's working on over our time together.

That's not something Kara does.

We both treat these nighttime hours of privacy together as important.

Unless it's a bleedin' emergency, I come home to Kara before midnight every night. And she is always here, ready to welcome me when I wake her.

I frown, trying to figure out what's going through my sweet wife's brain. "Is this a late-night study session? Have you got a big test coming up or something?"

She was still before. Now, she's frozen into immobility. "You know."

"About you going to college? Yes."

"How long?" she asks in a whisper.

"Since the beginning. There's nothing about you that I don't know."

She makes a sound of disbelief.

I shake my head. She doubts me? "I followed you."

"When?"

"The night you and Róise snuck out to celebrate her birthday."

Kara slides out of the chair and puts distance between us, but at least she's facing me now. "No. You couldn't have."

"I did. You're good, love. Our blackgloves couldn't have handled the cascading disabling of alarm triggers any better." I'm still proud of her ingenuity and intelligence.

"Then how did you follow us?"

"I watch you," I admit.

Her hazel gaze dark with an emotion I can't decipher, she asks, "What do you mean you watch me?"

"On the security feeds. With your phone tracker. I always know where you are."

KARA

I always know where you are.

Mick's words resound in my brain like a clanging bell. Only instead of feeling like the alarm they should be, they warm something inside me that's been cold since he left earlier.

The pain is still there, but this *attention*? *Obsession*? It implies that I'm not nearly the nonentity in my husband's life I've always thought I was.

But if he watches me so much, he should know I'm not taking any classes for the summer term. "You don't watch me all the time, or you'd know I don't have any classes right now."

I'm working on final plans for the big Labor Day celebration, not because they couldn't wait until tomorrow, but because I couldn't sleep.

"I forgot."

He forgot? "That doesn't sound like you."

"No one is infallible, *a stór*."

But Mick usually is. Did his dinner with Dierdre rattle him in some way?

That's not a question I want an answer to, so I ask a different one. "Why didn't you tell me you knew I was taking college courses?"

"Why didn't you tell me you were taking them?" he counters.

My hands fist at my sides, my fingernails digging into my palms. "I was afraid if I did, you would make me stop."

"I am not your father."

So, he thinks, like me, that Brogan would have insisted I stop? "I guess not."

"I'm glad you're still in therapy," he says, with the air of a man getting everything out there at once. "In fact, I think you should convince Fiona to see an online therapist too."

"You think..." I can't get enough air into my lungs right now.

My entire secret life is not actually a secret at all. And I have no idea how I feel about that. Contrary to my fears, Mick is not trying to make me give up a single thing I've kept from him.

Not even the therapist.

Mick shrugs. "It might help her."

"So my dad can marry her off to someone for another alliance?" I ask painfully.

"That can't happen. Brogan gave his word to your cousin. Fiona's freedom at the cost of hers."

"My father is good at getting around the intent of a promise by finessing the fine details."

He'd taken advantage of the fact that it was *seanathair* who made the promise to Róise's dad, both now dead, not to force my cousin into an arranged marriage. The promise had been predicated on the agreement of my uncle to take his rightful place as boss when *seanathair* died.

Only Uncle Derry died before my grandfather and never took over as boss, nullifying the promise. At least as far as Brogan was concerned.

"Do not misunderstand me, Kara. I will not allow him to arrange a marriage for Fiona."

"Why?"

"Because I keep my promises and I won't work for a man who doesn't keep his."

And the only way Mick stops working for my dad is for Brogan to retire. Or die.

Or for Mick to.

A shiver skates up my spine and I force the disturbing thoughts from my head.

"You agreed with him that he wasn't responsible for honoring *seanathair's* promise to Uncle Derry?"

"Yes. Derry should have planned for that eventuality and ensured a different wording on the vow."

"You think he should have planned for what would happen if he died before *seanathair*?" I ask, more appalled than I probably should be considering the life we live.

Mick unbuckles his belt and slides it out of the loops on his pants, catching his backup holster as it releases from the belt. "I have."

"What do you mean?" I lick my lips, watching in fascination as my husband begins disarming himself, one weapon at a time.

I've seen him do this hundreds and hundreds of times and it still makes me wet.

"Your father has signed a blood contract stating that if I die, neither he, nor any other Boss of the Shaughnessy Mob will attempt to force you to marry again."

"You never told me."

"I don't plan to die." He shoves his trousers down his legs, revealing muscular thighs that an action hero would envy.

"But you made arrangements in case you do." How do I reconcile this with the way Mick dismisses my feelings so easily about other things?

Like Dierdre.

Unbuttoning his shirt, my husband asks, "Are we done talking now?"

"Why?" I give him a suspicious look. "What else are you planning to do?"

He picks up his tie from the bed and lets it dangle from his fingers. "Do you really need me to tell you?"

"No." And I don't mean he doesn't need to tell me.

I mean no to the tie. No to sex. No to all of whatever he's got planned.

"No?"

"That's not how this works, Mick," I tell him flatly.

"What's not?" he asks, like he really doesn't know.

How could he watch me like he says he does and be this obtuse about how I feel?

But then he doesn't watch me for the sake of emotion. Clarity bursts in my brain. I'm not an obsession. I'm a responsibility and Mick watches *over* me.

"You don't get to leave with the cum still wet between my legs to go wine and dine your ex."

A strange sound comes out of his throat. Surprise maybe? "It wasn't a date."

"It was more of a date than you've taken me on since our sixth anniversary." And that was over a year ago.

Besides, duty dates on our anniversary don't count, even when they do manage to happen.

"It was business. I told you that."

Business that had to happen at a restaurant? I don't think so.

I've spent most of the night picturing my husband and Dierdre laughing over an intimate table for two. And business did not feature in a single one of the images tormenting me.

Ignoring his claim, I say, "You for sure do not get to come home acting like nothing happened. Like I'm supposed to be here, ready, warm and waiting for you, just because you decided to come back."

"There was never any question about me *coming back*. I never sleep away from you if I can help it."

He likes to be here in the morning to have breakfast with our son. That does not make *me* feel special.

"Kara, *mo chuisle*—"

"No." I put my hand up. "Just no. Not tonight, Mick. You already got your rocks off for the day. If you wanted to make love again, you would have stayed."

"That was not an option." Frustration laces my husband's voice.

It's weird. He doesn't usually show impatience.

But I'm not giving in.

"Do I have to say it?" I ask.

We both know what I'm talking about.

Red.

He jerks his head side to side. "I'll take a shower and leave you to whatever has you so enthralled."

I grab the urge to take back my words and stuff them down as deep as I can, past my hurting heart and deeper than my unrequited love for my contract marriage husband.

CHAPTER THIRTY

Ghost Guns & Ceremonial Skeans

MICK

I'm still in a piss-poor mood when I make it into the lab two days later.

For two nights, my wife has kept me at a physical distance. She allows herself to snuggle into me after she goes to sleep, but when I wake her to make love, she pulls away.

Feckin' Darakov.

Feckin' Dierdre.

They are both fucking with my marital peace and the thought of killing one, or both of them, is growing more attractive by the day.

They bleedin' deserve each other. That's for sure and certain.

Even the prospect of test firing the working prototype of the whisper gun doesn't penetrate my dark mood. I don't want to be here in the lab.

I want to be with Kara and I want her to look at me like she can't get enough. Not like she can't get away from me fast enough.

The air in the Bunker is filtered, but sometimes the scent of our DNA killing cleaner lingers in Interrogation. And the shooting range smells of spent powder and gun oil.

But the lab?

It doesn't smell like anything.

Hex doesn't use gun oil on the new weapon, only synthetic lubricant and thermal paste. Which can have a slight odor when heated, but right now, the air in the lab is as sterile as the workbenches.

The weapons engineer stands across from me, a steel gun case on the lab bench between us.

Her dark curls are pulled back in a messy twist, pencil jammed through the center like she forgot what century she's in. The coat she wears is supposed to be crisp and white, but it's rumpled and the lapel's smeared with graphite.

Arms crossed, expression somewhere between triumphant and exhausted, she nods toward the gun case.

But I don't pick it up. "Did something go wrong with the last prototype?"

"That's the same prototype."

"Why this?" I wave at her appearance.

"I'm working on a modular rail system compatible with pistols, rifles, and SMGs. The idea is a built-in nanocoating which slowly releases synthetic lubricant when internal friction increases."

"Sounds promising." I knew I got the right weapons engineer to head our research lab.

She grins tiredly. "It's pure soldier self-care, but I'm stuck on devising a mechanism that signals when it's time to dismantle and clean the weapon."

"Like the heat indicator on the whisper gun?" I can think of some soldiers who would benefit from the reminder.

Not on the crews under me. My men establish a weapons care routine that they learn never to deviate from.

Punishment for doing so is severe. I've never had a soldier forget more than once.

"Exactly like that. Everything I come up with is flawed though. I've barely slept in three days."

That explains the graphite.

Dr. Ximena Morales does all her drafting with graphite pencils on inch graph paper. Old school and un-hackable.

"After we fire the test rounds, you'll go home and change that. The whisper gun is a priority, but that big brain needs rest to keep coming up with brilliant breakthroughs."

"You don't have to tell me twice."

Which tells *me* that by barely slept, she means she hasn't slept at all.

Hex nods toward the gun case. "No interruptions during this test firing, boss."

Like *she's* the boss. Hex has got balls, I'll give her that.

I flip the latches and open the lid.

The whisper gun looks exactly like it did the day before yesterday. Sleek. Matte black. An elegant, if ordinary weapon.

Or so it would seem. I reach for it.

"Seven shots," she reminds me. "Before it needs a passive cool-down cycle."

I test the heft of the weapon in my hand. Not as heavy as a regular handgun, but more powerful than the smaller guns with a similar weight.

"What are we calling it?" I ask.

"Vanta." Hex pushes her glasses up with her forefinger.

I narrow my eyes. "What the fuck does that mean?"

Hex smirks like a kid with a matchbook. "Vantablack. Darkest material ever engineered. Absorbs ninety-nine-point-something percent of light. You don't see it. You don't hear it. Just disappears into the dark. Like this beauty."

I sight down the range, a small grin pulling at the corner of my mouth. "It fits."

"Yes." She smirks. "It's a hell of a lot better than calling it the whisper gun like some dumbass nickname from a Jason Bourne knockoff."

I take the dig without comment, my sour mood finally lifting as I sight down the barrel at the target.

The trigger pull is soft. No recoil. Barely any sound.

The slug punches through the steel target with no more drama than a whisper through a confessional.

Nothing but displaced air to mark its passing. This weapon is exactly as advertised. A whisper gun.

Vanta.

My heart gives a kick in my chest. We did it.

The second and third shots fly just as clean. Then I shift and aim at the layered ballistic gel and Vanta's bullet goes through it like it's air. Twice.

I pivot slightly, targeting a reinforced plexiglass dummy like the ones we use for training scenarios.

Final two shots...same result.

The handle is slightly warm, but no warmer than steel after being held in your hand.

I lower the weapon and glance back at Hex. "You've outdone yourself, Morales. Expect a hefty bonus for job well done in your next payment deposit."

"Thank you."

We will briefly discuss the next phase. Production of a cadre of weapons we can provide to handpicked soldiers to test in the field.

We're weeks, if not months, off from mass production.

And I'm sure as hell not ready for a Vanta to end up in the hands of a competitor for an attempt at back-engineering.

Brogan and I discussed this. We won't offer the weapons for sale to allies until we are on the cusp of mass production.

Now, it's time to test out another weapon.

Wraith stands in the center of his holding cell, sweat darkening the collar of his T-shirt, his breathing just starting to even out.

Brice nods to me. "He did good."

My lieutenant put our new recruit through his paces with his crew.

Weights, calisthenics, and hand-to-hand combat training. Nothing new for a man who was an Army Ranger.

"Hey, Kieran." I step inside the small room leaving the door open behind me. "How did you like training with strong Irish soldiers?"

His head jerks up.

"Besnik told me your legal name when I agreed to give him his nephew back in exchange for forgetting you exist."

Kieran Llesh's eyebrows raise and his mouth twists cynically.

"And a half-a-million dollar fine for being stupid enough to take a job that meant trespassing on our property." I sit down in the only chair in the room and wave toward the bed for him to do the same.

Sparse, but clean, these holding cells aren't for intimidation. But for a man who spent ten years in the Army, two of them working for the shadowy agencies connected to it?

It's a decent space.

Not that he'll stay here if things go the way I plan.

A barely-there smile flicks across Wraith's features. "Darakov only paid The Albanian Boys two-hundred grand for the job, and half was due upon successful completion."

"You know what they say. You get what you pay for. If he'd hired you directly, things might have gone differently the day before yesterday."

Wraith's jaw clenches, but he doesn't answer. Shifting into the classic military at ease position, feet shoulder-width apart, thumbs interlaced behind his back, he doesn't sit down either.

I can work with that.

"Your grandmother is Irish." Though we found no mob affiliations in her family. I was right about something else too. "Ranger Rick fits better than I thought, doesn't it?"

Our blackgloves did a deep dive on Wraith yesterday and nothing I learned has changed my mind about recruiting this man into the mob.

He'll be a good soldier.

"I prefer Wraith."

I nod. "Alright, Wraith. I can do that."

My new recruit relaxes infinitesimally. He really doesn't want to be called Ranger Rick.

Interesting.

"Besnik is pretty broken up over Luan's death," I say.

"No doubt. Luan was a better soldier than Gjon ever will be."

"I got that impression." Not that I regret letting Wraith kill the Albanian.

Wraith sighs. "He was also an asshole. My mother is not a slut."

"The Albanian Boys have some backward views on women."

"And the illegitimate children they give birth to." It doesn't sound like those views bother Wraith, but he's bleedin' good at hiding his thoughts so I can't be sure.

"Is that why you never joined the gang?"

"I was never invited."

"Did you want to be?"

"No." The disgust imbued in that single word isn't hard to read at all.

"And the Cosa Nostra? Your father didn't want you to get made?"

Wraith scowls. "My *sperm donor* can choke to death on his handmade Italian loafers."

"He abandoned your mother when she found out she was pregnant?" I ask, wondering if he'll tell me the truth.

"They were never together. She worked as a maid in his house. The one time they had sex was not consensual."

And because he was connected, no rape charges would have been filed.

I pull a knife sheath stamped with the Shaughnessy coat-of-arms from my inner breast pocket and offer it to Wraith, hilt first. The *skean* inside is ceremonial, but that doesn't make it any less lethal.

His gaze flicks from the knife to the open door, drawing the correct conclusion. I'm showing him trust.

What he doesn't know is that no matter how good he is, he's not as deadly as I am. He doesn't have his kit, but I'm wearing mine, including a knife in a spring-loaded sheath at my wrist. I will have it out and piercing his heart before he can finish taking a threatening step toward me.

But the illusion of trust is necessary at this stage and if my recruitment strategy works, that trust will be as real as it needs to be for him to be inducted into our mob by the end of the year.

His face a blank slate, he stares down at the *skean*.

I jut my chin toward him. "Take it."

He does, sliding the knife from the sheath. The Irish dagger is the same as the first one given by the first Shaughnessy Mob boss over a hundred years ago to his soldiers.

The blade is six inches long and so sharp when Wraith tests it with his thumb, a drop of blood wells. He makes a sound of surprise.

"There are no weapons just for show in the mob." We don't do pretty swords hanging on the walls that can't do their job of running an opponent through.

Or beheading him when necessary.

My father's sword has taken more than one finger from his soldiers in punishment.

Brogan prefers other methods.

Namely, sending them to dance with the devil. Me.

He runs his fingertip over the *claddagh* on one side of the hilt. "My mother has a ring with this on it, given to her by her mother."

"Every element symbolizes something to our clan."

"What?" he asks, his tone low.

"The heart is usually associated with love, but for us it stands for the lifeblood you are willing to sacrifice for the mob."

His eyes meet mine, his unreadable. "And the hands?"

"The hand of your brothers that will always be reaching toward you as yours will reach to help them. A mob is family, not just a group you join."

"Being in the Irish mob is a way of life," he says like he's repeating something he heard.

"Who told you that?"

"One of my Ranger brothers."

That tracks. From fighting for Irish liberation to protecting the country of their birth, there has always been members of the mob in the military. "He was right."

"I thought the Army was a way of life too."

"The crown symbolizes loyalty. No man gets inducted that isn't trustworthy."

"Not even someone born to the mob?" he asks, his tone disbelieving.

"Not even then. Family shouldn't be the weak link in a syndicate. They should be the strongest members." The deadliest. Like me.

Like Fitz will be one day.

He flips the *skean* over and makes another involuntary sound of surprise.

That side of the hilt is engraved with the Shaughnessy coat-of-arms. Below that is his name and below that is the year of his induction.

This year.

He'll either be part of the mob, or dead by December 31st.

"That means if you die on a job, we *bury* you. Properly. If you're captured, we come for you. If you're betrayed—"

His head comes up at that, his eyes burning.

"You are your own instrument of justice and if you can't be, your brothers take the job on for you."

"Luan believed my mom betrayed her husband." Wraith is testing me like I'm testing him.

"If that had happened to the wife of one of my men when he was in prison, I would have sent Rory to settle it."

"Rory?"

"He's our best stealth assassin."

Wraith doesn't blink. "What about the child she carried?"

"Would have been raised to serve the mob like the other sons of our clan."

"That's not how it is in The Albanian Boys. Pure bloodlines are prized."

And his wasn't considered pure. "The mob has always recruited from outside the clan. Keeps those bloodlines healthy."

Wraith almost cracks a smile at that. "They looked down on my mom before she got pregnant with me, because her mother wasn't Albanian."

"Your Irish blood is not something you have to be ashamed of," I growl.

"What about my Italian and Albanian blood?"

"You're in America, boyo. This country is filled with people whose bloodlines scatter to the four corners of the world."

"Not yours. You're Irish through and through."

"Don't you believe it. My great-grandfather was a Scot. You go back far enough and you'll find a Viking."

"So, you're saying it doesn't matter?"

"The only thing that matters, is if you are willing to bleed for your own." Wraith inclines his head.

"Being one of ours isn't about bloodlines, it's about brotherhood. Knowing someone has your six in a firefight, that you won't be hung out to dry when the feckin' feds or the Russians come calling."

"The Rangers was a brotherhood."

"But then they loaned you to covert ops for one of the alphabets. Those feckers left you for dead in a country ours denied sending you to."

"Ours?" he asks.

"I'm a U.S. citizen." I still have my Irish citizenship too.

"I won't ask how you know all that."

"Even if you were already mobbed up, I wouldn't tell you." It's a warning.

We keep secrets for the good of the clan. There are things I know that even Brogan doesn't.

He thinks there are things he knows that I don't. I let him live with his illusions.

"The only question that matters right now, is: do you want to earn that *skean*?"

Wraith's jaw flexes and he looks down at the knife again. "I was freelance for a reason."

"Because you didn't have brothers you could trust."

"How do I know I can trust you?"

"That's what training and initiation is for." Trust has to be built both ways.

He slides the *skean* into its leather sheath and hands it to me. "I'll earn it."

"I never doubted it but remember, when you fucked up in the Army, your CO made you do pushups until you puked or passed out. If you fuck up with us, that'll feel like child's play."

He doesn't look worried. I'd be disappointed if he did.

"And if you betray us, I'll put a bullet through your brain myself."

Wraith's mouth twitches again. "I would expect no less."

"Tell me about Darakov," I order.

Wraith is silent for several long seconds and I let him make up his mind.

Either he's loyal to us, or he's loyal to the man who paid for his services but refused him the distinction of brother.

"He wants the weapon prototype. He thinks you got it after a demo that went bad last year."

"He's right."

"He found the assistant that worked with the engineer who designed it. Darakov thinks he can get the electric gun working."

"That's what he called it? An electric gun?" Not a rail gun. Not a ghost gun.

"Yes. He said, it's like a taser, but it shoots an electric bullet with enough charge to stop the heart."

That is *not* the base design of the whisper gun, even before Hex got her hands on the schematics.

"That's what the assistant told him?" It doesn't sound like Darakov was at the demonstration.

"I guess."

"What's the assistant's name?"

"Denis."

"No surname?" I press.

"He never used one in my hearing." Wraith wipes his face with the bottom of his t-shirt. "The only other thing I know about the Russian is that he's trying to arrange a marriage with the daughter of one of the Northside Dublin Mob's leaders, but she's disappeared."

"He doesn't know where she is?" That could be useful.

"No. He tried to hire me to find her."

"You refused."

"If she ran, she had her reasons."

Aye. Dierdre wanted to come after me.

Even so, keeping her here will use Darakov's resources. A strategic positive.

"Why does he want to marry her?" I ask.

"He wants an heir, but negotiating the marriage alliance gave him the chance to get information he wanted."

Bleedin' feckin' hell.

Did my da tell Darakov about the Bunker?

And Brogan is probably the bigmouth who told Kelly about the Bunker. Or at least the tunnels used to hide Shaughnessy mob soldiers back in the day.

On the positive side, it sounds like Darakov's intel is both vague and inaccurate. He has no idea how close to production on the Vanta we are.

"Did your intel include information on the Bunker, or just the tunnels?" I ask.

"The tunnels. He assumed if you had tunnels under the city, you had storerooms too."

Gjon's comment that Darakov wanted the whisper gun prototype and anything stored with it makes more sense now.

He doesn't know about the lab.

And because of the way we played with Gjon's brain, he doesn't know any more about the Bunker than he did before sending a team in to steal from us.

CHAPTER THIRTY-ONE

Labor Day Ambush

KARA

The air smells like barbecue, the beach, and the sweet but dying blooms of the last of the summer roses.

The familiar scents of the annual Labor Day picnic on the grounds of the Shaughnessy mansion.

A holiday arguably bigger than Christmas for us, Labor Day is the one time a year that the entire Shaughnessy mob congregates.

Soldiers. Wives. Children.

Anyone and everyone connected to our clan's syndicate comes to rub elbows with the boss and his family.

Even Fiona and Zoey shared our picnic blanket to eat before my sister disappeared into the boathouse, locked against entry for anyone without the code for the door.

Heavily involved in the unions, especially the Longshoremen's Association, the connection between the mob and Labor Day goes back to the beginning.

Shaughnessy mobsters were at that first parade in 1882, organized by the Central Labor Union. We played our part in it becoming a federal holiday a little over a decade later after the Pullman strike.

To hear my father tell it, Labor Day exists because of the Irish mob. But then he also claims that Halloween started in Ireland, which okay...there are definite roots in the ancient Celtic festival of Samhain.

But according to Brogan Shaughnessy, if it's something good, it probably started with the Irish.

Laughter rolls across the lawn like music, carried on the breeze as children who see each other once a year chase one another through the grass and splash together in the pool.

I sit on a picnic blanket with my knees bent, my feet to one side, like the mob princess I've been trained to be. His long legs stretched out, his sexy feet bare, Mick sits beside me, looking relaxed.

We made love for the first time in over a week this morning. I needed his nearness and reached out for him. He accepted my tiny overture with a voracious hunger that left me spent and feeling much more relaxed.

He's in a better mood than he's been in days. And so am I.

Fitz races past with the twin sons of one of our dock workers, his smile full of mischief.

"Watch, da!" he crows as he leaps over a diaper bag on a nearby blanket.

The entire first level of the yard at the back of the house is filled with blankets and lawn chairs for the older family members. The lawn between the pool and the ocean is set up for badminton, bocce ball (the set gifted for the celebration by Miceli) and giant yard pong.

Teens are swimming off the dock and lounging on the shore. Splashing children have pretty much taken over the pool, that has two lifeguards on duty.

Enoch grins at me as he runs by too, clearly enjoying his first Labor Day.

According to Hope, the AOG didn't celebrate national holidays. Or Christmas. And the way they celebrated religious ones wasn't intended to give children joy and a sense of belonging.

Easter was a time to teach them about the physical and emotional sacrifice necessary to be a *good* Christian. The rhetoric of religious nationalism was shoved down Enoch and Esther's throats from infancy.

Hope's too for that matter.

But she broke away from the brain-washing and did her best to mitigate it with her children.

She's pretty amazing and I think maybe I should tell her that. From one mom to another.

Sitting with my father, on a picnic blanket smack dab in the center of the revelers, Hope's fairly glowing with happiness. Though I'm not sure if it's caused by the holiday or the fact my father has barely let her out of his sight since they got back from London the day before yesterday.

Moma (who insists she's not old enough for a lawn chair) is sitting with them. So is Dierdre, for which I am silently but utterly grateful. When she chose sitting with the boss over sharing our blanket, my day turned brighter for sure.

That she is attempting to appear as the hostess of the event isn't lost on anyone. That no one else sees her that way is entirely lost on her.

Róise's fiancé, Miceli, started out sitting with us, but after eating, he went to talk business with my father. I was surprised, but not in the least unhappy, when Mick didn't opt to join them.

Fitz collapses on the blanket in front of me and his dad, barely missing Róise' feet. "Can I have another cookie?"

Reaching out to wipe at the chocolate smudged across his cheek, I ask, "How many have you had?"

He makes a face, jerking away from my hand. "Mom!"

The title's new and it's not at my instigation. Dierdre-bloody-Kelly told Fitz that big boys don't call their mams mommy. When asked for his opinion by our son over-the-moon excited about starting *big boy* first grade, my clearly distracted husband agreed.

When I told him later I didn't appreciate it, Mick didn't even remember the discussion. But he pointed out that at some point Fitz was bound to stop using *mommy*.

Which is true, if not the point.

The point was that Mick had taken Dierdre's side over mine. Which I was smart enough not to bring up.

Because Mick seems to be really sensitive to anything that might indicate I'm jealous lately. He's not mean about it, but he goes out of his way to tell me I have nothing to be jealous about.

Like that has helped any woman ever to feel more secure in her relationship.

Anyway, I told Fitz that we might be Irish but we're not from Ireland. If he wants to call me something besides mommy, he can use *mom* like I did with my mother.

I won that battle at least.

"How many?" I ask again and wait for Fitz to answer.

He shrugs. "Four. Maybe five."

"Which is it?" Mick hands Fitz his water bottle.

Our son takes a drink and then sighs. "Five, I guess."

He looks so woebegone, I have to hide a smile.

Mick looks at me, his lips quirking too. "Well? What do you say, *mom*?"

"One more, but that is it." My stern tone could use some work, but it *is* a picnic.

Fitz takes off again, yelling for Enoch to race him, and my heart squeezes watching the two of them rush toward the food tables set up on the terrace.

Pure joy, tangled in a moment.

"You're such a good mom," Róise says with a grin.

Speaking of glowing. In her signature pink, my cousin is the epitome of happy bride-to-be.

Mick drawls, "She is that."

Warmth rushes into my cheeks. You'd think I'd stop blushing at my husband's compliments after seven years of marriage.

"Thanks." I smile at them both. "I try."

"You try so hard to be good at everything you do. Maybe too hard." Róise's words carry meaning I don't want to get into right now.

I'm enjoying myself.

"How are the wedding plans going?" I ask, to change the subject.

"You'd be better off asking *moma* or Aria. Not that I don't have opinions, but those two are operating on a single fixed track and it's all about the wedding."

"*Moma* was the same with my wedding." And back then, a completely overwhelmed eighteen-year-old, I hadn't minded a bit.

"She's obsessed. *Moma* even scoured Pinterest for the latest wedding trends. Aria was not impressed with the 'shades of brown' wedding idea." Róise laughs.

"I know, she told me about the 'love story notes' idea, but that doesn't really work for an alliance wedding does it? It's not like Mick and I had a meet-cute to share with our guests and yours with Miceli isn't exactly family friendly." I wink at my cousin.

This time her laughter is pure Róise wicked.

I grin at her. "You look happy."

There's no question that Róise and her mafioso are deeply in love, regardless of what brought them together.

"I am. It doesn't feel real."

"Three weeks until you're a De Luca." I waggle my eyebrows at her. "You ready?"

"More than. If you believe Miceli, I'm already a De Luca at heart."

"That's really sweet."

"Don't let him hear you call him that," Róise says with a laugh.

"How did the fitting with *moma's* dress go?" I ask.

I'm Róise's matron-of-honor, but we didn't have to go wedding dress shopping because she wants to wear our grandmother's dress.

My grandfather insisted I wear a gown designed by a big name fashion house. *Moma* made sure shamrocks were embroidered around the hem in matching white thread, so you had to really look to see them. But they were there.

She also made sure I had a tiny horseshoe nestled amidst the elegant roses in my bouquet. There'd been no sixpence in my shoe, but I'm determined that Róise has one.

We Irish mob princesses need all the luck we can get with our marriages.

Later, when everyone is visiting with everyone else, I go to check on Fiona in the Boathouse.

I don't find my sister, but an unpleasantly familiar voice lets me know I'm not alone.

"Kara." Dierdre stands in the open doorway, blocking the sun and my exit.

I knew I should have pulled the door shut behind me. "Hello, Dierdre. Are you enjoying yourself?"

"Yes. Your da really goes in for American Labor Day. My da and Micky's celebrate *Lá an Lucht Oibre* of course, but not with so much fanfare."

"It's an important day for our family."

"I'm sure. It really emphasizes how crucial heritage and family are for the Shaughnessy Mob."

I nod.

Glossy black hair, smooth despite spending the last couple of hours outside subject to the breeze off the ocean, she's dressed in a royal blue romper. The shorts show off her long legs and her sandals reveal perfectly painted toenails.

I'm wearing my favorite summer outfit: palazzo pants with a halter top. And somehow what usually feels cool and sophisticated, not to mention flattering to my generous curves, feels understated and almost frumpy.

No. Stop thinking like that. Mick's eyes didn't read frumpy when he looked at you earlier. They said he'd like to take you inside and do wicked things with you.

My inner cheerleader has good intentions, but my outer mob wife is facing off with my husband's ex-lover and wearing insecurity like cheap perfume.

"You play such an important role in this tradition, don't you?" Dierdre asks, false sweetness saturating her tone.

"We all do."

"But you especially..." She lets her voice trail off and gives me a look of pity. "What you had to sacrifice to guarantee an heir to your father."

My world tilts. I suck in a breath, but I feel like the oxygen isn't reaching my head.

Thoughts racing, I ask, "What do you mean?"

"It must have been so hard. A virgin undergoing IVF to guarantee a boy baby." She shakes her head, like she feels sorry for me.

I shake *my* head, trying to clear it. There's no way she can know this. No way, except...

Mick told her?

My heartbeat is a roar in my ears.

Mick told Dierdre something I've never even shared with my cousin or sister?

I want to scream.

I want to grab Dierdre by the hair and throw her off the dock in the cold water of the bay. After I kick her.

But most of all? I want to slap my husband right in his loose-lipped mouth.

"Oh..." She affects surprised concern. "Should I not have let you know that Mick told me?"

I grit my teeth to keep the words in that want out so desperately.

Dierdre's mouth thins. She's not getting the response she wants.

I latch onto that and use the knowledge to keep my perfect mob princess façade in place.

"I just wanted to tell you how much I admire your willingness to sacrifice for the sake of your family's heritage." She reaches toward me like she's going to touch my arm. "I don't know if I would have been so willing to go months without having sex with my husband."

I step back. "I don't know what you thought to accomplish by bringing up the past, but it's not to tell me how much you admire me."

"But—"

Putting my hand up, palm out, I shake my head. "Stop, Dierdre. There's no audience to play to here. It's just me and you and you have to know I'm fully aware of what a cold-hearted bitch you are."

Her eyes widen with shock, then narrow. "The kitten has claws, I see."

"I'm no kitten and you? *You're not anything*. Nothing to Mick. Nothing to me." I say the words like they are true, no matter how much I doubt them personally.

"I'm the woman Micky loves. He left me for a chance at being a boss, but don't kid yourself. He still wants me and I'm more than willing."

Mick *does not* love her. He can't. "If my husband loved you, he never would have left Ireland. He's not that weak or grasping."

"You keep telling yourself that. But now that he has Fitz, he doesn't need you anymore. When he files for divorce, don't forget I told you so."

Her words about Fitz are too much a reflection of my own fears, it's all I can do not to throw up.

But I still manage to say in an even tone, "Mick is not divorcing me."

"Go ahead and bury your head in the sand while I rebuild my relationship with the only man I want. And, Kara? What I want, I get."

"Not my husband." The words ring hollow inside me, but they sound confident and sure.

And that's all that matters.

"We'll see." Dierdre spins on her heel and walks back out into the sunshine.

While my heart dives into the frozen tundra of winter.

CHAPTER THIRTY-TWO

The Boathouse Reckoning

MICK

Kara comes back from checking on her sister with her spark missing.

What did Fiona say to her?

I force myself to wait to find out, to fix whatever it is, until the party ends.

The Labor Day guests are gone when I ask my wife if she wants to walk on the beach with me.

"Come for a walk with me." I put out my hand, expecting Kara to take it.

Fitz is spending the night with Enoch, watched over by a full complement of bodyguards.

I've given security their instructions to sweep every room, closet and nook of the mansion to make sure it's clear of revelers. The outdoor area has already been swept and the only people left are the cleanup crew.

My wife looks at my hand like it's a snake ready to strike. "A walk? Why?"

"Because I want to." Realizing that isn't exactly romantic, I add. "So, we can talk."

Kara likes talking. She likes romance. Which is why I try, even though it is not natural for a man like me.

More since I noticed the way she watches Miceli with Róise than before.

No Italian mafioso is going to make my wife think her Irish mobster isn't as good of a husband.

Instead of the soft look I'm expecting, Kara's expression goes frosty. "About the divorce you want so you can be with your first love? No thanks."

She turns to go and I'm so shocked by her words it takes me a second to reach out and grab her. Her body tenses when I touch her.

"What the hell do you mean?"

Kara yanks away from me and, not wanting to hurt her, I allow it. But then I swiftly step forward and swing her up into my arms.

She crosses her arms over her gorgeous tits, her expression mutinous. "Don't pretend like you don't know."

"How about *you* pretend like I don't know and tell me." It sounds reasonable to me.

Kara doesn't think so and tries to twist out of my arms. The daft woman is going to fall and break something.

I tighten my hold and start walking toward the boathouse. We need privacy and I still want to take her for a *romantic* walk on the beach.

My mouth twists at the thought. But I remember how impressed Kara was when Miceli did that with Róise.

"You told her. I can't believe you told her."

"I told who? What?" I pick up my pace until I'm jogging.

Something is going on with my wife and I need to figure out what.

When we reach the boathouse, I key in the code and let us in. Overhead lights triggered by the motion sensor go on.

Convenient for us when we want to use the boathouse at night and an additional security measure against anyone gaining entry to the property from it.

I installed them after my wife and her cousin snuck off the property to go into the City to celebrate Róise's 21st birthday with some friends.

They reveal the hurt and anger shimmering in my wife's hazel eyes.

Confused by what could have caused it, I carry her to one of the oversized armchairs and sit down, keeping her firmly in my lap.

"Now, explain please."

"You told Dierdre about the IVF."

Shite.

"No, *a stór*, I did not."

"Then how did she find out?" Kara demands belligerently.

I sigh. "She read the contract."

"How?"

"My guess is she broke into her father's safe."

"She had no right."

"I agree. I'll tell my father they need to increase security." No way should Dierdre have access to contracts.

As a woman who will most likely marry outside the Northside Dublin Syndicate, allowing her access to sensitive intel is unacceptable.

I've benefitted from that weakness in their security in the past when she shared what she learned with me. But they need to shore it up now, especially if she's going to marry into the Russian bratva.

Kara shifts on my lap and my body has a predictable reaction, but her demeanor says that's not on.

Not yet, anyway.

"She said you told her."

"She's stirring trouble."

"Then send her home."

"You know I can't do that. The Northies are our allies. Your father promised Dierdre protection."

There's the additional benefit of pumping Dierdre for information. We've already got her phone cloned and have combed through her phone logs and texts.

She's been texting with Ilya. Or more accurately, he's been texting her.

She engages. Flirtatiously. But noncommittally.

But like any smart mob princess, she has her locations services disabled on it. So, he's not finding her that way.

So far, she hasn't shared anything about us she shouldn't.

But I wonder if the same is true for her father or mine. Just because I didn't know about the Bunker before I came to New York, doesn't mean they didn't. Making them the most likely source of Ilya's information regarding it.

I don't think my father would knowingly give that information to Ilya, but we're not the only ones with effective drugs for interrogation.

And after discovering Brogan told my da about Kara's jealousy after Fitz's birth, I'm not sure that generation is nearly as circumspect as they need to be.

"Then send her to one of *our* safehouses. That would fulfill the terms of the alliance."

"If she wasn't the daughter of one of the mob's leaders, it would. But she's is and it won't." Kara knows this.

But her irrationality is understandable given the provocation.

"I'll speak to Dierdre and tell her not to bring it up to you again."

"Don't you dare!" Kara glares at me, fire and brimstone in her eyes. "You're not going to let her know she got to me. Not after I managed to keep my cool and not toss her in the bay by her hair."

The image of my sweet wife doing something so unproper and violent makes me chuckle.

She's not amused though.

Swallowing the urge to keep laughing, I kiss the corner of her mouth, then her temple, and finally her cheek. "I don't want a divorce. I told you, I will never let you go."

"She said she gets what she wants."

"Not me," I assure my wife. "I belong to you as surely as you belong to me."

"Do you mean that?" Kara asks, like there can be any doubt.

"Aye."

"What would you do if another man told you he intended to take me away from you?"

I don't even have to pause to think. "Kill him. Slowly."

"So, you won't mind if I kill your ex-girlfriend."

"I'll help you hide the body," I tease.

As if my gentle wife would ever kill anyone.

"I'll hold you to that."

"As long as you let me hold you."

She relaxes against me and my body takes that as the signal to prove my claim of mutual ownership.

My mouth covers hers and the kiss goes incendiary from one heartbeat to the next.

I have her naked and straddling my still jean covered thighs so fast, even I'm not sure how it happens.

Kara doesn't mind, giving her body to me with the generosity I crave and will never be able to live without.

Her perfect nipples are already swollen and turgid, dark as berries from her arousal.

Arousal that is teasing my nostrils and calling to the primal urge to fuck and conquer. The tantalizing fragrance of her body's lubrication, along with the scent of her skin.

I lean down and kiss each gorgeous peak, first softly with my lips closed. Left breast. Right breast. Then again with my lips parted, breathing hot air against the sensitive flesh. And once more with a swirl of my tongue, reveling in the taste of her skin as much as its petal softness. Finally I let myself taste her with carnal intensity, gently tugging with my teeth before sucking her nipple into my mouth.

She's squirming and moaning before I move onto her other delicious tit.

These baps are mine.

She knows it. And I know it.

She groans and presses herself against my mouth.

No more holding back. No more denial of the truth.

We belong to each other.

The invitation is too sweetly given to ignore. I pull back, taking her nipple between my teeth and teasing it with the tip of my tongue.

"Stop teasing me, Michael! You know what I need."

She needs to come.

But not yet.

She's so sensitive here. After giving birth to Fitz, that sensitivity only increased. Making her climax from nipple stimulation alone isn't something I always have the patience for.

But when I do, it is always worth it.

For both of us.

"You are so perfect for me, *mo chuisle*."

Whimpering, her breathing grows increasingly erratic.

I gently nip her swollen berry.

She arches up, making her pillowy softness indent against my mouth. "Oh, yesssss..."

I pull her nipple and the surrounding aureole completely into my mouth and start suckling hard.

Incoherent pleas fall from her lips, her fingers tunnel into my hair and yank. Not to get me away, but because she needs something to hold onto.

Concentrating all my expertise and knowledge of my wife and her responses, I move from one delicious tit to the other, savoring each over and over again.

Pushing her toward completion, but not letting her come.

Not yet.

She writhes in my lap, rubbing the apex of her thighs against my steel hard cock, unconsciously pleasuring us both.

Primitive need holds me back from giving her my fingers.

Sliding my hands over her backside, I press them between her fleshy cheeks, touching the sensitive rosebud.

She goes wild against me.

Someday, I'm going to claim this tight little hole, like I've claimed the rest of her. I don't know what holds me back.

A harsh laugh sounds inside my head, mocking me.

I know all right.

If I fuck her ass, she'll see the part of me that is more monster than man. The brutal need I hold in check every time we make love.

Just like I hold it back now. But I let my fingertip press, barely breaching her tight sphincter.

My wife is so responsive, incredibly beautiful in her passion.

How could she think for a second I want another woman?

There is no other woman.

They do not exist to me.

Only her. My Kara.

The pulse of my beating heart.

She writhes, alternately pulling my hair and pushing my head against her creamy curves.

"Michael! Please. It's too much."

A dark laugh rumbles in my chest and I suckle harder.

"No." An agonized groan. "Yes." She cries out, "Don't stop. Oh, harder, please, Michael, just a little harder."

I give her what she wants and when her body bows in ecstasy, I bite down more firmly on the tender bud in my mouth while releasing the hold on my most basic instincts enough to press my finger into her ass to the first knuckle.

She screams and comes with one body-racking shudder after another, while I keep stimulating her breasts and she dry humps me until I come in my pants for the first time since she got pregnant with Fitz.

I shout loud enough to wake the dead and she finally goes limp, slumping against me.

I pull her as close to my body as I can. "Mine."

"It goes both ways, Mick." She nuzzles into my neck.

Yes. It does.

CHAPTER THIRTY-THREE

Stage—Managed Affection

KARA

One of the best things about having a birthday in early September is that it means my father doesn't throw a huge party, doing syndicate business under the guise of family *bon homme*.

Too close to Labor Day, my birthday falling on the 10th is usually a nonevent.

Only not this year.

For some reason, my father decided his oldest daughter's 25th birthday requires over-the-top fanfare and decided to throw me a surprise party.

At Carnegie Hall.

Although, whatever reasons Brogan has for this gathering, I'm sure they have nothing to do with celebrating my birth.

Not in my family.

Big parties like this? Are always about the mob. The Labor Day picnic? A statement about mob unity and the power we wield in the unions.

It's always about my father's power and wealth. A chance to rub elbows with the people he knows and has access to and for everyone to see him doing it.

Showing off.

He doesn't brag. He considers *flahing* a sign of conceit and insecurity, but Brogan doesn't have to brag when everything around him is designed to *show* his superiority.

If my father wants to make a statement about his strength, security will be obvious and intimidating in their dark ops uniforms, weapons visible. If he wants people to see his sophistication and wealth, our men dress in suits and keep their guns under their jackets.

Today, security is in suits. Probably to impress the Italians. The mafia my cousin, Róise, will be marrying into at the end of this month are more formal than us and my father doesn't like to be shown up.

The De Lucas threw Róise's 21st birthday party on the VIP floor of an exclusive club in Manhattan.

Boss Shauhnessy has to go one better, of course.

So, we're celebrating *my* birthday with 200 of my not-so-nearest-and-dearest at Carnegie Hall. In the Weill Music Room, to be exact. Complete with a world-renowned concert pianist playing for the guests before dinner is served.

Her music almost makes this dog and pony show worth it. Because the pianist is one of my favorite musicians. I wonder if my father knows that?

Maybe Mick told him.

No matter how little time Mick spends with me, it would be hard for my husband to miss her prominence in my music collection. I have all of her albums. In vinyl *and* CDs because streaming services change.

Something flutters in my stomach at the thought of Mick making this happen, but only for a moment. Then I shut down those feelings hard.

You're way past getting butterflies over small things that may, or may not, mean Mick cares about you, Kara. You're too smart for that.

I started out as his means to an end. Then we discovered volcanic passion between us, but that's not affection. Mick likes me, but he doesn't love me and it's not going to suddenly happen after seven years of marriage.

"Mommy, open my present to you." Fitz tugs on the skirt of my Lela Rose floral embroidered midi dress.

Elegant and sleeveless, with a full skirt, the green dress that brings out the green in my hazel eyes has been tailored to fit my curvy frame to perfection.

The scoop neckline does amazing things for *the girls* and I can't help noticing how many times my husband's gaze has strayed to my cleavage since I got dressed for the party.

He's been insatiable since our little break from sex before Labor Day, coming home in time to tuck Fitz into bed and then taking me to ours for hours upon hours of mind melting sex.

I turn to my son with a smile. "I'm not opening gifts here, *mo stóirín*. I'll do it when it's just us at home."

"Please, mom." Green eyes, so like his dad's stare back at me imploringly. "Grandda said I could bring it."

Translated: I have permission to open the gift here.

Probably because his grandda wants a photo op, or something. I look around and sure enough, there's a photographer with his camera trained on me and Fitz.

Ignoring the way my stomach sours at even my young son giving me a birthday gift becoming a PR prop, I reach for the small box wrapped with lots of tape and uneven seams.

Fitz goes up on his toes and breathes excitedly over my shoulder. "I wrapped it myself."

My sweet boy. The best part of me and the mobster I married.

"You did a great job," I tell him. "It's almost too pretty to open."

"Mom." Fitz draws the words out over three long syllables.

With forced grin and wink, I tear away the wrapping paper to reveal a box the same emerald green as Mick's eyes. It's embossed in gold with the store's name.

A frisson of excitement goes through me. Every piece of the Irish jeweler's collection is individually designed and handmade, making whatever is inside mine alone.

I do nothing to suppress my gasp of delight when I open the lid. A delicate, bolo style, tree of life bracelet is nestled on the satin. Silver glints brightly against a fabric that is such a dark green it is almost black.

I run my fingers reverently over the bracelet. "I love it."

"Knew you would," he crows. "Da thought you'd want something with diamonds."

Fitz knows me better than his father.

Okay, to be fair, Mick probably wasn't thinking about what I would like. He'd be focused on adding jewelry to my collection of pieces that exhibit my wealth and standing. Thereby his own and that of my father.

"Your da already took care of that." I touch the pear-shaped green sapphire of perfect color and clarity sitting against my chest an inch above my cleavage.

This year's gift is going to be one of my favorite pieces. Not because of the size of the sapphire pendant, or the round cut diamonds and princess cut green sapphires of impeccable quality used in the setting.

But because the setting from which the pear-shaped sapphire dangles is made up of delicate leaves and tiny branches. Beautiful, it reflects my love for nature, despite my inner computer geek.

I would be feeling treasured and seen if not for the fact that Dierdre is also sporting a new necklace given to her by Mick.

He gave it to her the day after Labor Day. It's all I can do not to grimace at the memory.

"Oh, Micky, thank you. It's perfect!" Dierdre holds up a silver chain with a four-leaf clover charm nestled next to a medallion of St. Michael. "It's just like the one I lost."

Lost? She probably threw it away and then dropped enough hints my husband bought her a replacement.

Jealousy takes another swipe at my heart. In the past, it would have been a cut deep enough to draw blood. But not today.

Whatever my marriage was, or could have become, it's not. And I've finally accepted that fact.

If we had a different relationship, I would have told him about college and my therapist. If things were different between us, he would have told me he knew.

Mick and I are stuck together and we both have to make the best of it, but my heart is no longer on offer.

Sex, yes. Emotions, no.

That's my new mantra.

"You keep your 'mportant stuff in that box with the tree carved on the top," Fitz says, breaking into my thoughts. "And you're the most important to me."

My heart bursts with love, silly emotional tears pricking my eyes. "Thank you, Fitzy."

Pulling him in for a tight hug, the moisture in my eyes almost spills over when he hugs me back just as tightly. Getting hugs like this from him is pretty hit-and-miss these days.

I'm struggling to believe he's already in first grade. And loving it.

"Why don't you help your mam put the bracelet on?" Mick's deep, rich voice washes over me as his warm hand lands on my bare shoulder.

My heart rate surges a my nipples bead with inappropriate anticipation. Because emotions aside, my husband is my sexual catnip.

Utterly and totally irresistible.

I accepted that when I chose to make love to him again after the debacle of him leaving me to take Dierdre to dinner.

His forefinger slides over my collarbone, sending a shiver of arousal through me I try my best to hide. The possessive press of his thumb against my nape makes that almost impossible though.

I want to shrug off his touch almost as much as I want him to move those skilled fingers just a little lower. Neither would be acceptable right now.

What I can do is lean forward to allow Fitz to help me put on the bracelet and hope my husband gets the hint.

But Mick's hand only shifts so he's cupping the back of my neck in an even more possessive hold.

"What a pretty bracelet." Dierdre's voice surprisingly close grates against my ears.

I didn't notice her get up from the table she's sitting at with guests who are not family.

My shoulders go rigid, but I don't let the smile slip off my face. "Isn't it? My son has excellent taste."

"So does your husband." Dierdre taps the medal for St. Michael she hasn't taken off since Mick gave it to her.

"I have to agree," my father's voice booms. "He had the good taste to marry my daughter."

The look he gives Dierdre makes the gloating smile slip right off her face.

"Aye, there's no denying Kara is the perfect wife for me and I'm lucky to have her."

My stupid heart skips a beat.

Even knowing neither man means anything real by his words, for just a second I let myself wallow in the fantasy of being appreciated.

Treasured.

But reality's spotlight dissipates the glow of fantasy. Neither Mick, nor my father said what they did because they care about me, or how Dierdre's words affect me.

They care how her words impact the people around us. They're doing what they always do: protecting the image of the Shaughnessy Mob and our family.

It wouldn't do for it to look like my husband was open to Dierdre's blatant fascination with him.

Regardless of whether he is, or not.

His words say one thing and that pendant around her neck says another.

CHAPTER THIRTY-FOUR

Anger Management Mob Style

MICK

The mats in the training room reek of sweat and industrial cleaner. Brice's crew just finished their morning training session.

Rory's guys are filtering in because their time on the mats starts soon.

It will have to wait.

I need to burn off some anger before I start killing people. Dierdre is at the top of my list, but we need her for intel on Darakov.

Besnik and his people are getting on my nerves too.

Because they're still breathing.

Bleedin' politics.

"Wraith!" Training my new recruit is the perfect way to channel some of that aggression.

Kieran stops and turns toward me. He's sweaty, but he doesn't look tired. Good.

"You up for some one-on-one?" It's a question, but we both know there's only one right answer.

He nods, giving it.

Brice stops and turns to watch, the rest of his crew following suit. Our soldiers take up positions along the wall to watch.

Brice tosses a roll of athletic tape to me and Rory gets one for Wraith. We wrap our wrists and hands in silence.

"Gloves?" Brice asks.

I nod.

We don't use boxing gloves in training, but open-fingered ones like MMA fighters. They protect our hands enough that we don't usually break bones, but allow us to grapple and strike like we would in a fight with a real enemy.

Sometimes, I forego the gloves, but the fury that burns deep inside me is too close to the surface. I want to expend some of it, not kill my new recruit.

Brice hands me a pair of black MMA gloves. "Don't kill the new guy boss. I like him."

"He barely talks."

My lieutenant secures and tightens the glove on my right hand. "That's why I like him."

Rory helps Wraith and we're both gloved and ready to go.

I shake out my shoulders. "We go full contact, but no injuries that'll keep you out of commission."

Wraith circles me the moment I raise my fists.

He's smart and doesn't lunge. He watches, gauging my moves and speed as I warm up.

"You ever train in Krav Maga?" I ask.

He shrugs. "Some."

"Show me."

He moves first and fast, an efficient strike aimed at my ribs. I block, counter with an elbow feint and step into his guard.

He doesn't flinch.

Good. He knows that pain's part of the process and isn't trying to avoid it.

This might be the fight I need.

We trade blows, measured at first, then harder. He lands a hit to my jaw that snaps my head back.

Adrenaline surges and I grin at him through the sting. "That the best you got, fecker?"

Wraith doesn't waste his breath taunting me back. We circle again. The silence stretches, punctuated only by breath and movement.

Strike. Block. Feint. Hit. Repeat.

It's a lethal dance we both know the moves to. He's good enough that I start to release some of the frustration riding me like a pissed off jockey.

The more Kara pulls away, the harder it is to hide the monster inside. The need to stake a claim she cannot deny gets stronger with every beat of my heart.

She's upset about the St. Michael's medallion I gave Dierdre. What she doesn't know and I'm not about to tell her because it's mob business, is that I'm the one who *lost* the necklace.

I stole it and replaced it with one with a tracker in it. We need to know where Dierdre is going when she and her bodyguards leave the mansion.

I could have put the tracker on her necklace before *finding* it, but I knew if I gave Dierdre something new, she'd wear it every day to irritate my wife.

What I didn't expect was for Kara to be upset by it. We belong to each other on such an elemental level, Dierdre isn't even a buzzing fly in our life.

How does my sweet addiction not realize that?

I get the right angle and kick the back of Wraith's thigh.

He goes down to his knees, but he's up again a second later.

Punch. Kick. Feint. Block. Hit.

We're pretty feckin' evenly matched until I let the rage out.

Kara should know I have zero bleedin' interest in my ex. Even if she struggles to believe me, and that just pisses me off. I don't lie to Kara.

I withhold, but I never lie to her. Like she doesn't lie to me.

But even if for some feckin' reason I don't understand, she's decided she can't trust my word –

Wraith gets a solid punch into my solar plexus.

Pain explodes along my nerve endings and I welcome it.

This is what I need.

Not nearly as strong as the intensity of my need for Kara, but necessary to keep the façade in place.

The underboss who is only brutal some of the time.

How can my wife not realize there is no room for another woman's breath, much less her body in my life?

A sharp whistle pierces the air, bringing me back to the moment.

I've got my arm around Wraith's throat and he's choking out. He's not giving the signal for surrender though.

I let him go anyway and he falls to his knees.

There's respect in the other soldier's eyes. Not for me. That's always there along with a good dose of fear for some of them.

But for Wraith.

Kieran Lleshi is the only man in this room, besides my lieutenants, that has lasted longer than five minutes against me.

"And that, gentlemen, is how you fight." I walk out of the gym to the sound of my soldiers congratulating Wraith.

It's time to feed my addiction.

Kara's not expecting me. Brogan is. But his office isn't where I'm headed.

I need to see my wife. Confirm she's still there.

I pull up the camera feed from inside our place and find her in the bedroom working on the computer.

Classes started the day after her birthday. Odds are good she's studying this time.

I'm about to interrupt her concentration. Fitz is in school until 2:45. That means we have the apartment all to ourselves.

No interruptions.

I don't bother taking a shower before getting into my car and heading back to the mansion. Maybe I can convince my wife to take one with me.

Kara is more than willing to be distracted, but there's something different about our sex now. She's holding part of herself back from me.

That place I need to live inside of her is closed to me and no amount of pleasure and wild passion will open it

We're both getting dressed and I'm about to suggest another swimming lesson in the bay with Fitz, when my phone buzzes.

It's Brice.

Feckin' hell.

I have to take it.

"Yeah?" I shove an earbud in my ear and slide the phone into the pocket of my suite jacket.

Kara looks up from putting on her sandals. She doesn't ask who it is. That's not how it works in the mob.

But she watches me.

"Dierdre's on the move."

"Give me a second." I mute myself. Not something I usually do.

Before the debacle of leaving Kara to go to dinner with Dierdre after making love, I would have just walked out of the room.

Leaning down, I kiss my wife. "I have to go. I'll see you at dinner."

She nods, her eyes going wide, but doesn't say anything.

"We good?" I ask.

Now those pretty hazel eyes narrow. "Why wouldn't I be?"

I'm smart enough not to hazard an answer to that question. Instead, I kiss her again. This time I let it last and plunder her mouth with my tongue until she relaxes into me.

"We're good." It's a statement this time.

She nods like it was a question again.

And I smile.

She smiles back.

I have to force myself to walk out of our bedroom, going back to my phone call. "Where is she headed?"

"Could be Queens. Could be Manhattan. Both are east."

"Do we have someone on her?" I exit the apartment and give the guards on the door a death glare. "Keep my wife safe."

The men say, "Yes, sir," in unison.

"You worried about something happening to Kara?" Brice asks.

"We've got a feckin' viper in our bleedin' nest and a Russian with a hardon for our new gun in communication with her. What do you think?"

"Kara has a detail on her at all times," Brice reminds me. "Even within the mansion."

"I know. I assigned them." But shite happens.

"She'll be fine, boss."

"I wouldn't be walking away if I didn't believe that." Doesn't mean I like leaving her though.

"Dierdre is on the Long Island Expressway."

"Do we have someone tailing her?"

"Kieran and Sean."

"Part of Wraith's training?" I ask.

"Not that he needs much of it. Once he learns how to work within our power structure rather than the military, or as an independent contractor he'll be ready to take the oath."

"You're that sure of him?"

"When have you ever been wrong about a recruit?" He sounds resigned to losing a very good bottle of whiskey.

"You'd think you'd know better than to bet against me."

"Got to keep you on your toes, boss. You need to be challenged now and again."

He's not wrong. Part of being a good leader is having smart people at your back. Brice, Rory and Conor are intelligent and all three of them have the balls to question me when I need it.

I'm betting Wraith will fall in that category too. He's not afraid of punishment or pain. That soldier will give his loyalty because he chooses to, not because he's been intimidated into making a vow.

The strongest syndicates are made up of men like him.

I monitor the Dierdre situation from my office as I go over the contract Brogan negotiated in London and put the terms into the client dossier for the other company.

My phone buzzes.

I tap the side of my earbud to answer. "It's a decent deal."

"Of course it is. I negotiated it." Brogan's arrogance doesn't faze me.

"You didn't need me there after all." Am I rubbing it in to press the point home?

Yes.

He grunts. "Travel is part of your job as my underboss."

"Some can't be avoided, but from now on, I want to minimize my trips away from my family."

"You could have seen your family if you'd gone to London."

My wife and son are the only family that matters to me. "Did you meet with the Northies then?"

"Yes. Brian and Oisín seem genuinely worried about Dierdre's safety. They offered a favor in return for keeping her safe."

"She's in contact with Darakov."

"That's not a surprise if they're trying to negotiate a marriage alliance. Her mam is already making wedding plans."

"She'll have to cancel them. An alliance between the Northies and Darakov isn't good for us." Which means it will not happen, one way, or another.

"He could be a distributer for us."

"Nah."

"You're not the boss yet, Mick. Don't presume to tell me what to do."

"He can't be trusted." Which should be feckin' obvious after Darakov sent mercs to steal the original prototype.

"Who in this world can be?"

"There's watching out for a double cross and there's putting your hand around the wasp's nest and expecting not to get stung."

Brogan laughs like I'm joking.

I'm not.

"There are other options for distribution," he muses in the silence that falls between us.

"Starting with allies we already have strong bonds with makes more sense." Though I want to connect with the Greek mafia out of Portland.

They have some impressive weapons connections and a reputation for brutal but honest dealings. I can work with that.

My phone lights up with a text.

"I've got to go." I don't wait for Brogan's answer before disconnecting the call and putting one through to my lieutenant. "Where is she?"

"The Waldorf. Wraith followed her to a room on the concierge level."

I don't ask how he got the keycard to gain access to that floor. I expect my men to take initiative. "Who's staying in that room?"

"The blackgloves are hacking into the registration system now, but chances are it'll be booked under an alias."

And if Wraith had gotten a look at the occupant, Brice would have already told me.

"Her phone?"

"Whoever is staying there is using a jammer. We can't use the listening app we installed and there's nothing but muffled sound through those thick walls. Even our best targeted listening device isn't picking up distinguishable words."

Whoever is in that room excels at countersurveillance measures.

My money is on my least favorite Russian. Darakov.

Plans for Dierdre are going to have to escalate.

And that favor my father and Oisín promised Brogan for keeping her safe is going to have to go unfulfilled.

CHAPTER THIRTY-FIVE

The Breaking Point

KARA

The sound of a knock on the apartment door drags me out of the code I'm writing for my Advanced Python Programming class.

Standing, pain zings into my lower back. Sitting so long in one position never goes well, but I keep doing it.

It's too easy to get lost in my programming.

Stretching my neck from side to side, I hurry to answer the door.

Hope's probably looking for someone to keep her company. She seems pretty lost now that both Esther and Enoch are in school.

I don't mind taking a break.

There's a smile of welcome on my face when I open the door. "My boy definitely thanks you for the inter..."

My voice cuts off and my smile slides right into a scowl when I see who is on the other side.

Dierdre.

"Mick isn't here." Manners dictate I step back and invite her inside.

I don't.

Her baring of the teeth can't be termed a smile. "Are you going to let me in?"

"No."

"Come now, *cailín*, we need to talk and it's not a conversation you want anyone else overhearing."

I'm neither a girl, or a particularly young woman. Especially in relation to Dierdre's age.

"*Moma* might get away with calling me *cailín*. You will not." I make no effort to step back from the door.

Dierdre rolls her eyes. "You're too young for Micky, no matter what you'd like to believe."

"Funny, that's not how he acts when he's buried deep inside me and begging me to come with him." I can't believe those words just came out of my mouth.

Maybe super bitch is right.

This is a conversation better handled in private. I move back to allow her inside.

She gives me a pitying look as she passes me. "Ordering more like. Micky isn't one to beg."

She's right, darn it. But I'm not about to tell her so.

I shut the door and turn to face her. "I'm not going to offer you a seat, refreshments or to use my bathroom. Say what you need to and leave."

"You're holding Micky back."

"Again, that's not how he sees it."

"Of course it is. He's got too much honor to break his marriage vows, but he's completely out of your league and deserves a woman of equal strength to stand beside him."

"Agree to disagree."

Dierdre's eyes narrow. "Don't be a child. He's too much man for you and we both know it."

"Not true." He's just the right amount of man for me.

Even if he doesn't return my love, my husband craves my body like a drug.

"You need to give Micky a divorce."

It's like the woman cannot hear a word coming out of my mouth. Or she's not listening to them.

"You need to get a first-class ticket out of Delulu Land. I'm not divorcing my husband so you can make a play for him." Not that she probably hasn't made a play already.

Only Mick's pesky morality has gotten in the way. At least, that's how I'm sure she sees it.

"If you love him, you will let him go."

"Letting him go implies I'm somehow holding onto him, and let's be clear, Mick is the one that wants me tied to his side." Or at least to his bed.

"He's making the best of a bad situation, but it's been long enough. Everyone says you're so compassionate and sweet, shouldn't you turn some of that on your own husband?"

Even though I know she's talking out of her behind, her words hurt. I won't let her see that though.

"I can't imagine anything crueler than making it possible for Mick to play house with a woman like you. He deserves so much better." I turn Dierdre's words back on her.

And it hits home. Dierdre's look skewers me.

"If that's all..." I let my voice trail off and wave toward the door.

A vicious light enters Dierdre's eyes. "Divorce isn't the only way to end a marriage. It's not even the most expedient."

"Are you serious right now?" I laugh and it's genuine. "The minute I tell my father that you are threatening me, your best-case scenario is to be put on the first plane back to Dublin."

"Why would he believe you?" Dierdre asks snidely. "Your past irrational jealousies make your take on any situation between Micky and another woman unreliable."

Something cold shudders through me, but I don't let my dread at her words show. "Whatever gossip you've heard is old news. My father has no reason to doubt my word."

"If it's such old news, why was he bemoaning only last fall to Mick's da and mine about all the drama your jealousy caused?"

"I don't believe you." Only, I kind of do.

My father would sacrifice me in a hot minute to further his alliances. He already did. Sacrificing my reputation so long as it doesn't reflect badly on him is nothing.

"Why would I lie?" She taunts.

That forces another laugh from me, this one not quite as amused. "I could write a book – no make that a *series* – on the lies you tell."

The question with a much shorter answer would be why and when would the original vintage clingwrap tell the truth?

She shrugs, like my insult doesn't faze her. A manipulator like her is probably proud of her ability to sell a lie.

Which begs the question: would my father believe me, or her about this conversation?

A tiny fissure happens in my soul when I realize that I don't know the answer.

Why was he complaining about me last year? Did he tell Brian Fitzgerald and Oisín Kelly about my stay in The Marlowe Center?

No. If he had, Dierdre would have brought it up as an argument for me leaving Mick.

Not to mention it would make Brogan look bad.

"If that is all." I wave toward the door. "I'm busy."

"Do yourself a favor and ask Mick for a divorce." Menace imbues her voice and casts her face in wicked lines.

I refuse to be intimidated. "Not going to happen. Even if I wanted to divorce my husband, and I don't, my father would have to approve the dissolution of my marriage."

That's not about to happen. It would compromise his alliance with Mick and Dierdre's families.

"Once Fitz was born, you were no longer necessary for the alliance between the Shaughnessy Mob and the Northies," Dierdre says, like she knows exactly what I'm thinking. "If you die, the alliance still stands. You are now surplus to requirements."

That saying isn't nearly as charming coming from her than when my former roommate use to say it. The fact I've thought the same thing only makes the wound of those words more potent.

But you don't show weakness to a predator like Dierdre.

Forcing my feelings deep beneath my mob princess façade, I go on the offensive.

"If you have me killed my father *will* find out. But more importantly, so will Mick. What do you think he would do to the person responsible for the death of his beloved son's mom?"

A flicker of uncertainty passes through her gaze, but then it turns calculating. "More to the point, what would it do to your husband if his son became the casualty of your mob's current conflict with the bratva?"

We are having a conflict with the bratva? I shake my head. That is not what is important right now.

This bitch just threatened my son's life.

"Have you forgotten, but if Fitz doesn't survive, neither does my father's deal with Mick?" And Brogan proved with my cousin that a promise doesn't count in his eyes when the person who guaranteed it is dead.

"Does it? You used IVF to get pregnant the first time. A surrogate can carry one of the embryos. She could in fact give both the heir and the spare that your father wants." The *unlike you* hangs between us.

"You being the surrogate, I suppose."

She shudders with distaste. "No, but an appropriate one can be found. You're that easy to replace."

"You're a very stupid woman." I point to the door. "Leave."

"What are you going to do? Tell on me to Micky? He didn't believe you about you asking me to leave. He won't believe you now. He *trusts* me. And he thinks you're pathologically jealous."

I don't bother to reply.

Her stupidity isn't in her certainty Mick would believe her over me. Even I'm not sure on that one. Nor is it in believing that she can get away with murder undetected, because anyone can if it's planned right.

No, her idiocy comes from believing I will let her survive to harm me and my son.

That I won't take immediate steps to protect myself and Fitz.

Impatient for her to leave, I walk toward the door.

Her hand lands on my shoulder, jerking me to a halt. "What's the matter, cat got your tongue?"

I grab her wrist and turn, executing one of the moves Fabiana taught us, I flip the bitch onto her back.

Without giving her a chance to get over her shock at my move, I press the heel of my shoe right over her jugular. "How much pressure do you think it would take for my heel to break your trachea and leave you gasping for your last breaths right now?"

The temptation to apply that pressure is nearly overwhelming.

She glares up at me, but keeps her mouth shut for once.

Maybe how close I am to following through shows on my face.

The desire to kill her and end the threat to my son's life roars like an angry beast inside me.

But I need a plan to prevent war between our mobs. If I'm not sure how Mick would respond to me killing his ex-girlfriend either, that's my lookout.

I press down just enough that she has trouble getting air in. "You might be as venomous as a rattlesnake, but a mama bear will rip a snake to shreds to protect her cub."

I might be a born and bred city girl, but even I know that law of nature.

She chokes out a sound as her lips tinge blue from lack of oxygen.

The door to the apartment swings open.

"Stay away from me and my son." I lift my foot from Dierdre's neck and quickly step back before she can grab my ankle like she's tensing to do.

"What the hell is going on here?" Mick rushes past me and offers Dierdre a hand to help her up.

Like she needs it.

But that action tells me everything I need to know about how to handle her threats. And it's not by going to him, or my father for help.

"I'm so glad you're here, Micky." Dierdre's voice trembles and a convenient tear trickles down her cheek. "I told you Kara's irrationally possessive of you. I thought she was going to kill me."

"Kara's not a killer." Mick steps back from Dierdre.

What is he doing here? Is he expecting another *morning break* with me?

I'm so not in the mood after the confrontation I just had with his ex and the way he helped her off the floor.

"She had her foot on my throat." Dierdre coughs and breathes deeply for effect. "She attacked me for no reason. I was just warning her about how dangerous it is to let Fitzy play in the boathouse when he's so fascinated by the idea of swimming in the water beyond it."

Oh, she's such a good liar. She sounds so sincere, but she miscalculated with this whopper.

"Our son is too afraid to try to swim beyond the boathouse," I say scathingly. "And don't call him Fitzy."

Her calling my husband Micky is grating enough.

With an appealing look at Mick, she rubs at her throat. "I didn't know that. I was just trying help."

"If you have concerns about my son, bring them to me. You know Kara doesn't take well to what she considers criticism from you."

Seriously? "You did not just say that." I make no attempt to hide my fury at his words.

Mick jerks his head to look at me, like he's thinks I'm the unreasonable one right now.

"I'm sorry." Dierdre's voice hiccups on the word sorry like she's holding back a sob and effectively brings his attention back to her. "I just thought we were starting to be friends."

"In what world?" I scoff.

Mick looks between me and Dierdre and sighs. "I don't think you and my wife being friends is in the cards."

He freakin' sighed.

Again, like I'm part of the problem.

I guess, his ex-girlfriend wasn't mistaken about one thing. Neither my husband, nor my father, are going to believe a word I say about Dierdre Kelly.

That knowledge burns like bitter gall in my throat. But the jealousy they're all so worried about? Nowhere in evidence.

The only thing that matters is protecting my son and right now, Mick is in the way of that because of Dierdre's fixation on him.

Is it fair to blame him for that? Maybe not, but I can and do blame him for not sending her packing.

"Get her out of here before I have to take you up on the offer to help me hide the body," I say from between clenched teeth.

Mick winces.

He didn't like me saying that and revealing to the woman so intent on becoming his second wife that he made the offer. Not that she believes it.

The look of superiority on her face does not waver, until she turns toward Mick. "Don't worry. I'm leaving." Then she gives me an insincere look of sadness. "I'm sorry if what I said offended you."

"Fuck you, Dierdre."

Her eyes widen comically.

She didn't expect that.

The stiffening of my husband's spine says my words surprised him too. He frowns at me. "What has gotten into you, Kara?"

"Fuck you, too, Fitzgerald. Or better yet, why don't you both fuck right off together?" I spin on my heel and rapidly walk away.

They both think I'll fight to keep a marriage that is nothing but lust and contracts? That I'm jealous of him?

Not anymore.

I'm done.

Done trying to *handle* Dierdre.

Done with my marriage. Just done.

And if it means killing someone to protect my son, I'm enough of a mama bear to do it.

CHAPTER THIRTY-SIX

Fractured & Furious

MICK

What the bleedin' hell just happened?

My always dignified wife, who takes her role as highest ranking woman in the mob very seriously, and never so much as blinks in distaste at a rude guest had her foot on Dierdre's throat.

The woman who never swears, even in the throes of orgasm, just told me to fuck off.

With Dierdre.

That pisses me off more than the distance she's put between us lately.

All because of the pain-in-the-ass still trying to look wounded and put upon while spying on my family.

"Get the fuck out." I allow the mask I always wear to slip and let Dierdre see the deadly monster within.

The man who would feel no remorse about killing her and dumping her body in the ocean.

Her small gasp and the way she quickly puts distance between us says she realizes just how badly she miscalculated by starting more drama with Kara.

"I'm going." She puts her hands up in surrender. "But it's not my fault, Micky. Your wife is pathologically jealous."

"My wife is off-limits. Figure out what that means, or I'm going to forget about the alliance and send you home to your father in a box."

Her eyes widen, but it's not affected this time. She's scared. And she should be.

Her games are going to end, or she is. And I don't care what my father-in-law thinks about that.

The door has just closed behind Dierdre when Kara comes stomping down the hall. She's carrying her purse, laptop bag and a duffel.

I step into her path. "Where are you going?"

"Is Dierdre still a guest in my father's house?" she asks instead of answering.

This isn't the first time in the last few weeks that Kara has referred to the mansion as her father's house, not *home* like she used to.

I'd think she wanted us to get our own place, but there's no way she wants to move away from Maeve and Fiona.

Dry washing my face with my hand, I sigh. "You know she is."

She nods, like she expected nothing less. "I'm moving into my old room."

Everything inside me freezes. "The fuck do you mean you're moving into your old bedroom?"

"I need some space."

"From me and Fitz?" The last time she wanted space from us, she tried to take her own life.

That is not happening. Not ever again.

"From you." Her clarification is swift and certain.

Fuck. "You know I have no interest in Dierdre."

"Why keep her here then?" Kara demands.

"I told you. Business."

"Explain what kind of business requires keeping that viper sharing our living space." She says it like a dare.

One she knows I can't take up.

"Mob business."

Her laugh is harsh and without a drop of humor in it. "Believe it, or not, Mick, but I'm not stupid. I know it's mob business."

"Then why are you asking?" Frustration bleeds into my voice.

"Because I want to know specifically: what business could be more important than..." She shakes her head. "I was going to say *than me*, but we both know anything to do with the so-called good of the mob takes precedence over me."

"If it's good for the mob, it's good for you too, *a stór*." What is going on with her?

"Don't call me that. You don't treasure me. You never have and you never will."

"What the feckin' hell did Dierdre say to you?" I reach for Kara.

But she jumps back, making it very clear she does not want my touch. "You really want to know?"

"I wouldn't have asked if I didn't."

"She wants me to divorce you so you two can get married." Kara waits for me to react.

But I'm not surprised and frankly, I'm surprised she is. "Did you have to refuse with your foot on her neck?"

Not that seeing that tableau when I came in wasn't a hell of a turn on. But once Dierdre goes crying to her da, I'll be the one expected to sort it.

"That's not when I took her to the floor."

My sweet wife uttering those words takes my semi to fully hard and my interest in what Dierdre said is smashed under an anvil of lust.

But it's obvious Kara is not on the same page as me.

So, I ask, "What did she say that had you reacting with your new self-defense moves?"

I wish I'd thought to train my wife in self-defense. That could have been a lot of fun. Maybe I'll ask if she wants to practice on me.

"Your not-so-ex-girlfriend threatened to kill me as a more expedient route of getting me out of the way."

Dierdre's too spoiled to get her hands dirty with violence. "Are you sure you didn't misconstrue something she said?"

"Yes."

"Did she use the word kill?"

"No."

"So?" I ask leadingly.

Kara is a reasonable woman. She'll get there.

"So, how else am I supposed to take: *Divorce isn't the only way to end a marriage. It's not even the most expedient*?"

Cold fury brings everything into sharp focus. If Dierdre knows about The Marlowe Center, then those words have a much more sinister meaning.

She was trying to plant the idea of killing herself in Kara's head.

"I will talk to her." And I will talk to Brogan.

This situation cannot be allowed to continue.

"Because that did so much good before." Kara is looking at me like I'm a useless new recruit who can't even load my weapon yet.

"I'll sort it," I grit out.

She just shakes her head. "In case you're interested, when her threats against me didn't scare me into compliance, she threatened to kill our son."

Kara watches me, waiting to see how I'm going to respond to those fantastical words.

"You don't have to embellish your encounter to get me on your side, Kara. I said I would sort it, and I will." Dierdre is a lot of things, but stupid isn't one of them.

She has too much self-interest to risk harming Kara or Fitz.

But pushing my wife into harming herself? That's right out of the first year mean girl playbook.

"Why did I think that's exactly what you were going to say?" Kara asks with disgust.

"I don't know what is going on here." I move toward my wife. "But there's no way that she's going to risk my wrath, or your da's, by harming you or our son."

No matter what she said.

And I doubt after her takedown, Dierdre is going to be threatening Kara in any capacity again anytime soon.

Taking advantage of the fact that I won't touch her when she so clearly doesn't want me to, Kara sidesteps and moves around me.

When she has her hand on the knob to our front door, says, "I am not convinced. And that does not make me feel safe."

"If you're worried about being safe, you're more secure here in the apartment with me and Fitz." It's a solid, logical argument.

And with a few rare exceptions, Kara is a logical woman.

"You're assuming I believe that you will protect me from your ex-lover."

All the fury I bled off in the workout with Wraith comes rushing back. "I gave you my word I would protect you always."

"You didn't protect me from this. You didn't protect me from Dierdre hurting me."

"That's not the kind of protection I promised."

"Well, it should have been."

CHAPTER THIRTY-SEVEN

The Strategy of Survival

KARA

I've been holding the vial so long, it's warm in my hand.

The box *moma* gave me before my wedding sits open on my old bed. It's the first time in my seven-year marriage that I've opened it.

It stayed closed even when my mind was so chaotic and my emotions were so debilitating after Fitz's birth.

I never *wanted* to decrease Mick's ardor. Neither have I ever had need to threaten Mick with the dagger.

The Ethylene Glycol never even registered to my brain that dark day I took all the sleeping pills to shut down the cacophony of terrible thoughts in my mind.

Now, I'm holding onto it and not sure who I mean to use it on.

Dierdre...or Mick.

With him out of the picture, she won't have a reason to harm my son. And without her death, the Northside Dublin Syndicate will have no reason to withdraw their alliance.

Or worse, declare war on the Shaughnessy Mob.

The thought is so much like the way my father would think, it makes me sick. It's the exact way of thinking that led him to promising my hand in marriage to a complete stranger at the age of sixteen.

It's this kind of mob-is-all based logic that made Brogan think it was okay to blackmail my cousin Róise into a marriage alliance with the Italian mafia she despised.

These thoughts are not mine.

I may have sacrificed my future for the good of the Shaughnessy Mob, but I will never sacrifice the life of someone I care about for it.

Dierdre, on the other hand, is a different matter.

If I kill her, that will protect Fitz in the short term. However, it puts his father in danger from retaliation at the hands of his own family. My father too.

I may not like Brogan Shaughnessy, but I do love him.

There is only one way to protect everyone and make sure Dierdre dies. Divorce Mick.

Once I ask for a divorce, my father and Mick will know that jealousy isn't motivating what I tell them about Dierdre. They will both believe me that she threatened Fitz.

And that will be her death sentence.

While I have a bottle of Ethylene Glycol, they have the skills and means to *guarantee* her death is perceived as an accident.

All I have to do is convince both men I really want a divorce.

And I do.

No matter what my mob boss father and underboss husband believe, I deserve a husband who loves me. Who puts me first when my life and that of his son is on the line.

Who immediately believes me fully and completely when I tell him that's what's going on.

~

Brogan is at his desk and Mick is in one of the chairs facing it when I enter my father's office.

That's fortuitous.

And a sign, if I need one, that I'm doing the right thing.

My father greets me as soon as I walk through the door. "Hello, Kara. Mick was just telling me about your little run in with Dierdre."

Little run in? "Is that how you describe a guest in your home threatening the life of your daughter and grandson?"

His expression turns pained. "I know she has been making something of a nuisance of herself."

"Do you?" I ask.

"Hope told me." His eyes soften briefly when he says the other woman's name. "She doesn't like Dierdre either."

"Hope has discerning taste."

My father's mouth twists with disapproval. "You don't have to make up stories about Dierdre to get rid of her. She'll be going back to Ireland soon enough."

Mick makes a sound. Of annoyance? I'm not sure. But it definitely isn't agreement with Brogan's condescending words.

"I'm not here to talk to you about the Wicked Witch of the West." Not yet anyway. "I want permission to divorce Mick."

Eyes widening with discernable shock, my father opens and closes his mouth without anything coming out of it.

"No," Mick says with glacial finality.

I don't look at him. I can't. Not if I want to get through this meeting without crying, or doing something equally humiliating, like ask him why he doesn't love me.

But I do address him. "I wasn't asking you. We were married in the State of New York. That means, I can file for a divorce and it will eventually be granted, regardless of what you want."

"This is a discussion you need to be having with your husband, Kara." My father has found voice again.

I shake my head. "I disagree. As I said, Mick ultimately has no say over whether or not I can divorce him. However, you as the mob boss, do."

We all know that he has granted permission for a handful of divorces in his tenure as mob boss. Under the right circumstances, even my hidebound father acknowledges an individual's right to choose who they are married to.

"Like hell," Mick says.

But my father nods, his expression now troubled. "That is true. But you must know I'm not about to allow you to divorce Mick and destroy our alliance with the Northside Dublin Syndicate."

"Fitz is now the guarantor of that alliance, not me. I don't have to be married to Mick for him to be your underboss, or for him to take over from you when you retire."

"As much as I hate to even think about it, there's no guarantee my grandson will live to take over from his father," Brogan says heavily.

In other words, he wants more grandsons.

It's my turn to nod. "There are still male embryos in frozen storage at the clinic."

No female ones, but that's not a memory I want to relive.

"You are not going through IVF to get pregnant again." Mick's voice is deadly certain.

I shrug, still not looking at him. "I don't have to. An appropriate surrogate can be found to carry the baby."

Dierdre was right about that at least.

The astonishment on my father's face is almost comical. He was surprised by my request for a divorce, but my willingness to allow another woman to carry my child stuns him.

I'm not thrilled with the idea, but the reality is my father will not approve me beginning divorce proceedings if I'm pregnant. And he's not going to allow Fitz to be his only grandson.

The very fact he is the current mob boss instead of his dead older brother is evidence enough of the dangers to this life.

"Perhaps you should return to The Marlowe Center." My father doesn't sound condescending now.

He sounds worried.

"Some things cannot be therapied away. Believe it, or not, I am *not* jealous of Dierdre. I don't believe Mick wants to sex her up." Mostly. "I know she's still here because of mob business."

"Then what is the problem?" my father asks.

"The problem is that I deserve to be happy. I know my happiness means nothing to you, but it means something to me."

Brogan winces, like my words hurt him in some way. But I don't let myself go down that mental pathway. The only reason they bother him is that I'm not acting like the perfect mob princess puppet he wants me to be.

"You do not believe I will protect you from Dierdre. That is why you are pretending to want a divorce." Mick's voice is devoid of emotion.

"I want a divorce because I want to be happy," I say baldly.

"You love your husband, Kara. You're not going to be happy divorced from him." Brogan sounds so sure of himself.

"I don't expect you to understand. Or even to care about my happiness. But I expect you to be fair. I've done my duty. I went through IVF at the age of eighteen so you could have the grandson you and *seanathair* wanted."

My grip on the chair arms tightens to the point of pain. Talking about that time is still hard for me.

My therapist said it might always be triggering, but I'll say what needs to be said, if there's a chance it will sway my father.

"The hormone imbalance that came after – the reason for my postpartum depression – could have been linked to the hormone therapy I was forced to endure for the harvesting of my eggs at such a young age."

Brogan grimaces.

He doesn't like hearing that. Well, I didn't like living it.

"Did you know that the early mortality rate for women who give birth in their teens is over twice that for women who don't? That a second pregnancy in her teens will increase that number by 50%?"

The color leaches from my father's face. "No."

Is he wondering if that's the reason mom died? She married my father right after her eighteenth birthday and gave birth to me before she turned nineteen.

Pregnancy and delivery weren't easy on her and she suffered from anemia after.

My memories of my mom are of a kind, gentle, almost ethereal woman.

I realize as an adult, that her health was always fragile and that's why she seemed like she wasn't entirely tethered to this world.

Mom had a dangerous miscarriage when she was nineteen and was told by her OB to wait at least two years before getting pregnant again. Her next pregnancy was no kinder to her health than the first two and after she miscarried a second time, her doctor strongly recommended she not get pregnant again.

Ever.

She died giving birth to Fiona at the age of twenty-five.

"You will not die young," Mick says in a voice that sounds like ground glass.

I shrug. "I hope for Fitz's sake I don't."

"Stop talking like this. You are not going to die!" My father slams his fist down onto his desk.

"The point is not how old I will be when I do, but that you've already taken too much from me. I sacrificed my future for the good of your mob, and now I want to take some of it back."

Brogan's head rears back, like I punched him in the jaw. "It's your mob too."

"If it is, if I'm as much of a member as your soldiers..." I don't for a minute believe I am, but I do believe my father likes to believe he's a fair, if harsh, man. "Then in all fairness, you will honor my request."

"Dierdre will be leaving to return to Dublin soon." My father rubs his eyes, like he's tired.

Soon is not immediately and as long as she's here, my son is at risk.

"Dierdre's being here and the way she's treated me might be the catalyst, but she's not the problem." Being married to a man who places mob business ahead of my feelings and needs is.

That's not something my father will ever understand though, so I don't bother saying it.

Brogan sighs, suddenly looking every one of his fifty-two years. "If you want to divorce your husband, you have my permission on two conditions."

Of course there are conditions. "What are they?"

"The first is that you act as a mother to the sons born of a surrogate."

"I would have insisted on it. I am their legal mother, no matter who carries them in her womb."

My father nods, satisfied.

"The second condition is that if there are no viable pregnancies from the current embryos, you are willing to have your eggs harvested again."

"No way in feckin' hell!" Mick surges to his feet, his lack of emotion suddenly transforming into incandescent rage. "Kara will never be forced to go through IVF again."

I can't see my husband's face, but the way my father blanches looking at him tells me I don't want to.

"You need more than one son," Brogan says without his usual conviction.

Mick says nothing. He just stands there vibrating rage.

Finally, my father sighs. "Fine. I'll grant permission for the divorce if you are willing to discuss the option should it become necessary, Kara."

"Agreed."

Still silent, Mick returns to his seat.

My father avoids looking at him which makes me sneak a peek at my husband's profile.

His jaw is rigid; his entire posture is coiled violence ready to strike.

"You need to talk to your husband, Kara, but you have my permission to file for divorce if that is what you really want."

I can't believe it was this easy. I expected to have to argue a lot longer.

But I'm relieved I don't have to. Because I've got another unpleasant discussion ahead.

Convincing my father that Dierdre Kelly has to die.

CHAPTER THIRTY-EIGHT

A Womb, a Weapon, & a Warning

MICK

P rimal rage pushes against my control with the power of a rocket launcher.

If I speak, I will snarl.

If I move, I will kill Brogan. Then I will grab Kara and drag her back to our apartment where we will discuss her appalling request with our bodies.

I sit. I listen. And I plan.

My wife is not leaving me. Not to death. Not to divorce. Not ever.

"Now, we need to talk about Dierdre," Kara says, like she hasn't just taken an Uzi to our life together.

"I told you, she's going back to Dublin soon," Brogan says.

Then he looks at me with an expression that says he expects me to back him up.

I'm more likely to blow him up and I let that truth shine in my eyes. The only part of my body any emotion is getting through.

He frowns and turns his gaze back on his daughter.

"As long as she is living, she is a danger to Fitz." Kara's tone is implacable.

Brogan sighs. "She won't be living in the mansion for much longer."

He missed the point of what his daughter just said to him. I didn't.

For the first time since coming upon my wife and Dierdre in our apartment, I consider that Dierdre Kelly is egotistical enough to believe she can get away with harming my wife and son.

I thought she was too smart to sign her own death warrant, but if she threatened Fitz, that's exactly what she did.

"Mick." Kara says my name, trying to get my attention.

As if every molecule of my body isn't already consumed with her and only her.

I turn my head and our gazes collide. Hers is filled with emotion. Pain. Grief. Determination.

"What do you need, *mo chuisle*?"

Her lips twist like she's just sucked on a lemon wedge. She doesn't like me using endearments with her?

Tough.

She *is* the beat of my heart and if she is gone, so is my heart. Then no one is safe except my son.

I will kill them all. Starting with her father.

"You said you watch me on the video feeds sometimes."

More like all the time. "Aye."

"You have cameras in our apartment then, right?"

"Aye." There is no point in hiding the level of my obsession any longer.

After tonight, she is going to see how fixated I am, how tight I am willing to hold her to me.

"Do they pick up sound, or only images?"

"They have sound." I like to hear her voice, especially when she's talking to our son.

There's a softness in it I crave.

"Do you record, or only livestream?"

"Record." I have an 8-terabyte external hard drive filled with my favorites.

"Can you access the minutes before you walked in on me with my foot on Dierdre's neck on your phone?"

"Aye."

"Thank you." She's taking my willingness to do it for granted.

As she should.

Like she should take for granted that she is mine and I am hers and that is not going to change.

It takes a minute, but I find the segment she wants me to play. Assuming she wants her father to hear what was said, I put my phone on speaker and start the video.

"Your best-case scenario is to be put on the first plane back to Dublin." Kara doesn't sound worried. She sounds angry.

Dierdre's snide voice follows. *"Why would he believe you? Your past irrational jealousies make your take on any situation between Micky and another woman unreliable."*

"Whatever gossip you've heard is old news. My father has no reason to doubt my word." Dierdre wouldn't have heard the lie in Kara's voice, but I do.

I shift my gaze from my phone's screen to my wife. She's trying to hide her vulnerability, but it's shining in her hazel eyes.

The temptation to kill her father and then stab my own thigh in punishment for doubting her is so strong, my hands ache with the need to act.

"If it's such old news, why was he bemoaning to Mick's da and mine about all the drama your jealousy caused only last fall?"

Brogan jerks, his expression turning pained.

"I don't believe you." The words are right, and Kara probably convinced Dierdre, but her lack of confidence is obvious to me.

She does believe her father opened his big mouth yet again.

And the look on Brogan's face says he realizes that too. Regret and guilt are written all over my boss's expression, but Kara isn't looking at him. So, she doesn't see it.

She's watching me.

To see if I'm getting the point yet?

"Why would I lie?" Dierdre asks.

Kara's laughter is filled with mockery. *"I could write a book – no, make that a series – on the lies you tell."* I'm watching while listening, so I see the moment Kara has had enough. *"If that is all."* Kara's voice is colder now. *"I'm busy."*

"Do yourself a favor and ask Mick for a divorce."

"Not going to happen. Even if I wanted to divorce my husband, and I don't, my father would have to approve the dissolution of my marriage." She changed her mind pretty fast on that, didn't she?

She can change it back just as quickly then.

"Once Fitz was born, you were no longer necessary for the alliance between the Shaughnessy Mob and the Northies. If you die, the alliance still stands. You are now surplus to requirements."

There's a pause.

Then Kara's voice, tight and cutting: *"If you have me killed my father will find out. But more importantly, so will Mick. What do you think he would do to the person responsible for the death of his beloved son's mom?"*

Why did I think it was okay to subject Kara to this viciousness? She's abso-feckin'-lutely right.

I should have protected her from Dierdre's cruelty as much as the threat of any physical harm that could come to my wife.

"More to the point, what would it do to your husband if his son became the casualty of your mob's current conflict with the bratva?" Dierdre taunts calmly.

I pause the recording and look at Brogan to see if he caught it. He's not tracking. That regret? It's so strong, I'm not sure there's room for anything else right now.

Not even thinking like a mob boss.

"She knows about our issues with Darakov," I point out to him.

Which is confirmation that at some point they have communicated about things other than his pursuit of a marriage alliance with her mob through her.

Brogan's head snaps up, his eyes coming back into focus.

"I asked the wrong bleedin' questions." And I am feckin' furious at myself.

Believing her reason for being in New York was to make a play for me, I dismissed the potential for additional motives and didn't question her on them.

I don't make mistakes. Especially not ones that could put Kara or Fitz at risk.

Brogan gives a significant look toward his daughter. "We can discuss that later."

"Maybe if you had discussed whatever it is with me before today," Kara says drily. "This whole situation could have been avoided."

With my wife's words, another bullet point to add to my plan to keep her emerges.

She's been frustrated with me for withholding information from her for weeks. She wanted to know what business kept Dierdre at the mansion and I refused to tell her.

Because it's safer for Kara not to know.

At least that's what I've always believed.

However, I thought she didn't need my protection against Dierdre's words, and I was wrong about that.

It's looking like I was wrong about this too.

I meet my wife's eyes. "I'm sorry."

She jerks a nod, but there's no softening in her demeanor.

She's still stuck on getting the divorce then.

"You want me to kill Dierdre?" I ask.

"I don't care who does it, but yes, I want her and the threat she poses to Fitz gone. Permanently."

"You don't mention yourself," Brogan says. "But it's obvious she threatened you first."

"You already knew that, but it wasn't enough was it?"

Brogan doesn't answer.

I don't think he can. There's pain on his face I can't identify with. It's emotional, but there's no doubting it's real.

"I don't matter. You made that clear. I've never mattered. Not to you. Not to Mick. All I've ever been to either of you is a means to an end. A uterus to carry the heir and a spare." The bitterness in Kara's voice is laced with her own emotional pain.

And that pain bothers me.

It has to be fixed.

"You *do* matter, Kara. I'm sorry I didn't believe your version of what happened until I saw it for myself."

Kara's expression says she's not handing out any offers of easy forgiveness. "As long as you take care of the problem now without plunging us into war with the Northside Dublin Syndicate, I'll be satisfied."

"But not happy," Brogan says, sounding none too much in that state himself.

"There's nothing for me to be happy about in this situation. If Dierdre had acted on her desires before giving me a warning, either I would be dead and my son would be without a mother, or both of us would be."

And Kara holds both her da and I accountable for that.

Brogan shakes his head. "She wanted you to ask for the divorce and thought she could threaten you into doing it."

"It worked." And for that alone, Dierdre would have to die.

That she threatened my wife and son with intent only means her death isn't going to be quick.

Kara shrugs. "I guess we all learned a lesson from this."

"Yes, we did," Brogan says with sincerity.

"Fitz is going to be home from school soon." Clearly done with the meeting, she turns to walk out of the office.

"Kara," her father says with some urgency before she reaches the door.

She stops but doesn't turn to face him.

"I really am sorry. You are my daughter and I love you, even when I do a terrible job of showing it."

"I'm not sure it's love if you can't show it," she says quietly before leaving Brogan's office.

I send a text to Brice to pick up Dierdre and put her on ice until I'm ready to deal with her.

"I'll take care of Dierdre," I tell Brogan.

He nods. "She has to die."

"Aye."

"Kara deserves a better father than the one I have been."

I won't argue with that. He's a strong mob boss, but he has never valued his daughters like I value my son.

And I'm a sociopath.

He's not.

Or so I have always assumed.

I stop at the door on the way out of his office. "I will burn down this mob and everyone in it before I let my wife go."

"Good. My daughter deserves to be loved that way. But I'm not the one you have to convince."

Loved? I don't do love. But I need her.

And she needs me.

For a man like me, that's more powerful than any ephemeral emotion.

Brogan thinks I'm going to romance his daughter into staying with me, but that's not how a man like me works.

I keep what is mine no matter what the consequences.

CHAPTER THIRTY-NINE

The Kidnapping Clause

KARA

The room is pitch black when I wake up. I blink and then blink again, trying to make out shapes in the dark.

Usually, after I've been asleep, my eyes are adjusted enough to see the dresser on the far wall, the darker rectangle that is the entrance to the en suite.

Then I remember. I'm in my old bedroom. But I don't recall it being this dark when I went to sleep.

Trying to penetrate the stygian darkness, I turn my head and that's when I feel the constriction. I'm wearing a sleep mask. That's right.

I put it on in an effort to finally get to sleep. I don't take sleeping pills. Ever.

I lift my hand to take the mask off, but instead of free movement, I feel a tug against my other wrist.

There are cuffs on my wrists. The wide leather kind with a silk padded lining like the ones Mick uses on me when we get kinky between the sheets.

Panic should be my first reaction, right? But it's not. Arousal hits me right between my legs, making my thighs clench.

Ignoring the sensation, I try to sit up. That's when I realize my ankles are cuffed together too.

That's not what Mick usually does. He likes my legs free, so he can position me the way he wants me.

"Mick?" My voice only tremors slightly with the realization that this situation may not be down to my husband's doing.

My brain races with ways to get out of this.

A familiar hand presses against the side of my neck. "Don't freak out, *mo chuisle*, it's me."

One of his arms slides behind my back and then his other one underneath my knees, and he lifts me from the bed.

I reach up with my bound hands and rip the sleep mask from my face. My eyes are adjusted to the dark, but I still don't see much.

The outline of Mick's shoulders and head is visible because he's so close. Everything else is indecipherable because the room is darker than normal.

There's something over the window covering where cracks of light would usually slip through. The only light, as little as it is, comes from the soft glow of the nightlight through the cracked door to the en suite.

"What did you put over the window?" That's not what I really need to know right now but it's a start.

He takes a step away from the bed with all the confidence of a man wearing night vision goggles in a completely dark environment. Only there are no telltale lumps on his face.

The surety of movement is 100% my husband.

He shifts me against his chest and warmth tingles through me from where my arm brushes against his cotton covered pecs. "I closed the safety shutters."

Every room has them for security, but the walls won't withstand repeated firing, hence the multiple safe rooms in the mansion.

Because the mob isn't just a business like my father wants to pretend. It's an army and my family has many enemies with armies of their own.

"I slept through that?" The shutters aren't loud, but they aren't silent either.

"You slept through me putting restraints on you," he says in a flat tone. "I thought you would wake up."

"You sound disappointed." Which is a lie because there's no emotion in his voice at all.

"Why would I be?" His head comes down toward me and I'm sure he's going to kiss me, but he just inhales. "It made the first part of my plan easier to execute."

"Sometimes you sound more like a robot than a man." That's not something I would have said to Mick before.

I always pretended I didn't notice when he withdrew into an emotionless shell. That was my job, right? To be a good little mob princess and pretend everything was fine.

Even when it wasn't.

But I'm done pretending. My brain to mouth filter with him is as broken as our marriage.

"Why close the safety shutters? Are we under attack? Where's Fitz?" I demand frantically.

I don't know why Mick would feel the need to bind my wrists and ankles to take me to the safe room though.

"No."

Before the relief even has a chance to register, he adds, "I closed the shutters so you couldn't go to the window and draw attention by banging on it."

Fear slithers down my spine. Why would I need to try to get help?

Mick said in Brogan's office there would be no divorce. Does he plan to kill me?

I curl my fingers into fists and bring my bound hands up in an arc, hitting the side of his face as hard as I can, throwing myself backward as he grunts from the impact.

Landing hard, pain radiates through my body on the side of impact.

Mick curses. "Feckin' hell, Kara. You are going to hurt yourself."

"Better than letting you hurt me!" I try to put distance between us, but it's nearly impossible when I have to move like an inch-worm.

Mick swoops down and picks me up again, clamping my arms against my body. "You're going to have bruises tomorrow. Don't do that again."

"Bruises are better than dead."

The sound that comes out of his throat is pure animalistic aggression.

And my stupid body doesn't go into fight or flight mode. It goes into let's-get-ready-for-sex mode. My vaginal walls contract and the juncture of my thighs gets slick with arousal.

"You are not dying!" His voice doesn't sound robotic now. It's rough with fury. "And you are not getting a divorce."

"That's not your decision to make." I try to struggle.

His hold only clamps tighter. "Calm down. You know I won't hurt you, but you are feckin' going to hurt yourself if you keep this up."

"You already have."

He sighs. "Not like that. It is inevitable that a man like me would cause emotional pain for a woman with such a tender heart."

"What are you talking about?" A man like him? A mobster?

Maybe he's right. But then again, maybe he's not. Róise's mafioso doesn't hurt her like Mick hurts me.

But he loves her.

Even though their engagement started out the same way as Mick's and mine, there is no question that Miceli loves my cousin. Or that she loves him.

I'm happy for her, but their relationship has put marriage into perspective for me.

Mick doesn't love me and love on only one side only leads to pain.

"I have kept my monster locked inside, so you would not be afraid of me."

It takes me a second to parse what he's saying. But when I do, it doesn't make sense. What monster?

He sets me down on the bed again and turns on the light.

He's wearing snug fitting cargo pants, a black tactical t-shirt and boots.

He's armed. Overtly. A shoulder holster with a semiautomatic and another holster at the small of his back. I'm sure he's wearing his usual knives too.

I swallow, pressing my thighs together.

The fact he's prepared for battle should not send touch-me-now signals to my traitorous body.

Mick settles beside me and traces the lace edging on the neckline of my nightgown. "I like this."

My nipples go tight and hard from that single touch. It's all I can do not to scream my frustration.

How can such a small connection have such a big effect on me? But it's always been this way.

Divorce isn't going to change that.

"I got it to wear on our anniversary," I say punitively.

It's not sheer, or overtly sensual, but the slip style stretchy nightgown that barely reaches midthigh adheres to my plus size curves. The spaghetti straps and sweetheart neckline reveal a lot of skin.

It's my kind of sexy.

It's also comfortable.

I wore it tonight as a reminder of why I'm back in my old bedroom. Mick missed our anniversary because mob business came first.

Again.

Just like it did this morning with Dierdre.

My husband's thumb slides over my turgid peak and I give an involuntary shudder of delight. That only makes me mad.

"What do you think you're doing? We're not having sex, Mick." The pulse of want in my core says, *wanna bet*? But I ignore it. "We're getting a divorce."

"Wrong on both counts." Mick's hand slides down my side and along my hip to curve possessively over my backside.

"Stop it," I say as much to him as my own body bent on betraying my conviction to stay aloof. "You're not going to force me."

Ours may not be the love of the century, but one thing I know with absolute certainty: Mick will never harm me physically.

Not in any way, but especially not that way.

Regardless of my aberrant thoughts of a moment ago.

"To have sex? No." His handsome features don't register any emotion, but there's no mistaking the repugnance in his voice at the thought.

"You need to take the cuffs—"

"To leave with me?" He asks, interrupting my demand. "Yes."

Wait. What? Is he saying what I think he is? He *is* going to force me to leave with him? "You're taking me back to our apartment?"

Binding my wrists and ankles feels pretty elaborate just to get me to another wing of the mansion.

"No."

Well, that was helpful. Not. "Then where?"

"Somewhere we can talk things out."

Talk things out? "Since when do *you* want to talk things out?"

"Since you asked your father for permission to divorce me," he says like it should be obvious.

It's not. Not even a little. "But you don't care if we get divorced. It won't stop you inheriting control of the Shaughnessy mob when Brogan retires."

"Wrong." He doesn't say *again* but I hear it in the silence between us.

"I don't know where you think you're taking me, but we're past hashing things out to fix our marriage." It hurts to say the words.

But his reaction to my altercation with Dierdre today showed me just how little I matter to Mick.

"I don't agree."

"And because you don't agree, you're going to kidnap me?" I ask sarcastically.

"Aye." No humor there. Just pure Neanderthal mob underboss intent.

With a longing look at my breasts, he stands up, leaving me sitting against the pillows on the bed, my extremities still bound.

Mick looks around the room. "Where is your duffel?"

"In the closet." It won't help him make a quick and easy abduction. "I unpacked earlier."

His jaw goes taut and he heads into the closet.

Knowing I have maybe a minute, or two, while he packs my stuff, I quickly bend forward and try to find a release on the ankle cuffs.

If I can get them undone, I can run.

These may be like the cuffs he uses when we make love, but they aren't them. There's no discernable way to release them, or to unhook them from each other.

I try pressing against the leather, over and over, everywhere my fingers can reach. Then I run my fingers between the leather and my ankle, looking for a hidden release. Nothing.

"They require a key." Mick is standing in the doorway to the closet, the duffel dangling from one hand.

"Take them off me."

"No."

I try a different tack. "Where's Fitz?"

Mick heads into the bathroom, presumably to grab my toiletries. "In a helicopter on the way to where we are going."

"So, you kidnapped our son too?" I raise my voice so he can hear me.

"I didn't have to," Mick calls from the bathroom. "Fitz is happy to go on a trip with us."

Only he's not with us. He's already on the way there and I can't help feeling that's on purpose.

"What about school?" I demand.

Mick comes back into the bedroom, the duffel zipped. "I arranged to get his schoolwork and the learning goals for the week from his teacher. You will be able to work with him so he does not fall behind."

"We're going to be gone a week?" My voice rises, but I can't help it.

"We'll be away from the mansion as long as it takes."

I don't ask *takes to do what* because I've got a pretty good idea. Mick's a possessive guy. His outlook is pretty basic. Me and Fitz? We're his.

He says he's mine too, but it's not true. There's a big part of him I cannot touch because it belongs to the mob.

He doesn't acknowledge that and in his primitive view, marriage is for a lifetime. Even if that marriage is nothing but a contract and good sex.

Okay, mind-blowing sex, but that's not love.

"How do you plan to get me out of the house without me screaming my head off?"

"It would be easier if I could drug you, but I can't," he says conversationally.

"Because of what happened before." For the first time ever, there's something about that time in my life that works in my favor.

"Because a man does not drug his wife."

"Uh..." I'm seriously at a loss as to what to say to that.

It's okay to kidnap me, but not drug me?

"I don't want to kill our men, but I will if they try to stop me." His face reflects not a single regret for making that threat.

There's something different about him. That thing that lurks underneath his easy Irish charm is on the surface. I always assumed that it was the mobster, the man willing to commit criminal acts for the good of the syndicate.

But it's something more.

I'm not convinced the men would come to my aid if they saw Mick carrying me out of the house, no matter how loudly I screamed. But am I willing to take that chance?

"You're insane," I accuse.

"It's called antisocial personality disorder, and it is not accompanied by delusions or paranoia."

Which apparently is supposed to mean he's *not* insane.

"You're a sociopath?" How can that be possible?

He loves Fitz. I know he does.

"Aye."

"You're deluded if you think I'm going anywhere with you," I inform him.

"I thought you would prefer I not kill your father either." He says it so prosaically.

Like he didn't just threaten to murder his boss and friend.

"Why in the world would you even threaten that?"

"He gave you permission to file for divorce. Once I am boss, that permission will be rescinded."

"No. No. No." This is not happening.

Mick, the affable, but scary underboss, is not threatening to kill my father to keep me married to him.

"You can't kill my father. He's your boss. You took an oath."

"He betrayed that oath when he agreed to the divorce," Mick says implacably. "Just as your *seanathair* did when he ordered the disposal of our girl embryos."

That is not a memory I want to revisit, but he can't be saying what I think he's saying. "You killed my grandfather?"

His health began to deteriorate months before Uncle Derry's death and more rapidly after. Everyone put it down to *seanathair's* grief.

"Aye."

My brain cannot take this in. "Why?"

"He stole from me. That is an unacceptable betrayal of the oath between boss and soldier and negated the oath I made to him."

Because the girl embryos belonged to me and Mick, not my grandfather. Only *seanathair* hadn't seen it that way.

"I don't understand." My brain is spinning like hard disk drive gone amok. "How did you kill him?"

"Thallium poisoning. I wanted to use arsenic, to prolong his suffering because he made you cry. But your grandfather was old school Catholic which meant no cremation. And arsenic can be detected in the body too long after death."

My husband's eyes reflect a complete lack of emotion, including re-morse. This is the real Mick. Not the charming facade he puts on to fool people.

I always knew it was there, but he held this part of himself back from me.

"If I had known the full cost of his actions toward you, I would have made him suffer much worse before death."

"You think I took the pills because of *seanathair*?" I ask, aghast.

"Aye. Because he made you believe you had no value when your value to me was and is immeasurable."

"That can't be true. You don't love me."

"You are my addiction, Kara. I *need* you."

"That's not love."

"Nah, it's not. But it is real."

"You love Fitz."

"Aye."

"But you don't have those kinds of tender feelings for me."

He shakes his head. "Addiction is not a feeling."

I'm not sure that's true, but what do I know? I never even realized my husband was obsessed with me.

The fact he has been stalking me since the early days of our marriage gives credence to his claim though. I'd only been guessing about the cameras in our living room earlier today.

But they're there and Mick had recorded footage of me and Dierdre from them.

How long does he keep the recordings? Does he have favorites?

And what is wrong with me that my mind is going there right now? "You can't kill my da."

"You stopped calling him that. After you came home from The Marlowe Center."

"I did." I don't know why I slipped now.

Or maybe I do. Because when it comes down to it, I don't want him hurt. He's still my father, even if I don't think of him as my da.

"Why?" Mick asks.

"A da is someone who loves his children. Nurtures and protects them." Even Mick with his ASPD, is a da to our son. "Regardless, Brogan is your father-in-law. He's family."

"You and Fitz are my family." Emotionless implacability stares back at me from Mick's green gaze.

"We might be your primary family, but he's still your father-in-law."

Mick shows no softening.

"He's your friend," I claim desperately. "Like Brice, Conor and Rory. You wouldn't kill them."

"If they threatened you or Fitz I would." He pauses, thinking. "Or if they betrayed me."

I can't help noticing me and Fitz came first, but I shake my head. "My father didn't betray you."

"Aye, he did. And Kara, Brogan is not my mate."

"Well, according to you, Dierdre isn't your friend either. She threatened to kill me and you told her I *don't take criticism from her very well*. Why does she get a pass?"

My grandfather didn't. And I'm not sure how I feel about that.

Life for *moma*, Fiona, Róise and me has been better since his death. Brogan Shaughnessy may be a ruthless mob boss too, but some part of him cares about us.

For all his talk about family loyalty, I'm not sure any part of *seanathair* ever did.

"She doesn't. Brice is doing a chemically enhanced interrogation on her with our newest recruit. After that, she'll be sent back to Dublin with no memory of the interrogation."

"Sounds like a pass to me." And that's not what my father promised.

"Once she is back in Dublin, she will disappear. Her family will believe she has been kidnapped by Ilya Darakov. Both will die in a plane crash while he is trying to get her to Odessa."

It's a good plan for killing her without starting a war with The Northside Dublin Syndicate. "Who's Ilya Darakov?"

"The Russian bratva leader trying to steal new weapon technology from me."

Me. Not us. Not the mob. Me.

Whatever is going on, Mick is taking it personally.

"Why aren't you doing the interrogation?" And why is Mick telling me all this?

It's mob business even if I have a vested interest in permanently removing the threat of Dierdre to my son.

"Because I fucked it up the first time and didn't ask the right questions. I won't let that happen again." He said something like that in my father's office.

"Funny, I thought you'd say because you're busy kidnapping your *wife*!"

"That too. Our marriage takes precedence."

"I don't believe that for a minute."

"You will."

I ignore his claim and say, "Brogan is your boss. You can't kill him without serious repercussions."

"None more serious than allowing you to leave me."

CHAPTER FORTY

Reflections During a Kidnapping

MICK

K ara glares at me in silence as I wait for her to understand the ramifications of her screaming for help.

"If you're so worried about me yelling," she says, her voice meaner than I've ever heard it. "Why don't you just gag me?"

"You know why."

Seven Years Ago

I walk into the clinic treatment room expecting my wife to be dressed and ready to return to the Shaughnessy estate.

But she's standing in her nightgown, her expression dazed as silent tears track down her cheeks.

I don't know why, but I do not like seeing her cry. "Kara?"

Her head turns toward me, but she doesn't speak.

"The nurse said the implantation procedure went as expected." I take a slow step toward her, my atavistic instincts telling me that any quick movement will cause her distress.

Causing her upset is unacceptable.

Again, I don't know why. I do not react to any of the other women in my life like this. My mother's tears do not affect me. My sisters getting upset only impacts me if the reason for it is something I deem worthy of handling.

My father and older brothers would prefer I let them handle insults to the family. They always have.

My solution usually involves death. Or at the very least, copious amounts of pain.

Pain. Ah. Kara told me she was worried the procedure would be painful.

"You were anesthetized for the procedure, weren't you?" I gave very clear instructions in that regard.

At first, the doctor tried to assure me there would be no more than minor discomfort for Kara. But after my subsequent *talk* with him, he agreed putting her under for the procedure would be best.

If he did not do so, I will keep every promise I made during that *discussion*.

"What?" Then her eyes focus on me, and she nods. "Yes."

The anesthesia might explain her disorientation, but not the tears. "Was there more pain than you expected when you woke up?"

I'm within touching distance now and my muscles are rigid with the need to reach out and do so.

We've been married for six weeks and I'm still getting used to the compulsion I have to physically connect with her whenever she is in the same room. I don't act on it unless we are in our bedroom, but it's there all the same.

Once she is pregnant with our son and we are able to have penetrative sex, the inexplicable need will decline sure as certain. But right now, my primitive instincts to claim her completely are going unfulfilled.

And they're growing stronger by the day.

Instincts I understand. They're base animal urges, not born of the emotions I don't feel.

"I..." Kara shakes her head.

"What's wrong, *a stór*?" That is not a question I ask.

Because I don't care.

However, I am Kara's husband and watching out for her is my duty.

"They just threw them away." The last word ends on a sob. "In the g-garbage."

Feck this. I pull my tender-hearted wife into my body and wrap my arms around her. "What did they throw away?"

Whoever threw away something of Kara's that is this important to her will lose more than their job by tomorrow.

"The girl embryos. They're gone. Tossed out with the trash like they were never even there." Another sob wracks her body.

The girl embryos? We only need boy embryos for the in vitro. However, I have enough intelligence not to say that.

I may not understand why she is so distraught, but she is and that is what matters.

And something primal in me is furious the clinic had the audacity to dispose of what belongs to me.

"I knew I didn't matter to *seanathair*. To any of you. But this..." She pounds on my chest. "They mattered to me."

"If you want daughters, we don't have to use in vitro to make them." After our son is born, Kara is never going through this process again.

Taking the fertility drugs has been hard on her. She's had almost every negative side effect the doctor warned us about: irritability, increased anxiety, headaches, nausea so bad she can't eat some days, hot flashes and even pain around where they gave her the shots.

"They're gone," she says again, sounding heartbroken.

I have no heart to break, but that does not mean it is okay with me that someone broke hers.

Plans for her grandfather's future begin to form in my head as I rub her back. I've never done this before, but I've seen my father do it for my mother and I'm very good at mimicking.

It works and eventually, Kara's tears ebb. I release her and she steps back, the desolation on her face filling me with fury.

"We'll have daughters one day." It's the only thing I can think to say.

But she shakes her head. "No. I won't give birth to a child who will have no voice in her own life."

Is she talking about herself? "You have a voice, Kara."

"No, I don't. I never have."

"You do with me." It's a vow.

Lethargic and acquiescent she lets me help her dress.

It takes more effort than normal to keep my *normal mobster* façade in the face of the rage that fills me at the lost look in her eyes.

The Present

I would remember that haunted look six months after Fitz's birth, when I walked into our en suite to find my precious wife unconscious on the cold marble floor, an empty bottle of pills by the sink.

"I don't break my promises."

"What do you call this?" She lifts her bound hands with a scowl.

"Expedient."

"You would really kill one of your men for trying to stop you from kidnapping me?" She bites her lip, eyes narrowed as she studies me.

"Aye." I could pretend to feel badly about that, but there's no point.

My true self is on display for my wife and there's no putting that genie back in the bottle.

"Fine," she grumbles. "I'm not going to let you keep my son from me."

"That was never going to happen." I send the command for the safety shutters to retract.

She harrumphs. "Like our divorce is never going to happen?"

"Exactly like that." I bend down to lift her, but she rears back.

"You can take the cuffs off. I already promised not to scream."

"But you did not promise not to run." And my wife is just wily enough to have done that on purpose.

"I'm not going to run. I want to see Fitz. Make sure he's okay."

"You know he is."

"Maybe." Her expression is not friendly. "But I still want to be sure."

"Good." That should make getting her into the SUV without incident easier.

She lifts her bound hands and wiggles them in my face. "So, undo me."

"No." I lift her into my arms again, this time holding her tightly so she cannot try to throw herself from them.

Her expression mutinous, she holds her soft curves in rigidity against me.

Which does not make them any less tempting. I regretted missing our anniversary this summer, but never more so than now when I see the tempting nightgown she bought to wear that night.

Apparently, her plans changed when I stood her up for dinner.

When I came to bed on our anniversary, long after she fell asleep, she'd been wearing sleep shorts and a t-shirt. If she had hoped I would not find the outfit sexy, it had been in vain.

I thought when she thanked me for the roses with that emotional catch she gets in her voice sometimes that all had been forgiven.

The fact she is wearing the nightgown on the night she planned to start her life without me would indicate that it is not.

More recently, she showed anger that I took Dierdre to dinner but had not done the same for my wife.

Apparently, Kara wants us to have *date nights*. Not that she's ever said anything like that to me, but it's clear she sees it as a lack in our marriage that we don't.

If she wants dates, I will take her on dates.

CHAPTER FORTY-ONE

Undone by Addiction

KARA

When we are at the door about to step into the hall outside my old bedroom, I say sweetly, "You may have forgotten, but I prefer to sleep without panties."

Mick goes absolutely rigid and swears. "Get a blanket to cover my wife."

Conor, who has been waiting in the hall, rushes past us. Soon the throw-blanket from the end of my bed is covering me from neck to ankle. The other man is careful not to touch a single centimeter of skin while he's doing it too.

Are his men aware that I am my husband's obsession? Maybe they are. Maybe they only know he's over-the-top possessive.

Whichever it is, the soldiers under my husband's direct command are careful never to look at me below the neck and they keep their attention brief regardless.

It never bothers me when they're on sentry duty and I'm swimming with Fitz in the pool or sunbathing with Fiona. Some of the other men make me wish I wore a wetsuit to swim in.

"If you'd taken the cuffs off, I could have gotten dressed for this little jaunt," I snark.

"I like you in cuffs," Mick says in a sensual rumble.

My ovaries sit up and take notice.

Darn it.

Even furious with him, Mick is still my ultimate catnip.

He finally removes the cuffs once the SUV we are traveling in clears the mansion's gates.

Then he hands me my duffle. "You'll be more comfortable in clothing that covers more of your body for the helicopter ride."

"You'll be more comfortable if I don't show so much skin to your men, you mean." But he's right.

As respectful as they are, I don't want to flash my cooch to any of his men.

I dig in the duffle, shocked when I see my box from *moma* in there.

"You could have used the Ethylene Glycol instead of asking for divorce," he says, like talking about his own murder doesn't bother him at all.

Maybe it doesn't.

I pause in my rummage for clothes to wear. "How long have you known I had it?"

"Since the week after we were married."

"You went through my things?" What am I asking? "Of course you did. You're my stalker."

"I am your husband." His tone reminds me he plans to stay that way.

"The knife and the Ethylene Glycol make sense, but what is the blood pressure medication for?" He doesn't sound the least bit worried I had what amounts to a deadly poison in my possession the entirety of our marriage. "It's an unreliable poison and the amount necessary to cause death would show up on a rudimentary tox screen after death."

"It's not meant to kill, or even maim."

"Then what?"

"If a woman's husband is too demanding in the bedroom, I have it on good authority that the right dose will introduce him to his new friend, Ed."

An arrested expression takes over Mick's features. "Erectile dysfunction?"

"You catch on quick." I grab a pair of underwear and slide them on under the blanket.

"You have never used it on me."

"No, I haven't."

"You didn't use the Ethylene Glycol either."

"No." Then a memory stirs. "You're the reason I couldn't find my box when I first got back from The Marlowe Center."

When I'd finally come across it in the top of my closet behind a storage container of mementos from my years at boarding school, I'd assumed I put it there and forgot.

There were a lot of things I forgot or remembered like they were a dream from the months after Fitz's birth.

"Aye."

"I never even thought about using it. When I took the sleeping pills, I wasn't trying to kill myself. Not consciously. I just wanted the pain to stop, for the chaotic and negative thoughts to be quiet for a while."

We've never talked about this. I never thought we could.

I'm not sure why I feel like now is the right time to do it though.

Mick's jaw clenches. "If you had tried, you would have found it completely ineffective."

"You replaced the Ethylene Glycol with a placebo?" I don't know why that shocks me.

He would not have been willing to risk me killing him.

"Aye. The blood pressure medication too. And the knife is so dull, it'll barely cut butter."

I don't know why, but that makes me laugh when really, nothing should be funny right now. "You're very thorough."

"Always. You kept the box on a high shelf, but one day Fitz might have found it."

"I know." I squirm under the blanket, tugging a pair of leggings up my thighs. "That's why I started locking it in the drawer in my vanity. But Fitz was just a baby when you made the switch."

"I wasn't worried about Fitz when I did it."

"You were worried about me."

"Your emotions became erratic when you started taking the fertility treatments."

He's right. They had. "If there was a negative side effect I didn't experience, I don't know what it is."

"You were too young to be put on those drugs."

"I was an adult."

"If I had known about the increased chance of early death for a woman who gets pregnant as a teenager, I would have insisted on waiting until you were in your twenties." A glimmer of something shows in Mick's eyes.

Not emotion. He doesn't feel that as he's pointed out so clearly tonight. But something.

I shrug. "My grandfather would never have allowed it. Besides, I don't see you going without penetrative sex that long."

"If necessary, I would have, but it wouldn't have been. You could have gone on birth control."

"That would have really sent *seanathair* into a tizzy fit." I pull off my nightgown and the blanket slips showing my naked shoulder.

Mick touches my bared skin. "You're so soft. The closest I will ever come to Heaven is touching you."

There's a snarky comment about poetic sociopaths on the tip of my tongue, but I swallow it back. There's too much implacable honesty in that statement to mock it.

"If I had known, I would have ended his ability to cause you harm before it happened."

"That sounds a lot like regret for a sociopath."

"Apparently, I am capable of feeling it, though this is the first time in my experience."

Like he felt love for the first time when Fitz was born.

"You weren't obsessed with me back then."

"You are wrong. My addiction started on our wedding night. Why do you think I left you alone in our bed?"

"Because my grandfather called you."

"I lied. He did call, but not until later."

"Then why leave?" I ask with remembered pain at the abandonment.

"I never lost control during sex, but that night I came close. I had given my word that I would not come inside you but if I had stayed with you, I would have broken it."

"You don't break promises." Unless the one he makes the vow to breaks faith with him.

Then, apparently, all bets are off.

"And I don't lose control."

"Except with me." And for me.

He killed my grandfather for hurting me, even if Mick justifies it to himself that it was because *seanathair* had stolen from him. And he's willing to kill my father in order to keep me.

A normal woman would find that reprehensible.

But it warms something inside me that has been cold for too long.

We are all products of the lives we've lived. Mine hasn't been normal and I refuse to feel bad that the way I think and feel don't necessarily fall on the normal scale either.

And one thing I can't deny, if only to myself: I never said red when he was kidnapping me.

CHAPTER FORTY-TWO

Operation: Date Night

KARA

"I'm taking you out." The words precede Mick into the bedroom where I am putting away the rest of our clothes in the dresser.

I'm not sure why Mick insisted on bringing my duffel. He packed a month's worth of clothes for me in the matching luggage.

Straightening, I push the drawer shut with my foot. "Like...to dinner?"

"Aye."

My brain stutters. "With me?"

His jaw flexes. "Who else would I be taking out, Kara?"

I give him a sour look he has no trouble interpreting.

"That was not a date. It was business and I'll tell you all about it at dinner."

"You'll tell me about business? At dinner? At a restaurant?" I ask, just to be sure.

"Aye."

He wants to take me on a date after kidnapping me and bringing me to the vacation house in Martha's Vineyard?

We arrived near dawn this morning and I didn't even argue about going to sleep in the bed we shared on our wedding night. Mick joined me, but he didn't try for sex, so I didn't knee him in the balls.

After all the revelations of the early hours of the morning, I needed to be held and he was the only one around to do it.

At least that's the story I'm telling myself.

We woke around eleven and spent the day with Fitz. Both of us.

Apparently, my husband explained to our son that we are on a *family vacation*. And Fitz is so excited about spending a week together, there's no way I was going to burst his bubble.

Hence the unpacking.

Trying to ignore the frisson of excitement the thought of a date with Mick – not on our anniversary – causes, I ask, "What about Fitz?"

"He's having a slumber party with Conor and Rory."

That stops me.

"With your two top lieutenants?"

Mick nods. "They're bribing him with popcorn and a late bedtime. Gobby is invited."

"Your top men are babysitting our son and his cat?" It's not such an outlandish idea.

Fitz adores all three of Mick's lieutenants and calls them uncle. I'm not sure how Mick didn't realize those men are his friends when they're as close as brothers, but they've never watched my son overnight.

Apparently, there are a dozen more men staying on the grounds to watch over us too, as Mick makes his obsessed sociopath bid to save our marriage.

"According to Fitz, Gobby is the best movie buddy. Don't ask me what show they picked." He says it so seriously, like I might actually quiz him on what animated feature our son talked his honorary uncles into watching.

A laugh slips out before I can stop it. "You're serious."

"I am."

"You planned a date night?" My voice comes out way softer than I mean it to.

He frowns. "Is it that hard to believe?"

"Mick, we don't date. I can count the number of times we've gone out together on one hand." This past anniversary was the second one he missed.

The other one was the year after Fitz was born. With everything happening then, I barely notice that one.

"You're exaggerating."

"I'm not. We don't do date nights. We do dinners with important people where I play my role and you play yours. Required appearances. The only time we eat alone together is breakfast sometimes when Fitz sleeps in."

"You enjoy those mornings," he says like a challenge.

I don't bother trying to deny it. He'd know me for the liar I would be. "That's not the point."

"That is exactly the point." He crosses his arms, unmovable.

My heart gives a ridiculous little lurch, and I hate how easy it is for him to undo me with five words and a tight jaw.

I lean back against the long dresser, now filled with mine and Mick's clothes, and cross my arms. "What makes you think I want to go on a date with you now?"

"You said you did."

He's talking about the Dierdre debacle.

All the softness his words engendered disappears. "That was before."

"There will be no divorce, therefore there is no *before*," he says, proving he knows exactly what I meant. "There is now and always."

"And you think if you say that, it makes it true?" I demand, making no effort to hide my crankiness.

I'm not the perfect paragon Kara anymore.

His expression says *yes* but he's smart enough not to say the word out loud.

"Why now? If you wanted to go out with me, you would have said so sometime in the last seven years."

"Dining in restaurants creates a security risk I prefer not to take with you." Suddenly, he's invading my personal space.

How did he get so close?

"What do you mean? We eat out for our anniversary." As well as the events I just mentioned.

His hand settles on my waist, like he needs to touch me. "I prep the locations beforehand."

"In what way?" I ignore the breathiness of my own voice.

"By the time we arrive, there are two full teams of security dedicated to your safety in place. One inside the restaurant, or venue, including the kitchen to oversee the preparation of our food. The other team stays outside, with two snipers in place."

No wonder we don't go out to dinner on a whim. "Isn't that overkill?"

"Nothing that keeps you safe is too much."

"Did you make those preparations for your dinner with Dierdre?" Somehow, my hand is holding his belt and I'm standing even closer to my husband.

Desire flares in his green gaze. "Nah."

"Why not?"

"Because she's not worth the effort."

"But I am?"

"Can you doubt it?" His hand not holding my waist cups my nape under my hair, completely surrounding me with him.

"I wouldn't have asked for the divorce if I didn't."

Understanding dawns. "You don't think I value you?"

"I know you value me, but you don't prioritize me, so that puts low currency on that value." I think, even with his ASPD, he cares about me.

As much as he cares about anyone besides Fitz. But that still doesn't make me *important* to him.

"Not taking you on dates made you believe this?" he asks, no inflection in his tone.

I have to get used to that. Mick not masking his true nature.

"Abandoning me for work on our wedding night, taking phone calls in the middle of sex—"

"I explained about our wedding night."

"But if you'd gotten the call from my grandfather before you left the bedroom, you would have gone."

Mick nods. "And that bothers you?"

"The fact you would do it at all? No," I spell out very clearly. "The fact you would do it on our wedding night, or miss our anniversary for mob business? Yes."

"Because our anniversary is the only time I take you out to dinner, just the two of us."

"That, and it's our anniversary Mick. If you don't want to celebrate our marriage, how am I supposed to believe it, or I am important to you?"

"You need to make me a list of the dates that are important to you."

"They're not some big secret. Our anniversary. My birthday—"

"You want me to spend time alone with you on your birthday?" he interrupts me to ask again.

It's on the tip of my tongue to say, *duh*, but I don't. Maybe what is obvious to me, and other people isn't to my sociopath. And maybe that list he wants is his way of prioritizing my feelings.

I simply nod and say, "Yes." Then a thought comes to me. "It would be just as special if that time included Fitz."

"But no one else."

"No one else."

"Not even Fiona or Maeve?" he checks.

"Not even them. Our time together as a nuclear family is at a premium. You making it happen for my birthday would feel special."

"Noted."

I can't believe he's got me talking like we have a future already, but this whole Mick showing me who he really is and listening to my every word? It's heady stuff.

He pulls something out of his trousers pocket. A flat jeweler's box. "I know jewelry is just part of the armor you wear, but this made me think of you."

"You have to step back so I can open it."

He does with clear reluctance.

I flip the top up on the box and gasp. It's a garnet cut in the shape of a heart and wrapped in yellow gold wire, creating a tree of life in the center. It's set in an oval setting decorated with tiny foliage accented with small round brilliant cut emeralds and diamonds.

Like my birthday gift, this necklace feels special. As if it was made just for me.

There are earrings made with the same yellow gold and gemstones but simple and elegant to compliment the pendant.

"It's beautiful." I touch it reverently. "I can't believe you just saw something like this and it made you think of me."

"I saw a heart shaped stone wrapped in the tree of life and told the jeweler I wanted something like it, but befitting my queen."

"Garnets symbolize passionate love and devotion," I tell him.

So do emeralds. Diamonds symbolize enduring love, commitment and strength.

"I know."

"Are you trying to tell me something?" I ask, my heart beating wildly in my chest.

"There is no stone that is associated with addiction, but enduring devotion is close. You are my pulse, my treasure."

He says it in English and I feel like that's purposeful. He wants me to know he's not just using an endearment. But that the words carry a deeper significance for him.

"And the love?"

He brushes my hair back from my face and behind my ear. Touching me again. Because he needs to? "I don't feel emotion."

"That's not true. You love Fitz and while you may not love me you react to me with emotion. Pleasure. Anger. Frustration. Happiness."

"The anger and frustration are new," he says with one of his genuine smiles.

The smiles he reserves for me and Fitz indicated a level of joy that Mick shows with no one else.

Addiction.

I wonder. Is what Mick calls addiction what I might call love?

"If you're really intent on staying married, you need to know I'm done being the obedient perfect mob princess," I warn him.

"Is that how you see yourself?"

"Yes." I lick my lips and watch his gaze fixate on them. "Isn't that how you see me?"

He shakes his head a little, like he's clearing it, and our eyes meet. "No."

"How do you see me?"

"Stubborn. Rebellious."

I laugh out loud until I realize he's serious. "How do you figure that?"

"Would you have ever let me use the cuffs again if I didn't start turning off my phone when I had you bound?" he asks in return.

"No."

"Stubborn."

"Self-protection."

"Exactly. When something is important to you, you don't back down about it. Like Fitz getting therapy after Róise's kidnapping."

"It's a good thing he didn't see you carting me from the mansion bound wrist and ankle." My words sound a lot more amused than angry.

Gah.

He's getting to me.

Mick shrugs. "There's a reason I sent him ahead in the helicopter."

"You could have just not kidnapped me," I suggest.

"Nah. It was necessary."

Not willing to argue that designation with him, I ask, "How do you think I'm rebellious?"

"You kept seeing a therapist after you came home from The Marlowe Center even though you knew your father didn't want you to."

"You called him my father."

Mick's brow furrows. "Aye."

"You usually call him my da."

"Not now that I understand why you don't."

Obsession. Devotion. Loyalty. I might be deceiving myself, but Mick's definition of his feelings for me are sounding more and more like love.

"One rebellion does not a rebel make."

Mick laughs and the genuine humor in the sound makes me smile too.

"You are going to college secretly, you hacked our security feeds so you and your cousin could sneak off the property, you taught our son to read despite his teacher telling you not to."

"Expecting me to hold my son's natural development back for her convenience was ridiculous. Besides the deed had already been done."

"You read the letter she sent to parents about what she expected our son to be proficient at before coming into kindergarten, just like I did."

"His first-grade teacher is much more focused on challenging his students," I say with approval.

"You like him."

"I do." I roll my eyes at the danger vibes now emanating off my husband. "Not like that. Rein it in psycho boy. The *only* man I like in *that* way is you."

"I don't want you to like other men at all."

"Not going to happen. But you never have to worry about me flirting with other men, or allowing them to try to undermine our marriage."

Mick winces. "I miscalculated the damage Dierdre could do because I knew I wasn't interested in her."

"Would you make the same choices again?" I ask, because this really matters.

"Not a chance in hell, even if my men call me the devil."

"That's good to know." Maybe my husband can learn to be the man I need him to be in our relationship. "So, you think I'm a stubborn rebel?"

"I think you've been selective about your intransigence and rebellions, but that is going to change."

"It's almost like you know me," I tease, feeling a little overwhelmed by that truth.

"Better than anyone else. But understanding you is something else entirely," he admits.

But he wants to.

And that counts for a lot.

"What should I wear for this date?"

CHAPTER FORTY-THREE

Unmasked at Altitude

MICK

We take the helicopter back into the City because Kara likes Asian Fusion food and the restaurant with the best reviews is here.

Although there is virtually no noise inside the cabin of the S-92, we don't try to talk. Kara watches out the window, her expression reminiscent of the one Fitz got when we took him to the fair in the summer.

Now, that was a logistical nightmare, but Kara was determined to take him. So, I made it happen.

Does she understand that was as much for her as it was for Fitz? My gut tells me she doesn't.

We're about twenty minutes into the flight when she turns her gaze on me. I haven't had my eyes on anything but her the whole flight.

Her eyes widen, like she's surprised to find me looking at her. Where else would I be looking when she's so feckin' sexy?

Her black dress has sleeves that reach right past her elbows, but her shoulders are bare and there's a deep V showing off her cleavage. She's wearing the necklace I gave her earlier, the bottom tip of the heart just touching the top of the deep crevice between her gorgeous baps.

It's some kind of stretchy fabric, so it clings to all her womanly curves and my dick is telling me what an idiot I am for this date thing. If we were back at the house in Martha's Vineyard, we could be getting naked.

We have nominal privacy in the private lounge of the helicopter, but the divider between the other part of the cabin with our security team and the lounge is half wall, half curtain.

Not soundproof.

Regardless, if we were still in Martha's Vineyard, Kara wouldn't have that sweet smile playing over her lips. Her eyes wouldn't sparkle like they're doing now.

And no matter how hot our chemistry, she'd be as apt to douse the flames between us as fan them.

I fucked up royally with the Dierdre situation. That's no reason to ask her father for permission to divorce me, but I hurt her. And that is not okay.

She doesn't feel valued and she's one of the two people I treasure above all others.

When the psych books talk about people like me finding *their person*, they're talking about Kara.

A strange look comes over her beautiful face.

"What is it?" I search her eyes, trying to figure out what she's thinking.

Just lately, that's not as easy as it used to be.

"It just hit home that my husband of seven years is taking me out on a date for the first time," she says wistfully.

"We've been on dates before."

"No, we haven't. You've taken me out to dinner for our anniversary. Out of duty, but this is the first time it's a real date."

And she likes that it is.

I may not know why it's so important to her, but I can see that it is. "It won't be the last."

"Is that a promise?" Suddenly she's looking vulnerable.

I don't hesitate. "It is."

"Zoey and Fiona date, even though they don't leave the house." Kara's hands fidget in her lap.

There's a message there and I take my time figuring out what it is. I don't jump to a lot of conclusions. That's not how my brain works.

But it's more than that. Getting it right matters.

Because I am not giving my wife a divorce and I'd much rather she was okay with that than fighting me on it.

"If I had realized that dating was important to you, I would have taken you for a picnic on the beach." Zoey and Fiona did that at least once a week during the summer.

And it clicks.

Zoey's a mafiosa, but she still makes time to spend time one-on-one out of the bedroom with Fiona. She's not an underboss, but even with my schedule, I could have made that happen.

I know why I didn't. My wife does not.

Pulling one of her fidgety hands into mine, I lace our fingers. "Spending time alone with you outside of our bedroom was too risky."

She gasps. "What do you mean?"

"My need for control. My intensity. You didn't question it when we were making love."

The look she gives me says not to be so sure. "You hold something back then too, though. I can tell."

She's right. "There are things I want..." I shake my head. "If I let go of my control, I would devour you."

"Maybe I want to be devoured."

"I hope so." Her threat to leave me all but destroyed the leash I have on my primal urges where she's concerned.

"Tell me what you're really afraid of, Mick." She's so earnest.

So open.

So different from me. "You probably think I didn't touch you last night because I was respecting your boundaries."

"And maybe you were a little worried I'd knee you in the groin if you did." She winks.

That thought hadn't occurred to me, but I'm glad it did to her. Because if she'd done that, it would have had the desired effect.

Not because she hurt me too much for me to perform, but my tender-hearted wife doesn't cause pain to others. If she does, there's a compelling reason why.

I could not have ignored her overcoming her basic nature to get my attention.

"I didn't touch you other than to hold you, because if I did," I tell her. "I was worried I would destroy all the boundaries between us." Like I've wanted to do so many times.

My lizard brain doesn't understand why I can't fuck her in the ass, or shove my dick down her throat. My need to protect her has been stronger than those instincts though.

Up to now.

"What kind of boundaries?" she asks, her voice catching, her pupils dilated.

Feckin' hell. She's turned on by the idea, not repelled.

"I want to come in your tight little ass and make you climax while I'm doing it."

Her mouth makes a perfect O, but nothing comes out. Not even a breath.

"I want to fuck your throat and see the tears run down your temples from choking on my cock." Said cock is hard as a rock and raging right now.

Kara licks her lips. "You do?"

"Aye." Fuck. How can she doubt it?

I pull her hand over the console between us and press it against the pipe trying to break my zipper.

She squeezes.

My hips buck.

"Stop." But I don't move her hand away, do I?

"I don't want to." She squeezes me again and rubs her hand up and down the log in my pants. "I want you to lose control, Mick."

She doesn't know what she's asking for. "You're going to get your wish if you keep that up. I'll fuck you right here."

"With the pilot and the security team just on the other side of the curtain?" She doesn't sound appalled by the idea; she sounds excited.

Fuck. Me.

Kara's hand strokes me through my trousers like she owns me – which she does – and I bite back a groan.

"You want me," she whispers.

"No feckin' idea how much," I rasp, the muscles in my thighs locking up with restraint. "Get in my lap."

She hesitates.

I undo my seatbelt. "If you want this, get your tight pussy over here."

I don't talk to her like this. That's not part of our sex life.

But instead of offending her, it turns my wife on. She unbuckles her seatbelt and jumps up before reaching under her dress and pulling off her panties.

This version of Kara is going to kill me dead, but I'll enjoy every second on my road to hell.

"Come here, *mo chroí.*" The words rumble from deep in my chest.

Tugging her sexy dress up to her hips, she scrambles onto my lap. Without hesitating, Kara swings one leg over, straddling me. Her knees settle on either side of my hips on the soft leather seat, her dress riding up over her thighs.

I drag my palms over the silky skin of her legs, so warm and soft.

Breathing hard, she leans forward and braces her hands on my shoulders.

I kiss her. Hard.

Her mouth parts with a gasp, and I take full advantage. Our tongues collide, and everything I've been holding back – everything she's just given me permission to unleash – pours out of me.

She rocks against me, and my hands slide to her backside, gripping the generous curve and pulling her tight to me. I grind against her, and she moans into my mouth.

"I need you now," she pants. "I need you *in me.*"

That's all it takes. I yank at my belt, then my zipper. Then I line myself up, the head of my cock brushing against her wet heat.

"This is what you want?" I growl, my voice low and rough in her ear. "You want me to fuck you in a helicopter, knowing my men are just feet away?"

"Yes," she whispers, and that one word damn near undoes me.

She sinks down slowly, taking me in inch by inch, her breath catching as I stretch her open. But I'm not going slow. She said she wants me to devour her. So, I do.

Taking her mouth like the marauder I am, I surge up, forcing myself inside her to the hilt in one brutal thrust.

She cries out against my lips, but she doesn't try to pull away. Her hips cant back and forth pressing her needy little clit against my pelvis.

My fingers dig into her hips as I guide her body up and down on my swollen dick.

"You're so tight," I mutter against her lips. "So bleedin' hot and wet."

"You make me that wa—" Her words cut off in a wail when I yank her downward as I shove upwards, hitting her cervix.

Fuck. I have to slow down.

Regain control.

But Kara's vaginal walls tighten around me, and my wife's body goes rigid in climax.

What the bleedin' hell just happened?

I rip my lips from hers and our gazes lock. She's moving against me, riding out her ecstasy, not a single sign of distress on her pleasure flushed features.

My lips find her neck. Her jaw. Her mouth again.

I'm not done. And neither is she.

Surging up, I carry her across the small lounge and lay her flat on the bench seat there. Then I start to piston in and out of her, forcing her body to take more pleasure.

Yanking her dress down her arms, I expose her generous curves. I want to squeeze her tits. Play with her nipples.

And that's what I do as I ride her pussy with all the power in my body so much bigger than hers.

"You were made for me," I growl. "Everything about you."

Pupils blown, she demands, "Say it again."

"You. Were. Made. For. Me."

She moans, loud enough I know even the pilot heard it. Good. Let them know who she belongs to.

Our bodies slap together, the wet sound of our joining loud in the otherwise silent cabin. Her dress is bunched up like a corset from just below her boobs to the top of her mons. The necklace I gave her glints in the soft light, a message and a claim.

She is mine.

Always.

"I'm coming again! Oh, Michael," she gasps, her voice tinged with awe.

It's not the first time she's climaxed so close together. Something else is making her sound like that.

"Let go," I growl. "Right now, Kara. Let me feel you."

She does.

Her whole body trembles as she falls apart under me, clenching around me in rhythmic spasms that drag me right over the edge with her.

I thrust once, twice, and then empty myself inside her with a low, guttural curse.

We cling to each other as we come down. I roll off the bench, landing on the floor, Kara on top of me. She laughs and it makes her swollen pussy clench around my still hard dick.

Then Kara slumped against my chest, both of us panting, sweaty, and completely wrecked.

"I hope your team enjoyed the soundtrack." Her giggle is soft. Sweet.

So like my wife, but the vixen who seduced me into fucking her on a helicopter full of soldiers has a dark side too.

"If they did, I might have to perforate their eardrums."

She rears up and stares down at me. "No." That's all she says.

And fuck if the jealous and raging beast inside me doesn't calm down.

"You didn't keep anything back from me this time." Her eyes glisten. "You were all here."

"I'm always all here when I'm with you."

"But you don't always let me see that all. In fact, you never have before."

Is that why she was so happy she orgasmed a second time with almost no stimulation? Hell, the first time she came didn't take any time at all either.

Is she that turned on by the real Michael Fitzgerald?

For the first time in my life, shock has my tongue completely tied.

One truth reverberates through my mind. If I want to keep my wife, I have to give her my true self, not the one I think won't scare her.

Bleedin' hell. I'm not sure *mo stór* is afraid of anything.

Who would have guessed the key to her willingness to stay with me would be me giving her full access to the sociopath she's married to?

CHAPTER FORTY-FOUR

Confessions of a Mobster & His Mob Princess

KARA

I'm still reeling from what happened on the helicopter ride into the City when the armored SUV glides to a halt in front of a building near the Meatpacking District downtown.

What *I* instigated.

And I'm not embarrassed. Not that the men know what we did. Not that I was so hot for my husband, I came twice and close together.

None of it.

Because Mick didn't hold anything back and I loved every second of it.

I glance up and see a *Hisashi* above open double doors. There are three stylized letters in all capitals on the wooden awning: TAO.

"I've heard about this place." But I never thought I'd get a chance to eat here.

It's huge and even I know security is a logistical nightmare in a restaurant of this size and as busy as it is. But it's one of the top Asian fusion places to eat in the City.

I blink up at Mick. "You're taking me here?"

"Aye." He doesn't tease me for asking, since where else would he be taking me?

But I'm still having trouble taking it in.

"You don't even like Asian fusion." I take his hand.

He laces our fingers and holds my hand tight. My heart goes kathump.

"Nah. I prefer a good Irish stew any day," he says. "But you like it and this is a date."

I think I maybe mentioned how much I like this style of food once in his hearing. And he remembered.

Because he's obsessed with me.

Heck, he's probably aware of every single time I've ordered food from my favorite Asian fusion restaurant on Long Island for lunch.

"I guess being stalked by my husband isn't all bad," I tease.

He leans down and kisses me. Right there on the sidewalk in front of the passers-by.

It doesn't last long and the tension in Mick's body tells me he never loses full awareness of our surroundings. But he still does it.

And that causes another kathump in my chest.

The closer we get to the main restaurant area, the louder it gets. Until we're standing in front of a pretty woman giving Mick a warm smile.

She welcomes us to the restaurant and she turns her head enough to encompass me with her smile as well.

I smile back, but it's forced.

Not because she's not lovely. I'm sure she is, but the music and voices in loud conversation to compensate for the volume of it create a wall of sound that presses against me like a physical force.

Mick pulls me closer and leans down. "Okay?"

I want to say yes. He's made a real effort to bring me someplace special, but I have an inexplicable urge to cry. I don't understand this.

No, I don't go places like this. Even the bar we went to for Róise's birthday wasn't as loud as this, with sound echoing all around me. The club for her party was louder, but still not like this.

This cacophony is outside my normal experience, but that doesn't mean it should be this overwhelming to me.

"It's loud," I say.

The hostess isn't smiling now. She's looking at me with concern. "Are you alright?"

Do I look that bad?

"Would you like to get our food to go and eat somewhere more quiet?" Mick asks.

I sag against him and nod. Mick tells the hostess what we want to do, and she gets us menus to look at before calling a waiter over to take our order.

By the time I've picked out my food, I'm practically crawling out of my skin. Leaving one of his men to get our food when it's ready, Mick leads me back outside.

As soon as we are back on the sidewalk, my entire body shudders in relief.

"I would understand Fi having this reaction," I say to Mick as we start walking. "But I'm not prone to anxiety."

"Or you are not put in situations that trigger it for you," Mick replies.

That's something I'm definitely bringing up in my next therapy session.

"The acoustics in there amplified everything," I say, trying to explain it both to myself and my husband.

Mick nods. "When I train my men on interrogation techniques, they have to learn that everyone has a different level of pain tolerance."

"Uh. Okay." Where is this going?

"What barely registers for one person might break someone else. Circumstances matter too. Pain inflicted in an environment that causes mental distress is more acute."

I get the analogy he's trying to make. "But I wasn't distressed."

I'm not distressed. Am I? This is what I've wanted for my whole marriage. For Mick to take time to spend with me like a normal couple.

"But you were excited. Heightened emotion of any kind can increase our reaction to stimuli."

And I don't like loud noises. I've never equated that with anxiety, or anything like that. Only, given a choice, I always go for the quieter alternative.

The alternative where sound is measured and pleasant, not a roar of noise assaulting my eardrums.

And while I have to deal with crowds in my role as my father's daughter and Mick's wife, I don't like them. I never make a big deal about it because protecting Fiona is always more important than my low-level discomfort.

If I didn't step in and do the socializing, her need to escape every social gathering would become more obvious.

"I'm going to talk to my therapist about this. I can't react that way in a social setting where others could see it as a weakness." I am Kara Fitzgerald, ranking female in the Shaughnessy Mob.

"Now that I know that type of noise is overwhelming for you, I will not allow you to be placed in a situation where you have to deal with it," Mick says resolutely.

I sigh. "That's not realistic."

He stops and faces me. "You need to understand that I will protect you in every way I learn you need it. Every. Single. Way."

"I'm a grown woman. I should protect myself."

Mick's answer is to kiss me. Right there on the sidewalk. He takes his time and when we start walking again, pleasure and warmth are popping like bubbles in my bloodstream.

We walk down 9th and are turning down W 15th Street before I ask where we are going.

"Pier 57's Rooftop Park."

"You had a backup plan for my totally unexpected reaction?" I ask with disbelief.

"I had planned to take you to the park to see the view of the harbor after dinner."

Wow. When he decides he's going to take me on a date, my husband doesn't half-ass it.

"And if I'd wanted to dance at TAO's nightclub?"

"Security was in place and the doorman apprised of our possible intention."

"I'm impressed."

"I'm good at logistics," my sociopath says not-so-modestly.

"You are that." I look around us but don't see anyone I recognize. "Your guys are following us, aren't they?"

"Aye. Two went ahead to scout a safe location for us to eat."

"Are we going to sit on the grass?" I'm not sure how I feel about that in my dress.

"There are benches."

"We'll be lucky if any of them are empty."

"I'm the underboss to the Shaughnessy Mob, *mo stór*. We don't need luck."

That's new. Mick usually calls me treasure and I'm beginning to understand he means that literally, but calling me *my treasure* makes it more personal.

I decide I like it.

Mick's right of course. There is an empty bench with a radius of about ten feet around it free of other people when we get to the south side of the park.

Not having planned to do any real walking in my four-inch pointy-toed heels that do great things for my calves while squishing my toes, I can't wait to reach the bench. My feet nearly cry with gratitude when I sit down on it.

The view is too beautiful to focus on my sore toes though. We're about a quarter of a mile out over the water and whatever direction I look is a feast for my eyes.

The skyline of Lower Manhattan. The Hudson River and New York Harbor. I can even make out the Statue of Liberty in the distance.

"It's beautiful here," I breathe.

"Nothing is more beautiful to my eyes than you *mo chuisle*." Mick's hand clasps the back of my neck the way he does so often lately.

A blatant statement of connection. Our connection.

"You called me *mo chroí* on the helicopter." He never has before.

His heart. It's a little different than calling me his pulse. Closer to the word I'm afraid he'll never use.

Love.

Will he remember? Will he admit it if he does.

"Aye. Before you, I had no heart to speak of."

"That can't be true. You love your parents." Even as I say the words, I doubt them.

We have been married seven years and we've never gone to visit his family once.

He's been to Dublin on business without me, and I'm sure he sees them then, but when I ask about it, he never has much to say.

They came for the wedding, of course.

His parents came to visit after Fitz was born, but I don't remember a lot about that time. His mom sends gifts for birthdays and Christmas. She video calls once a month, but Sheila hasn't been back to New York.

Brian comes for business with my father and Mick a few times a year and always stays at the mansion. He's always charming to me and respectful of Mick.

He's good with Fitz, but not doting.

I like him, but I don't have any affection for him.

Mick told me once that his family did not approve of our son being given the surname of Shaughnessy.

Maybe that's why Mick and his da aren't close. They're not antagonist, but if I didn't know Brian was Mick's da, I'd never guess it by how they are together.

"No, I don't love them. I did not experience love before you gave me Fitz."

"I guess I did give you a heart then." I remember the first time he called me *mo chuisle*.

It was when I woke up in the private hospital after taking the sleeping pills.

He'd told me I had to live because I was the beat of his heart. I'd thought that meant he might love me, but he never said anything like that. And he always held part of himself back from me.

I still clung to the possibility for the first couple of weeks I was in The Marlowe Center because Mick was there every day with Fitz. They stayed at a rented property nearby along with his crew at the time.

It was during those weeks that my heart finally bonded with my six-month-old son.

And I found a reason to live.

I also discovered what showed on his face when my husband looked at someone he loved. Because that softness? It only came over his features when he was looking at our son.

Not me.

When we returned to the mansion, Mick's work schedule was brutal and we stopped connecting except in the bedroom.

Again.

I accepted that being his pulse wasn't the same as being his love and did my best to lock my own feelings deep inside me.

Moma told me later that Mick found me on the floor of our bathroom. She'd reiterated her willingness to protect me from him if I needed it. Something about him scared her then.

Now I realize he let his façade slip.

With her bloodthirsty attitude, I don't know how *moma* held herself back from putting the Ethelyn Glycol in *seanathair's* Irish whiskey.

I will take my sociopathic husband over my narcissistic grandfather any day of the week.

"What are you thinking about?" Mick asks me. "You've gone silent."

I tell him, omitting the part about preferring his ASPD over *seanathair's* narcissism. But I'm pretty sure it's implied.

Mick kisses my temple. "I took care of it for her."

"That should bother me, right? That you..." I look around us. No one is close by, but I still say, "Did *that* to him. Only it makes me feel protected."

"I will always protect you."

"I'm starting to believe you again."

"There will be times you will have to point out that your feelings are at risk from others. I won't always see it."

He sure hadn't with Dierdre and he hadn't listened when I tried to tell him. "Will you hear me? Will you care?"

"Aye. Now that I understand the cost to you of me putting business ahead of your emotional wellbeing, I will not do it."

"Don't go making promises you can't keep, but if you try...if I come first some of the time, that would be good."

"You don't understand, but you will. I will never again risk losing you."

The words send a tendril of warmth through me and there's nothing I can do to stop it from reaching my heart.

When his soldier arrives with our food, he brings a portable table as well and we eat our dinner looking out over the Hudson River. At least I do.

Mick looks at me.

When we finish eating, Mick hands me a pair of no-show socks and my favorite lightweight tennis shoes that cushion my feet like clouds. "Put these on so we can walk."

"They don't exactly go with my dress." But I'm already slipping off my heels and handing them to him.

He gives the Christian Louboutins to one of his soldiers for safekeeping, then offers me his hand.

I take it and we start walking along the park path.

"Why did you stop coming to my office?" Mick's voice breaks the comfortable silence between us.

"You didn't even notice I was there."

His hand tightens around mine. "I bleedin' well noticed when you didn't come anymore."

"Did you miss me?" I ask facetiously, knowing he didn't.

"Aye."

I stop walking to stare up at him. "You did?"

He nods, his jaw taut.

"Why not tell me? Why not ask me to come?"

"At first, I thought it was because you needed the time to take care of Fitz. He started crawling and he needed space to play."

I nod. Because that *had* been part of it. But I would have figured out a way to make it work if I thought my husband *wanted* me there.

"When I was in group therapy one of the other residents at The Marlowe Center asked me what I did while I hung out in your office all day. Like *why* was I there?"

"None of his feckin' business."

I smile wryly. "That's not how group therapy works. Anyway, I realized I didn't do *anything* useful. Anything that had to be done in there with you."

"I didn't care."

"I did." I shrug and then change the subject. "I've never understood how you convinced my dad to let you move to Maine with Fitz to be near me."

"I didn't. He told me no. That you didn't need us there."

"But you came anyway. With your crew."

"Aye."

"That could be seen as betrayal."

"And he could be seen as dead." Knowing now what I do about how Mick's brain works in regard to taking care of me and *anyone* standing in the way of that, I don't for a second think he's joking.

Worried Mick is going to start dwelling on his desire to kill Brogan for agreeing to the separation, I return to our earlier discussion against my better judgement. "You said at first it was about Fitz."

"Aye. It took me a few months to realize you were actively avoiding coming to my office."

"And that didn't bother you?"

"Oh, aye, it bothered me alright. But I know what I am and I figured you were looking for some freedom from me."

"Is this an ASPD thing, a guy thing, or just a you thing?" I ask, not so facetiously. "Because that doesn't make any sense to me. Why would I want freedom from you?"

"You didn't have a choice about marrying me or doing it right out of high school."

"Neither of us had a choice. If you didn't marry me, *seanathair* would have married me off to someone else."

"Aye, I realized that right off."

"And you weren't about to give up the chance to advance in the Shaugh- nessy Mob like you couldn't in the Northies."

"I wasn't about to let another man get his mitts on you."

"You said I became your addiction on our wedding night."

"That's when I recognized the threat you were to my self-control. From the moment we met, I knew I wasn't going to let any other man bask in your innocence."

"You have a poetic streak, did you know that?"

"I might be a sociopath." He winks. "But I'm an Irish one."

I laugh softly, content to stand there and look up at my handsome husband for the next millenia.

Which is a ridiculous truth, but it is my truth.

"Anyway, I wanted you to have what freedom I could give you."

"That's why you never told me you knew about me pursuing a university degree." He wanted me to feel the freedom of doing something entirely on my own for myself. "You're a pretty special sociopath. I'll give you that, but I would still rather have known you missed me."

"That's when I started watching you on the security feeds."

"And installed cameras in our apartment."

"Aye." He doesn't look even slightly repentant.

And *that* at least is not surprising.

CHAPTER FORTY-FIVE

The Obsession of Love

KARA

After our date, we don't head back to the helipad. Instead, Mick takes me to The Tower Room at The Plaza.

After one of our men lets us into the security cleared hotel suite and leaves, I spin in a slow circle taking in the lavish décor.

Yes, we live in a mansion, but this is a very special hotel room. The gilt furniture breathes opulence and elegance. And all I want to do is make a beeline for the big round bed I can see through the opening to the tower.

"Fitz gets to enjoy his sleepover. I thought we could enjoy ours." The sensual promise in my husband's voice makes it clear *we* won't be eating popcorn and watching a children's movie.

A pulse of want thrums in my core as a shiver of desire snakes up my spine.

Without either of us saying a single word, we move into the bedroom in one accord. I kick off my shoes and toe off my socks while watching my husband tear his clothes off like we didn't have sex only hours before.

Tugging my dress up my body and over my head, I toss it aside, now completely bare to the emerald heat in my husband's eyes.

Stepping forward, I lay both hands on Mick's hair roughened chest and push, guiding him back toward the bed. He stops when the backs of his legs bump the bed.

His eyes never leave mine. They're heavy-lidded, dark with intent and desire, but there's something else in them too.

Restraint. Control. The very thing I want to take away from him.

Because now that I know what it is like to have all of him, I'll never settle for the façade again.

I push a little harder against his chest. "I want to taste you."

It feels like everything stills around us. Even the air.

We've never done this.

I've wanted to. So many times. But I never had the courage to try.

Mick's the only lover I've ever had and even back when I was a naïve eighteen-year-old, I knew he'd had sex with much more experienced women.

Meeting Dierdre only confirmed that.

"Let me," I say, and slowly drop to my knees.

Mick spreads his legs, making room for me between them, tacit agreement to do what I want.

I wrap my hand around his thick shaft again, pumping once, slowly, watching how his abs contract and his hand fists at his side.

The sight of him like this – so powerful, so undone – makes my whole body clench with need.

"The girls in my high school used to talk about this." I lick my lips. "They said boys complain if they didn't do it right."

"Boys might, but I'm a man, *mo chroí*. There is no doing it wrong when I crave the touch of your mouth on me and have for the past seven years."

"Then why haven't—"

He puts his finger against my mouth, stopping my words. "I wanted to fuck your throat and I doubted my control to stop myself."

My clitoris throbs at his words. "I want you to lose control."

"I will na hurt ya." Mick's Irish brogue is so thick it would take a knife a lot sharper than the one in *moma's* box to cut it.

"I know you won't. You didn't hurt me on the helicopter." My intimate flesh can still feel the hard use he gave it, but I like the ache.

It's a constant reminder that with me, this man with nearly supernatural control, loses it. And only with me.

"Do whatever ya want." Mick's hands fist in the duvet.

I smile inside, but keep it off my lips. My predator doesn't need to think I'm challenging him.

I'm so not. I'm challenging us.

To be what I need us to be as a couple.

When I lean in and press my mouth to his tip, he groans and lets his head fall back.

Salty and hot, he tastes like power, like possession, and I want all of it.

Fantasies I've had about this over the past seven years run through my mind like a montage. One in particular playing over and over again.

Acting on it, I lean forward and drag one of my tight, aching nipples up and down the length of his thick, pulsing shaft.

It feels so good, I moan.

He does too, only his sounds more like a growl – low and raw.

I do the same with the other nipple, the sensation streaking through me like lightning, a direct line from the tip of my breast to the hot, desperate ache between my legs.

"I like this," I murmur, breathless.

"I feckin' glory in it," he rasps.

I smile, then do it again. It feels even better the second time, but it's not enough. I want more. I want control.

I want to surround him.

I press my breasts together around his thick erection, the weight of him nestled between them as I start to slide them up and down the length of him.

One hand lands on my shoulder in a tight grip and his hips jerk upwards, not letting me draw too far away.

"Fuck my bod with those big baps, *mo chuisle*!" he demands.

The need in his tone mixed with the heavy Irish brogue excites me as much as our bodies touching in this intimate way.

"You enjoying this?" I tease, just before dipping down to lick the viscous fluid beaded on the angry red tip of his penis on the next stroke.

Salty, like tears, but there's sweetness too. Unique. Intoxicating.

"Aye! Feckin' hell, Kara, do it again!"

I do. This time I let my tongue swirl over his crown, tasting more of him and prolonging the pleasure for both of us.

His fingers clamp onto my nipples, tugging, fondling, as I stroke him with the tunnel of my breasts. My hips rock back and forth in need, but there's no relief in empty air.

Each time his broad head brushes against my lips, I linger longer, licking, teasing, learning what makes him moan, what makes him shake. He starts moving in sync with me, his urgency growing by the second.

I want that urgency as unbearable as mine is. I need it.

I kiss him again, letting my parted lips linger over the head of his cock, before releasing my breasts. Wrapping my now free hands around his straining flesh, I lower my mouth over his head, stretching my lips wide to take him in.

I suckle gently at first, savoring the taste of his precum. Then more firmly, allowing my tongue to circle and stroke.

His fingertips tighten on my nipples to the point of pain and my own pleasure grows more urgent.

"Don't stop. Kara!"

Like I'm going to. My clitoris is aching for direct stimulation, but the tightening in my womb tells me I'm not going to need it to go over the edge into ecstasy.

I revel in the power I have over him, in knowing that right now, this lethal man is completely at my mercy. My predator, undone by his heart.

I slide my mouth down slowly, letting my tongue trace the sensitive underside of his thick shaft. He grits out a dirty curse in *Gaeilge* and it makes me want to smile in triumph, but my mouth is too full for that.

I take as much of him into my mouth as I can before sucking hard. He thrusts up reflexively, hitting the back of my throat, gagging me a little.

I don't mind. I want this. I want *him*. All of him.

His words from earlier play through my brain in a sexy litany. *I want to fuck your throat and see the tears run down your temples from choking on my cock.*

I pull back, then push down again, taking him a little deeper each time. My hands move with my mouth, the rhythm a little awkward, but he doesn't seem to care. If anything, his wild, frenzied movements say he's right there with me.

He lets go of my nipples to fist his hands in my hair, guiding my movements, pushing me further and further until I'm not just gagging. I'm choking and moisture trickles down my cheeks.

"Jesus, Mary and Joseph, *mo stór*, you're gonna make me lose it." As out of control as he sounds, he pulls my head back so I can take a breath between each thrust.

Taking care of me even when his lust nearly consumes him.

Remembering one of the conversations about how to *do it right* from my high school days, I hum around him. The results are more than a little gratifying. Swearing, his hips jerk and his hands pull on my hair.

I tighten my grip at the base and take him deeper, swallowing when he hits the back of my throat this time.

He goes deep, blocking my airway and I love it. He thrusts once, twice and then he pulls back, allowing me to breathe again.

I look up at my husband. His eyes are wild, feral. His chest rises and falls like he's run a marathon.

Then in one smooth motion, he pulls his erection all the way out of my mouth and hauls me up off the floor, before tossing me onto the bed.

I cry out in shock.

"Spread your legs." The command is rough, a growl scraping from his throat.

It thrills me.

I obey.

Mick climbs between my thighs pausing for a second that feels like a minute while his gaze consumes every fold of my intimate flesh.

"You're glistening for me, *mo chroí.*"

I arch, utterly shameless in my need. "I want you."

He lowers his head and licks me from my perineum to my clitoris, in one long, slow stroke with his hardened tongue.

Already over sensitized, I shriek.

His smile is diabolical. And then he eats.

There's no other word for it. He devours me like a starving man. Tongue wicked, hands possessive, arms pinning my thighs so wide there's plenty of room for his broad shoulders.

He circles my clit, flicking, sucking, teasing, and every time I get close, he backs off. Again and again.

Desire wars with remembered pleasure.

There have been times he's kept me bound and on edge for hours. I've come so hard, I passed out. More than once.

I don't think I have the stamina for that tonight. I need.

"Michael," I whimper.

"You'll come when I say."

I want to argue, to beg, to demand. But all that comes out is a cry as he sucks harder, and thrusts two thick fingers inside me, hitting that perfect spot.

And I shatter. Screaming my throat raw as my body seizes around his fingers, stars bursting behind my eyes.

Before I can come down, he shifts and flips me onto my stomach. Bruising hands yank my hips up and back, and he plunges his huge erection inside me in one brutal, beautiful thrust.

I scream into the sheets, and he curses, gripping my waist like he owns me.

Because he does.

"This is mine," he growls, thrusting so deep, so hard, I swear I can feel him in my throat.

"Yes," I gasp. "Yours."

The rhythm is ruthless. Punishing. Perfect. My whole body tightens again, climbing impossibly high, impossibly fast.

"I want you to come again," he grits out. "Let me feel it."

I reach under myself, rubbing my swollen, needy clit. My orgasm hits like an earthquake, splintering me into a thousand trembling pieces.

And it hits me. More than the pleasure. Something deeper. Something fierce.

Crimson. Intense.

"I love you, Michael!" It comes out on a sob and I wallow in the profound rightness of the words.

This is not with the pale pink affection that grew in those early months for the man I married.

This is mature. Molten, heated, and consuming. This is the kind of love that doesn't come with safety rails.

And I tremble with the enormity of it.

Mick goes rigid above me, growling my name as his hips jerk and he floods me with his heat.

For long minutes, neither of us move and the only sound in the luxurious hotel suite is our harsh breathing.

Then he sinks down on top of me, nuzzling my neck. "So feckin' perfect for me. I'm bleedin' lucky, even for an Irishman."

I smile, utterly boneless beneath him. And for this moment in time, I let myself believe I'm not just his wife.

I'm his everything.

CHAPTER FORTY-SIX

The Bunny Boiler Betrayal

MICK

I don't look away from the screen.

Not even for a second.

Because if I do, I'll end up fantasizing about walking into that room and peeling the skin off Dierdre Kelly with my bare hands.

And I need to pay attention to what's being said, no matter how satisfying those fantasies might be.

She sits slumped in the steel interrogation chair, lashes fluttering like she's on the edge of sleep. The drug makes her docile, not unconscious. Her eyes are open, her pulse steady.

Her mouth, at last for the moment, incapable of lies.

Good.

Brice stands off to the side, arms crossed, quiet and imposing.

Wraith leans in, voice low and calm. His hands stay open and relaxed, not threatening. He doesn't need to be.

Not when Dierdre's will is compromised, chemically.

I couldn't be in that room. I know that. I'd crush her windpipe the second she spoke my wife's name. And that would defeat the purpose of the drug. We need answers.

Without starting a war.

Kara's helping Fitz with his schoolwork. I've got a live feed of them too. It's playing on my phone and when I need to lower my blood pressure so I don't give the order to kill Dierdre, I look at it.

My fingers flex beside the laptop. I should've asked the right questions when I interrogated Dierdre myself. My sins of arrogance nearly cost me my wife.

Never again.

"You've been in contact with Ilya Darakov since coming to New York," Wraith says.

Dierdre's mouth twists in distaste. "My da wants me to marry him."

"Why?"

"Darakov has connections the Northies want. Access to weapons the Shaughnessy Mob doesn't trade in."

Wraith's muscles bunch under his snug fitting tactical t-shirt, a subtle indication of tension. "What kind of weapons?"

"Biological. Brian Shaughnessy doesn't like the idea of using them, but da says staying on top means using what's necessary."

"What do *you* think?" Wraith asks, using an effective drug induced interrogation technique.

Ask the subject their opinion and other pieces of information will be revealed.

"I think Brian Shaughnessy is soft. He refuses to do business with syndicates that are involved with human trafficking. We're losing millions in revenue from deals we could have made."

She recites the words like a well learned lesson, no doubt learned at her father's knee.

Oisín Kelly isn't the loyal friend my father thinks he is.

"When my da and Nevan are in charge, the Northies will prosper like never before."

Her father and brother? What about my brother, Adam? Do they expect him to go along with their plans? To step aside?

No chance on either.

"How's that going to happen then?" Wraith invites Dierdre to share her knowledge.

To feel smart and superior.

"Once Brian Shaughnessy is gone..." Dierdre taps the side of her nose. "Well, no one lives forever."

Fuck.

I send a message to Brice.

Mick: *Ask if there's a plan to assassinate my father.*

But even before my text reaches Brice, Wraith asks, "Does your da have plans to help Brian on his way?"

Sounding more like Kieran than his moniker Wraith, my new recruit slides into a creditable Irish lilt, giving Dierdre a false sense of being among friends.

"No. He's loyal. But once Brian is dead, da will take Nevan's advice."

So loyal he talks shite about the code of honor the Northies have lived by for generations. Limits my father still adheres to.

Though maybe not if he's willing to be talked into using biological weapons.

"If not your da, then who?"

"My brother knows if we don't move with the times, we'll be left behind. He's the one that talked my da into the marriage alliance with Darakov." For a second her clear admiration of her brother wavers. "That was a mistake. There are other ways to form the alliance."

"Your brother has plans to kill Brian Shaughnessy?" Wraith asks, still talking low and gentle, his Irish lilt perfect.

Dierdre blinks and Wraith has to ask the question again.

Then she nods. "Uncle Brian has a heart condition. No one will question when he has a heart attack after eating all the rich foods at Christmas dinner."

The diabolical siblings even have a timeline for the assassination attempt that is never going to happen.

"Your brother confides in you a lot," Wraith says with false admiration.

"We see things the same way."

Like psychopaths with no honor.

"What about Mick's brother. Isn't he supposed to take over for his da?"

Dierdre frowns. "He's in the way."

Which is not an answer. I want Wraith to shake the disloyal cow, but that wouldn't help in an interrogation like this one.

Unless we were using the drug to induce fear and paranoia...the thought is a tempting one, but answers given out of fear aren't always reliable.

"Does your brother have a plan for how to deal with that?"

"No. Nevan thinks he can convince Adam to go along because he's more ruthless about business than Uncle Brian."

I always knew Nevan was a *gobshite*. Adam is ruthless, but like all of us Fitzgerald's he adheres to his own code of honor and that includes the one established for the Northies.

Dierdre leans forward. "He's wrong, but I have a plan."

"I bet it's a good one," Wraith encourages her.

"It is. Once Micky's brothers are out of the way, he can take over. He won't hesitate to do what's best for the mob."

My wife is right. Dierdre is delusional.

"You plan to get rid of all of Mick's brothers?" Wraith asks, flicking a glance at the camera recording the interrogation.

"Over time. I can't do it all at once, but by the time they're all dead, he'll be in charge of the Shaughnessy Mob too and we will rule Dublin and New York."

We. Like I would ever allow that woman to stand beside me. She's not even worthy of licking the dirt off the bottom of Kara's shoe.

Wraith draws the conversation out, getting as much detail as possible about Dierdre's demented plans.

"Ilya and I have a deal," she says at one point.

"A good deal?" Wraith asks, managing to sound admiring while his body is rigid with disgust.

Dierdre's eyes lose what little focus they had. Her voice is flat, like she's reading from a script. "He said if I helped him get some gun prototype, he'd back out of the marriage alliance."

She's already revealed she can't back out because her da threatened to cut her off financially if she didn't marry Darakov.

Brice makes a sound and I shift my focus to my lieutenant leaning against the wall. He's not leaning now though, he's standing away from it, his hands fisted at his sides.

Wraith glances at his crew leader and shakes his head infinitesimally. "How were you supposed to do that?"

"I told him about the Bunker."

"How do you know about the Bunker?" Wraith asks.

Motherfucker.

My jaw clenches so tight I think something cracks.

She licks her lips. "I overheard Uncle Brian and my da talking."

Dierdre is even better at earwigging than I gave her credit for. No way did my da and Oisín discuss mob business like that in her hearing on purpose.

"Everyone thinks the Bunker is a myth, but Uncle Brian told my da that it's real. An underground safe house in Queens the Shaughnessy Mob has been using since they emigrated to New York. Uncle Brian has met with Brogan there."

It's time my father-in-law retired to the legit side of the business. He's gotten too arrogant for proper caution to run a criminal syndicate.

First, he tells my da about Kara's jealousy back in the day and now I learn he's shown the Bunker to da. At least it was before we started working on the Whisper Gun project.

Da hasn't been to New York since the month before renovations on the Bunker began.

"What did you and Darakov talk about in the Waldorf suite?" Wraith's voice drops even lower. Lethal and intimate.

"Since his men failed to get the gun prototype, he wanted more information."

"What kind of information?"

She sighs like it's obvious. "A different way into the Bunker. He wants me to search Micky and Brogan's offices for information on the gun."

No wonder she came to my office so often. Only problem for her is, there's no information about the Vanta in there.

Only on my phone and laptop and the NSA isn't going to break that encryption, much less Dierdre feckin' Kelly.

"Did you find anything?" Wraith asks.

Dierdre pouts. "No."

"Was Ilya happy about that?" Wraith's voice is pitched low with commiseration.

"No. He threatened to back out of the deal if I didn't tell him something."

Wraith's eyes narrow. "What did you tell him?"

"I lied." Dierdre taps her nose again. "I told him I thought the information was in the boathouse because no one is allowed to go in there."

"What else?" Wraith prompts, clearly as aware as I am that Ilya Darakov wasn't going to be satisfied with supposition.

Sighing again, Dierdre's head lists to the side. "I had to tell him the number of soldiers guarding the mansion and their security rotations."

No way does she know that stuff. Even her bodyguards don't know it. We don't stick to a set schedule for rotations. Routines make you vulnerable.

"Did your bodyguards give you that information?" Wraith asks.

Dierdre winks at him. "Nope. If they knew I was spying for Ilya, they'd tell my da I turned rat." She shudders. "So, I lied again."

"Did it work?" Wraith asks, an underlying buzz of excitement in his tone.

Dierdre's lies can work in our favor. If Darakov is planning an attack on the mansion, we can take him out then and Dierdre can be a casualty in the crossfire.

It's more elegant than my plan, but not as fun. I planned to drug them both with a paralytic and then put them on his private jet after sabotaging it. They would have had two other guests on the plane with them.

Siberian pit vipers.

Darakov is known for using their venom on his enemies. He is reputed to have several living in terrariums in his home and rumors say he travels with one on his plane in case he needs it.

But this new development would allow me to torture and then kill Darakov without retribution. Problem is, any signs of physical torture on Dierdre could lead to war.

Psychological torture it is then.

Dierdre's lips twitch upward, smug. "Ilya said he'd get my father to back off. No marriage. No threat of being cut off."

"Is that all you talked about?" Wraith asks, showing an ingrained thoroughness that will benefit our mob in the years to come.

Dierdre shakes her head. "I told him Kara was in the way. That I needed her gone."

Even though I know Dierdre threatened Kara's life, hearing that she asked for help from that scum, Darakov to make it happen snaps something inside me.

My chest hurts. It feels like I'm going to have a heart attack. I cannot lose Kara.

Not ever.

Feckin' hell. I love her.

It's not how I love Fitz, but there is no other word for this feeling. It's too big for addiction, too encompassing for lust, too much to be anything other than the miracle of a sociopath loving his woman.

"What did he say to that?"

She rolls her eyes. "Well, after the blowjob, he said he'd take care of it."

"You ordered a hit on Mick's wife?" Brice asks, speaking for the first time.

"No," she says, sounding indignant. "I didn't order anything. I just said it would be better for everyone if she disappeared. He said he'd take care of it."

This feckin' cow is bunny-boiler crazy.

She thinks she can take my heart from me? Never going to happen. I'd rip Dierdre's from her chest first.

Brice is the one who asks, "Why do you want Kara dead?"

A rapturous smile covers Dierdre's face. "Because Micky is mine. He always has been. And once Kara is dead, he and I will rule New York and Dublin together."

I close the laptop with a bang.

If I watch one second more, I'll find a way to teleport myself through the screen and make her scream.

I *am* going to bury her.

But I'm going to do it in a way that protects my wife and son. The two people I love.

CHAPTER FORTY-SEVEN

Even Sociopaths Love

KARA

Over the next couple of days, it gets easier and easier to believe that I *am* Mick's everything. Me and our son.

Mick tells me all about this new weapon he's been overseeing the development of for almost a year. It sounds like something right out of a sci fi novel.

When I told him that, he said my father said the same thing.

He also tells me that Brogan told him that I deserved to be loved fiercely. And I'm starting to think that maybe I am.

Because if there's a difference between Mick's obsessed craving for me and the love I feel for him, I can't see it.

When he tells me why he kept Dierdre at the mansion and how his *soft* interrogation of her ended, I laughed my head off.

"I wish you'd gotten pictures."

Mick flashes his devil's grin. "You think I didn't know you'd want to see?"

He pulls out his phone and shows me.

I laugh so hard it brings Fitzy out of the pool where he's been swimming with Rory. "What's so funny, mom?"

I put my arms out for a hug and my son gives me an exuberant one before he remembers, he's a big boy and too cool for that.

"Aww, mom." He draws out *mom* until I'm laughing again.

Before I can stop him, Mick shows the picture of Dierdre facedown in her plate of Dublin Lawyer.

"She fell asleep in her dinner?" Fitz rolls his eyes. "She's not strong or smart. Not like mom."

Mick ruffles Fitz's hair. "You got that right, boyo."

Rory yells to ask Fitz if he's done swimming and our son rushes back to the pool edge before cannon balling right into the water in front of Rory.

The big bad mobster gets splashed with an almighty spray of water right in his face.

Happiness fizzes inside me as I turn back to Mick. We're sharing a double wide pool lounger he bought the day after we arrived.

"You planned to tell me all along?" I nod toward his phone, indicating the picture of Dierdre.

Confusion flashes in Mick's green gaze. "Nah. I didn't."

"Are you sure about that?"

"I'm not." And that stuns him.

Mick is always sure.

"Maybe you were growing as bothered by the walls between us as I was," I suggest gently.

He nods, this time showing zero uncertainty. "I want you back in my office. I've already got a desk set up for you to do your schoolwork at. Once you graduate, you can work there."

"You want me to work for you?" I ask.

He shakes his head and my heart squeezes painfully.

"I want you to work with me. I don't share your father's antiquated views of a woman's place in the syndicate."

"So, you'd be okay with our daughter growing up to be a soldier like Zoey?" I ask.

Mick yanks me right into his lap, our gazes locked. "You want to have a daughter?"

He remembers what I said that terrible day when I realized my grandfather had ordered all the girl embryos to be thrown away.

So do I. And I remember the feelings that made me say that. That made me believe there was nothing worse than bringing a girl into this world.

"You would never take away our daughter's voice, or allow anyone else to," I say with conviction.

"No, I wouldn't. And no daughter of mine is getting married right out of high school either."

"She gets a say about who she marries and when she does, if she *ever* does it," I say.

Mick nods. "Chances are, it will be an alliance marriage because she won't be exposed to men outside our world."

I know he's right and I don't dispute that. But there's a difference between being told who you must marry and being given a choice about who it will be.

Or if you ever will marry.

"And Fitz?" I ask.

"Will always have a say in his future. We are born to this life, but that doesn't mean our destinies are written for us. Mine changed when I married you."

And mine changed when I married Mick. No other man would ever have held my heart like he does.

"I might not have a girl," I warn him.

"But you do want to get pregnant with me again?" he asks, his tone more hesitant than I've ever heard it.

"Yes. I love you, Mick. And I know you will love our daughter like a child deserves to be loved."

"Like I love her mother."

My heart swells in my chest as tears wash into my eyes. "You love me?"

"I have since the beginning. I didn't recognize it for what it was. Addiction I understood, but love? That was a total mystery to me."

"Then Fitz was born."

"And I knew I loved our son. Every feeling I had for him was fierceness tempered by tenderness."

"Not the way you felt about me."

"Nah."

"I don't love you the same way I love our son either. Or Fi, Róise or *moma*, for that matter." That love is fierce, but it's not passionate.

It's not accompanied by a need I don't think I'll ever be able to deny.

"Or your father."

"Or him." Yes, I love my father.

And maybe someday, if he really believes the words he said to Mick and acts like it, I'll even like him.

"I didn't understand the nuances of love."

"Because you've never loved anyone else."

"Not even my family."

"But especially not Dierdre."

"Fuck no! Not that disloyal piece of shite."

"Tell me how you really feel," I tease, but I won't pretend I don't like him saying that.

"She was working with Darakov."

"The Russian?"

"Aye. In exchange for information on our mob, he promised to back out of the marriage alliance."

"Why didn't Dierdre just say no?"

"Because her da threatened to cut her off financially if she did."

"I could almost feel sorry for her. It's a horrible feeling to think you're powerless in choosing your own future."

"Don't waste your tender heart on her. She planned to kill you. Even if she hadn't been a traitor, I would have killed her."

"Because you will always protect me."

"Always."

"Because you love me to the depths of your sociopathic soul."

"I'm not sure I have a soul, *mo chiste is a stór.*"

"Your cherished love? You're pulling out all the stops now." I'm teasing him, but my throat is thick with tears.

Because there's not a single bit of me that doubts that is exactly what I am to my ruthless mob underboss.

His cherished love. His treasure. His heart and its pulse.

His everything.

Later that night, after we've tucked Fitz into bed, Mick asks me if I want to go swimming.

Loving how he's making it clear he wants to spend time with me, not just in the bedroom, I say yes.

When we get to said bedroom, Mick holds up the tiniest green bikini I've ever seen.

"You can't wear this back at the mansion." His tone is a mix of warning and heat. "It's hard enough for me to let you wear your tankinis where the soldiers can see you. This? This is for when it's just us."

I arch a brow. "What about Brice and the others here?"

"*My* crew know better than to look."

I believe him. But it still sends a little thrill through me that I'm the one who can make this man come undone.

When we get outside, the sun's gone down, the moon is rising, and the water glows under soft deck lights.

It feels magical. I'm floating on my back, enjoying my view of the night sky when a hand closes around my ankle.

That's the only warning I get before I go under. I come up sputtering and glaring to find Mick grinning.

Carefree and happy and that just does my heart in.

"You'll pay for that," I threaten, launching myself at him.

I try to dunk him, and I definitely tickle him, but he's too strong. He flips us both underwater and when we come up, we're wrapped around each other.

His mouth finds mine with the unerring accuracy of lovers who have shared a bed and their bodies for seven years.

We kiss and tease and laugh until I'm breathless, and my entire body is buzzing. I wrap my legs around his waist, locking my thighs around him, trapping the hard length of his erection between us.

"You surrender?" he asks, grinning down at me, his hands roaming along my back and cupping my bottom under the water.

I rest my head on his shoulder, letting myself melt against him. "If this is surrender, syndicate wars would end before the first soldier dies."

"Nothing else can feel like this, *mo chiste is a stór*. What we have is unique."

That endearment again. And the way he says it makes my heart flip.

I press a kiss to his neck. "You think we're the only sociopath and mob princess who love each other more than life?"

"Doesn't matter. That love can't be duplicated."

"You're not competitive at all." I rub myself against his erection.

"You ready to go inside?" he asks.

"I'd rather go in the hot tub." I've got plans.

He agrees like I expect, because he would do pretty much anything to make me happy. And just knowing that infuses every breath I take with joy.

We reach the pool steps, and I try to unwrap my legs, but he tightens his hold on my backside. "No. Let me carry you."

I glance around. I don't see anyone, but I know they're out there – his men, watching. Protecting.

"All right," I murmur.

He carries me across the pool deck, the blunt tip of his hard sex rubbing against the apex of my thighs with every step. My mind drifts to a dozen scenarios that end with us naked, still in this exact position.

But first...I have my plans.

Mick starts the jets, then steps down into the bubbling hot water with me still in his arms.

I tense. "It's hot."

"You'll get used to it." He dips us both down until the water reaches our necks. "This is the quickest way."

My body fights the shock of the heat at first, but it doesn't take long before I'm sighing. "That feels heavenly."

We settle side by side on the bench, warm water and jets working out the tension in my muscles. It should be relaxing. And it is – for a while.

But I'm too aware of his nearly naked body. Of how good he smells. Of how safe I feel, even with danger always one breath away in our world.

Snuggling into his chest, I slide my hand up his thigh, slow and deliberate. When I brush my fingers against the hard line of his sex, he goes rigid beside me. I smile, as if I'm not up to anything at all.

My hand drifts beneath the waistband of his swim trunks.

"Keep your eyes on the stars, Michael," I murmur.

His hand grabs my wrist before I get too far. "What are you doing?"

"Can't you tell?"

"My men are on patrol," he reminds me. "I know you can't see them, but they're here."

"I love how you keep us safe." I curl my fingers around the top of his shaft. "But relax. The bubbles hide everything."

"You don't think my shout of ecstasy will give you away?"

I grin. "Do you care?"

"Do you?" he counters.

"No." And I don't. I'm not ashamed of this. Of us.

"If you keep your face blank, no one will know what I'm doing." I stroke him again. "And you're really good at that."

He has lots of practice.

"You make it hard," he growls, so turned on he doesn't catch his own pun.

"I know," I whisper.

His grip slackens. I slide my hand deeper, curling around his thick length and stroking slowly, savoring the weight and heat of him in my hand.

"You are pure pleasure," he breathes. "But I'm not sure this isn't torture."

I keep my eyes on the stars and work him with deliberate, steady strokes. It's heady, knowing I can bring this powerful man to the brink and none of his men will be any the wiser.

Until he shouts when he cums.

His chest rises and falls faster. His thighs jerk.

Then suddenly, he erupts out of the water, lifting me with him.

"Mick!"

He ignores me, carrying me at full tilt across the deck, his face wild with intent.

Feral. Focused. Mine.

He doesn't slow down when we get in the house. He pounds up the stairs and kicks open the door to our room. It slams shut behind us with a reverberation I feel in my chest.

"I want you," he growls, and his mouth claims mine with a heat that threatens to consume us both.

I don't fight it. I kiss him back like he's my oxygen and I've been drowning. We lose track of everything – time, breath, the world around us – until he breaks the kiss and steps back, his gaze dark and dangerous.

"Take it off," he says, his voice more animal than man.

"What?"

"Take off your swimsuit."

"Is that an order, underboss?"

"Yes."

CHAPTER FORTY-EIGHT

No More Boundaries

MICK

I wait.

Forcing myself not to touch her, gripping tight onto my iron control.

But it's different now. Because I know that when it slips its leash, I won't scare Kara. My perfect wife will revel in it.

She reaches around to untie the string holding the bottom of her top in place. The fabric falls down her sides, clinging to her generous tits, teasing me with glimpses of the underswell of her breasts, but not giving me what I crave.

Her hands drop to her sides, waiting, taunting.

"Now the other one," I order, my voice a low growl.

She reaches up and unties the bow at her neck and then peels the wet fabric down with agonizing slowness, provoking me.

It falls away completely, landing with a soft splat on the hardwood floor. My eyes stay riveted to the raspberry pink, swollen nipples revealed, now tight with arousal.

Cupping her breasts in both hands, she rolls her palms over those puckered peaks, and feckin' hell – I nearly explode in my trunks.

My wife's self-assurance in her own sexuality is the biggest turn on I've ever known.

This is Kara confident in my love. An emotion I was so feckin' sure I didn't feel for her, but saturated my heart and soul from the beginning.

I spent so much time hiding my true self from her, I didn't let myself see what lurked under the surface either. Another man might think love weakens him. I don't.

It's new and different to think about having, but one thing I know: the feelings Kara elicits in me make me more dangerous. I will do anything to keep *mo chroí* safe and with me.

I am not weak because of my love for her and Fitz. I am stronger.

Her head tips back, mouth parted, breath stuttering out of her.

"This feels good, Michael," she says on a soft sigh. "But not nearly as good as it does when you touch me."

Those words go through me like a steel pike.

I step forward.

But she lifts her hand, stopping me. "Not yet." Then she breathes. "Please."

Every muscle in my body vibrates with the effort it takes not to haul her into my arms and bury myself inside her. But I stop.

"I'm not finished following your orders." Her hands drop to her hips.

She tugs at the bows holding her bikini bottom together.

My fists clench at my sides. Sweat breaks out on my brow as she unravels the ties with slow precision. The fabric clings to her, still wet, still teasing.

"Pull it off." My voice is hoarse. Raw with primal need. "Now."

She uses both hands to tug the damp fabric away from her skin as she spreads her legs. The green scrap drops to the floor like silk sliding off a goddess.

She's naked. Glorious. Mine.

The light brown curls at the apex of her thighs glisten with her arousal. I take a deep breath, inhaling the delicious scent mixed with the salt water from the pool.

She's ready. Needy. Wet.

I drop to my knees in front of her and press against her inner thighs until she widens her legs further, my name a whisper on her lips.

Spreading her pussy lips with my thumbs, my eyes are fixed on that sweet feminine flesh. And there. There it is. Her clit, deep red and swollen, completely popped from its hood and glimmering with her honeyed arousal.

I lean forward and taste her.

She says my name again, this time in a strangled shout. Her hands tangle in my hair, yanking tight.

I swirl my tongue around her clit, teasing and devouring, and she grinds her hips forward, chasing more. I give it to her. Change my angle and go deeper, licking straight into her slit until my jaw is covered with the proof of how much she wants me.

She's feckin' delicious. I could stay right here and feast forever.

She rides my tongue with a desperate rhythm, panting, begging with her body, but I know she's right at the edge and I want to be inside her when she falls.

But not in her perfect little cunt. I look up at her until her eyes, dazed with lust, meet mine.

"I want to fuck your ass," I tell her, my voice guttural.

She nods and breathes, "Yes. I want to be with you every way there is for us to join our bodies."

I damn near come right then.

I surge to my feet, and lift her up against me, her legs automatically wrapping around my torso again. "I need you every way there is for a man to need his woman."

She clings to my neck. "Yes."

I claim her mouth with a kiss that gives no quarter and she takes all of it and gives it right back, kissing me with a fervency born of ungovernable passion.

Wanting to give her an orgasm to make her pussy as sensitized as I need it to be, I angle myself so my head kisses her opening.

"Michael?" she asks with confusion. "I thought..."

"Trust me."

"Always. In all ways."

Feckin' hell. This woman.

She sinks down, slick, swollen and ready and I press upward. Gravity and the power of my thrust leave her with no choice but to let me all the way in.

Her arms lock around my neck and she kisses me, hot and hungry. I grip her hips and move her on me, using the full strength of my body to take her the way I need to.

Four thrusts. That's all it takes before she explodes around me, crying out, her body clenching and convulsing. I don't stop, pushing her to keep taking me as her body tries to pull away from me.

But she doesn't say red. She doesn't say anything.

My sensual wife just moans, her face twisting, and then she's biting my neck and coming again, her whole body shaking with a second orgasm. She whimpers from the over stimulation.

Perfect.

I walk us to the bed and lift her off of my painfully hard cock.

She makes a sound of protest, her pussy lips clinging to me.

I place her on the bed, and she lays there, acquiescent and beautiful.

It only takes a few seconds to get the cuffs around her wrist and then attach them to the white wrought iron headboard with one of my ties.

Kara looks up at the cuffs. "Where are the ones you used when you kidnapped me?"

"In the closet." I watch her with unrelenting hunger.

"You could use them again, sometime. If you want."

The offer astounds me. "No bad memories?"

"No. As marriage rescues go, getting kidnapped by my husband was a pretty spectacular one."

"I'll remember that." I trail my fingers down her arms.

And Kara relaxes into the bed like she always does for me, her body going boneless.

Her trust in my sensual mastery over her is absolute. I will never betray that trust. And now that I know even my darkest desires are welcome, I'm determined she will enjoy every moment of every one of them.

I bring her to the edge of another orgasm while I work one finger into the tight ring of muscle, stretching her. She gasps as my finger penetrates her, hips jolting upward, but not away.

"Easy," I soothe, dragging my thumb over the throbbing pearl at the apex of her folds. "Let me open you."

The tight heat around my finger clenches, trying to expel me. I press deeper, then stop to let her adjust, to feel every inch I give her. She moans, low and desperate, pulling on the cuffs.

"You're doing so well," I whisper, voice gone hoarse. "You're letting me in, *mo ghrá*. Letting me own this part of you."

Her eyes flutter shut, and I feel her body melt into the mattress again, breath hitching as I slide a second lubricated finger in beside the first.

She cries out. In pain? Or pleasure?

I stop and to let her body adjust to the new intrusion.

But she squirms against my fingers. "Green, Michael, green!"

If I last until I get my dick inside her, they're going to have to call the bishop, because it'll be a bona fide miracle.

Scissoring my fingers to stretch her tight opening, I go back to massaging her clit. It pulses under my touch, her thighs trembling.

"Don't come yet," I warn, as I withdraw my fingers. "Not until I'm inside you. Not until you feel what it means to truly be mine."

She whimpers my name. Not as a protest.

As a plea.

And I give her more.

A third finger.

Taking her to the edge of yet another orgasm.

And another.

We are both covered in sweat and shaking with need by the time I turn her onto her stomach and press the head of my cock against her backdoor.

"Relax for me." I press a tender kiss to the back of her neck.

She makes a soft sound and her body goes limp under me.

I push forward again, but her sphincter seizes and I stop.

"I'm going to slap your ass. The shock to one set of nerve endings will help those around your tight little hole relax." I don't ask if that's okay, but I do wait to see if she says, *yellow* or *red*.

We've played a little with spankings, but not often because doing it brought too much of the primal monster inside me to the surface.

Kara loves that primal monster though.

She loves *me*.

Then I hear the word I crave in a low whisper, but unmistakable. "Green."

I deliver a stinging slap to her left butt cheek and push an inch inside her as soon as her asshole loosens. Then I spank her right cheek and gain another inch.

Her ass is rosy red and she's sobbing in pleasure, pleading with me to let her come by the time I'm seated fully inside her forbidden channel.

Only then do I start fucking her with the powerful thrust of my hips my body craves. I need release. But I need her with me. Not just her body. I want her soul.

Kara becomes frantic in her need and I lay down over her, covering her body completely with mine as I reach around and slide my middle finger between her wet pussy lips.

I rub circles around her clit until she's screaming for release as we move together, frantic, lost in each other.

The pleasure builds sharp, unrelenting, inevitable.

"Come with me," I demand.

Then I pinch her abused little pearl of pleasure as I fill her back passage with my hot cum.

Her body tries to rear up, but mine holds her in place as she screams out her climax.

We exist together in that perfect moment, a cataclysm of need, surrender, possession and release.

So much more than sex.

It's us. No walls. No hiding.

She is fully mine and I am fully hers.

Forever.

Finally, I can give the right label to this feeling inside me.

Love. Tenderness. Devotion.

Fixation. Addiction.

Because I'm still a sociopath and that's how my emotions, or what there are of them, work.

But a sociopath who loves with the very depth of that addiction.

CHAPTER FORTY-NINE

The Queen Takes Her Throne

KARA

M y father is already in the meeting room when Mick and I step in, two of his lieutenants behind us.

Despite the space age level security in the Bunker, four more of Mick's men are guarding the hallway outside the room.

He's leaning over a long metal conference style table with a floorplan of the mansion spread out in front of him. A red pen sits beside a half-drunk mug of black coffee.

Looking up at the sound of our entrance, Brogan swears.

"What is she doing here?" he demands of my husband.

I don't give Mick a chance to answer. "That's a good question considering I've never been here before."

Which is not to say the women in my family don't know about the Bunker. We all do and when Róise was kidnapped she was headed to it for safety.

Not that she knew how to get inside.

Which is not okay.

"Of course not," my father dismisses. "We conduct mob business here."

"You conduct it at the mansion too, but I'm allowed to live there."

"That's different."

"Is it?" I shake my head. "I don't think it is. The mansion is fortified for our safety. But this place is even more secure. Why do mob soldiers have access to it for sanctuary, but not the women in your family?"

I know the answer to my own question: because we aren't as important as his soldiers.

But the expression on my father's face is arrested. "It's always been this way."

"I wonder. I have no doubt that *seanathair* had that policy, but maybe the bosses before him valued the Shaughnessy women more than he did."

Instead of getting angry and blustering like I expect, Brogan sighs and nods. "Maybe they did. I know I do."

"And yet you never told me or Fi about it. Never gave us the codes to get in if we needed to."

"We keep you safe without it." There's the bluster I expected.

But I'm not impressed. "Protecting us means making it possible for us to protect ourselves."

"Is this about those self-defense courses Miceli insists you all take?" My father sounds agrieved.

He doesn't like the training, but the only person he could have forbidden from taking it is Fiona and he was too enamored with the idea she would willing leave the mansion to do so.

"It's about treating us like equals and not little dolls you want to keep on a shelf until you have use for one of our uteruses."

"That's crude."

I shrug.

"You're right."

Shock expels from my lungs in a gasp. "I'm right?"

"Yes. I've made mistakes raising you girls. I see that now. You *should* have access to the Bunker and the armory for that matter." He puts up a hand. "But first you take gun safety and shooting lessons."

Stunned, I just nod like a bobble-head.

"That said, you do not belong in this meeting, Kara."

I stop nodding abruptly and my spine stiffens, but this time Mick speaks before I can. "She stays."

"This is mob business," Brogan says, like maybe Mick didn't get the memo.

Mick settles his hand on my lower back in a statement of solidarity. "Kara is now privy to all my business."

"That is not wise. We've always kept the women in the dark for a reason." His voice is rough with conviction. "We keep them safe by keeping them separate."

Mick shrugs. "And if that is how they choose to live, we respect that. Kara is my equal and she chooses to know."

That word I like so much that my former roommate used to say perfectly describes the look on my father's face.

Gobsmacked.

"We've always done it this way," he says and runs his hand over his face. "For their protection."

"I don't care how it's always been done. That's not how it's going to work with me and Kara. I can protect my wife better by telling her the truth when she wants it. There will be no secrets between us." The deep satisfaction in Mick's tone when he says those words have nothing to do with mob business.

He is happier than I've ever seen him now that he doesn't have to hold part of himself back from me. Our lovemaking is off the charts.

And coming back to the mansion hasn't changed that. It was good before, but it's different now. We're both our true selves, hiding nothing.

After Fitz left with his bodyguards to go to school, Mick stayed. He swooped me up and carried me to bed, to the floor, to the wall – any surface strong enough to take us. I came hard and fast and often.

And when I told him I loved him again, it felt like the most natural truth in the world.

Because it is.

It was his words after that blew a hole in my heart and filled it back up again.

"Thank you for loving me for the sociopath that I am and not the man I pretend to be for everyone else." Then he told me he loved me.

And we made love again. No handcuffs. No edging. Just two bodies moving together in love filled pleasure as he said *thank you* to me over and over again, between kissing every inch of my face, neck and shoulders.

Mick needed the walls to come down between us even more than I did and I'll never forget that. I will never allow him, or me, to erect them again.

Right now, my father stares at my husband like he's lost his mind. "That's not how it works in our world."

"It is in the one I'm creating with Kara."

I'm so pleased by his response, I turn my head and reach up so I can kiss the underside of his jaw. "Yes, it is."

"This is what you really want?" my father asks me.

"Yes. From now on, I get a voice in my own life and the life of this family."

"You're a strong and intelligent woman, one I'm proud to call daughter. I'm sure you'll only make us stronger." He grimaces. "But you can't blame me for worrying about you."

"If you worried about my emotional wellbeing as much as you do my physical, we'd have a very different relationship."

"If I change, if I show that you and your sister matter to me more than the mob, more than anything..." He pauses, almost diffident. "Do you think that relationship can change?"

"If your actions match your words and intentions, it's possible. I don't trust you, but if you really want to change that, you will."

His eyes glisten, but he blinks away the moisture and nods. "I will."

For some reason, I'm too choked to speak, so I merely nod.

"Darakov thinks the plans for the prototype are in the boathouse," Mick says with an abrupt subject change.

Done with emotional watersheds for the moment, I'm grateful. "So, we set a trap."

"I don't want my family put at risk," my father says. "We need to draw him into targeting the Bunker again."

"That will only net us more hired mercs, or his own men."

"We want Darakov to come, right? So, you can kill him and explain Dierdre's death away as a lover's spat gone wrong," I say.

Mick's brows furrow. "That wasn't the plan. She dies in the crossfire when he tries to kidnap her again."

I shake my head. "That makes it look like we didn't protect her like my father promised to do. But if Dierdre sets up the assignation and somehow ends up dead when she changes her mind and refuses to leave with him..."

I watch my father and husband, to see what they think.

Mick's face is blank, but my father looks impressed.

"You've got her phone cloned, right?" If they don't, I can easily do it by replacing her charging cord in her bedroom with one that sends data directly to a cloning program.

Mick guides me into a chair and then sits down in one he tugs to a position right beside me, our thighs touching. "Aye."

"Send him a text telling him that she's going to get him the prototype, but will only hand it over to him."

Mick's eyes narrow in thought. "They've been too cautious to text about their deal."

"So, couch it in terms that he'll understand but make it obvious what she means. Stress her need for secrecy, that she's worried you're onto her and she's going to keep their contact to a minimum."

"If we make it look like a romantic assignation in the boathouse, we'll be able to show the texts to her father as proof of the scenario we are creating," my father says with admiration.

We discuss the best way to word the texts and then my father suggests that I handle the exchange because I'm a woman.

I stifle my sigh. Baby steps.

My father isn't going to change overnight and I'm doubtful he'll ever be anywhere near being labeled a feminist.

But he's trying.

The text exchange goes well. I make it clear, as Dierdre, that I won't hand *myself* over to anyone else. Only him.

I make it sound like she's agreed to the marriage and wants to spend time with him away from her family, or my father's watchful eye to be certain of their physical compatibility.

We agree to meet at 2 a.m. in three days at the boathouse for our rendezvous.

To be safe, all texts and calls will be funneled through the clone program in case Darakov contacts her before then.

He shows he knows it's a ruse for getting the prototype with his final text.

Ilya: *I look forward to fulfilling all the terms of *our* deal. I keep my promises. I'm glad you keep yours.*

Which I'm grateful for, because after she gave him a blowjob to convince him to have me killed, the idea of her being willing to have sex with him isn't that big of a stretch.

The next three days are fun.

For me.

Not so much for Dierdre.

Mick goes from never showing me affection in public to touching me whenever we're together. Which is pretty much 24/7. I start doing my schoolwork in his office and we're making out on his desk one time when Dierdre walks in without knocking.

He's kissing me up against the wall the second time she does it.

He puts his arm over my shoulder during dinner, intermittently pressing his lips to my temple. He holds my hand as long as we have our security detail around us.

He explained why he didn't before, and I tell my sociopath that he's sweet.

That leads to an impromptu episode in the sunroom with men outside the doors to the terrace and hall to prevent anyone interrupting us.

He is not at all sweet and I end up with a sore bottom, but only in the best possible orgasm inducing way.

I help Mick's blackgloves comb through camera footage from in and around the mansion, identifying everyone Dierdre and her two guards have spoken to so they can be debriefed, according to my father.

Or interrogated, according to my husband.

Mick's interrogating a man who showed up in several conversations with Dierdre and even entered her room on one occasion. I wouldn't want to be him.

Even if he didn't divulge anything to her, he's been unknowingly consorting with the enemy and Mick has no mercy when it comes to our safety. If the man turns out to be a rat, I don't envy me, because security is going to get boa constrictor tight around here.

I'm taking a break to read, ensconced in my favorite chair in the sunroom, when Dierdre comes storming in.

She slams the door and glares at me. "I don't know who you think you're fooling, but all this lovey-dovey bullshite with Micky is just that."

"I don't know what you're talking about." I lay my eReader on the table and shift my weight in the chair.

I know there are security men around me, but I'm not taking any chances. My life is finally what I want it to be and this woman is not taking that away from me.

One of my security detail is on the far side of the room, to give me privacy. Mick insists if I'm not in our apartment that I have a bodyguard with me at all times.

And the men have all been instructed to prevent Dierdre access to our apartment, no matter how big a temper tantrum she throws.

My bodyguard is silently making his way toward us, but I'm not worried.

Dierdre isn't armed with anything but her poisonous words and they can't hurt me now.

She's not besting me a physical altercation and we both know it. Still, my muscles are bunched and I'm prepared to jump up if I need to.

"Did you forget what I told you would happen if you didn't divorce my Micky?" she demands, her eyes lit with a fanatical gleam.

I stand up and step right into her personal space. "Did you forget what I said I would do if you threatened my son?"

She takes an involuntary step back, but scoffs. "Like you're going to kill me."

"I don't need to kill you, Dierdre. You're already dead."

"What's that supposed to mean?" she asks belligerently.

The door opens and Mick enters, sliding his phone into his pocket. "Just what it sounds like, Dierdre."

"Stalking me again?" I tease my sociopath.

"Always."

"Your wife just threatened to kill me," Dierdre screeches at top volume.

"Not exactly, boss," my bodyguard pipes up.

Dierdre's head jerks around and she stares at the man she didn't realize was in the room with us.

"I know," Mick says calmly. "She told Dierdre she's already dead."

"I'm not dead," Dierdre yells.

I tilt my head. "Aren't you?"

"You thought you could come between me and the woman I love. The only woman I could ever love. The only woman who could ever match me strength for strength. Passion for passion."

"You really are sweet, Michael." I smile dreamily at my husband.

Dierdre lunges for me, but Mick is lightning fast and has her hands cuffed behind her back in zip ties in less than a second.

He shoves her toward the bodyguard. "Put her in a holding room."

Like I told my father, mob business happens here when it has to. Not everyone who shows up at a mob boss's door is his friend.

We've got a subbasement I've never been in, but I'm assuming that's where the holding cells are.

The soldier grabs Dierdre by the upper arm, but she screams and kicks him. Then he tosses her over his shoulder fireman style and carries her from the room, her caterwauling all the way.

"Isn't that a little conspicuous?" I ask.

"He's one of my men."

As opposed to one of my father's men who Mick does not trust as much. His lieutenants and their crews know stuff even Brogan doesn't. But I know it all.

Now.

Mick grabs me, picks me up the same way and starts jogging.

Only I'm laughing and his hand is squeezing my thigh suggestively as he jogs up the grand staircase.

"Where are you taking me?" I smooth my hands over his toned backside. What's a girl to do? It's right *there*.

"We need to have another discussion about how very *not* sweet I am."

CHAPTER FIFTY

The Lovers' War Plan

KARA

S nuggling with Mick postcoital orgasm is one of my favorite things. It's the only time his body is completely free of tension and the dark aura that surrounds my husband dissipates.

I never named that dark aura before, or even consciously recognized it as being there, because I told myself that Mick was the man I saw on the surface.

Now I know the truth, and that dark aura doesn't bother me. Because it's real.

It's Mick.

And I love every atom of Michael Fitzgerald and his tarnished soul.

Mo diabhal

I trace the words on the tattoo over his heart. "What's wrong?"

He jolts. "You know something has me fashed?"

"I know you better than anyone else, just like you know the very depths of me." I press my hand over his slow-beating heart. "Now, tell me."

"I have to decide whether or not to tell the Northies about Dierdre and her brother's plans for my father, or simply kill him quietly and eliminate the threat."

"Why not tell them?" I ask.

"If his father refuses to kill him, I will anyway and that could cause a schism between our two mobs."

"Because even though you don't feel love for your family like you do for me and Fitz, you're loyal to them." Mick's loyalty is better than a lot of people's love if you want my opinion.

I'm just lucky enough to have both.

"I cannot allow a threat to my father's life to continue to exist."

Trying to understand why there's a quandary then, I ask, "What are the downsides of not telling your father about Dierdre and his plans?"

"He may have things in motion that Dierdre doesn't know about."

"So, interrogate him before you kill him." Unless I'm missing something, that seems like the obvious solution.

"Interrogation will lengthen the amount of time I have to be away from you and Fitz."

Warmth suffuses my heart. This man.

My sociopath.

"We'll go with you." I nestle closer to my husband's warm body. "A trip for Fitz to meet the rest of your family and us to offer condolences on the Kelly's loss of Dierdre will be a good cover for you being in Dublin."

Mick sits up and pulls me with him, right into his lap.

His green gaze bores into mine. "You're okay with that?"

"I don't like being away from you anymore than you like being away from me. From now on, Fitz and I travel with you."

"When it's safe," Mick temporizes.

I smile at him with all the confidence I feel in *mo diabhal's* strength. "You'll keep us safe wherever we are."

"I will." He agrees. "But I won't knowingly take you into situations that carry unacceptable levels of risk."

"Okay." We'll discuss what an *unacceptable level* is later.

"I'll have to employ drugs for the interrogation like I did with Dierdre. He can't die while we're in Dublin."

"You sound disappointed you can't torture him," I tease.

Mick shrugs. "If he wasn't the instigator of Dierdre's plan to get rid of you, he approved of it."

And that puts an even bigger bullseye on the man than his plans to kill Mick's father.

"Someone had to feed Dierdre's delusional beliefs," I say in agreement. "My guess is it's her brother, and he has his own reasons for doing so."

Maybe to destabilize the Shaughnessy mob. To what end I don't know and really don't care. Despite being part of an ally mob, he's our enemy and that's all that matters.

"Anyone who is a threat to you or Fitz has to die," Mick says implacably, echoing the tone of my thoughts.

"Agreed, but the same goes for you." I grab his face and stare right into the fathomless depths of his eyes. "No one is taking my sociopath away from me. If there is a monster inside you, it's a gargoyle. Stony and silent until it comes to life to protect the people who matter to you."

Mick slams his mouth against mine with a renewed passion that at first startles and then consumes me. Our hands are everywhere on each other, and I shift so I'm straddling his lap.

I pleasure us both rubbing my sensitized and swollen clit against his steel hard erection. And he lets me, making no move to take over.

My ovaries are exploding at the power this predator allows me to have over him.

It stuns me how natural this feels now. How powerful. The first time I did this, I was tentative. Shy.

I feel anything but shy right now. I feel like the mob queen I am.

Breaking the kiss, I meet emerald eyes glittering with lust, I take his hardon in my hand, anticipation thrumming in my core.

His grips my hips, fingers digging in. "Look at you. Feckin' hell, you're breathtaking."

I glory in his words and how tight his grip is on me. Like he's afraid to ever let me go.

Shifting upward, I let the head of his penis press against my opening and then sink down onto him. My body is ready for him, already slick and stretched for his girth from earlier.

Not that I don't feel the stretch now.

I do. And it's delicious.

The apex of my thighs presses against his groin as he is fully seated in my body.

We both groan at the same time.

His eyes shut, but not for long. He opens them again, needing to see me. Needing to watch.

"You're so fucking tight," he grits out, his voice gravel. "So perfect around me."

I start to move, slowly at first. Rolling my hips as I brace my hands on his shoulders.

Mick lets me set the pace. "You ride me like you were made for it."

"I was," I promise him.

"You're the strongest woman I've ever known. Smart. Loyal. Vicious when you need to be." His words fall out between clenched teeth. "And so bleedin' beautiful, you bring me to my knees without even trying."

The stretch, the fullness, the way his voice wraps around me like silk and sin is almost too much. And I lean forward, grabbing the headboard behind him, my aching nipples rubbing against his chest as I move faster.

Dipping his head, he grazes first one, and then the other with his teeth before taking it into his mouth and sucking.

Ecstasy arrows to my core. "Mick..."

"That's it," he growls against my breast. "Ride me, Kara. Take what you need. Show me who you are."

"You know who I am." And he's the only one who really does.

Not even *moma*, my sister or my cousin know me like Mick does. And it's taken me seven years to realize it.

He suckles me with harsh pulls until I'm riding him with no finesse and utter abandon.

Lifting his head, he cups both of my breasts, playing with both turgid buds now. "You look so good like this. Hair wild. Skin flushed. Tits bouncing as you fuck yourself on me."

This constant vocalized praise is something new and it started after Mick showed me his true self. I love it. Almost as much as I love him.

But I have no breath to reply, so I kiss him with carnal ferocity.

The pleasure inside my body coils tighter and tighter. I know what's coming and still the intensity of the pleasure takes me by surprise as I scream his name and come.

His hands slide back to my hips, his grip tight and he holds me against him as my orgasm implodes through me.

"You make me lose my mind, *a chiste is a stór*." His voice is almost reverent now. "You make me better."

"You don't need to be better," I gasp out. "Just you."

"You were born to rule beside me." His voice cracks as his hands grip harder. "No one has ever matched me until you. No one has ever touched my soul until you."

He flips us, so he's on top and he pistons his hips without mercy, driving me to another pinnacle of pleasure with no respite from the one I just had.

"You're mine, Kara," he grinds out, eyes wild and feral. "All of you. Every feckin' inch."

"Yours." And then I break apart.

Pleasure rockets through me, explosive and total. I cry out into his neck as I come, my walls pulsing around him in wave after wave of ecstasy.

He surges up into me, groaning as he follows, his climax hitting with the force of everything he is: dominant, devoted, and entirely mine.

We collapse together, still joined, still gasping.

His body blanketing mine, he whispers the only words that matter. "I love you. I'll love you through my last breath and into eternity."

CHAPTER FIFTY-ONE

For Kara. Always.

MICK

Dierdre is pacing the cell when I release the biometric lock and walk inside.

"Micky, what am I doing here? I don't know what that devious woman you married told you, but I love you. You must know that." She throws herself at me, clinging in a way no woman but Kara has a right to.

I shove Dierdre from me hard enough that she lands on the cot across the small room. Eyes wild, she jumps up again.

But I put my hand up. "Stay there."

For once, real tears fill her eyes and spill over. Unlucky for her, the only woman's tears who matter to me are Kara's.

"You tried to take my heart from me," I inform her dispassionately. "You will die. And you will be in excruciating agony when you do it."

Dierdre starts screaming and I leave the cell.

She's still alive because she has one more job to perform, but when that's done, she will die in terror and pain.

A just ending for someone who wanted to kill my wife and threatened my son.

Later that night, I stand in the shadows of the boathouse watching the water on the bay. The access door for the slip connected to the main room of the boathouse is open and Dierdre is sitting in a chair bathed in the light of a single lamp like she's waiting for someone. What she is, is drugged.

Just Special K this time. I only needed her malleable and suggestible.

Despite my warning about her death, when I tell her I need her to do something, the drug makes her willing. Her delusions make her eager.

But by the time Darakov realizes the trap, it will be too late for him to escape.

The sound of an outboard motor reaches me before my eyes tune to the dark shadow crossing the water.

We've turned off the alarms on the bay side of the boathouse and the guard underwater is one of my men. No word of tonight's events will reach Northie ears from any mouth but my own.

And that narrative will only have a loose resemblance to what actually happens.

Darakov waves at Dierdre and like the well-prepped, drugged-up bunny-boiler she is, she waves back.

He moors the boat at the edge of the pier and steps out.

"You got the prototype?" he asks when he's only a few feet from her.

She nods. "In the duffel."

He moves forward quickly to grab it and that's all I need.

I give the signal and the two guards he brought with him are taken out with head shots, the only sounds the thud of a body hitting the decking and the splash of the other going into the water.

Darakov turns to see what's happening and I strike. Taking him down is almost anticlimactic. Clearly too used to having his men do all the fighting for him, his resistance is pathetic.

I have him cuffed at the wrist and ankles with a gag shoved in his mouth and duct tape over it in less than a minute.

It's ridiculous.

"With a leader as weak as you, no wonder your bratva is about to get wiped off the face of the earth." By me.

I shove the aerosol mask prepped with the benzo compound over his nose and wait for him to inhale before pressing the release on the canister.

He stops squirming after his third inhale. The cuffs on him are designed not to leave marks even if he struggles against his bonds. But I'm not taking chances.

If something is worth doing, it's worth doing right. And the stage I'm setting for this narrative precludes bondage or interrogation marks on his body.

I instruct Conor to dispose of the two dead bodies of Darakov's men and transfer him and Dierdre to holding cells in the mansion.

Getting the information I want from him, and a lot more that might prove useful in the future, will take too long for us to accomplish step two of our plan before the bay gets busy with potential witnesses this morning.

It's after dinner the next day and I'm finishing up Darakov's interrogation when my phone buzzes in my pocket.

I pull it out and realize it's a video call. Connecting, I step into the hall. The subbasement is one of the few parts of the mansion that don't have video surveillance.

That Brogan is aware of.

I have cameras down here, but the only people with access to their feeds are my lieutenants and me.

"*Mo chroí*, you look beautiful." Her natural curls frame her face.

She stopped straightening her hair and pulling it back into ponytails all the time. More evidence my queen is settling into herself and her rightful place.

Her smile is warm and intimate. "Thank you. I know you're busy, but Fitz wanted to talk to you."

She wouldn't have called me like this before, even if our son asked her to. It fills me with satisfaction that she does now.

"I'm always happy to talk to our son."

"Told you he wouldn't mind, mom." Fitz's voice comes through clearly though I can't see him yet.

Kara rolls her eyes and then the video feed shows the wall, the ceiling and finally my son's eyes and nose. He's holding it too close to his face again.

"Hi, da."

"Hello, *a mhac*. Are you and your mom having fun?"

"Mom is letting me watch three episodes of *Spidey and His Amazing Friends* before bed." My son's voice is soaked with glee.

"Your mom is a pretty wonderful woman, isn't she?"

"Aye, Da," my son says, mimicking my Irish burr. "She's savage craic."

"Who taught you that one?" He didn't learn Irish slang at school.

"Uncle Rory. He says the best stuff."

"Well, that's bang on. Your mom *is* savage craic." And in ways my son will never know about.

"Will you be home soon, da?"

I calculate how long the rest of the interrogation should take and nod. "I'll be there in twenty minutes."

I make it to the apartment in time to watch the third episode of my son's favorite show before Kara and I tuck him into bed.

Kara wants to know how the interrogation went and I tell her. "He wanted the whisper gun prototype, but he hasn't told the pakhan about it. His bratva is the only one involved in the attempt to steal it from us."

"Except that Albanian gang leader you told me about."

"His gang was hired for a job. He doesn't have any information." Which won't stop me destroying his gang.

Helping me with that will be Wraith's final test for induction into our mob.

But I have more pressing thoughts to attend to right now.

Like how many times can I make my wife orgasm before she passes out?

The answer is four.

I gently clean her body, my cock giving a jerk as I wipe the combination of my spend and her juices from her thighs. But I let her sleep and force myself to shower and dress. After checking on Fitz, sleeping with Gobby beside him on the pillow, I return to the subbasement for the next step in my plan to rid the earth of Dierdre and Darakov.

Without going to war with the Northies.

Brice steps out of the holding cell when I reach it. "He's ready, boss."

Only the men in my crew, those under my lieutenants and my private security detail, call me *boss*. The rest of the Shaughnessy soldiers call me underboss.

But my men's loyalty is to me first.

I already run this mob, even if Brogan thinks he's doing it.

"Good." I enter the cell and find a naked Darakov strapped to a chair, the clarity in his eyes testament that he is indeed ready.

The benzo compound has mostly worn off, so he'll appreciate what I'm about to tell him fully.

I slap Darakov first on the left cheek, then on the right. He'll be dead before a bruise can form on either.

There are no overt marks on him.

"Wraith is as adept as you or I at doling out pain without leaving bruises behind," Brice says with approval.

I nod toward Wraith. "Good to know."

He inclines his head. "I prefer using those techniques on bastards like him who deserve it."

I don't ask him what he means. I don't care. "I prefer to use my skills on behalf of my family too."

Wraith's gaze probes mine. "You meant it when you said that when I'm inducted into the mob, I'll be part of the family?"

"I did. That's how we work in the Irish mob. Soldiers are soldiers, but they're also family. Their wives, their children, they're all our responsibility."

"That's not how Besnik sees it."

"He's a waste of space. And his chosen heir is going to take down his syndicate from within if an enemy doesn't do it first." An enemy like me.

Wraith doesn't smile, but there's a lift at the corner of one of his eyes. "You're right about that, boss. You're right about that."

Darakov stares up at me. "You can't do this. If you kill me, you'll be declaring war with my bratva."

"You declared fucking war with the Shaughnessy Mob when you tried to break in and steal what is not yours. I'm already working on the destruction of your bratva."

He tries to look like he's not affected, but I can tell that hit home. "You can't destroy us. We're too strong."

I laugh with some humor but more cruelty. "You mean the Odessa Mafia is too strong."

Not that I believe any syndicate is too strong to take down, but Odessa isn't my enemy. Darakov and his bratva are.

"Your bratva is just a tiny part of their organization," I deride.

"An important part. I'm the best weapons dealer they have."

"You'd sound more impressive if your tiny dick wasn't shriveled and on display," Brice mocks.

Darakov glares at my lieutenant. "I'm still part of Odessa and if you kill me, you're declaring war on them."

"Nah. I spoke to your pakhan."

Darakov doesn't look afraid yet. "So? Then you know he stands by his vor.

Vor being what they call their soldiers.

But I shake my head. "Not this time. I showed him proof of your attempt to steal from me. If you had gotten away with it, he would've praised you. But now? You make him look bad. You make him look weak."

He starts yelling at me in Russian.

I just shake my head in mock sympathy. "If you had asked permission, or told the pakhan about the Whisper gun, maybe. He thinks you put his neutral relationship with the Shaughnessy Mob at risk for a nonworking prototype of a more reliable weapon undetectable to security scanners."

"You lied to him!"

"And?"

"He won't let you get away with killing me." This time, there's desperation, not confidence in Darakov's tone.

"On the contrary. He doesn't want war with us. Where Odessa has uneasy truces, the Shaughnessy Mob has allies. All over the world."

There it is. That look of terror that feeds my dark soul.

"Don't kill me. I can get things for you. Things no one else can."

I don't bother to reply to that or his other begging.

Finally, I taze him just to shut him up. It works. "Dress him now or after?" I ask Brice his preference because he'll be the one doing it.

"Now. The venom might trigger instant rigor mortis. Some do."

"Venom?" Darakov croaks.

Brice administers chloroform and then he and Wraith dress the unconscious man.

Darakov comes to as the two men lift him to hold him between them.

"What are you going to do with me?" Darakov asks groggily.

"Well first..." I grab a syringe and lift it. "I'm going to inject you with this."

His face pales. "What is that?"

"You're well known for using the venom of the Siberian pit viper on your victims. I thought you would enjoy dying the same way." I didn't have to give up my favorite parts of my original plan after all.

He starts to struggle, knowing what's coming: excruciatingly painful death that will leave no marks on his body.

Important, because the best way to get rid of him and Dierdre is to continue the ruse of star-crossed lovers.

Their boat will capsize in the bay, and they will both drown.

Conscious, but unable to save themselves.

I give him enough venom to incapacitate him and cause him excruciating agony. It would probably result in death after a few hours, but he'll drown in the bay first.

After going to the cell next door and injecting Dierdre with a paralytic, we take her and Darakov down to the boathouse. We used Kara's program with some modifications for the new security programs to temporarily disable motion sensors and cameras outside, replacing their feeds with the one of Dierdre walking down to the boathouse the night before.

That footage was replaced with the back acreage devoid of movement.

Once we get our victims onto Darakov's inflatable raft, Brice and I row it out to the middle of the bay, no outboard motor to attract attention. Then, while Brice dons his scuba gear, I take care of business.

Dierdre is aware, but completely unable to move her limbs. She looks at me with terror in her eyes and I smile.

It's not a nice smile.

Most of mine aren't.

The only people who get good smiles from me, smiles that reflect real feeling, are Kara and Fitz. And hopefully one day, there will be another child for this sociopath to love.

"You're going to drown. And the entire time you're drowning, you will know that you brought this on yourself. Because you threatened the only woman who matters." I shove Dierdre over the side.

There's no flailing, just a splash as she sinks in the cold, salty water.

Turning to the now convulsing Darakov, I say, "I will kill every vor in your bratva."

Unfortunately, with the two already dead, there are only five more to dispose of.

"I will destroy the biological weapons you wanted to sell to my old mob. My blackgloves will dissect your computers. We'll raid your inventory stashes and take what we want."

Even in his state my words reach him, and he swears at me in Russian.

It's his turn to be the recipient of my less than friendly smile. "We'll destroy everything I don't want and erase you from existence."

After that pronouncement, I push him into the water. He tries to swim, but his convulsing body won't let him and I watch while he flounders and eventually drowns.

I put on my scuba gear while Brice drops into the water and disconnects our DPVs from the boat. The inflatable raft might be painted dark for stealth, but it's inferior design is easy to capsize.

Brice and I use our DPVs to return to the boathouse unseen.

I shower before climbing back into bed with Kara. Sensing my presence, she turns naturally to me in her sleep.

Like she always does.

Because I'm her sociopath.

And Kara? She is my everything.

Epilogue: No Loose Ends

KARA

We travel to Dublin for Dierdre's funeral with Fitz and my father.

Brian and Oisín were furious when they discovered that Deirdre and Ilya Darakov had been in contact while she was in New York. His capsized inflatable raft was discovered by a fishing trawler. Then their bodies washed up on the beach a day later.

Both deaths were ruled accidental drownings and warnings were issued again about the use of a pleasure craft without lights in the bay at night.

Recovery of Dierdre's phone records confirmed Mick's account of events.

Things got rocky between my father and the Northie leaders, Oisin demanding to see the security footage from that night.

My father played the role of furious and offended very well before finally handing it over. Of course, it had been manipulated to back up our story about her death as well.

The lack of alarms on the water was explained by the ability to disarm them from the yacht inside the boathouse. No one was supposed to know about that, but Dierdre was good at sussing out secrets and her family knew that.

Nevan vehemently denied the narrative, but couldn't divulge his knowledge of Dierdre's fixation with Mick and desire to get rid of me without repercussions from Brian Fitzgerald.

She hadn't told him about her deal with Darakov, so eventually, even he had to accept our version of events. On the surface anyway.

Dierdre's bodyguards were recalled immediately to Dublin where I'm sure they were interrogated and killed for dereliction of duty.

My father told Oisín that he was capable of protecting Dierdre from outside threats, but not from herself. He even said it with what sounded like genuine regret.

Eventually, Brian and Oisin agreed that Dierdre's death was a tragic accident resultant of her headstrong nature.

Not that either of them verbalized the last bit, but Dierdre's personality was well known to them all.

Now we are here to pay our respects and for Mick to interrogate Nevan.

We stay with his family, but their reserved demeanor toward us and Fitz is even more obvious when I see how they interact with the rest of their children and grandchildren.

We're a subdued group gathered in the drawing room before dinner, the night before the funeral. Most of the Fitzgeralds and all of the Kelly family are here.

Fitz walks up to Oisin and pats the man's arm. "I'm sorry for your loss." He sounds so grown up it makes me tear up.

Six years going on sixty sometimes.

Oisin clears his throat. "Uh, thank you, Fitzgerald."

"My da would cry and cry and cry if I died," Fitz goes on and turns to Mick. "Wouldn't you?"

"Aye, *mo leanbh*, I would at that." Mick's words seem to electrify the others in the drawing room, who stare at him with varying degrees of shock and disbelief.

"Dierdre was real pretty and she smiled a lot," Fitz continues, ignoring the way everyone in the room is now hanging on his every word.

"Aye, she did," Oisin says, his voice catching.

Fitz lifts his hand toward Oisin. He's holding his two favorite figurines. "This is Spidey and Miles. They help me when I feel sad sometimes. They'll help you too."

Ashlynn lets out a sob and Sheila hugs the other woman to her.

Oisin's eyes are filled with tears when he takes the toys from my son. "Thank you, Fitz."

After that, both families warm up to my son. And I'm glad for their sakes that they do. Because if they'd hurt his feelings by continuing to keep their distance, it wouldn't only be Mick's wrath they'd have to worry about.

My father returns to New York the day after the funeral, but Mick, Fitz and I stay on in Ireland.

I spend the next week getting to know Mick's family while Fitz bonds with his cousins. I like Mick's family and now that they dote on Fitz like they should, I'm even starting to feel affection for them.

A couple of days after the funeral, Sheila invites me to share a morning cuppa in her favorite room. It's a cozy room that reminds me of *moma's* sitting room. Five people at the max could sit in here comfortably.

Right now there are four. Mick's mom, his older sister, Chivon, and his younger sister, Brigid.

I like Brigid the best because she's giving her father fits and that makes me feel a kinship with her.

Sheila serves us all cups of teas and offers a plate of *biscuits*. Which are not fluffy, carby goodness served with butter and jam, but crispy cookies.

Just like *moma* serves with her tea and talk with us girls. There's more than just the layout of this room that reminds me of *moma's* space.

I take a cookie. "Thank you."

"The other night..." Sheila's voice trails off.

Chivon continues her mother's thought, like they've discussed this before inviting me to tea. "My brother said he would cry if Fitzgerald died."

I nod slowly. "First, he would probably kill a lot of people and maybe burn down the city, but yes, he would cry."

Brigid frowns at her mam. "That's why I don't want to marry into this life. Did you hear how matter of fact Kara talked about her husband murdering people. And she's a sweetheart."

"My aunt, who I loved like a second mom, was gunned down in front of me, my sister and her daughter, my cousin. My uncle was shot and killed after I married Mick. My cousin was kidnapped right in front of me and

Fitz in August. Our lives are hemmed in violence, but I wouldn't give up being married to Mick for anything or anyone."

The silence that follows my pronouncement lasts for nearly a minute.

"You really mean that," Brigid finally says.

I sip my tea and smile at her. "I do."

"But he's..." Chivon's voice trails off.

"He doesn't feel love," Sheila says. "He pretends, but he's my son. I raised him and no matter how he and his dad worked to hide it, Mick isn't normal."

I shrug. "We live in a world of violence, crime and justice that has nothing to do with government laws. None of us is normal."

"But he's *different*," Chivon says. "Scary."

"Not if you're part of his family," Brigid says firmly. "He'd never hurt one of us."

"You really believe that?" Sheila asks her youngest, hope lacing her voice.

"I know it for a fact," I say. "Mick is absolutely loyal to those he considers family and he loves me and Fitz."

I don't claim he loves them. He doesn't and I'm not going to lie to my in-laws unless I have to.

"Brian pushed him to accept the marriage alliance because he was worried Mick might..." Her voice trails off again.

I set my teacup down on the small table and lean forward. "Never! Mick would never harm family."

Not unless they betrayed him and negated his sense of loyalty. I don't mention that because it's never going to happen and it would hinder the argument I'm trying to make.

"But he's so emotionless." Chivon shakes her head. "The only living thing he ever loved was Toby."

"That's not true any longer," I remind them. "Who was Toby?"

"Mick's dog. A drunk driver ran him over. My son killed him. Mick was eleven." Sheila says this like it should shock me.

It doesn't, but then I know my husband's dark nature and accept it for what it is. Part of him.

"My son has a cat. His name is Gobby. His uncle, Rory, is cat sitting while we're here. If someone ran over Gobby while driving drunk, my son wouldn't have to kill them. Mick would do it for him."

Chivon frowns. "You say that like you think it's a good thing."

"He calls Rory uncle?" Brigid asks.

"Mick has one of his lieutenants cat sitting for your son?" Sheila asks.

I pat Chivon's arm. "Yes, it is a good thing. Mick will protect us from anything, including my son feeling the need to exact vengeance at an early age."

Then I turn to Brigid. "Yes, he calls Rory, Brice and Conor uncle. They're family."

I focus my gaze on my mother-in-law. "They're more than his lieutenants, they're his brothers. Brothers who would die for him or to protect our son and me. Not because he asks them to, but because we're family."

Sheila rears back like I struck her. "We're his family."

"Yes." It's true. "But so are they."

"And they're the family he trusts. That's what you're saying," Chivon says.

"Yes."

"You don't think he trusts us?" Sheila asks, her voice laced with sadness.

I don't ask what there is to trust about a family who basically banished him out of fear because I want Mick to have a better relationship with his parents and siblings.

"Do you trust him?" I counter. "I do. In all things and every way."

"Mick really does love you, doesn't he?" Chivon asks. "That level of trust doesn't come from anything but knowing you are loved on a cellular level."

Chivon's husband has been dead longer than I've been married, but I wonder if she trusted him like I trust Mick. If he loved her.

Arranged marriages are common in our world. Love? Not so much.

"I know my family loves me that way," Chivon says, as if I asked the question.

"But Mick doesn't," I say.

"I didn't think he needed our love," Sheila says.

"I think every child needs love." And maybe my sociopath would have developed tender feelings for one or more of them, if they'd given it.

But Mick scared them, it sounds like from a very young age.

"He was so emotionless when he was little. He only cried if he was hungry or wet. Never because he wanted attention. He ignored us most of the time."

"He didn't ignore me the day he broke that bully's arm," Brigid disagrees.

They tell me a story about Mick exacting retribution for an older boy knocking Brigid off the monkey bars.

"That's Mick. He protects the people he considers family." If I say it often enough, maybe they'll believe me.

"Then I wish he'd known what my husband was doing to me," Chivon says grimly.

Her mother gasps, but Brigid nods vehemently. "Mick would have gotten rid of Jack after the first time he hit you."

"Did you tell anyone what was happening?" I ask Chivon gently.

She shakes her head. "I thought it was my duty to take it, to endure."

"It wasn't," Brigid says with vehemence.

Sheila reaches out for her daughter. "Is that why you never came home during your marriage?"

"Jack wouldn't let me travel without him. He barely let me leave the house."

The look on Brigid's face says she knows all this and I think maybe that has more to do with her refusal to marry into another syndicate than anything else.

"If you'd told us..." When Sheila's voice trails off, we all know it's because she knows what she was going to say would have been a lie.

I tell them about *moma's* box then.

"I had no idea Maeve was so blood thirsty," Sheila says.

"She'd kill to protect us girls." And I'm just realizing how lucky I am to have been born into a family with her as my grandmother.

"I want a box like that," Brigid declares.

"You're never getting married, why would you need one?" her mother asks with some asperity.

Chivon's face sets with determination. "I wish I'd had one and I guarantee my daughter will if she ever gets married."

"That's enough talk about murder boxes," Sheila says. "Tell me more about Mick and your lives together in New York."

We stay in Dublin for two weeks while Mick gathers intel and we all get to know his family better. Most importantly, they start to get to know Mick.

MICK

I don't know what Kara said to my mam and sisters, but they treat me differently.

The wariness that's always been there is gone. Before we came to Dublin, I would have said it didn't matter, but I find that I like it.

That it makes me happy.

Not happy like I am with Kara, but not neutral either.

My father and brothers are the same and that doesn't bother me, so I haven't had some epic emotional epiphany.

Still, I like not scaring my mam and sisters.

Maybe it's seeing me with Fitz too. I show tenderness for him and Kara that I don't show anyone else.

Once I've gotten the information I need on Nevan's schedule and social patterns, I'm able to nab him and interrogate him using the benzo compound.

I discover no one else in the Northies is privy to his plans to kill my father. I also learn that he's doing business that his father and mine know nothing about.

I assign his assassination to Rory with the instruction that his death should lead to the discovery of those behind-closed-doors dealings.

Rory makes it happen on the night of Samhain.

Just in time for Kara to go off her birth control and us to start trying for that daughter she wants so badly. If we have another son, we'll rejoice in his birth and enjoy the hell out of trying again.

Because Kara and me, we're that epic love story I always believed was a fairytale.

The one where the sociopath in tarnished armor lives happily ever after with his mob princess.

And kills with prejudice anyone who so much as breathes a threat toward that happiness.

The End

If you enjoyed Sins of Arrogance, please leave a rating or a review and give my other spicy mafia romance series, Syndicate Rules, series a try:

Convenient Mafia Wife (Prequel)
Urgent Vows
Demanding Mob Boss
Ruthless Enforcer
Brutal Capo
Forced Vows
Assassin's Obsession
A De Luca Family Christmas Carol

Watch for new books coming in the Syndicate Sins series, starting with *Sins of the Past* in December.

Want to read about Kara and Mick renewing their vows in a wedding he surprises her with on their next anniversary? It will be posted to my bonus content as soon as this book reaches 500 reviews/ratings.

For access to all free bonus content, sign up for my newsletter on my website:
https://www.lucymonroe.com/

Irish Glossary

a chiste is a stór – my cherished love

a chroí – my heart

a chuisle – my pulse

a ghrá - love, dear

a leanbh – my child

a mhac – son

a stór - treasure

an diabhal – the devil

athair mór – grandpa (big father)

bod – penis

cailín – girl/young woman

ceannaire – leader/chief

flahing – boasting/bragging

Gaeilge – Irish (language)

gléas – asshole

máthair – mother (mom or mam for mom)

mo – mine

mo stóirín – my little treasure

moma – grandma

seanathair – grandfather

Ní hionn sé, stop chun an scaidín a ghéilleadh. – It's not a delay to stop and sharpen the scythe.

Tá tú chomh álainn. – You are so beautiful.

Lá an Lucht Oibre – Labor Day/May Day (celebrates worker's rights) in Ireland

Acknowledgments

With sincere and heartfelt gratitude to:

My husband, Tom, who spoils me like the best romantic hero. He took such good care of me through a personal medical emergency that lasted several weeks, I was able to get back on my feet so I could finish the revisions on this book.

Andie, my amazing editor at Beyond the Proof who excels at catching dangling threads and inconsistencies. Her insights make my books better. Full stop. Her ability to catch timeline inconsistencies is her secret superpower. This time she realized the book was missing some scenes and it's so much better for having them. Thanks, Andie!

Two very special ARC readers who take the time to proofread after the copyedits are done before writing their reviews, Dee Dee & Haley. Massive hugs to you both!

Any remaining typos, mistakes, or translation errors are my fault and mine alone.

 USA Today bestselling and award-winning author **Lucy Monroe** has published over 90 romance novels, with more than 12.5 million copies in print worldwide. Her stories have been translated across the globe and span contemporary, historical, and paranormal subgenres—often with a twist of suspense, always with heart and heat.

After a successful career in traditional publishing, Lucy transitioned to indie and now writes the emotionally rich, spicy romances she's most passionate about—including her newest series, *Syndicate Rules*, which features morally gray mafia heroes, bold heroines, and all the danger, desire, and redemption readers crave.

A lifelong romance reader and story lover, Lucy enjoys connecting with fellow book lovers online. Her stories prove one thing above all: love conquers all... but not easily.

For info on her books and series extras, visit Lucy's website:
www.lucymonroe.com
Subscribe to her newsletter:
Substack: @lucymonroeauthor
Follow her on Social Media:
Facebook: LucyMonroe.Romance
Instagram: lucymonroeromance
Pinterest: lucymonroebooks
goodreads: Lucy Monroe
YouTube: @LucyMonroeBooks

ALSO BY LUCY MONROE

Syndicate Sins

SINS OF ARROGANCE

Syndicate Rules

CONVENIENT MAFIA WIFE
URGENT VOWS
DEMANDING MOB BOSS
RUTHLESS ENFORCER
BRUTAL CAPO
FORCED VOWS
ASSASSIN'S OBSESSION
A DE LUCA FAMILY CHRISTMAS CAROL

Mercenaries & Spies

READY, WILLING & AND ABLE
SATISFACTION GUARANTEED
DEAL WITH THIS
THE SPY WHO WANTS ME
WATCH OVER ME
CLOSE QUARTERS
HEAT SEEKER

CHANGE THE GAME
WIN THE GAME

Passionate Billionaires & Royalty

THE MAHARAJAH'S BILLIONAIRE HEIR
BLACKMAILED BY THE BILLIONAIRE
HER OFF LIMITS PRINCE

LUCY MONROE

CINDERELLA'S JILTED BILLIONAIRE
HER GREEK BILLIONAIRE
SCORSOLINI BABY SCANDAL
THE REAL DEAL
WILD HEAT (Connected to Hot Alaska Nights - Not a Billionaire)
HOT ALASKA NIGHTS
3 Brides for 3 Bad Boys Trilogy
RAND, COLTON & CARTER

Harlequin Presents

THE GREEK TYCOON'S ULTIMATUM
THE ITALIAN'S SUITABLE WIFE
THE BILLIONAIRE'S PREGNANT MISTRESS
THE SHEIKH'S BARTERED BRIDE
THE GREEK'S INNOCENT VIRGIN
BLACKMAILED INTO MARRIAGE
THE GREEK'S CHRISTMAS BABY
WEDDING VOW OF REVENGE
THE PRINCE'S VIRGIN WIFE
HIS ROYAL LOVE-CHILD
THE SCORSOLINI MARRIAGE BARGAIN
THE PLAYBOY'S SEDUCTION
PREGNANCY OF PASSION
THE SICILIAN'S MARRIAGE ARRANGEMENT
BOUGHT: THE GREEK'S BRIDE
TAKEN: THE SPANIARD'S VIRGIN
HOT DESERT NIGHTS
THE RANCHER'S RULES
FORBIDDEN: THE BILLIONAIRE'S
VIRGIN PRINCESS
HOUSEKEEPER TO THE MILLIONAIRE
HIRED: THE SHEIKH'S SECRETARY MISTRESS
VALENTINO'S LOVE-CHILD
THE LATIN LOVER 2-IN-1 with
THE GREEK TYCOON'S INHERITED BRIDE
THE SHY BRIDE

SINS OF ARROGANCE

THE GREEK'S PREGNANT LOVER
FOR DUTY'S SAKE
HEART OF A DESERT WARRIOR
NOT JUST THE GREEK'S WIFE
ONE NIGHT HEIR
PRINCE OF SECRETS
MILLION DOLLAR CHRISTMAS PROPOSAL
SHEIKH'S SCANDAL
AN HEIRESS FOR HIS EMPIRE
A VIRGIN FOR HIS PRIZE
2017 CHRISTMAS CODA: The Greek Tycoons
KOSTA'S CONVENIENT BRIDE
THE SPANIARD'S PLEASURABLE VENGEANCE
AFTER THE BILLIONAIRE'S WEDDING VOWS
QUEEN BY ROYAL APPOINTMENT
HIS MAJESTY'S HIDDEN HEIR
THE COST OF THEIR ROYAL FLING

Anthologies & Novellas

SILVER BELLA
DELICIOUS: Moon Magnetism
by Lori Foster, et. al.
HE'S THE ONE: Seducing Tabby
by Linda Lael Miller, et. al.
THE POWER OF LOVE: No Angel
by Lori Foster, et. al.
BODYGUARDS IN BED:
Who's Been Sleeping in my Brother's Bed?
by Lucy Monroe et. al.

Historical Romance

ANNABELLE'S COURTSHIP
The Langley Family Trilogy
TOUCH ME, TEMPT ME & TAKE ME
MASQUERADE IN EGYPT

LUCY MONROE

Paranormal Romance

Children of the Moon Novels
MOON AWAKENING
MOON CRAVING
MOON BURNING
DRAGON'S MOON
ENTHRALLED anthology: Ecstasy Under the Moon
WARRIOR'S MOON
VIKING'S MOON
DESERT MOON
HIGHLANDER'S MOON

Montana Wolves
COME MOONRISE
MONTANA MOON

Made in United States
North Haven, CT
20 January 2026

87035469R00232